KU-274-822

UNTIL YOU COME HOME

UNTIL YOU COME HOME

by

Ellie Dean

WARWICKSHIRE
COUNTY LIBRARY

CONTROL No.

Magna Large Print Books
Long Preston, North Yorkshire,
BD23 4ND, England.

British Library Cataloguing in Publication Data.

A catalogue record of this book is
available from the British Library

ISBN   978-0-7505-4608-9

First published in Great Britain by Arrow Books in 2017

Copyright © Ellie Dean 2017

Cover illustration © Ildiko Neer/Arcangel by arrangement with
Arcangel Images Ltd.

Ellie Dean has asserted her right to be identified as the author of this
work in accordance with the Copyright, Designs and Patents Act, 1988

Published in Large Print 2018 by arrangement with
Random House Group

All rights reserved. No part of this publication may be reproduced,
stored in a retrieval system, or transmitted in any form or by any
means, electronic, mechanical, photocopying, recording or otherwise
without the prior permission of the Copyright owner.

Magna Large Print is an imprint of Library Magna Books Ltd.

Printed and bound in Great Britain by
T.J. (International) Ltd., Cornwall, PL28 8RW

To Georgina Hawtrey-Woore.
We're all beside you in your battle.

1

Barnham Green, Somerset, 1944

It was the last day of February, and bitingly cold. Anne Black tried not to shiver as she stood next to the headmaster, George Mayhew, while her friend and colleague, Belinda Frobisher, kept an eye on her class of little ones who were rather sullenly awaiting their turn to be seen by the district nurse. She watched as Nurse Mary Higgins combed through their hair and felt the ominous itch in her own which she had to force herself to ignore. None of the children liked being seen by the 'Nit Nurse', as they called Mary, but with so many of them packed into the overcrowded classrooms, it only took one louse-ridden head for the infestation to spread right through the junior school and across the entire village.

'I wish the school board would give us the money to build another two classrooms,' muttered George, digging his scarred and withered hand into his jacket pocket. 'We're overstretched as it is with so many evacuees, and it's hardly surprising we've got all sorts of health problems to deal with.'

'At least we cleared up the impetigo and ringworm those poor London children arrived with, and that's down to the good country air, a decent diet and proper hygiene.' Anne smiled at him, able now to look into the fire-damaged side of his face without feeling the initial twist of pity that had previously made every conversation awkward. 'Let's just hope we can clear this quickly before the nursery is infested as well. I don't fancy having to treat my two's hair; not with them both going through a tricky stage at the moment.'

She had a brief vision of trying to deal with three-year-old Rose's thick, dark curls as well as Emily's, and the tantrums that would no doubt follow. Emily might only be just over a year and a half, but she'd quickly learned from her sister that tears and temper could quite often be the path to getting her own way if Anne was tired after a long, busy day.

As the last child endured being examined and doused with DDT powder, Belinda chivvied the others outside to the playground where they immediately let off steam by racing about and shouting at one another. 'That's me for the day,' she said cheerfully, flicking back her cloud of blonde hair and then reaching for her hat and coat. 'I'm off home to get ready for my date with Hank Simmons. He's promised to take me out to dinner and then to a club in Taunton. Will I see you both at the village dance tomorrow night?'

Anne rather envied Belinda's hectic lifestyle, for there seemed to be a never-ending stream of young men wanting to take her out, and it had been years since Anne had gone dancing with her husband Martin. 'I promised to help with the food, so as long as we're not snowed in I shall be there,' she said. 'Can't let the WI down now I've been elected onto the committee.'

'I might pop in for a minute or two,' said George. 'It's not really my sort of thing,' he added shyly.

'You should give it a try,' Belinda teased, her blue eyes bright with daring as she looked up at him. 'You never know, you might enjoy it. Well, ta-ta for now.' She sashayed out of the room on her impractical high-heeled shoes.

'I don't know where she finds the energy,' sighed George. 'But I do admire her joie de vivre.'

'We could certainly do with some of her enthusiasm for life.' Despite being only in her twenties, Anne felt suddenly rather matronly and staid. 'But it isn't easy when you have two small children to look after at the end of a long day.'

The nurse turned to Anne and George with a rueful smile. 'I'm sorry,' she said, 'but I'm going to have to check you too. Nearly every child is infested, and I suspect they've spread through the families as well.'

Anne sat down and felt the heat of embarrassment as Mary slowly combed through her long dark hair, knowing what she'd find. 'I've got them too, haven't I?' she asked.

'You certainly do, which means you'll have to take these combs and packets of DDT powder back with you to Owlet Farm and treat everyone – including the land girls. I know it's a bind, but we have to get it under control.'

'I feel so dirty,' muttered Anne, resisting once again the terrible urge to scratch.

Mary calmly combed the DDT powder through her hair before turning to examine George's. 'Lice attack clean hair too,' she said, 'so there's no

11

shame in it. Just make sure you use the powder as per instructions on the packet – even on those who are yet to be infested – and comb the dead lice and their eggs out onto newspaper every morning and night, and then burn the paper. Prevention's the watchword.'

'Even the little ones?'

'Especially the little ones,' Mary said firmly, combing the powder through George's neat brown hair. 'Keep it on for as long as possible and then wash it out with strong coal-tar soap. At the first sign of itching, do it all over again.'

George dipped his chin, clearly as embarrassed as Anne. 'It looks as if you'll have your work cut out for the next few weeks, Mary.'

'Don't I know it,' she said on a sigh. 'I'll have to visit every house and farm in the village. I just hope my stock of powder doesn't run out – it's the very devil to get hold of with the rationing so tight and the Bristol suppliers constantly under enemy attack.'

She handed George a finely toothed comb and he slipped it into his top pocket. 'Would you stay for a cup of tea?' he asked.

'I don't have time,' she said regretfully. 'Perhaps after my next visit.' She finished packing her medical bag, then headed out into the brisk wind which was scattering leaves across the now deserted playground.

'What about you, Anne? Time for a cuppa before you go home?'

He looked so wistful that she couldn't refuse, despite the fact that there was a pile of marking to do once she'd treated the children's hair and

12

fed and bathed them ready for bed.

'Why not?' she replied, stowing the comb and packet inside her bulging briefcase. 'I could do with a sit-down before the evening chaos, and as Sally is working at the village nursery today she'll take the little ones home.'

They fetched their coats, hats and gas-mask boxes and wrapped up against the raw wind, then Anne followed his tall figure across the playground towards the tiny cottage provided for the school principal.

Squadron Leader George Mayhew had once been engaged, but the girl hadn't loved him enough to stick around after he'd been disfigured during the Battle of Britain when his plane was shot down, and he cut a rather lonely figure around the village. He'd come to Barnham Green six months ago, straight from the hospital at East Grinstead where he'd endured months of skin grafts and rehabilitation under the care of the talented surgeon Archibald McIndoe, and had taken over as head when the previous incumbent had enlisted in the navy.

There had been some consternation at first, for despite the reconstruction of his face he was still badly scarred, and although there was great admiration for the man, some of the parents were worried his appearance might frighten the children. To her shame, but like so many others, Anne had been almost afraid to look at the terribly burnt tissue on the left side of his face and the tortured waste of his hand and arm, for fear that he might see how much it affected her. But his quiet command and gentle ways soon put everyone at ease, and after the children's initial stares and open curiosity had been satisfied, they no longer pestered him for stories of his time as a Spitfire pilot and how he'd come to be so injured.

Anne glanced across at him now, once again experiencing that twist in her heart as she pictured how handsome he'd once been, and how much he reminded her of Martin who was no doubt at this very minute putting his life in danger on a bombing mission over Germany. She hastily tamped down on the dark thoughts that plagued her constantly. Her husband would survive; he'd come through – he had to.

She blinked back the tears, blaming them on the icy wind, and concentrated on the cottage ahead. Like the other buildings in the village, the two-bedroom cottage was of mellowed cream stone, with a small front garden which had been turned into a vegetable plot, a sturdy wooden door and four windows overlooking the narrow lane that ran through the village to the nearby hamlets.

The thickly entwined branches of wisteria curled over the door and along the wall, leafless now, but a riot of purple droplets in the spring. St Augusta's square Norman tower could just be seen through the trees that formed a boundary between the churchyard and the cottage, and to the rear was a magnificent view of the snow-capped Mendip Hills beyond the broad, sweeping valley of ploughed farmland and drystone walls.

George opened the door and stood back to let her pass into the narrow flagstoned hall where a steep flight of wooden stairs led to the upper floor. She walked past the doors of the two front

14

rooms and went straight to the tiny kitchen at the back where the range fire emitted welcome heat after the rawness of the winter's day.

While George went to the sink to pump water from the well into the tin kettle and set it on the hotplate, Anne put her briefcase on the table and warmed her hands at the range before removing her scarf and beret. She was no stranger to this kitchen with its wooden draining board, stone sink and rows of shelves which housed cooking utensils and mismatched china, for she, Belinda and George often shared a cup of tea in here after school.

It was very neat, which she supposed was only to be expected from an ex-serviceman, but it could have done with a woman's touch – like curtains at the window, and beneath the sink to hide the cleaning materials, and perhaps a plant pot or two to brighten up the place. She had thought to offer to make him curtains, but realised he might find that a step too far in their relationship, and it could make things awkward.

'Have you heard from your husband recently?' he asked, pouring boiling water into the large brown teapot to warm it.

'Not for a while,' she replied. 'But you know how erratic the mail is, and he's so busy at the moment, I doubt he has the energy to do anything but sleep when he's not on ops.' She turned from his steady gaze and looked out of the window. 'Still,' she sighed, 'no news is good news these days, don't you think?'

Clearly regretting bringing the subject up, he changed tack. 'How are you all coping out on

15

Owlet Farm now the weather's closing in?'

'Well enough,' she said, grateful for his tact. 'The three land girls are doing a sterling job with the cattle and now he's left school, my brother Bob has taken on the ploughing and planting of the south field for the first time as well as learning to repair the stone boundary walls. My other brother, Charlie, although he's only thirteen, is managing to keep the machinery going with a good deal of advice from old Fred and Bert, and Sally and I muck in with whatever's needed.'

Her smile was soft with affection. 'As for Auntie Vi... She's revelling in the fact she has so many little ones about the place after all those childless years, and we all count ourselves very fortunate that she took us in.'

'I thought Violet was related to Sally and Sally's brother Ernie? Surely she had no other option but to take them in?' He poured the tea into mugs.

'She's their aunt, but no relation to my lot, and I have the feeling she'd have taken anyone in who needed a home. In that way, she's very like my mother.'

She sat at the scrubbed table and cupped her hands around the mug for warmth as she thought wistfully of her mother, Peggy. 'Sally was one of my mother's first evacuees. She and her brother Ernie came down to Cliffehaven from London – a right pair of little waifs they were – who, of course, Mum immediately took under her wing.'

Swept by the familiar wave of nostalgia for her mother and Beach View, she went on to tell George how Ernie had once worn callipers following a polio attack, and how Sally had set up a

16

home dressmaking business and then married the local fire chief.

'Their father brought Ernie down to Barnham Green to his sister in 1940, and Sally joined him once she'd had little Harry. Cliffehaven is right in the flight path of enemy bombers, and with Cliffe Aerodrome only a few miles away, none of us liked risking our children's lives.'

'Ernie's certainly no longer a crippled waif,' said George with a twinkle in his eye. 'He's never still and rarely silent, and can give most of the others a good run for their money on the football pitch. And although he's a pain in the neck during lessons with all his questions, I'll rather miss him when he goes up into the senior school in September.'

He sipped his tea carefully, always aware that the left side of his mouth didn't work properly because of the tightly puckered skin.

'He and Charlie are a couple of scallywags, forever getting into trouble – and with four-year-old Harry watching every move they make, it won't be long before he's a handful too,' Anne said dryly. 'All Sal and I can hope for is that senior school calms Ernie down – although it hasn't seemed to work on Charlie.'

'They're both extremely bright boys, with engaging characters. I rather hope they don't lose that lust for life. The world is far too serious, and we need boys like that to remind us what this war is really all about.'

Anne finished her tea and rinsed out the mug, then peered out at the lowering sky. 'I have to go, George. It'll be dark soon and looks like it'll snow again.' She wrapped her scarf around her neck and drew the knitted beret over her hair which was now white with DDT powder, and picked up her briefcase.

'Would you like me to escort you? Only I don't like the thought of you walking alone in the dark.'

Anne smiled. 'That's very sweet of you, but I know the way and it's not that far.' She began to head for the door. 'Why don't you come to the dance tomorrow night?' she asked tentatively as she reached for the latch. 'It's not as if you're a stranger to the village, and I know Belinda's dying to teach you the Lambeth Walk.'

He looked down at his highly polished shoes. 'I feel awkward amongst a lot of people,' he confessed quietly. 'And I'd hate to spoil the fun.'

'Oh, George,' she sighed. 'You wouldn't spoil anything. Everyone here admires you and is only too willing to bring you into the village fold if only you'd let them. Please reconsider.'

He looked up then, his brown eyes regarding her intently. 'If you think it would be all right, then perhaps I might just pop in for a bit. You will be there, won't you?'

She nodded and then opened the door to be met by a blast of cold air. 'I'll knock on my way to the village hall and we can go together. Thanks for the tea.'

Anne hurried away so he couldn't see the sadness in her eyes. The poor, brave man had sacrificed so much for his country, but despite the medals and commendations he had become terrified of social events to the point where he preferred to hide away in his cottage. She and Belinda had to help ease him back into society, she decided as she bent against the wind and picked her way quickly through the muddy puddles of the country lane. He was a hero – one of Churchill's 'few' – a casualty of this terrible war which had already claimed so many lives. It was the duty of every man, woman and child to ensure that he overcame his fear and was brought into the community.

Her footsteps faltered as she reached the end of the tunnel of trees which arched over the lane. Despite the weather she was reluctant to return to the noise and demands of Owlet Farm just yet, and as it was unusual to have time alone, she climbed over the stile and tramped along the high ridge which sat above the valley, needing these few moments to gather her thoughts and steel herself against the nightly terrors of bad dreams which kept her awake and constantly on edge.

Her breath clouded momentarily in the frosty air before being whipped away as she looked out at the vista spread before her. She pushed her hair out of her face and turned once more into the wind that blew across the empty miles of dark ploughed fields and rolling green hills. Her eyes were watering with the cold, her heart aching for home and news of Martin as she regarded the leaden sky and the ploughed fields already spark-ling with frost in the strange light that always comes before it snows.

She dug her gloved hands in her pockets and blinked back her tears, thinking of Martin and the tiny cottage they'd bought near Cliffe Aerodrome. They'd only lived in it for a few short months before enemy bombing raids made it too dangerous to stay there once she'd had Rose Margaret.

Her sigh was tremulous as she looked up at the threatening sky and wondered how long it would be before she saw him again. Rose Margaret hardly remembered him despite the photographs Anne kept by her bed, and little Emily Jane had only just been born when he'd had his last very short leave. As for herself – she'd become independent, making her own money and decisions, doing as she pleased within the boundaries of motherhood; her routine rarely set in stone unless in the classroom. She'd been Martin's wife for four years, but since she'd come down to Somerset, they'd had to snatch rare moments of his leave together, which simply hadn't been long enough to get used to one another again before they were torn apart by duty and commitment.

It was as if she was single, and the short honeymoon period in the cottage had been just a lovely dream involving two people who were now almost strangers – strangers who'd been changed by the war and the separate lives they'd been forced to lead, and who could never return to what they'd once been. Time and distance didn't allow for the necessary intimacies and domestic routine of marriage, and her greatest fear was that this enforced and lengthy separation would be the undoing of all their hopes for a future together – a future hard-won against his parents' relentless disapproval.

She tried to cheer herself by thinking about the recent news. Things were becoming more hopeful every day now the Russians were pushing back the Germans in Poland, and the 900-day siege of

Leningrad was over. The British and Americans were advancing against the Japs in Burma, and the Allies were fighting against Jerry in Italy – and she had to hold on to the hope that it would soon be over and they could try and begin their married life again as a proper family. It would be a struggle to adapt for both of them after all they'd experienced these past years, and it could take a long time, but if their love proved strong enough she had to keep the faith that they would come through this and find something even deeper and more rewarding.

Martin had been promoted to Group Captain and Station Commander of RAF Cliffe, and having already completed four ops missions over enemy territory, had just embarked on his fifth, which meant he'd flown over 100 flights in battle, and was the rightful possessor of a Distinguished Service Order and a Distinguished Flying Cross and bar.

Now Bomber Harris had begun his blanket bombing of Germany, the lists of those dead or missing in action were growing longer by the day, and the new recruits were raw boys who simply hadn't had the time or experience to really know what they were doing. Martin constantly fretted over them, trying to protect them, but too many had perished before their first op was over, and although it wasn't the done thing to talk about it, Anne knew how deeply their sacrifices had touched him.

It was all very well for the men under his command to regard Martin as their lucky mascot, but Anne was realistic enough to know that the odds of him surviving were becoming shorter with every raid. She shivered with the cold that seemed to have settled around her heart, turned her back on the view and began to plod towards the broad valley and Owlet Farm which had been her home for almost three years.

For all her loving kindness, Auntie Vi wasn't a relation and certainly couldn't replace her mother, and although she was almost twenty-eight, it was at times like this that Anne really needed Peggy's reassuring arms about her and to hear her soothing voice telling her she wasn't alone – that there were thousands of women living with the same fears as they kept the home fires burning, cared for their children and waited for their men to return.

She knew that there were numerous evacuees living in Somerset and the village school was bursting at the seams – and her own mother was doing her best to bring up young Daisy all the while her father, Jim, was out in India. But there were moments when self-pity, fear and longing became too overwhelming, and like a small child, she needed her mother. However, Peggy was far away in Cliffehaven with Grandad Ron and her baby Daisy – who was ten months younger than Anne's Rose Margaret – and no doubt fretting over Jim. Peggy ran the Beach View boarding house in Cliffehaven, and nothing would convince her to leave her home and her evacuee 'chicks', not even the Luftwaffe. Anne could picture the boarding house kitchen; warm and cosy and ringing with the laughter of the girls who'd found a home and shelter there, just as she had here with Vi, and the yearning to be there was a deep internal ache.

Dashing the ready tears from her eyes, she found a sheltered spot beneath an overhang of rock, folded her thick coat around her and sat down on a clump of frosty grass. She hugged her knees, glad to be out of the biting wind, but not yet ready to return to face the others with the delights of lice treatment and the usual chaos of the evening ritual of baths, tea and bed.

Owlet Farm belonged to the widowed and childless Vi – a homely, plump woman in her late fifties, who'd opened her heart and her empty, echoing rooms to Anne and her children as well as her younger brothers. Her niece, Sally, had moved into one of the farm cottages with little Harry and her brother Ernie, who'd just turned eleven, but everyone ate together at the large kitchen table, and with Bob and Charlie constantly arguing over something and nothing, and Rose Margaret getting more uppity by the day as Emily threw tantrums, it was hardly surprising that they got on each other's nerves occasionally. Yet there was a profound sense of togetherness, and warmth in working as one to defy their common enemy and make the very best of things until their men came home.

Anne wondered then how Vi would feel once the war was over and she was left alone again, for it had brought her companionship as well as the chance to mother the little ones, and she would struggle to cope on her own in that great house. Perhaps she could be persuaded to sell up and move closer to Cliffehaven where she could stay involved with Sally and the children.

Not wanting to dwell on what the future might hold, Anne looked up and realised that the light was fading fast, the clouds thickening and threatening snow. She got to her feet, brushed down her coat and began the long descent towards the farm. Her gaze drifted over the sprawling stone farmhouse, the line of cottages and the large barns and sheds which encompassed the milking parlour, the byres and the winter feed and hay stores. The three land girls occupied one of the smaller barns which had been kitted out with bunks and washing facilities, and there were two ancient farmhands who lived in the other cottages, too old for anything much but to offer advice – but too much a part of Owlet Farm to pension off.

Anne dismissed the homesickness and the ever-present worry over Martin. This was her home now until the war was over, and her children were waiting for her.

RAF Cliffe

The daylight was fading as the second-in-command pointed to strategic targets on the map and went through the briefing for that night's op. Sitting next to him, Group Captain Martin Black regarded the men who'd congregated in the room and did his best not to show the deep concern that had become a daily torture to him over these past months.

The silent, attentive gathering was made up of bomber crews and the fighter pilots who would escort them. They had come to Cliffe from all corners of the world – Poland, America, Czechoslovakia, France, Rhodesia and Australia – with one aim: to fight for freedom against Hitler's tyranny. To Martin they looked painfully young and fresh-faced; eager to do their bit; seduced by the glamour bestowed on the airmen who were hailed as heroes by Churchill and the media; wanting to be part of it.

There were few heroics in reality, he thought sadly; just sheer bloody-mindedness to get the job done; skills honed by experience or from natural ability – and a damned good dose of luck.

He smoothed his moustache with a finger, studying the faces before him as they eagerly noted down their orders. He knew everyone by name – for he made a point of getting to know each man and his family background. Since they were willing to die for their country, then it was the very least he could do. And so many had not returned, their ghosts lingering, their voices and laughter echoing still in the darkest hours of a sleepless night.

They had not been forgotten, but to acknowledge their departure; to mourn and reminisce over even the good times was too stark a reminder of what fate might have in store for those they'd left behind – so the empty beds, the erasing of a name chalked on the duty board, or the absence of a drinking companion were never remarked upon. It was a tacit code they lived by, but Martin knew that beneath those stiff upper lips was tightly held nerve – and with every operation, the strain increased.

He looked across to Wing Commander Roger 'Tash' Makepeace and caught his eye momentarily before the other man returned to jotting down his orders. They'd been friends since joining the RAF back in 1939 and by some miracle both of them had so far come through with barely a scratch. But now Martin noted the dark shadows beneath Roger's eyes, the weariness in the lines that were now etched in his drawn face, and knew they mirrored his own.

Roger was a tall, broad man who'd once had a ruddy complexion and boisterous nature; who'd always been the first to suggest a drinking match or a game of pirates in the mess – now the stresses and strains of responsibility and the many losses of his men had aged him, and even the handlebar moustache he was so proud of didn't look quite so jaunty.

Martin tuned into what was being said, but as he'd already carefully studied the maps and read through the instructions that had come from High Command HQ, he let his mind and his gaze wander again.

Sitting next to Roger was Squadron Leader Freddy 'Pedro' Pargeter, a naturally gifted young pilot whose family lived in Argentina, and who'd come to England at the start of the war to do his bit as well as cause mayhem amongst the British women with his handsome looks and winning ways. He'd settled down with a lovely wife, Charlotte, but that didn't mean he'd settled down in any other ways. Freddy could be as gung-ho and reckless as any of the Polish airmen, and he was brave – rather like his sister Kitty, who was

26

married to Roger and flying for the ATA, the Air Transport Auxiliary, despite having lost a leg in a plane crash. He'd certainly earned his DFC and bar.

Martin regarded the young man sitting next to him. Squadron Leader Matthew 'Pinky' Champion still looked like a schoolboy with his light brown hair, freckles and impish grin. Despite his habit of blushing when the centre of attention he was now a veteran Spitfire pilot, and beginning to show the signs of terrible strain. Martin made a mental note to have a frank chat with him, for he was well overdue some leave.

Bomber Harris might be adamant that all leave should be cancelled during his campaign of blanket bombing over Germany, but there came a point when it was necessary to insist upon a break for the safety of his crews. From his own experience, Martin knew that a tired man lost concentration, his reactions became sluggish, and that could be deadly when you had the Luftwaffe dive-bombing you or chasing your tail.

He realised the briefing was drawing to a close, and once again studied the young airman at the back of the room who'd arrived that morning. Pilot Officer Jack Newbury was barely nineteen and fresh out of training. His records stated he'd had less than twenty hours' solo flying experience – which was about average for such sprogs – and although he was putting a brave face on things, this would be his first op, and he would need careful watching.

As his second-in-command fell silent, Martin stood and thanked him and then dismissed his men before leaving the hut. He lingered outside and then rounded up Roger, Freddy and Matthew. 'A word in my office,' he murmured, his gaze following Jack Newbury who was determinedly swaggering along with the other youngsters.

They trooped into the Nissen hut that replaced the original wooden admin building which had been blown to smithereens following an enemy bombing raid the previous year. Martin sank into the worn leather chair behind the ferociously neat desk, took off his highly decorated peaked hat, and waited as the others helped themselves to coffee from the pot and flopped into the less comfortable chairs usually reserved for those about to get an earwigging.

Cigarettes were lit and caps removed as darkness fell beyond the blackout blinds and the weak glow from the desk-lamp struggled to chase away the gloom of the chilly office. They were uniformly wearing the bluish-grey, rough woollen battledress which everyone called 'Hairy Marys', because they made them itch – but they provided warmth to beat the freezing conditions once in the air.

'I don't suppose you've got a tincture of something hidden away, old chap,' said Roger hopefully. 'A nip of something in this coffee to combat the cold, before we freeze our backsides off up there?'

Martin shook his head. 'You know the drill, Tash. No booze until you get back.' He could have done with a slug of whisky himself, but he straightened a pen which was already perfectly in line with the others and cleared his throat instead.

'As you can see, we have another sprog flying with us tonight. This will be his first experience of going solo into battle, and I'd like him back in one piece, so I'm putting him with you, Roger.'

'Thanks,' Roger muttered. 'It's not as if I don't have enough to do up there in the beehive, without having to nursemaid some kid who probably doesn't know his arse from his elbow.'

'I have every faith in you, Tash,' Martin said. 'You've done it before – as we all have.'

'I'm a man short,' protested Freddy. 'Why can't I have him?'

'Because I don't want him learning your bad habits, Pedro.' Martin shot him a wry smile. 'Besides, you've already got two sprogs of your own – that's enough to keep an eye on. Speaking of which, how's young Forbes shaping up?'

Freddy grinned, his dark eyes dancing in his handsome face. 'A chip off the old block,' he said proudly. 'I have high hopes for that one.'

'Good. Just keep tabs on him and don't let him get overambitious,' Martin warned.

He turned back to Roger. 'Keep Newbury behind you so he can shadow you. If you run into Bogeys, then it's every man for himself as usual, and he'll have to take his chances. But if all three of you could keep an eye out for him and the others, I'd be grateful,' he finished on a sigh.

'We'll do what we can,' said Roger. 'But you know as well as I do that there's no time to even breathe up there when the Luftwaffe come at you.'

Martin nodded, fully aware of what it was like when under attack. He looked at his watch. As long as the weather didn't close in they were due

29

to scramble in less than an hour, then they'd form a 'beehive' – a close formation of bombers and fighters – and head for Stettin to bomb the hell out of its vast munitions factories.

'Go and get prepared, while I have a quiet word with Pinky.'

Pinky went bright red and Roger and Freddy looked alarmed. 'What's he done now?' demanded Roger, who'd been Matthew's mentor during his initial flights and still kept a fatherly eye on him.

'Nothing I'm aware of,' Martin replied. 'I just need a word, that's all. Now clear off.'

They shot Matthew looks of sympathy and stomped out in their heavy flying boots, parachute packs swinging from their shoulders, their sheepskin-lined leather jackets tightly fastened against the bitter night.

Martin waited until they'd closed the door behind them and then turned back to an anxious Matthew. 'After tonight, I want you to take a forty-eight-hour leave,' he said without preamble. 'I realise that won't give you time to visit your family, but I'm sure young Rita will be delighted to have your company. You'll billet with Mrs Wright, who always keeps a room spare for such occasions. It will do you good to have some civvy-kip for a change and get away from this place.'

Matthew protested vehemently, but Martin was adamant. 'You're a credit to the team, Pinky, and I'd like it to stay that way. Take leave, and come back refreshed.'

He pushed back from his desk to signal the end of the conversation. They exchanged salutes and Martin watched the younger man leave before sinking back into his chair. He was weary beyond belief, and in need of not only a decent night's sleep, but respite from the never-ending fear for his men, the awful letters he had to write to their bereaved families – and a leave long enough for him to get down to Somerset to his own little family. But the chance of any of those things coming to fruition was about as remote as a heatwave in January, so it was pointless to even think about them.

He scrubbed his face with his hands and reached for the pipe he always took with him on ops as a sort of talisman. Having packed it firmly with tobacco, he got it going satisfactorily, and sat puffing away on it as he thought about his family in the stillness that always came before an op.

Anne's letters were full of all the things she'd become involved in as well as containing photographs and news of the children. Rose Margaret was growing into a little beauty, just like her mother, and baby Emily was as sweet as a button. But he'd only held Emily for an hour following her birth on his last leave, which had been so long ago he doubted if Rose would even remember him the next time he saw her. His only comfort was that they were safe with Violet.

As the hands on the wall-clock clicked towards the hour he set aside all thoughts of home and family, gathered up his parachute, rammed on his hat and fastened his flying jacket. The scramble bell began to clamour as he closed the door behind him and steeled himself once more to lead his men into battle.

2

Cliffehaven, March 1944

Peggy Reilly had ensured that she and Daisy were well wrapped up against the bitter wind before they left the stationmaster's cottage and headed home to Beach View. She'd spent a lovely couple of hours catching up on the gossip with Ethel and young April while she cuddled baby Paula. Stan had tried to keep Daisy amused with a giant jigsaw puzzle he'd made in his spare time out of offcuts of wood, but she was much too interested in April's baby, and determined to garner some of the attention she was receiving.

The raw weather was a sharp contrast to that cosy little kitchen, and Peggy set off smartly wheeling the pushchair down the hill, feeling the bite of winter nipping at her face. She thought of Ivy – one of her evacuees – up in that draughty munitions factory, and wondered how she was coping with the cold.

Daisy was snug under her blankets, but she hated the pushchair and was now kicking as hard as she could to be free of the reins holding her in, and her blankets. 'Walk,' she demanded crossly. 'Wanna walk. Now.'

'It will take too long to get home if you do,' Peggy said firmly. 'And Grandad Ron will be waiting for his tea. Here, cuddle Dolly and keep her warm.'

Daisy was not to be mollified and she flung the rag doll to the pavement.

Peggy sighed and picked up the doll, then crammed it into her string shopping bag, stoically ignoring Daisy's continued protests as she carried on down the almost deserted High Street. The entrances to the Town Hall and government buildings had been shielded by great stacks of sandbags, and every window had been covered in tape to protect it from bomb-blast, and a quick glance into Plummer's department store display proved that the utility clothing was as plain and unflattering as ever and didn't stir any desire to go shopping.

Daisy was going through the 'terrible twos' and everything had become a struggle, just as it had when her other children had been that age. Peggy could only hope it wouldn't last too long, for with rationing tighter than ever, air-raid warnings going off in the night, and the constant racket of the RAF thundering overhead on their way to bomb Germany, life was hard enough without having to put up with temper tantrums.

Determined to remain cheerful, she continued on past the bombed-out Odeon cinema where her husband Jim had worked as a projectionist; the wreckage of what had once been Woolworths, and the unscathed Home and Colonial Store which her brother-in-law Ted managed. Ted and her elder sister, Doris, were now divorced, and it was rumoured that he was courting Frances Albright, a pretty war widow who worked at the labour exchange – but if he was, then he was keeping very quiet about it, which was most frustrating, for Peggy liked a romance and Ted was a lovely man who deserved some happiness.

With Daisy still kicking her heels against the metal footplate and yelling in fury, Peggy continued to close her ears to the racket and kept walking at a brisk pace in the hope they didn't meet anyone she knew. It was always embarrassing when Daisy played up like this – people must think she was a terrible mother, but there really was very little she could do about it.

She looked across at the ruins of the lovely old church which had once stood on the other side of the road and was now completely flattened by an enemy bombing raid. The ornate iron railings that had once encircled Havelock Gardens had been uprooted long ago and sent somewhere to help make bits of aircraft, and there were bullet holes stitched along walls, and empty plots of rubble that had once been someone's home or business. The signs of war were everywhere, and although there was a glimmer of hope in the news, it seemed to Peggy that these long, colourless, cold days of struggle would never come to an end.

She reached the corner of Camden Road and glanced past Havelock Gardens to the grey, heaving sea and Havelock Road, which was regarded as one of the poshest areas of Cliffehaven. Doris lived there in a large detached house which overlooked the promenade, still smarting from the fact that Ted had dared to leave her, but too proud to admit that it was probably her own fault that he'd done so.

Peggy had always been perplexed by Doris, for

unlike her and their younger sister, Doreen, she was an overbearing snob. She constantly denigrated Peggy's home, choice of husband and her continued closeness to her father-in-law Ron and his lady-friend Rosie Braithwaite, who owned the Anchor pub. Doris had absolutely nothing to be snobbish about and yet seemed determined to climb the greasy pole of the upper echelons of Cliffehaven's society, and Peggy suspected she'd made Ted's life a misery – which had led to him having an affair with a woman who'd worked on the fish counter, which ultimately led to him discovering that life without Doris was rather pleasant.

Peggy turned into Camden Road and grimaced at the thought of the awful women Doris tried so hard to emulate. They sat on every town and charity committee and looked down on just about everyone, making a point of advertising all the good works they did for the war effort while they swanned about in their diamonds and furs, lived in their luxuriously appointed houses and stuffed their smug faces with black market smoked salmon and tinned peaches.

Neither she nor Doreen would have given them the time of day, but Doris was a different kettle of fish entirely and yearned for nothing more than to be part of their clique – even though she too had been born and raised in Beach View Boarding House by loving working-class parents.

Unfortunately, because of the scandal over Ted's affair and then the divorce, she'd been shunned, and although Peggy had tried to make her see that they weren't true friends and not worth the effort, Doris was determined to claw her way back in.

Peggy was drawn from her musings when they reached the fire station. 'Oh, look, Daisy. There's Rita,' she said in the hope it would shut her up for a minute.

Daisy immediately perked up as Rita waved to them from beneath the fire engine she was servicing. 'Rita, Rita. Wanna play.'

'I'll play with you after tea,' the dark-haired girl called back with a wave of an oily hand. 'I've got to get this fuel pump sorted first.'

Ivy's boyfriend Andy poked his head out to wave to them before the Fire-Chief, John Hicks, emerged from the depths of the fire station garage with a broad smile. John limped over to Peggy and made a fuss of Daisy, who immediately stopped being a demon and smiled angelically up at him as if butter wouldn't melt.

'And how are you today, poppet?' he asked.

Daisy giggled with practised charm and batted her eyelashes as she prattled back to him. She was definitely her father's daughter, thought Peggy in amusement.

'I got a letter from Sal today,' he said, turning to Peggy. 'They seem to be coping well down there in Somerset despite the hard winter, and of course having milk, eggs, butter and cheese in abundance makes life a lot more pleasant.'

'Lucky them,' she replied wistfully.

Conversation ceased and they all looked up as several squadrons of heavy-bellied Allied bombers thundered overhead accompanied by fighter planes. The sound reverberated through the streets, making the tiles rattle on the roofs and sending the screeching seagulls into panicked flight.

Peggy had little doubt that Martin was up there – probably Rita's chap, Matthew, too, and she sent out a silent plea that they would all return home safely. The raids had been going on for days now, and although the press and the radio reports banged on about the successful completion of their missions, they said very little about the fatalities incurred. Peggy shivered, for she knew Martin spent most evenings writing to the families of the boys he'd lost – and knew how deeply he was affected by the task.

'It looks like there's another raid on Germany,' muttered John. 'I almost feel sorry for the blighters.'

'Well, don't,' retorted Rita. 'Look at what they've done to us.'

'But too many civilians are being killed,' John protested.

'Like they were in London and Coventry,' she snapped back.

Peggy didn't want to get into the debate, for it could only get heated and would solve nothing. 'It's too cold to stand about,' she said, 'so I'll be off. Don't keep her too late, John, or her tea will spoil.'

As Peggy began to walk away Daisy immediately yelled in protest and squirmed furiously in the pushchair, kicking at her blanket and tearing off her woolly hat. Peggy calmly gathered both from the pavement and, ignoring this to-do, hurried down Camden Road towards Beach View and the warmth of her kitchen. Rita, Ivy and the other two girls would soon be home, and if she didn't get a move on nobody would get fed on time.

She passed the hospital where Fran was working as a theatre nurse, and then the bomb site which had once been a block of flats and the junior school which all her children had once attended and where Anne had started her teaching career. The thought of her scattered family sent a wave of loneliness through her – a yearning to have them all safely at home and sitting around her kitchen table. But with Anne, Bob and Charlie down in Somerset with Rose and Emily; Cissy living in barracks up at Cliffe Aerodrome; and Jim somewhere out in India, it was as if she'd been abandoned. Cards and letters never seemed to be enough, and the rare and too short telephone calls merely left her feeling more bereft than ever.

Peggy blinked back the ready tears. She'd become adept at hiding these inner sorrows; squaring her shoulders and putting on a brave face for Daisy and Cordelia and all the girls who'd come to live at Beach View. They too had their own sadness and fears, and they looked to her for strength and unquestioning love and comfort, which she was glad to give. Yet there were times when she felt she might break beneath the weight of all that responsibility.

She had a sudden memory of Martin's haggard face the last time he'd managed to visit Beach View and silently berated herself for being so feeble. Her worries and responsibilities couldn't begin to compare to his, and it was time she grew some backbone and got on with things instead of feeling sorry for herself.

Determined to shrug off her dark thoughts, she glanced up and caught sight of her friend Rosie Braithwaite, who was looking out of the top window of the Anchor. Peggy returned her wave. Rosie and Ron were still courting – even though Rosie kept him at arm's length and wouldn't commit to him until she was free to marry again. Her poor husband was still in the asylum, and the law of the day meant she couldn't divorce him, and only his death could free her to start a new life.

It was a tragedy, but Rosie kept cheerful, and Ron seemed quite happy with the arrangement – although there were times when he got quite grumpy. But then that was his nature, and like his dog, Harvey, his bark was worse than his bite, and beneath that dour exterior beat a sturdy, loyal heart and a wicked sense of humour.

Peggy waved to Alf the butcher, and Fred the Fish who were cleaning up in preparation for closing their shops. Reaching the bomb site on the corner, she waited while a convoy of American army trucks rumbled up from the seafront on their way to the Cliffe Estate.

The Yanks had taken over Lord Cliffe's fine manor house, but the rest of the forest and farm estate was being managed by the Women's Timber Corps, and her evacuee Sarah was working up there in the office. Sarah and her younger sister, Jane, were still waiting for news of their father, Jock, and Sarah's fiancé, Philip, whom they'd last seen on the quayside in Singapore as their ship sailed away and the Japs overran the

39

island. But at least their mother had also managed to escape and she and their baby brother, James, were safe in Queensland, Australia.

Peggy waited impatiently in the freezing wind for the convoy to pass, wondering fleetingly what Jane was doing since she'd left Beach View on some mysterious posting for the MOD, but had to accept she'd probably never find out. That was the thing about war – everyone had secrets, and it was the devil's own job to try and get to the bottom of things.

The convoy finally came to an end and she crossed the road. She struggled to push the pram uphill, hampered by Daisy's rigorous wriggling and the buffeting of the wind coming off the churning sea that crashed against the chalk cliffs which had given the town its name. At last she made it to the alleyway that ran between the tall Victorian terraced houses and stopped for a moment to catch her breath now she was out of the wind.

The lines of once-elegant Victorian villas laced the eastern hillside of Cliffehaven from the crescent-shaped bay up to the main road which led out of town. Now there were gaping voids in the terraces; sheets of hardboard covered shattered windows and doors; tarpaulins were tethered over damaged roofs and the pockmark scars of bullets were visible on nearly every wall.

Peggy approached the back gate and looked at the house which had been her home since childhood. Beach View had suffered some damage during a bombing raid, and it was only by the grace of God that she, Daisy and Cordelia had survived when the blast had all but wiped out the scullery and back wall. The neighbours had been marvellous, coming to do repairs without being asked and even kitting out her scullery so it was as good as new.

That was the one good thing about the war, she thought warmly as she opened the back gate and walked past the Anderson shelter. People had lost that British reserve and had come together to help one another regardless of class and circumstance to fight a common enemy and show Hitler they would not be bullied into submission. The bulldog spirit was alive and well and stronger than ever in these dark days, and with Churchill leading the way, Peggy had absolute faith that they would eventually see the light of victory.

She went down the path through Ron's vegetable garden towards his shed and the outside lav. Unstrapping Daisy, she grabbed her quickly before she could run off and opened the door to the outside lav. Holding on to her as she perched on the wooden seat, Peggy eyed the fancy porcelain handle on the chain, and the even fancier decoration on the cistern. Proof, if ever she'd needed it, that Ron had probably nicked it from the bomb site of the Imperial Hotel – although he'd sworn blind he hadn't.

Once Daisy was comfortable again, she opened the back door and parked the pushchair in the scullery. Closing the door on the weather, she was greeted by the lovely smell of stew cooking in the range, but Daisy was demanding to see Gan-Gan Cordy and it was a bit of a struggle to get her out of her outdoor clothes before she wriggled away and eagerly clambered up the concrete steps on all fours in search of one of her favourite playmates.

Peggy heard Cordelia's little cry of welcome and the tap, tap, tap of her daughter's running footsteps across the kitchen floor and smiled. Cordelia Finch was eighty now, and had been boarding at Beach View for many years. She wasn't related in any way, but she'd become so much a part of the family that she'd taken on the role of grandmother to Daisy and all the evacuees, as well as becoming something of a mother to Peggy. Cordelia had been enlivened by the arrival of the girls, and Daisy's birth two years ago, and although she and Ron were constantly arguing, there was no harm in it, for they both enjoyed a good exchange of banter and it kept them on their toes.

There was no sign of Ron or his dog Harvey, and a quick glance into his basement bedroom showed an empty ferret cage, piles of discarded clothes, boots, fishing tackle and poaching aids, and an unmade bed covered in dirty paw prints and cat hair on which lay a well-chewed meat bone and a sleeping Queenie.

Ron had brought Queenie home from his mate Chalky's smallholding – a tiny abandoned kitten with a withered leg, a determined attitude and an infestation of fleas. Now she was plump and as nimble as any other cat despite her crippled leg, her black fur sleek and long, her fluffy tail curled tightly over her white paws as two green eyes opened to regard Peggy with annoyance at having her snooze so rudely interrupted.

Peggy shook her head and gave a deep sigh as

she gingerly retrieved the bone from the tangle of sheets.

It seemed the animals had taken over, for Harvey did as he pleased – rather like Ron – and Queenie was constantly demanding to be fed or made a fuss of. Both of them emulated Ron by getting under her feet, eating her out of house and home and making a mess – which meant life was even more complicated than it needed to be.

She turned her back on the chaos of Ron's room, determined not to do anything about it until morning. Throwing the bone out into the back garden, she shrugged off her coat then carried her shopping bag upstairs to the kitchen, drawn by the promised warmth and the delicious aroma of stew.

'I thought Bertie was taking you somewhere nice this afternoon,' she said to the birdlike little woman who was carefully holding a cup of warm tea to Daisy's lips.

'It isn't rice, dear. It's tea. And of course the cup isn't dirty,' she replied, eyeing Peggy over her half-moon reading glasses. 'I am aware of how important it is to keep things clean, you know.'

Peggy smiled and made winding movements with her hands to encourage Cordelia to turn up her hearing aid. Once this was achieved, she tried again. 'Didn't you go out with Bertie today?'

'Yes,' she replied with a nod, still concentrating on helping Daisy to drink from the cup. 'We had lunch in a country hotel, but with the weather being so cold and dismal, we decided to cut the outing short and he brought me home.'

Peggy smiled, glad that Cordelia and Bertie Grantley-Adams – 'Bertie Double-Barrelled', as

43

they all called him – were friends again. There had been a time the previous year when they'd fallen out over some stupid gentlemen's club, but thankfully that seemed to have folded and nothing had been heard of it since. 'You should have asked him to stay on for tea,' she said, pulling on her wrap-round floral apron. 'I'm sure we could eke the food out for one more.'

'I did ask, actually.' Cordelia rescued the cup from Daisy and put it out of her reach now she'd finished the tea. 'But he's arranged to play bridge at the golf club and will eat there. I could have gone with him, but this weather doesn't agree with me and my arthritis is playing up.'

Peggy glanced down at the misshapen knuckles on the older woman's hands and felt a stab of pity for the pain she must be suffering. 'I'll make you a hot water bottle,' she said. 'That should help.'

'Don't fuss, dear. I'm fine, really.'

Peggy knew she was just being brave. After she'd checked the saucepans and taken them off the hot plate since they were in danger of boiling dry, she filled the kettle. The stone bottle was under the sink, and once the kettle had boiled, she filled it and made sure the stopper was tightly screwed in at the top. She didn't want Cordelia getting scalded. Wrapping the bottle in a clean tea towel, she snuggled it onto Cordelia's lap and covered it with a blanket. 'There, that should keep the nasty old cold out of your bones,' she said affectionately.

'Bless you, dear. You are good to me.' Cordelia patted Peggy's cheek, her blue eyes suspiciously, bright.

Peggy kissed her soft cheek, her emotions

bubbling up and making it hard to reply. She moved away to open the slow oven and prod the stew she'd prepared that morning. Consisting of a few scraps of cheap cuts of meat mixed with a lot of vegetables and lovely thick gravy it would be rich, warming and filling on such a bitter day. She added the dumplings she'd made earlier from the suet Alf the butcher had managed to sneak her under the counter, and then closed the oven door.

Daisy had absolutely no desire to be read a story and began to race about the kitchen and hallway with her wheeled horse which badly needed some oil to stop it from squeaking.

Peggy rootled about along the shelves beneath the sink for the little oil can and set it to one side in preparation for the moment when Daisy grew tired of her horse and turned to something else. It didn't take long before Daisy's attention was grabbed by the sight of her rag doll peeking out of Peggy's shopping bag, and as she fussed over her and tucked her in the doll's pram, Peggy quickly oiled the horse's wheels and dabbed the drops off the lino before someone slipped on them, then washed her hands in the stone sink.

Discovering that the teapot was still hot, she poured out a cup and leaned against the sink to regard her favourite room and garner some welcome heat from the range. The kitchen was the heart of her home, and despite the shabby state it was in, she looked at it with great affection.

The walls needed a fresh coat of paint, the ceiling was brown from tobacco smoke and cooking grease, and the lino Jim and Ron had fitted before Jim had left for India was already showing

45

the wear and tear of many feet. The furniture was mismatched and scarred by years of heavy service, and the woodwork needed scrubbing down and revarnishing – a job she'd asked Ron to do without any success.

As for the oilcloth on the table, it was so faded she could no longer make out its flowery pattern, and the table-legs had been gouged by Queenie's claws into deep ridges when she'd used them as scratching posts. One of these days they'd be sitting down to their tea and the blessed thing would simply collapse.

Peggy sipped her tea, thawing out from her cold walk and contemplating the line of photographs on the mantelpiece below the framed picture of the King and Queen. There were her boys Bob and Charlie, arms about one another, laughing about some bit of mischief as they stood in the back garden – and Cissy looking very glamorous in her WAAF uniform, the fetching peaked cap placed at a jaunty angle over one neatly shaped brow.

There was a snapshot of the girls who'd boarded with them, again taken in the back garden with Cordelia almost two years ago. As she looked fondly at the smiling faces of her chicks, Peggy thought how very young they all seemed – especially dear little Kitty Pargeter as she'd been then, so courageous and determined to carry on delivering planes for the ATA despite having lost a leg. She was married now to Roger Makepeace, one of Martin's officers, and although her letters were always cheerful, Peggy could read between the lines and knew how very much she fretted over

Roger and her brother Freddy as this seemingly endless war continued into yet another year.

Next in line was a photograph of Anne and Martin on their wedding day, and then another of Anne with her children, taken by the window of Vi's lovely, homely farmhouse. Peggy hadn't got to know Rose Margaret properly before they'd left for Somerset, and her single visit there had been too short to improve that situation. She had yet to even meet Emily Jane, which made her feel very sad; and the sadness intensified as her gaze drifted to the studio portrait of Jim looking so very handsome in his army uniform.

Beach View was not the same without him. Their bed felt empty at night, the rooms echoing now she could no longer hear his laughter and his soft Irish brogue ringing through them. At least he'd been at home long enough to welcome Daisy into the world, but she was growing up without him now he'd been sent to India, and they would be strangers to one another when he finally came home.

'Oh, dear, I am silly,' twittered Cordelia. 'I completely forgot that some letters arrived for you with the afternoon post. I put them in your bedroom.'

Peggy cheered up immediately. 'Who from?' she asked eagerly.

Cordelia's eyes twinkled behind the glasses. 'I do believe there's one from Jim, so why don't you go and read it while I watch Daisy and keep an eye on supper?'

Peggy's heart did a little skip at the thought. 'Thanks, Cordelia.' She gave her shoulder a gentle squeeze, mindful of her brittle, aching bones. Once she'd made sure Daisy was occupied with her toys, she hurried out of the kitchen and into her bedroom, which was off the hall.

The letters were in a neat pile on the bedside table, and she snatched them up eagerly, shuffling through them to see who'd sent them. There was indeed one from Jim, two from Anne, one from Kitty and one each from Bob and Charlie – a treasure trove for her delight.

Prolonging the sweet agony of leaving Jim's until last so she could really enjoy it, she swiftly read through Kitty's short letter, thrilled to discover that she and Roger had managed to snatch a twenty-four-hour leave back in November, and were now expecting their first baby.

This exciting news was being kept under wraps, for it was early days – but eventually it would mean she'd have to leave the ATA. As her family home was in Argentina, and her brother Freddy was based at Cliffe, she wondered if Peggy might have a room spare in a few months' time? She realised it could be a bit of bind for Peggy, but if it was possible, then it would give her a chance to find more permanent accommodation close to Cliffe Aerodrome where she might be able to see Roger and Freddy more frequently.

'Oh, you silly girl,' breathed Peggy. 'This has always been your home for as long as you need it. I won't hear of you going anywhere else.' She set the letter aside, making a mental note to send Kitty a telegraph first thing in the morning. Ivy hadn't been living here during Kitty's stay, but Cordelia and the other three girls would be thrilled to welcome her back, especially Sarah, for they'd become very close, and Peggy had a suspicion that the girl was feeling rather lonely now that Jane was living away.

Next she turned to the letters from her sons – not so young now, and probably growing taller and more mature by the day.

Bob wrote that he was delighted to be free of the classroom and very proud that he'd been given the important task of ploughing and seeding, and that although he wasn't yet fully expert, old Fred said he'd done a good job of the drystone wall he'd repaired on the top field. He'd left the scouts now and had joined the local Home Guard as well as the junior army corps, where he was now the champion at target shooting and map-reading. He was doing his stint of firewatching and was even helping out one of his former teachers to spot enemy planes and report them to the headquarters of the local Observer Corps. It was something he could fit in between his work on the farm, and if push came to shove, he'd apply to join the OC when he turned eighteen.

Peggy's heart clenched at the thought that in less than a year's time Bob could be fighting for his country – just as his father was – and her hand trembled as she turned over the page to read what followed.

It seemed Bob had no desire to join the army, although he was hugely patriotic, and far from being a pacifist – for the farm had become extremely important to him and he wanted to do his bit by providing the food, milk and grain that was now in such short supply due to the never-ceasing attacks on the Atlantic convoys. If Vi agreed, he was planning to assist her in managing the farm, since he felt he would be of more use to the country on the back of a tractor than carrying a gun – and would therefore be exempt from call-up.

Peggy breathed a trembling sigh of relief, though she knew that others might see his ambitions as a sign of cowardice. Still, Bob was proving to be as determined and mulish as his father when he got an idea into his head, and he would certainly be capable of dealing with any detractors. If it meant that her boy was safe, then it was all to the good as far as she was concerned.

She read through Charlie's scrawl, managing to decipher that he was keeping the farm machinery going with the help of old Fred and wanted to be an engineer like his father when he got older. He was playing football for the junior village team, and enjoying the rough-and-tumble of rugby at his senior school. But he wasn't too happy about the strict discipline enforced there, and hated maths.

Peggy giggled. 'Nothing much has changed there then,' she murmured. She turned over the page – torn from an exercise book – to discover that Charlie and Ernie had got into trouble because they'd taken little Harry out to go bear hunting in the woods like Davy Crockett, and managed to get lost. It had been a bit scary once it got dark, and they got a right ticking off from the leader of the search party that had finally found them, and had then suffered the indignity of a clip round the ear by the local copper, followed by another from Sally. He didn't think this was at all fair, since Harry had really enjoyed himself and was asking when they could go again.

Peggy shook her head. They were a couple of scamps, and it was a good thing someone was around to keep them in control, for left to their own devices they'd simply run wild.

She returned the letter to the envelope and tore open the first of Anne's which, joy of joys, contained photographs of Rose and Emily, and another of them all grouped outside the snow-covered farmhouse wrapped up against the winter.

Tears pricked as she saw how quickly the babies were changing and how much her boys had grown. Bob towered over the three women, and Charlie wasn't far behind, both of them looking very grown-up – especially Bob, who was wearing long trousers and seemed to have the shadow of fuzz on his chin and upper lip. It seemed like only yesterday that he was a little boy messing about in the back garden with his dad and Ron – and yet, here he was, rapidly becoming a handsome young man. It was enough to break her heart.

Anne's two letters were quite short because her days were filled with her school duties, the WI and of course looking after the children and helping on the farm, but she assured Peggy that she'd sent copies of the photographs to her father as well as Martin, which should perk them up a bit. Everyone was well, but the snow had made it difficult to get about, so they'd had to use the tractor to get the children to school and nursery – and because the coal truck couldn't get through, Bob and the land girls had gathered wood from the nearby forest to keep the fires going.

She wrote about George Mayhew and how his poor damaged face and arm were reminders of what might happen to Martin, and then went on in a lighter tone to describe the mayhem caused by a plague of nits, and how they'd all had to go about with hair whitened by DDT powder – even to the village dance, which had caused some hilarity. But at least they'd managed to persuade George to attend, and it seemed that with her and Belinda's encouragement he was slowly coming out of his shell.

She'd received some airgraphs from her father, and the occasional letter and telephone call from Martin, but there hadn't been any communication from Martin's family, who obviously were maintaining their disapproval of her and, more unfortunately, of their children.

'Oh, you poor love,' sighed Peggy. 'Nasty people. I simply can't understand how they managed to have such a lovely son in Martin – and as for completely ignoring their grandchildren... Words fail me.'

She heard the scrabble of paws on the kitchen floor and Ron's rumbling voice through the dividing wall and realised she didn't have long to read and digest Jim's letter before the others came home, so she quickly tore it open.

He'd been transferred to yet another regiment but was still mending the Americans' trucks and tanks; still enduring the awful heat and rains of the jungle; and still making the best of things with his mate, Ernie, even though they were constantly attacked by mosquitoes and what he

52

called Delhi Belly.

But the good news was that, on his transfer, he'd been promoted to Warrant Officer First Class, which meant he could send more money home. The drawback was that this promotion was only one step away from becoming a commissioned officer and he wasn't at all sure if he wanted to leave the ranks for the dubious pleasure of mixing with the 'Ruperts'.

Peggy smiled at this, for Jim had never thought much of his senior officers, even in the first shout. It was their private schooling and the old club ties that got his goat, but she put that down to inverted snobbery – which could, at times, be even worse than Doris's sort.

Jim continued that there was always the possibility the commissioned officers might be sent home sooner than the lower ranks – but there again, he could be sent home earlier anyway, because he was a married man and if this war went on for another year or so, he'd have served three years and be eligible for repatriation.

Peggy felt a sharp stab of hope as she quickly turned the page.

Jim warned that it could just be a rumour doing the rounds about this new repatriation law, which might or might not prove to be true – and she was not to hold out too much hope. The army marched on hearsay and bull-dust, the government changed its mind every five minutes, the Japs seemed determined to prolong the war by bringing in hordes more troops, and the officers couldn't be trusted to tell them anything straight, because he suspected they were as much in the dark as everyone else.

Peggy's hopes plummeted, and as she continued to read, she started to feel a little uneasy at his change of tone. He loved her, missed her and was very frustrated that sometimes the mail would be so delayed that he didn't receive a thing from anyone and then they all arrived at once. He asked if she was going out in the evenings to the parties and dances the other men's wives had written about – was the town still full of servicemen, and who did she go to the pictures with? Did the men from the aerodrome drop by – and what were the Yanks up to over at the Cliffe Estate? Was Sarah still bringing some home?

Peggy clicked her tongue at this. As if she had the time or energy to go dancing or even to the pictures, with Daisy, Cordelia and everyone else relying on her. As for entertaining Yanks and airmen, they were far too busy fighting the war – apart from the fact that she only had enough to feed her own household without entertaining the troops. What *was* he thinking?

She gritted her teeth. Jim might be a long way away, and it was clear he was fretting over what she might be up to without him, but he should know by now that she'd never dream of looking at another man – unless it was Ronald Colman, of course, which might be a temptation too far.

'In your dreams, Peggy Reilly,' she muttered crossly. 'Jim should look to his own conscience. When I think of all those parties and dances he's been to during his R&R in Calcutta ... I bet he's having a whale of a time with those nurses, without a thought in his head about me.'

54

She stopped mithering and returned to his letter, noting with some amusement that he'd picked up the Americans' slang, for each page was littered with words like 'swell', 'cute' and 'honey'.

It seemed that the last flight to Calcutta hadn't been very successful, and although he'd looked around the markets for something pretty to send her, he couldn't find anything decent. He suggested she used some of his wages which were being sent straight from the army to her bank account to go and treat herself to something nice.

This brought a sad smile. Every last penny Jim sent had to be used to buy clothes for Daisy and food for the larder as well as forking out for repairs around the house. But it was odd he hadn't found anything, like a bit of silk, or some jewellery or leather, because the other wives in Cliffehaven whose husbands were serving out there had received such things.

She gave a sigh. Jim hated shopping at the best of times, and she had to accept that if it was that hot and uncomfortable, he probably hadn't tried very hard.

Folding the letters into the shoebox she kept in the bottom of her wardrobe, she noted how many there were, and that soon she'd have to find a second box – which proved the point that he and their daughter had been gone for too long and that it was time for this blasted war to end so they could all come home.

She straightened the bed covers and went back into the kitchen to discover that although there was no sign of him, Ron had tramped mud all over her clean lino, left dead rabbits on the draining board for Queenie to nibble at, and dumped his filthy old cap in the empty fruit bowl she still kept on the kitchen table despite the fact there was no fruit to be had for love nor money.

Having shooed the cat away from the rabbits and hidden them in the larder, she vigorously wiped the floor with a cloth, removed the cap, and then noticed that Daisy was looking suspiciously sleepy as she sat on Cordelia's lap with a book. As it was getting close to bedtime, she gathered up the child and carried her upstairs to wash and change her into her nightclothes before tea.

The day might be over for some, but for Peggy the end was nowhere in sight. Yet, at least being busy stopped her from fretting over Jim's ridiculous suspicions and her far-flung family.

3

Somerset

Anne finished washing up the breakfast dishes and anxiously glanced up at the large kitchen clock. She'd been up since five, but having helped with the milking, getting the children dressed and breakfast on the table, time had sped past; now they were in danger of being late for school.

She left the dishes to dry on the drainer, checked that the collie and her puppies had enough food and water, and their basket was far enough from the range so they didn't get too hot, then turned her attention to her children.

Rose Margaret was sitting at the scrubbed pine table with her colouring book and crayons, while Emily wriggled about in the battered old high chair banging a spoon on the tray and yelling to be got down. There was no sign of Charlie, who was probably getting his school uniform filthy by poking about in some engine, and Bob was taking the milk churns down to the gate on the back of the tractor so they could be collected by the local dairy. As for Aunt Vi, Anne had insisted she go to bed and nurse the heavy cold she'd come down with overnight. But at least the nit problem had been solved, which meant one less thing to worry about.

'Do stop banging and yelling,' she pleaded, hoisting Emily out of the high chair and setting her on her feet. 'And come along, Rose. You need to stop that now and get your outdoor things on.'

'Don't want to,' she said grumpily, continuing with her colouring. 'Nursery's for babies, and I'm a big girl now.'

She's certainly big enough to answer back, Anne thought wearily, for they'd been through this performance most mornings recently. She gathered up the book and crayons, ignoring Rose's howls of protest, and stowed them away on a high shelf. 'Coat, wellies, hat and gloves,' she said sternly. 'Chop-chop.'

Rose stood defiantly with her arms crossed, her dark eyes glaring from beneath her fringe of black curls. 'Won't.'

Anne regarded her steadily for a moment and then rounded up Emily who was tottering about in pursuit of one of the puppies around the flagstone floor. Keeping a firm hold on her, she wrestled her into her warm coat and hat and helped her into the wellingtons. Her gloves had been stitched to a long twist of wool which ran down each sleeve, and once these were on her tiny hands, Anne gave her a kiss.

'Good girl, Emily,' she praised, well aware that Rose was closely watching her every move. 'Bob will be here soon and then you and I can go for our ride with Harry on the tractor.'

'I wanna go on the tractor,' shouted Rose, stamping her foot.

'Then you'd better get ready,' said Anne calmly, 'or we'll go without you.'

Rose glared at her defiantly and saw that Anne wasn't about to change her mind. She grabbed her coat and struggled into it, then squashed the woolly hat over her curls before sitting on the floor to drag on her wellingtons.

Anne quickly pulled on her own overcoat, rammed on the beret and wrapped the knitted scarf around her neck. She picked up her brief-case, heavy with the homework she'd marked the previous evening, and then collected everyone's indoor shoes from the doormat, stowing them in her string bag along with their sandwich lunches and the thermos flasks of soup. Noting that Rose had put her wellies on the wrong feet, she decided not to interfere as it would probably bring about another fit of pique.

Rose was first out of the farmhouse door, running awkwardly in her boots through the puddles on the cobbled yard and shouting for Harry. As

Sal and Ernie emerged from the cottage, Harry was almost knocked off his feet by Rose's enthusiastic hug and smacking kisses.

Anne caught Sally's eye and they grinned in amusement as Harry pushed Rose away and stomped off down the track in high dudgeon. 'I don't think he's too keen on being the object of such adoration,' Anne murmured.

Sal laughed and tucked her brown hair under the knitted bobble hat. 'He'll change his mind when he gets older. All boys do.' She pulled on her gloves. 'I meant to pop in and see 'ow Auntie Vi were this morning – but with one thing and another I ran out of time. She didn't look too clever last night.'

'I sent her back to bed with a hot water bottle and a cup of Bovril. She's got a nasty cold, and I didn't want it getting on her chest like it did last year.'

'Thanks, Anne. I'll come over tonight and keep her company.'

Anne peered into the gloom of the barn where the machinery was kept. 'Charlie? Time to go,' she called.

When he emerged, his forehead was streaked with oil and there was a suspiciously dark spot on the front of his gabardine mac. She eyed him with barely contained patience. 'How many times have I told you not to mess about with engines in your school clothes?'

'Every blooming morning,' he replied cheerfully and ran off with Ernie before she could give him a clip round the ear for his cheek.

'Little brothers, eh?' chuckled Sally. 'Ernie can

59

be a right pain too, so you ain't on yer own.'

'They need their fathers around to keep them in order,' said Anne briskly. She held firmly on to Emily's little hand to stop her jumping in the puddles as they walked down the muddy track, the ice cracking beneath their feet.

Sal gave a deep sigh, no doubt thinking about her John running the fire station back in Cliffehaven, and the little cottage they'd bought down by the seafront. 'Yeah, but that ain't gunna happen, is it? Not 'til this blooming war's over, anyway.'

They fell silent, each wrapped in their own thoughts of loved ones. When they reached the five-bar gate, they found Bob waiting for them with the tractor. The weather hadn't improved since the heavy snow in February, for now everything was made sodden by the seemingly endless rain which made the long trek over the hills into the village almost impossible with such young children. But at least the ride there and back had become something of a treat for them, and anything was a bonus if it kept Rose in a good mood.

Clambering up onto the trailer, they sat on the planed lengths of wood Bob had fixed to both sides, and with a wheeze, a jolt and a puff of smoke, they were off. Anne kept hold of Emily who was inclined to lean too far out in her excitement, and Sal did the same with Harry, while Charlie and Ernie sat in a huddle behind Bob, no doubt plotting some sort of mischief for later in the day. Rose got as close to Harry as she could and gazed at him in adoration. She'd already declared that she'd marry him when they grew up, and it seemed to Anne that her passion for the little boy couldn't be diluted by his determination to keep well away from her.

When they reached the top of the hill and felt the bite of the wind on their faces, they all drew up their coat collars and scarves. Anne gave a sigh of pleasure, for the landscape was quite glorious in the early sun, glittering with frost, green from all the rain, the rich brown of the fields already showing the first signs of new crops as flocks of small birds hunted for berries and insects in the hedgerows. On this crisp, sunny, late March morning there was no better place to be, for this was her England, and worth all the sacrifices to keep it free.

The tractor chugged along the deep ruts and finally reached the village lane. The older boys jumped down, grabbed their indoor shoes and began to race each other to the other end of the village where Charlie would be catching the special bus to the secondary school in the nearby town.

Anne watched them, warmed by the huge advances Ernie had made since arriving at Beach View crippled with polio. She gathered herself and helped Sally get the little ones down and then Bob turned the tractor round in the gateway of a neighbour's field before heading back to Owlet Farm.

Anne kissed Rose and Emily goodbye and handed over their lunches and shoes to Sally as they reached the deserted farm cottage that had become the local nursery school for the duration.

'Don't stand any nonsense from Rose today,' she murmured. 'She's getting far too bossy and

61

demanding by half.'

Sal nodded, keeping a tight hold of Harry who was almost yanking her arm off to get to Ernie, who was now puffing his way back down the lane. 'Mrs Booth will sort her out,' she said. 'She stands no nonsense, and is an absolute godsend when it comes to tantrums.'

Agatha Booth was an imposing woman in her sixties who marched about the village like a galleon in full sail, and was in possession of a booming voice and imperious manner which she used on anyone over the age of five. She had once been a nanny up at the manor house, and having been retired from her post once her charges no longer needed her, had made it her business to set up the nursery school for all the younger children whose parents were working in the town factories and on the nearby farms. Like most people in the village, Sal was rather in awe of her.

Anne followed Ernie across the playground and left him playing football with the other boys as she stopped to chat with George. 'It's a cold one, isn't it?' she said.

'It certainly is, but at least the children are keeping warm by dashing about.' He looked down at her and smiled. 'There's a treat for you inside,' he said rather shyly. 'It's my way of thanking you for all you've done for me.'

Anne frowned. 'But I haven't done anything.'

His expression softened. 'You've stopped me hiding away,' he said quietly, 'and given me back my life in these past few weeks.'

Anne felt awkward at the intensity in his gaze, and was aware of the colour rising in her face. 'I think you're being a bit overdramatic, George,' she said lightly. 'It was just a village dance, and it was Belinda who got you involved with the church jumble sale and the village fund for raising money for a Spitfire. You did it all yourself, really. You just needed a bit of encouragement, that's all.'

She realised she was babbling and stopped, not quite sure what to do next.

He took a step closer to her. 'But I wouldn't have been able to do that without you knocking on my door and insisting I accompany you to that dance. It's been a long time since I've danced with a pretty woman – and I have you to thank for that.'

Anne saw something in his expression that worried her deeply, for although she'd enjoyed dancing with him that night, she didn't want him getting the wrong idea. She edged towards the door. 'Well, it's very sweet of you to give me all the credit, even though I don't deserve it,' she said, looking at her watch. 'Goodness me, is that the time? I'd better get indoors and sort myself out before assembly.'

'Will you stay for a cuppa after school?' he asked, following her to the door.

Relieved that she had a genuine excuse, she shook her head. 'I'm sorry, George, not today. I have the church flowers to arrange, and as Agatha Booth is in charge, I daren't be late.' She shot him a tentative smile to soften her rejection.

'I'll see you later then.'

Not wanting to prolong the conversation, and unable to bear his crestfallen expression, she hurried indoors to change out of her wellingtons and hang up her coat. Stuffing her beret, gloves and scarf in one of the pockets, she carried her briefcase and string bag into her classroom, still rather shaken by the realisation that George was beginning to show all the signs of infatuation.

Which was ridiculous. He knew she was married and still very much in love with Martin, and although he was lonely and shy in mixed company – and they were both far from home during a terrible war – it was no excuse. Their relationship as colleagues and friends had blossomed because they shared many interests, including their links with the RAF, but they were professionals with responsibilities, and there were certain boundaries of conduct which she wasn't prepared to cross.

And yet it was probably her own fault, she admitted silently. Her natural warmth and caring nature had been misinterpreted, and her innocent intentions to get him back into society had backfired. The situation could get very awkward unless she dealt with it swiftly.

Taken up with her thoughts, it wasn't until she'd unpacked the homework books and stowed away her sandwiches and flask in her desk that she realised there was a proper coal fire burning brightly in the hearth. 'Oh, what bliss,' she breathed, holding out her hands to the very welcome warmth.

'Yes, isn't it? Utter heaven,' sighed Belinda as she came into the room, her blue eyes shining, her fair hair glowing like a halo around her elfin face. 'There's one in all three classrooms. George managed to get hold of some coal and thought we all deserved a bit of heat on such a cold day.'

Anne returned her smile, thankful that George's treat was something they all could share. 'That was very good of him,' she murmured. 'But I hope it doesn't mean he'll go short. It's difficult enough to get hold of at the best of times with the demands of the war and most of the miners having enlisted. Not that I blame them – anything has to be better than being buried underground all day.'

'I agree, but it's hardly fair to conscript boys by lottery to take their places. My brother's barely eighteen, with hardly any experience of life, let alone coal mining, and yet he's been sent to some place in Wales and told to get on with it.'

Anne had read about the Bevin Boys, as the newspapers were calling them, but hadn't really taken much notice since it didn't directly affect her or her family. 'Surely he can refuse and enlist in another service?' she asked in horror.

Belinda shook her head, her expression, usually so lively, now serious. 'Once they're chosen, that's it for the duration.'

'But that's awful,' breathed Anne, thinking of Bob, who so loved the clean fresh air of the outdoors. 'Then I can only hope that Bob doesn't suffer the same fate when he turns eighteen. It would kill him.'

'I doubt he will,' said Belinda, flicking back her fair curls and checking her appearance in her powder-compact mirror. 'His farm work will keep him at home, you'll see.'

Their conversation came to an abrupt end as George rang the bell and the children poured into the largest of the three classrooms with their tramping feet and loud voices to take their places for assembly.

Belinda grinned, slipping the compact into the pocket of her pencil-slim skirt. 'Here we go again,' she said cheerfully. 'I'll see you during the mid-morning break for a cuppa and a good gossip. I have lots to tell you.'

Anne returned her smile, knowing her friend had probably ensnared yet another suitor with her big blue eyes and infectious smile. How she did it, Anne had no idea, for there were very few young men about – and most of those were German POWs who worked on the farms and were therefore totally out of bounds. Although there was the occasional Allied serviceman who'd come to Somerset for rest and recuperation – both of which were in short supply once Belinda got hold of them.

It's just a great pity she hasn't set her sights on George, she thought as she followed Belinda's trim little figure into the main room and headed for the small stage at the end where he was waiting at the piano to begin the morning's assembly.

Yet a glance at the pair of them proved to Anne that it wouldn't work. They were chalk and cheese, and Belinda would probably terrify him should she make any advance on him. Perhaps the district nurse Mary would be a better match?

Anne smothered a sigh and joined in the morning hymn, her thoughts still wrestling with the awkward situation she'd found herself in, and how she might resolve it without hurting his feelings and making things even worse.

Cliffehaven

Ron tramped up the hill behind Beach View, his breath clouding in the frosty air as Harvey and his pup Monty raced ahead of him. Rosie had taken Monty in when it became clear that Peggy was at the end of her tether, and Beach View was too crowded to have two boisterous dogs about the place. Monty was no longer a pup, really, Ron mused, for he was as big as Harvey, with the whippet speed of his mother in those long legs, a fine brindled coat, and his sire's talent for sniffing out prey, as well as mischief.

Ron crested the hill, noticed that for once Queenie had opted to stay in the warm and not accompany him, and took a moment to light his pipe and admire the view. He never tired of looking out to the white cliffs that soared above the arc of the shingled bay, even though there was a line of shipping traps beyond the low-water mark now, the beach had been mined, and rolls of barbed wire ran along the edge of the promenade.

There were gun emplacements down on the seafront and in the surrounding hills, and the poor old pier looked forlorn, stuck out in the water, untethered from the seafront to prevent enemy landings, the rusting remains of a German fighter plane firmly embedded in its fire-blackened ribs. But the sky was as blue as the water on this bright, cold day, the gulls wheeling and mewling over the roofs and church towers of Cliffehaven, the scene deceptively tranquil.

Ron puffed on his pipe, his thoughts roaming

67

as his gaze trawled along the bay to the green hills that swept right down to the sands at the western end of the town. There had been many changes to Cliffehaven since he'd arrived with his family as a boy, and not all of them pleased him.

Where there had once been green fields there was a vast factory estate shielded by silver barrage balloons and high wire fencing; the Cliffe Estate where he'd done most of his poaching had been taken over by the Timber Corps and the Yanks, the boundaries now closed to him by tall chain-link fences topped with barbed wire; and the small fleet of fishing trawlers he'd once run from the beach beneath the cliffs was gone but for the single small boat his eldest son Frank had beached in Tamarisk Bay when he'd been called up.

His gaze drifted to the rough chalk track which ran down to the sheltered bay on the other side of the headland. Frank and Pauline lived in one of the fishermen's cottages right by the water's edge, the boat slowly mouldering from lack of use now all fishing had been confined to the Irish Sea and the Scottish islands.

Unwilling to dwell on the unhappiness that had befallen his son and daughter-in-law, he looked away and focused on the distant remains of the farmhouse where he'd earned a bit of extra money as a farmhand when the weather made it impossible to fish. The army had commandeered it, using it as a firing range to train recruits, the family sent to another farm all the way up in Scotland somewhere. They would have wept if they could see it now, he thought sadly, for it had been reduced to rubble.

Turning his back on the view he pushed his way through the scratchy gorse and long grass into the woodland that sprawled along the boundary fence to the Cliffe Estate. The land here was of no use to the Timber Corps, for the trees were spindly and weak from the wind that tore across the hills, their roots buried in brambles, ivy and clinging weeds. It was the ideal location to set traps for rabbits, and if he was lucky he might even find a game-bird or two which had escaped the watchful eye of the estate gamekeeper, and was hiding in the undergrowth.

Ron checked each trap as the dogs eagerly raced about, noses to the ground, tails whipping back and forth in excitement at the scents of fox, rabbit and badger. He would have preferred them to move more stealthily so as not to disturb a roosting pheasant or grouse, thereby alerting the gamekeeper on the other side of the fence to his presence, but they'd caught sight of something and were off, crashing through the trees in quick pursuit.

It was a while later before Harvey returned alone, panting fit to bust and covered in muck, having no doubt been rolling in something disgusting.

Disturbed by the racket he'd made, a cock pheasant thundered out of the undergrowth with sharp cries of alarm and heavily beating wings to fly straight over Harvey's head.

Harvey leapt high, easily catching the bird by the tail feathers and bringing it to earth, where he pinned it down with one determined paw.

The bird's alarm calls rang through the trees

and Ron moved swiftly. He grabbed the flapping bird, wrung its neck and stuffed it into one of his deep coat pockets before the gamekeeper was alerted. He quickly placed the third rabbit he'd snared into another deep pocket, reset the trap and then gave a low whistle to call Monty as he patted Harvey's head.

'To be sure, y'are a fine fellow, so rare, but it's time to be away before we're both in trouble.'

Harvey didn't need telling twice and he shot off, Ron tramping behind him in a circuitous route which would take him away from the boundary fence towards the old farmhouse ruins.

Upon reaching open ground again Ron paused for a moment to watch Monty who was in hot pursuit of a hare. He admired his speed and agility as he twisted and turned, his gaze fixed firmly on his quarry. And then Harvey joined in, chasing down the hare, herding it towards Monty every time it seemed about to break for freedom.

Ron watched in admiration for all three creatures, and although a hare would have been a real treat for the pot, he almost applauded the animal's cunning when it turned sharply and disappeared into the undergrowth.

Harvey and Monty whined in frustration, their noses and paws getting pricked by the thistles and barbs of thick bramble as they tried to go in pursuit.

'Come out of there, ye heathen beasts,' Ron growled. 'The hare won today, and you'll not be catching him now.' He grabbed their collars and dragged them away, then let them race free in pursuit of something else that had caught their eye in the grass.

Ron gave a sigh, wishing he had the energy to run about like that, and then headed for the wreckage of the farmhouse where he'd arranged to meet Frank.

Frank was six foot four and built like a tank – rather like his maternal Irish grandfather, but thankfully not possessing his fiery temperament. He'd recently returned to Cliffehaven to complete his final two years of call-up as a volunteer for the Home Guard and Civil Defence. It was rather sobering for Ron to realise that his son was almost fifty – but then he'd only been seventeen when the boy was conceived.

Ron smiled as he sat down on a rotting roof timber and contemplated his youthful indiscretion and the shotgun wedding that had followed. Her father had been a red-faced, muscular Irishman with a quick temper and a fearsome right hook honed from years of bare-knuckle boxing in fairground rings. Ron had been a skinny, spotty youth who was not about to argue with him – but despite the haste of the ceremony they'd had a happy marriage, with Jim arriving a few years later to complete their family until the cancer had taken her too soon and left him alone to raise their sons.

'What's making you smile, Da? Been up to your old poaching tricks again, I'll bet.'

Ron looked up at his enormous son who was being joyously welcomed by the dogs, and grinned. 'Now that would be telling, boy.' He patted the crumbling beam. 'Come, sit awhile. It's been too long since we've had time to talk without

71

women hanging about listening in.'

Frank made a fuss of both dogs before sitting down. 'Aye, you're right there,' he said on a sigh. 'Pauline won't let me out of her sight unless I'm on fire watch or warden duty, and I've not had a moment to meself since coming home.'

'You can hardly blame her,' Ron replied softly, remembering his two grandsons who'd been killed on one of the Atlantic convoys. 'Since losing those boys and having you so far from home, she's found it very hard, Frank.'

'It's been hard for both of us,' he replied, staring out towards the sweeping valley that had now been ploughed into farmland. 'But at least one of them survived, and we have to be thankful for that.'

Ron nodded, his memories of those three little boys making his heart ache. For like his own sons, he'd carried them on his shoulders as he'd tramped the hills, and when they were older he'd taught them how to tickle trout, to train the ferrets and hunt for eels. And when they were older still, he'd taught them how to man a fishing boat and read the tides and moods of the sea; to dry the nets, fix the engine and prepare the fish so they could be sold straight off the beach to the eager housewives. Now two of them were gone to a watery grave somewhere out in the Atlantic.

''Tis not a good time to be a parent,' Ron murmured, idly scratching Harvey between the ears. 'Especially not for a mother. Your Pauline has had to bear the brunt of coping on her own while she's grieved for those boys and fought to carry on. And Peggy's the same. She might put a brave face on things, but I know she's suffering inside with all her children and grandchildren so far from home – and Jim out in India.'

'I know it hasn't been easy,' Frank murmured, 'but it's the same for us, Da. I hated being away from home.' He took out a cigarette and lit it before changing the subject.

'How's Jim really getting on over there?' he asked, the cigarette bobbing at the corner of his mouth. 'His letters don't say much, but by the sound of it, it's not pleasant, what with the humidity, the monsoons and bugs, and the Japs pouring in on all sides.'

Both dogs perked up as Ron unfastened his poaching coat and dipped his fingers into the inside pocket of his old tweed jacket. They subsided into a disgruntled slump when they saw they weren't about to get their usual treat of biscuits.

'This is his latest letter,' he said, handing it over. 'Once you've read it, I'd like your opinion as to what I should do about it, because Peggy has yet to learn the truth of things.'

Frank frowned, took the letter and swiftly read through it. His dark blue eyes were troubled as he looked back at his father. 'Dear God,' he breathed. 'How the hell did he get involved in that? And how come Peggy doesn't know?'

Ron shrugged. 'He doesn't want her to fret any more than she already is, but it doesn't sit easy with me, Frank. I think she should be told.'

'What she doesn't know won't hurt her, I suppose,' muttered Frank. 'But I'm surprised someone else hasn't already let the cat out of the bag. There must be other wives in Cliffehaven whose husbands are serving out there.'

'It's all been kept under wraps until a few weeks ago when the MOD decided the families could be told. No one was supposed to know anything, even while they were in training.'

Frank studied the postmark on the envelope which clearly showed that Jim's letter had been sent from India. He gave a low whistle which made both dogs prick up their ears. 'Bloody hell, Da. Why Jim of all people? He's hardly in the first flush of youth, and when he was enlisted he was far from fit.'

Ron shrugged and tucked the letter back into his inside pocket. 'The ways of the military have always been a mystery to me, son. I can only guess it was his experience in the last shout that earned him this posting. And to be sure they'd've got him fit by the time they'd finished training him.'

He chewed on the stem of his unlit pipe, the memories flooding back of his own training before he and his mates had been sent across the Channel to the mud, terror, gore and carnage of trench warfare. That had been kept secret too, for to talk about it merely raised the spectre of his lost comrades and gave him nightmares which he still suffered from occasionally, even after all these years.

'Then he should have the balls to tell Peggy himself and not leave it to you,' said Frank, breaking into his dark thoughts. 'If she finds out from someone else it will hit her really hard. You know how soft she is when it comes to Jim.'

'Aye. And that's why I think I should tell her, face to face – and not have her read it in a letter or overhear it from strangers.'

'I don't envy you that task. But in the circumstances, perhaps it would be wise to tell her.' Frank paused and patted Monty who'd come to rest his nose on his knee. 'Would you like me to send Pauline over to hold her hand while you tell her? She might appreciate the company of another woman.'

'Ach, to be sure there are women enough already at Beach View,' Ron muttered. 'She'll not be alone. But thanks for offering, Frank. I do appreciate it.'

They sat in silence and Ron relit his pipe as Frank finished his cigarette and ground it out beneath his heel. 'Jim's an eejit to get involved in something like that,' Frank exclaimed some time later. 'You'd've thought he'd had enough of heroics during the first shout.'

'Maybe he wanted one last go at proving he isn't past it.' Ron himself was constantly denying his advancing years, trying to prove he was still as fit as the next man. 'There again, you know what the army's like – he might not have had a choice.'

'Either way, he's still an eejit,' said Frank crossly. 'We've lost too many already in this family, and if anything should happen...'

The silence stretched between them until Frank broke it. 'Changing the subject, Da. Have you seen this?'

Ron snapped out of his worried thoughts and took the printed leaflet. It was stamped with the royal crest, and had been issued by the Ministry of Labour and National Service, but the printing was all over the place.

CAN **YOU** MAN A **BOAT?**

As an extension of a Yachtsman's Emergency Scheme already in existence, **YACHTSMEN AND OTHERS** with motor boat or steamboat experience, either as seamen or engineers, **ARE INVITED** to put their services at the disposal of the Royal Navy for short periods of duty during the next six months.

Volunteers would be required to serve in harbour service craft and other small vessels, thus releasing trained naval ratings for general service.

Ron scanned the rest of the leaflet and then handed it back. 'You've done your bit, son, and you've got your duties here.'

'But each period of duty only lasts three or four weeks.'

'I read that, but it also says you have to get permission from the Home Guard and the Civil Defence Authorities to take part – and as you're already involved with both and not yet fully released from the army, I don't rate your chances.'

'I was hoping you'd put in a good word for me with them both seeing as how you're so involved,' said Frank. 'I'm sure the army won't mind if I do something for the navy.'

Ron snorted. 'I doubt that very much. The army and navy are oil and water and don't mix. My advice is to stick to what you're doing, and then, when you're finally demobbed, you can consider this again.'

'I hope to God the war will be well and truly over by then,' Frank retorted. 'They need volunteers *now*, Da,' he said impatiently. 'I reckon this call's gone out because something big is being planned – possibly even an invasion into France – and I want to be a part of it, not sitting about here with a bunch of old men and boys playing at soldiers.'

Ron glared at him from beneath his thick eyebrows. 'Some of us might have snow on the roof, son, but the fire is far from out – so mind your tongue. As for playing at soldiers, we keep this town safe. If anyone should volunteer for this it should be me.'

'Now it's you being an eejit,' snapped Frank. 'It's bad enough having Jim put himself in danger, without a man of your age going to work in marinas and ports that are Jerry's prime targets. I'll not hear of it – and neither will the rest of the family.'

'It's not up to them,' Ron retorted. 'If I decide to volunteer, then that's my business, and I'll hear no more from you or anyone else.' He fixed his son with a penetrating glare, defying him to argue.

Frank was the first to look away. He drew his tin of cigarettes from his trouser pocket and lit one before getting to his feet. 'I didn't come here to argue with you, Da,' he said quietly before shooting his father a grin. 'But to be sure, 'tis like old times, and I'm glad of it.'

Ron stood and clapped his son's arm, having to look up at him as he towered so broadly above him. 'It's good to have you home,' he said gruffly, 'and although I'm of a mind to think you're the eejit, if the army lets you volunteer to man boats, then I give you me blessing.'

'Thanks, Da.' Frank grasped his father's shoulders and regarded him affectionately. 'And please promise me you won't do anything daft. We'd all like to keep you a while longer – even though you're a complete pain in the rear end most of the time.'

Ron chuckled. 'To be sure, I have enough to do to keep me in mischief. I'll not be manning boats, unless it's our old trawler – and that won't happen until we've got rid of Jerry and the Japs.'

Frank swamped him in a bear hug. 'I do love you, Da,' he said, his voice breaking. 'It's good to be home arguing with you again.'

Ron blinked back his tears and held his son close, thanking God that he was safe, and praying that Jim also survived to come home. 'Aye, son. I love you too.'

They drew apart, unashamed by the emotion of the tender moment they'd shared, for Ron had always been a tactile father and his sons had grown up knowing the value of showing affection.

'I'll bring Pauline over next weekend,' said Frank gruffly. 'She needs to get out of the house more, and a bit of company will do her good.'

With a smile and a nod they parted, Ron heading for Beach View and the difficult conversation he had to have with Peggy – and Frank disappearing down the track which led to Tamarisk Bay and the home he shared with his wife Pauline and the echoing reminders of their lost boys.

4

Peggy and Rita were hanging out the washing while Daisy trundled up and down the garden path with her wooden cart, upon which lay curled a stoic Queenie.

'I'm amazed the cat puts up with it,' said Rita.

'She seems to like the vibration, and she'll get off when she's had enough.' Peggy wrestled with a wet sheet that the wind seemed determined to blow into her face. She didn't usually do the washing on a Friday, but it had piled up something awful when she'd cleared out Ron's room earlier, and would have proved a daunting task on Monday if she'd left it any longer.

'It's lovely having you home for the day,' she said to the small, dark-haired girl as they managed to firmly tether the sheet to the line. 'But I'm sure you have better things to do on your day off than help me with the washing.'

Rita shrugged. 'Ivy's at work with Ruby, there's nothing in the shops to buy even if I had the money, the motorbike doesn't need anything done on it for once, and Matt's probably sleeping in after the raid last night.'

She smiled and gave a deep sigh. 'I can't believe that almost a month has passed since he last had leave. It was such a treat to see him, even though he was billeted in a terrible dump with a dragon for a landlady and our time together was so short.'

79

'Well, I hope you behaved yourself,' said Peggy, biting back a smile. 'I know it's all exciting and so on to be together, but we don't want any accidents, do we?' She raised a questioning brow, her gaze steady on the girl's face.

Rita went pink and bent down to pluck a pillowcase out of the laundry basket. 'It's difficult, Auntie Peg,' she said, holding a pair of wet socks to her chest, her gaze still on her feet. 'We love each other very much, but have so little time together, and with him up there and putting his life in danger every day...'

Peggy gave her a swift hug. 'I do understand,' she murmured, dropping a kiss into her riotous dark curls and retrieving the wet socks. 'Me and Jim were just the same, but we got into a right pickle and no mistake. I was just lucky he was an honourable man and did the right thing by me. Otherwise, I could have ended up like dear little April.'

Rita bit her lip and still couldn't quite meet Peggy's eyes. 'Ivy and me had a long chat with Ruby, then went to see the doctor at the clinic to get fixed up,' she confessed softly. 'After what happened to April, we both realised it was better to be safe than sorry.'

'Very wise,' said Peggy, feeling a pang of something akin to sorrow at the thought of her chicks being so grown up and sensible. 'But war or not, the rule of no men upstairs still applies, Rita,' she added firmly.

'Yeah, we know that.' Rita finished pegging out the underwear and hoisted up, the basket, finally meeting Peggy's gaze. 'You don't think badly of us, do you?' she asked tentatively. 'Only we couldn't bear it if you did.'

Peggy put her arm about her shoulders. 'Of course not, Rita. You and Ivy are young girls caught up in a time when nothing is certain except for how you feel about your boys, and I'm just relieved that you're both being so mature about it.'

Drawing her close, she murmured, 'Things haven't changed so very much since I was your age, you know, and I'm the last person to criticise. But I wouldn't discuss any of it in front of Cordelia. She's from a very different generation, and probably wouldn't be quite so understanding.'

Rita pursed her lips. 'She came right for April, though. Maybe she's got more modern ideas than you credit her for, Auntie Peg.'

'She supported April because she had no one else to turn to,' replied Peggy 'But I happen to know she didn't really approve of what she'd done – especially as baby Paula's father was black.'

Rita blew out a breath. 'Life can be so very difficult, can't it, Auntie Peg?'

'It certainly can,' she replied affectionately. 'But everything looks much better after a cup of tea and a fag, so why don't you go upstairs and put the kettle on?'

Rita nodded and grinned impishly. 'We'll drown in tea before this war's over,' she teased.

'Not a bad way to go,' replied Peggy. 'But once we've had that cuppa, Rita, I suggest you go and tidy your room. The last time I looked in there it resembled a bomb site. I don't know what you and Ivy get up to, but I do wish you'd at least remember to bring down your dirty crockery.'

'Sorry. It's just that we never seem to have any time, what with Ivy doing her shifts at the factory, and me in and out every time the blooming siren goes.'

'Well, you've got plenty of time today,' Peggy reminded her gently.

As the girl went into the scullery, she smiled. Rita and Ivy were a couple of imps; their idea of tidiness was to throw everything into the wardrobe and shut the door on it. If she hadn't known better, she might have thought they were related to Ron, for he was as bad – if not worse.

She regarded the washing flapping in the brisk wind above the neat lines of turned earth in Ron's vegetable garden. There were already green shoots appearing, a sure sign that spring would soon be here even if the wind was bitter and yet more rain had been forecast for tonight. At least the weather had meant they'd had respite from enemy raids this week, but that hadn't stopped the boys up at Cliffe from setting out on their bombing campaign over Germany – and the racket they made was enough to waken the dead.

Peggy wrapped her cardigan more tightly about her as she wandered down the path towards Daisy, who was now covering the long-suffering Queenie with a doll's blanket and rather bossily telling her that she mustn't catch cold, because it would mean having to take yucky cowlibber boil.

Peggy smiled at this, for it was a struggle to get the daily dose of cod liver oil down Daisy at the best of times – and the thought of trying to get Queenie to swallow anything she didn't want in her mouth was laughable.

Needing a few moments alone, she leaned against the flint wall by the back gate where she was protected from the wind by the neighbouring fence, and dug in her wrap-round apron pocket for a cigarette. Having lit it, she watched the chickens peck about in their run, and then eyed the Anderson shelter without affection.

The corrugated iron hump had been erected by the council at the beginning of the war, and Ron had covered the roof in turf to grow parsley and mint for the kitchen. It was an ugly thing, and they'd spent too many hours in its dark, dank confines just lately, because Jerry bombers were now seeking vengeance for the RAF raids over their industrial towns and railways. It was inevitable, she supposed, but this tit for tat was wearing everyone down, and it would just be nice to have some peace and quiet and unbroken sleep for a change.

She felt the tension tighten the muscles in her neck and shoulders and made a concerted effort to relax. She always seemed to be on edge these days, for it was getting harder by the week to make ends meet – what with the rationing stricter than ever due to the tragic loss of so many supply ships in the Atlantic, the lack of coal and the price of everything going through the roof.

Jim's money was coming through all right, which was a blessing, and of course the government paid for her evacuees' keep, but it never seemed to be enough to get through the week. The girls were marvellous, bringing home bits and pieces they'd managed to buy or purloin from their various canteens, and of course Ron's foraging up in the hills did provide things for the pot. But Daisy was growing fast and needed new shoes and clothes – and the list of repairs needed around the house was lengthening by the day.

Ron had little time as it was with all his Home Guard duties, his stints at the Anchor to help Rosie and whatever other mischief he was involved in, to see to the loose roof tiles, the wonky guttering, the damp in the dining room chimney breast, and the mould growing on the bathroom ceiling and under the kitchen sink. But to get someone in would cost money, and she just didn't have it.

She stubbed out her cigarette impatiently and threw the butt into the dustbin which stood by the gate. There was many a time that she wished she'd been born a man, with the strength and know-how – and the right tools – to get on with things, and not have to sit about watching her home fall down around her ears. If only she'd done plumbing and woodwork at school instead of cooking and sewing, things would have been very different, she thought in despair.

However, an idea had been blossoming for some time now, and although Jim wouldn't like it and Ron would raise all sorts of fuss, it seemed to Peggy to be the ideal solution to her problems. Having mulled it over for weeks she finally made up her mind to see if her plan was possible, and felt instantly better.

'Come along, Daisy,' she said brightly. 'Leave Queenie to sleep, and come indoors for some tea and a biscuit.'

Daisy liked this idea and Peggy carried her up

the concrete steps into the kitchen to find that Rita was helping Cordelia unravel her latest disastrous attempts at knitting and a fresh pot of tea was steeping nicely on the table. She wouldn't say anything of her plans for the moment, she decided. It would be best to see if her idea bore fruit before she had to face the music.

They were sitting at the table drinking their tea and nibbling on the broken biscuits Ivy had brought back from the factory canteen a few days ago when they heard the back gate clatter, and heavy footsteps coming down the garden path.

Thinking it was probably Ron returning with Harvey, Peggy poured out a cup and added just a smidgen of precious sugar before hiding the bowl back in the larder. Ron was a glutton for sugar, and would quite often sneak in far more than he should before she caught him at it.

The back door was opened and quickly slammed shut against the blast of wind that tore up the steps, making the flames dance in the range's meagre fire.

'Hello? Anyone at home?'

'Martin!' Peggy jumped to her feet as he filled the kitchen doorway, and flung her arms around him. 'Oh, Martin, what a lovely, lovely surprise.'

He hugged her back until she could hardly breathe and tickled her ear with his bushy moustache as he kissed her cheek. 'I hope you've got more tea in that pot,' he said cheerfully, 'because I've brought a couple of pals with me.'

Peggy's eyes widened as she looked round Martin's sturdy figure, and saw her daughter, Cissy, and young Matthew Champion beaming at her from the steps. 'Oh, oh, darlings,' she gasped, the tears of delight welling as she was swamped in their embrace. 'Rita, Rita, look who's here!'

She continued to cuddle Cissy as Rita flew across the room and into Matthew's arms, and Martin paid court to a twittering Cordelia before making a huge fuss of Daisy.

Drawing back from the embrace, Peggy drank in the sight of her lovely daughter – so fair and blue-eyed, and as slim and glamorous as any film star. 'You look marvellous,' she breathed, taking in the neat uniform, the perfect make-up and the way she'd done her fair hair in a 'victory roll' beneath the fetching peaked hat. 'This is a wonderful surprise,' she managed through the lump in her throat. 'But you look too thin. Are you sure they're feeding you properly up there?'

Cissy giggled. 'I eat as well as anyone, Mam. I've just lost all that baby fat, that's all.'

'You were never a fat baby,' Peggy protested.

'Don't worry about it, Mam,' she soothed. 'I'm fine, really I am, and I don't want to spend what little time we have talking about my weight.'

Peggy fumbled a handkerchief from her cardigan sleeve and dabbed at the tears streaming down her face. 'Oh, dear,' she said shakily. 'Silly to get so emotional, I know. But it's been such an age since you were last home.'

'We can't stay very long, I'm afraid, Mam,' she replied regretfully. 'Martin managed to wangle an hour off, and as I'm his driver now and Matt was hanging about doing nothing, he thought we could all do with a bit of your special spoiling.'

Peggy gave her a swift hug and began to bustle about the kitchen in blind panic. The tea was easy to provide, but there was very little bread and marge, no jam or cake, or proper biscuits – not even a tin of spam to be shared.

'Please don't fuss, Mam.' Cissy returned from hugging and kissing Cordelia and her baby sister, Daisy, and put her arm about her waist. 'A cup of tea will be just fine. It's you we've come to see, not the contents of the larder.'

She glanced across to where Matt and Rita were squashed together in one of the fireside chairs exchanging sweet nothings. 'Or, at least, some of us have,' she added with a wry grin. 'Where's Granda?'

'He's out with Harvey. I think he was planning to meet your Uncle Frank, so he might not be back before you have to leave – which is a terrible shame, because he would have loved to see you all.'

Peggy wiped away her tears, fetched more cups and refreshed the teapot with boiling water before making sure Cordelia had her hearing aid switched on, and that Daisy wasn't making a nuisance of herself with Martin. She sat down, thinking how wonderful it was to have them home, to hear them chattering away in her kitchen just like the old days – except it wasn't the old days, she realised as fresh tears ran down her face.

Cissy seemed to sense the reason for her tears and reached for her hand. 'Please don't cry, Mam,' she said softly. 'We'll all be home soon, I'm sure of it.'

Peggy nodded and determinedly held back her

emotions. She didn't want to spoil these precious moments.

She gazed across at Martin who was sitting at the table with Daisy on his lap while he listened to her prattling on about Queenie and Harvey and tried to drink his tea. She could see how tired and drawn he'd become, and could tell by his expression how much he was missing his own little girls and her heart was heavy at the thought of them being forced apart.

'You look done in, Martin,' she said fretfully. 'Is there no chance of you being able to get down to Somerset for a break?'

'Not as long as we're on this campaign,' he replied, wincing as Daisy tugged on his moustache. He gently prised away the grasping fingers and handed her a scrap of biscuit, which she promptly tried to stuff into his mouth. Having reluctantly swallowed this, he continued, 'But there's the glimmer of hope that I might be able to snatch some leave before long.'

'Oh? Why's that, then?' Ron came clumping up the stairs as Harvey barged past him to get into the kitchen first. 'I thought you fly boys had had all leave cancelled.'

Before Martin had a chance to reply, the dog threw himself at Cissy, trying to climb into her lap and lick her face, his tail threatening to sweep everything off the table. Then he spotted Martin and repeated his enthusiastic welcome, almost turning himself inside out with delight, squirming at his feet and groaning in ecstasy as Martin heartily patted and rubbed his stomach.

Cissy brushed the dirt from Harvey's paws off

her pristine uniform skirt and checked her make-up in her compact mirror. 'Honestly, Granda, you should teach Harvey better manners. He's as bad now as he ever was.'

'Aye, maybe I should,' he rumbled, dropping a bristly kiss on her smooth brow, 'but then he wouldn't be the Harvey we know and love.' He regarded her with twinkling blue eyes from beneath his wayward brows. 'To be sure, wee girl, you're looking well, so y'are. How's that Yank of yours?'

'Randy? He's fine as far as I know,' she replied, her smile fading. 'I don't get to see much of him now he's over at Biggin Hill with the USAAF. But we write all the time, and occasionally we even manage to have a telephone conversation.'

'Well that's good,' he muttered.

Cissy eyed her grandfather with amusement. The poacher's coat was scarred and stained from years of use, his old tweed jacket was missing several buttons, his shirt collar was frayed and his baggy corduroy trousers were held up by a length of garden twine. He clearly hadn't shaved for a couple of days, his hair was a wild tangle and his eyebrows were so long they stuck out like wings. 'It's good to see nothing's changed with you,' she said, chuckling.

Ron shot her a cheeky wink, fished out the three dead rabbits and strangled pheasant from his coat pockets and placed them on the draining board before hanging his coat over the back of the chair and plumping down at the table to call Harvey to heel.

'Be still,' he barked. 'Sit and behave, ye daft eejit.'

89

He slurped some tea, made a face because it wasn't sweet enough for his liking, and then turned his gaze to Martin. 'To be sure, Anne and the wains will be glad to see you if you can make it down there,' he said. 'But I thought Bomber Harris was keeping you occupied?'

'For now,' Martin said carefully. 'But with the Yanks coming in on it, I'm hoping to get away for a proper visit soon.'

'Oh aye?' Ron's gaze sharpened. 'Something afoot, is it? Softening up Jerry before you go for the big push into Europe?'

'You know I can't tell you anything, Ron,' said Martin.

Ron grunted and slurped more tea. 'I'll take that as a yes, then,' he muttered.

'Ron, do stop baiting poor Martin,' said Peggy. She turned to her son-in-law. 'It would be marvellous if you could take time off – goodness knows, you need a break. But it would take hours to drive all that way and back, using up all your precious time together.'

'If I do get the chance to see them then I'll cadge a lift from the ATA,' he replied. 'There's always a plane being delivered somewhere, and I'm sure I can borrow a service vehicle for the short drive from either of the local aerodromes to the farm.'

He ran his hand affectionately over Daisy's dark curls as she leaned against his knee, before smoothing his ruffled moustache. 'But I'd appreciate it if you didn't tell her,' he said. 'It's not guaranteed, and could cause her great disappointment. Besides, I want it to be a surprise.'

Cigarettes and pipes were lit and the teapot replenished as the talk continued around the table, with absolutely no input from Matt and Rita, who were too taken up with each other to even notice they weren't alone.

Peggy held Cissy's hand, capturing each golden moment together as she heard about her life up at Cliffe. It was clear her girl was having a whale of a time with all her fellow WAAFs, and the attentions of the dashing young men who worked up there – yet her daughter's laughter was a little brittle, there were telling shadows beneath her eyes, and for all her lively chatter, Peggy could see that she'd experienced loss and great sadness, as well as the stresses and strains of trying to survive the war while under constant threat.

'How's Da getting on in India?' Cissy asked. 'He doesn't say much in his airgraphs, and most of the time I can't even read his writing.'

'He's bearing up,' said Peggy. 'You know your father, Cissy, he's probably wangled himself a comfortable billet and is getting others to do his work for him. He has native servants, you know, and he and his mate Ernie are making sure they want for nothing.'

Cissy's blue eyes were concerned. 'And you, Mam? How are you coping?'

Peggy's smile masked her worries. 'I'm fine,' she said lightly. 'The girls and Cordelia help out when they can, and Jim's money's gone up now he's been promoted. Daisy's getting a little harder to cope with now she's a bit more independent, but I manage, just as I did with the rest of you at that age.'

She glanced fondly at Ron, who was in deep conversation with Martin. 'Your granda is as untidy as ever and gets under my feet, but he's proved to be an absolute rock when I've needed him.'

'I wish I could get to see you more often,' said Cissy. 'But it's full-on up there, and I hardly have a minute to myself.'

Peggy cupped her powdered cheek. 'Bless you, love. You take care of yourself and don't worry about me.'

The visit was over too swiftly, and Peggy had to battle with her tears again as her visitors slowly went down the steps to the back door, reluctant to leave, but already focused on the job they had to do back at Cliffe Aerodrome.

'I'll walk with you to the car,' said Ron, dragging on his coat. 'Rosie's expecting me to help change the barrels before tonight's rush.'

Peggy held Daisy on her hip, and she and Rita followed them down the path, anxious to keep them in sight for as long as possible. With final hugs and kisses they climbed into the large staff car.

Cissy gave a couple of beeps on the horn before driving up the hill and out of sight. The silence they left behind was almost numbing.

'I think I'll go and tidy my room now,' said Rita, her eyes bright with unshed tears.

'Yes, love, you do that.' Peggy hitched Daisy further up her hip as they went through the back gate. 'I have to go out later, so would you mind keeping an ear out for Cordelia?'

Rita was so taken up with her own thoughts that she merely nodded and didn't ask Peggy where she was going – which was a relief, for Peggy didn't really want her to know just yet.

Somerset

Anne stood in the playground watching the children race around following their lunch break. Belinda would come to relieve her in five minutes, and then she planned to nip down to the nursery to eat her lunch with Rose and Emily. She didn't usually interrupt them during the day, but she needed to keep away from George until she could figure out if she'd just been imagining things, or if there really was a situation she needed to deal with.

She'd spent the mid-morning break with Belinda, who was as adept as any newspaper reporter at picking up snippets of gossip and had enough stories to tell about the group of Americans who were in Taunton for R&R to fill an entire day.

When Anne had first taken up the teaching post in Barnham Green, she'd been concerned that Belinda would earn herself a bad reputation, and there was nothing so harmful as village gossip – especially if it involved the local primary teacher. However, Belinda conducted her social life well away from here, and Anne suspected that most of her adventures were totally innocent, and she just enjoyed embellishing her stories. There was a sweetness about Belinda, a sense of vulnerability, despite the hair, the clothes and the make-up, and Anne had come to like her very much.

Anne watched Ernie as he and his classmates chased a football about, and then let her gaze drift over the knot of little girls awaiting their turn for the skipping rope or a game of hopscotch, and the gathering of small boys playing marbles near the bicycle shed.

She loved her job, had made friends in the village and become a part of the community, but her separation from Martin meant she'd been drawn to George, not only for his pleasant company, but because they were two lonely people trying to make the best of things during a time of turmoil.

'You're looking serious, Anne,' said Belinda. 'What's troubling you?'

Anne shook her head. 'Nothing more than usual,' she replied, not really wanting to reveal her suspicions to her friend. 'I'm just hungry, that's all. It's been a long time since breakfast.'

Belinda frowned and put her hand on Anne's arm. 'Well, if you need to talk, you know where I am.'

'Thanks, Belinda. You're a real pal.' She caught a glimpse of George standing in the doorway and returned his wave, then hurried off down the lane towards the nursery, wishing she had the courage to face him with her suspicions, and hopefully put them to rest. But it was almost the weekend and Monday would come round soon enough. She'd learnt long ago it was always wise to sleep on things instead of reacting too quickly.

5

Peggy had dressed carefully in her best navy skirt and the pale blue twinset her sister Doris had handed down to her once she'd become bored with it. She'd put on some discreet make-up and tidied her hair, and then pulled on her overcoat and good shoes. Tying the headscarf firmly under her chin, she left Cordelia snoozing in the fireside chair while Rita was upstairs, and slipped out of the house with Daisy in her pushchair. She didn't like the idea of sneaking around, but really she had a perfect right to come and go as she pleased. This enterprise was for her, and her alone, and she didn't want to share it with anyone just yet.

She'd only reached the end of the alleyway when she realised it had been a mistake to bring Daisy. After all the excitement of the morning, Daisy was tired and crotchety, her grizzling and complaining making Peggy's already stretched nerves jangle. But it would have been unfair to ask Rita to look after her on her day off, and although Cordelia was very willing to babysit, she simply wasn't spry enough to keep up with an energetic and wilful toddler.

She steered the pushchair over the road, buffeted by the strong wind that was tearing up from a sea darkened by the racing shadows of rain-filled clouds. The gulls were screeching as they wheeled overhead or sat on roofs and lamp posts,

95

and the awnings over some of the shops in Camden Road slapped and cracked against their moorings. It was a good thing she'd brought in the washing and remembered her umbrella, she thought distractedly as Daisy's heels drummed on the metal footplate, for it would certainly rain before nightfall.

As they approached the Anchor she wondered briefly if perhaps Rosie would take Daisy in for a while – and then swiftly dismissed the idea. If Ron was still there he'd ask endless questions, and as she wasn't good at lying, he'd soon discover what she was up to and lay waste to all her plans. With a sigh of annoyance, she carried on walking.

'Hello, Peg. What are you doing out on a day like this?' As if Peggy's thoughts had conjured her up, Rosie Braithwaite appeared at the entrance to the pub's side door, looking as glamorous as ever in her smart coat and high heels.

'I have to be somewhere,' she replied, glancing towards the door in case Ron was listening.

'It must be important to bring Daisy out when she's in such a foul mood,' said Rosie, tying her headscarf over her platinum curls and smiling at her god-daughter, who scowled back.

'Not really,' Peggy hedged. 'I just thought a breath of fresh air would shut her up.'

Rosie lifted a neat eyebrow. 'Well, that hasn't worked, has it?' She chuckled and hitched her shopping basket over her arm. 'You always were a terrible liar, Peggy Reilly. What are you really up to?'

Peggy went pink and couldn't look her friend in the eye. 'Something and nothing really,' she said.

'Would you like me to have Daisy while you're doing this something and nothing?' Rosie asked in amusement.

'Is Ron still with you?'

Rosie frowned. 'He left about half an hour ago to take a group of young Home Guard recruits through their paces at the drill hall.' She stepped closer to Peggy so she wouldn't be overheard by the three approaching housewives, her blue eyes sparkling with curiosity. 'What are you up to, Peg?' she murmured. 'I promise I won't tell.'

Peggy caved in. 'I'm going to see Solly Goldman and ask for a job,' she said in a rush. 'But you're not to breathe a word to anyone – especially not Ron.'

Rosie's eyes widened in astonishment. 'Blimey, Peg. Are things that bad at Beach View?'

Peggy didn't like to admit it, even to her best friend, so she just gave a shrug. 'I've got to do something to help the war effort,' she said, 'and as Solly's wife has started a crèche at the factory, it seemed an ideal opportunity to do my bit. Besides, I am going to see Solly out of necessity but I can't pretend I'm not excited about the idea of having a job. All my chicks have jobs, and sometimes I wonder what it would be like to be a modern woman like them.'

'But you look after everyone at Beach View and help out at the WVS and the WI. I'd say that's a job in itself; you're doing your bit and more besides, without going to work in a factory.' She regarded Peggy evenly and her expression softened. 'Oh, Peggy, why didn't you tell me you were struggling? I could let you have a bit of money each week so you don't have to do this.'

Peggy felt a wave of affection for her friend which didn't quite swamp the uncomfortable feeling of admitting that she actually did need the money. 'I have to stand on my own two feet like you do, Rosie,' she managed. 'But I appreciate the offer.'

'Jim won't like it,' said Rosie.

'Jim will have to lump it,' Peggy retorted. 'As for Ron, if I get a job, then I'll deal with him later.' She looked at her friend. 'Did you mean it, about looking after Daisy for a bit?'

'Absolutely. She can come with me to the shops and then, if she's a good girl, I'll treat her to something in the Lilac Tearooms.' Rosie smiled. 'When you've done with Solly, come upstairs and you can tell me how it went. Ron isn't due back until later this evening to help behind the bar, so we won't be disturbed.'

Peggy nodded. 'That would be lovely,' she said.

Rosie's smile faded as she reached for Peggy's hand. 'I hope you know what you're letting your-self in for, Peg. Those girls can be vicious little cows at times, and if you don't stand up to them, they'll make your life a misery.'

Peggy gave a nervous chuckle as she squeezed Rosie's fingers. 'I'd like to see them try, but I do know what it's like there. Sally worked for Gold-man, remember?'

Rosie nodded and took charge of the push-chair. 'You'd better get on, then. Good luck, Peg. I hope it all goes according to plan.'

Peggy hoped so too, and as she headed down Camden Road towards Goldman's clothing factory her heart was beating so rapidly she was finding it hard to breathe. She'd never had a proper job earning a wage in an office or factory, for she'd helped her parents run the boarding house straight from school. Once the children had come along, she'd simply been a wife, mother and boarding-house keeper – working all hours at keeping the house clean and her family and boarders fed. What on earth she thought she could do at the factory, she had no idea, and as she approached the daunting red-brick building that took up an entire block at the end of Camden Road, she began to have second thoughts.

She dithered by the imposing gates at the entrance, arguing silently with herself that she had no business being here – that Jim would be furious, and Ron would blow a fuse. She had responsibilities at home, a baby to look after, evacuees to feed and care for – as well as the elderly Cordelia who suffered so terribly with her arthritis in the winter.

There again she needed the money – and time away from Beach View could only be a good thing, for although she loved her home and everyone in it, there were times when she felt as if the walls were closing in, and that had made her want to break free – to be more than just Peggy the housewife and mother. She'd make new friends, do something useful for the war effort, and be revitalised with a new interest and her own money in her pocket to spend as she saw fit.

She took a deep breath and walked across the yard to the long flight of metal steps that went up the side of the building to the office on the top floor. If she didn't do this now, then she never would.

She opened the door to be met by a blast of fumes from the paraffin heater, which was belting out warmth and causing streams of condensation on the large window overlooking the factory floor. Peggy took in the outer office at a glance, noting the line of filing cabinets, the rota of shifts on the wall beside a large calendar, the worn carpet and the flourishing spider plant in a pot on the windowsill.

She smiled at the middle-aged woman sitting behind an enormous desk littered with files and stacks of correspondence. They'd known each other since infant school, and like Peggy's Jim, Madge's husband was serving abroad. 'Hello, Madge. Is he in?'

Madge's eyes widened. 'Hello, Peg. This is a surprise, and no mistake.' She grinned. 'You're not here for a job, are you?'

Peggy was getting used to explaining herself. 'I am, actually,' she said firmly. 'I thought it was time I did my bit.'

Madge frowned momentarily. 'I'd've thought you were doing more than enough already, but I admire your enthusiasm.' She became more business-like as she shuffled papers on her desk. 'You've certainly come to the right place. We're snowed under with orders, and Solly's tearing his hair out – what he's got left of it – trying to get staff.' She grinned again, her grey eyes warm with humour. 'I'll let him know you're here.'

Peggy stood at the window and wiped away a patch of condensation so she could look down at the line upon line of machinists, the great stacks of distinctive forces blue and khaki material at the far end, and the bustle of workers packing boxes with the finished uniforms, while the expert cutters worked at the large tables off to one side.

Solly had once made women's clothing, but his keen eye for the main chance had led him to obtain government contracts for uniforms before the start of the war, and now he was one of the largest employers in the town.

Peggy watched the girls singing along to *Workers' Playtime*, which was being piped down to the factory floor, and felt a flutter of excitement, in spite of her trepidation. It could be fun working here, she thought.

'Well I live and breathe. Peggy Reilly!'

She turned swiftly at the familiar voice, gravelled by too many cigars, and smiled back at Solly Goldman, whom she'd also known most of her life. He was a big man in his early fifties who made the office seem suddenly smaller – not just through his bulk, but with his immense personality. A large cigar was wedged in his thick-lipped mouth, his brown eyes were heavy-lidded, but sharply intelligent above his bulbous nose, and his beautifully tailored three-piece suit fitted his generous girth like a glove. His bald pate shone in the bright light, the friar's fringe of silver hair glinting like a halo.

'Hello, Solly,' she replied warmly. 'I hope you don't mind me turning up like this.'

'It's always a pleasure to see you, Peggy,' he replied, enveloping her hand in his warm, soft fingers. 'I can tell you're very well, but how's Ron and the rest of the family doing?'

'Ron's up to no good as usual,' she said dryly. 'The family are well, but scattered, and Jim's out in India of all places.'

He shook his head, his expression sorrowful. 'We live in troubled times, Peggy, but our sacrifices are necessary if we're to free the world of that devil Hitler.'

Peggy nodded, suddenly ashamed that her troubles were minor compared to what Solly and his family must be going through. She knew he had relatives and friends in Poland; and had heard awful rumours about what had happened to the Jews in the Warsaw ghettos and across Europe.

Solly made a visible effort to return to his usual ebullient self, but his smile didn't quite diminish the sadness in his brown eyes. 'You must give Ron my best regards and tell him to call in some time. It's been too long since we've had a chance to share a good whisky and put the world to rights.'

'I'll tell him. The chance of a whisky and a good chat is his idea of heaven.'

Solly asked Madge to bring them some coffee, then ushered Peggy into his large, comfortably appointed office and closed the door. 'Sit down, Peggy, and tell me what I can do for you.'

She sat in front of the huge, tidy desk and regarded him with affection as he plumped into his leather chair on the other side. It was so typical of Solly to get to the point without making you feel you had to explain yourself. He might have a reputation for being a hard taskmaster when it came to running his business, but she knew that under that imposing and rather daunting façade he had a soft heart. He gave generously to dozens of charities, and although it was a closely held secret, Ron had told her he'd been heavily involved in getting several hundred Jewish children out of Europe to sanctuary in England and America.

'I feel awkward at having to ask, Solly,' she began hesitantly. 'But I want a job.'

He raised both his eyebrows and took the cigar out of his mouth. 'Want, or need?' he asked gently.

She dipped her chin, feeling the heat rise in her face. 'Need,' she admitted.

He remained silent, and when she looked up she could see concern in his expression. 'I'm saddened to hear that, my dear,' he said on a sigh. 'And I would like to help, of course. But let's be practical for a moment. As far as I know you've never worked anywhere but at Beach View.'

'Then it's time I did,' she said firmly.

The discreet tap on the door heralded Madge's arrival with their coffee. She placed the cups before them as they sat in silence, and then closed the door softly behind her.

A diamond glinted in the gold ring on Solly's fat finger as he stuck the cigar back in his mouth and continued their conversation as if the interruption hadn't occurred. 'But I need skilled cutters and machinists, and mechanics to keep the machinery going,' he said carefully, puffing great clouds of noxious smoke into the stuffy room. 'I'd feel ashamed to offer you something as menial as packing boxes or sweeping the floors.'

'I can sew a bit,' she said hopefully.

He shook his great head. 'It would need to be

on a par with a tailor's finish. Those uniforms are expensive to make.' He sat forward. 'But because it's you, I'm willing to give you a trial and see how you get on.'

Peggy bit her lip. It had been years since she'd used a sewing machine, and in fact she'd given her Singer to Sally when she'd started her home-dressmaking business back in 1940. 'I'd like to give it a go,' she said hesitantly. 'But I could be a bit rusty until I get the hang of it again.'

He regarded her thoughtfully through the cigar smoke, and then pressed a button on the inter-com. 'Madge, could you see if Loretta's back from her break? If she is, then tell her I'm sending someone down for a trial run. Nothing com-plicated, mind. Shirt hems will do for now.'

Peggy perched on the very edge of her chair, butterflies in her stomach. The coffee cup rattled in the saucer as she placed it carefully on the desk. 'I really don't mind sweeping floors,' she said breathlessly.

Solly smiled then. 'Oy vey, Peggy Reilly. I never thought I'd see the day you'd be frightened of anything. The machine won't bite you. Loretta's my niece, and she's a good girl with lots of patience. I'm sure you'll be fine.'

She should have felt better at his confidence in her, but the butterflies were increasing and she only just managed to finish the delicious cup of milky coffee without choking on it.

Madge knocked and came back into the room, her gaze flying to Peggy with barely disguised curiosity before returning to her boss. 'Loretta said she'll come in a bit early from her break to do a test run. Is it Peggy doing the try-out?'

Solly nodded. 'Take her down for me, would you? And tell Loretta to go easy on her. She's a good friend of mine, and I'd like her to feel at home here.'

Madge raised an eyebrow but made no comment.

Peggy stood and smoothed her perspiring hands down her coat, the nerves making it hard to breathe, let alone get her legs to work properly. 'Are you sure about this, Solly?'

'We've been friends since I was in short trousers,' he rumbled. 'And I've never known you to fail at anything you've put your mind to. Now get out of here and show Loretta what you can do. When you've finished, come up and we'll discuss wages and a nursery place for Daisy.'

Peggy nodded and followed Madge out of the door. 'Oh, Lord,' she breathed. 'I hope to goodness I don't let him down.'

Madge stopped halfway down the stairs and turned to look at her. 'We both know Solly well enough to realise he wouldn't have offered the trial if he didn't think you were capable of passing it. Just take a deep breath, Peggy, and remember all the other things you've got through when you thought you couldn't.'

Peggy took a steadying breath, remembering how she'd thought she'd die alongside Daisy and Cordelia when they'd been buried under the rubble in her scullery – and how she'd managed to get to Anne when she'd been knocked into a cellar by a bomb blast and gone into labour. She'd survived all that, so why on earth did she fear this?

She took another breath and then grinned. 'Lead on, Madge. Let's get this done.'

The noise on the factory floor hit them as they walked through the door. The sound of sewing machines whirring, the radio blaring out and the chatter of the girls echoed in the vast space with its high ceiling and bright lights.

Peggy was daunted by the size of the machines, which looked so much bigger than they had from upstairs, but she squared her shoulders, plastering on a smile as heads were lifted and curious eyes watched them cross the floor. No one looked in the least familiar, but at least they seemed friendly enough, and a good many of them were her age or even older, so she wouldn't feel too out of place.

Solly's niece, Loretta, proved to be a pretty, dark-haired girl in her mid-twenties, and her beaming smile of welcome went part-way to easing Peggy's nerves. Madge introduced them and went back to the office, and Peggy sat down at the large machine next to the girl.

'I understand you haven't used one of these before,' said Loretta. 'So I'll run through what each bit is for and then show you how to thread it. It's a bit of a rigmarole, but you'll soon get the hang of it, and there's always someone next to you who will help if you need it.'

Peggy concentrated hard. The machine was like her old Singer, but much bigger, with more attachments – but she soon managed to thread it on her own, and very quickly learned how responsive the treadle was as she pressed her foot

106

down and the needle raced across the scrap of waste material. She nearly skewered her finger beneath the needle because of the speed it was going, but eventually got the hang of regulating the rate, and sewed a straight line.

Loretta left her to practise for a while on other scraps of material, and then returned with a white shirt. 'This is for a sailor serving in the tropics,' she explained. 'See how light the fabric is? I'd like you to finish it off by doing the hem.'

Peggy took the shirt with trembling hands and almost made the mistake of turning the hem the wrong way before she saw her error, clucked in annoyance and carefully eased it beneath the needle. Her concentration was such that she forgot to be nervous, and once she'd finished, she cut the thread, examined her work with a critical eye then handed it to Loretta.

'Not bad,' she murmured. 'Let's try another one, and this time make sure you don't get a fold in it at the corner.'

Peggy felt more confident with each shirt Loretta brought her. After she'd sewn five shirt hems, Loretta nodded and smiled. 'Well done, Mrs Reilly. You're a quick learner, and I'll be pleased to have you working with us. Now, I'll give you a short tour round the factory so you'll know where everything is when you start, and show you how to clock in and out.'

Peggy was brimming with confidence and delight as she returned to the office. 'I did it, Madge,' she said. 'I actually managed to sew proper straight hems on shirts.'

Madge chuckled. 'I had no doubt of it,' she

said. 'And neither did Solly. He's waiting for you in there.'

Peggy tapped on his door and at his gruff reply, went in.

'I knew you wouldn't let me down, Peggy,' he said, taking in her beaming smile. 'You've got the job. So when can you start?'

'I'd like to start on Monday,' she replied. 'But I'll have to work my hours in with my home duties, and of course I'll need a place for Daisy in the nursery.'

Solly beamed back at her. 'Consider it done.'

'Thanks, Solly, for giving me this chance. It means a lot to me.'

'Don't thank me just yet,' he replied with a twinkle in his eye.' 'I haven't told you what I pay.'

Peggy's pulse raced when he told her she could earn three pounds and ten shillings a week if she did enough hours, and that Daisy's nursery place would be free.

'But I thought there was a fee which came straight out of my wages,' she protested.

He threw his hands in the air. 'Oy vey, now she argues,' he said to the ceiling. He regarded her evenly, his brown eyes bright with good humour. 'This is my factory and I make the rules. Daisy will be looked after for free.'

'Oh, Solly, you are kind,' she sighed. 'But I'm not so badly off to have to accept charity.'

'Believe me, Peggy, it's not charity. Jewish wives are worse than Jewish mothers, and my Rachel would make my life even more impossible if I charged you, so let's hear no more about it.'

He rose from behind his desk to signal that the

conversation was over, and took her hand. 'Go and sort out your hours with Madge, and then she can arrange the same for Daisy before you go down to inspect the nursery.'

Peggy could have kissed him, but managed to restrain herself. Thanking him again, she hurried out to Madge.

It was raining quite heavily by the time she left the factory, but nothing could dampen her spirits today, and so she opened her umbrella and almost danced along the pavement as she headed for the Anchor.

Hurrying into the side alley, she let herself into the pub, left her sodden brolly by the pushchair at the bottom of the stairs and ran up to Rosie's cosy sitting room. Rosie was curled up on the sofa with Daisy in her lap and Monty sprawled alongside them, snoring, as she read aloud from a story book.

'I can see you were successful,' she said with a smile. 'What job did you get?'

'A machinist,' Peggy replied breathlessly, sinking onto the sofa and gathering Daisy into her arms for a hug. 'And would you believe it? He's paying me over three quid a week if I can put in the hours – more if I do night shift.'

'That calls for a gin and tonic,' said Rosie, giving her a delighted hug before clambering to her feet and heading for the tiny kitchen. She returned quickly with bottles and glasses and poured generous measures.

'Here's to your new career,' she said, raising her glass.

'And here's to having my own money,' said Peggy.

Daisy looked at them in bafflement as they drank deeply and collapsed into giggles. 'Want wee-wee,' she demanded.

Peggy wrapped her in her arms and kissed the top of her head, still giggling. 'Well that's brought me back to the reality of being a mum, and no mistake.' Carrying Daisy into the small, neat bathroom, she dealt with her needs and then returned to the sitting room to finish her drink and go into more detail of what she'd had to do to get the job.

'I'll have to go,' she said after a while. 'They'll all be wanting their tea, and I've yet to face Ron.'

'And I have a pub to open,' said Rosie, glancing at the mantel clock. 'I don't know how you're going to manage running the home as well as working for Solly – but knowing you, you'll find a way.'

She finished getting Daisy dressed for the outdoors and gave her a kiss. 'She's been really good today, despite the earlier tantrum, so if you need me to babysit again, you only have to ask.'

'Thanks, Rosie, you're a diamond. But she has a place in Rachel's crèche when I'm working. She's hired a very efficient retired Norland Nanny to run it, and having met her briefly this afternoon I have no doubts Daisy will soon learn to behave herself. But I'll definitely bear you in mind if there's a hiccup in the arrangements.'

They went down the stairs and Peggy strapped Daisy into the pushchair, pulled up the hood and fastened the weatherproof apron at the front. She manoeuvred it through the side door, then turned to Rosie and gave her a firm hug.

'Thanks for today, Rosie,' she murmured. 'I couldn't have got the job without your help.'

'Nonsense. It was a pleasure – and I enjoyed it, really.'

Peggy opened her umbrella and steered the pushchair down the street, her excitement tempered by the fact that she would soon have to face the music – and use every ounce of determination she possessed to defend her decision to go out to work.

Her faith in her ability to make a stand faltered the moment she entered the scullery and heard everyone talking, and the trepidation mounted as she carried Daisy up the steps into the kitchen.

Ron was cutting and boning the rabbits he'd caught earlier for tomorrow night's stew, closely watched by Queenie from her favourite vantage point on a shelf above the drainer. Rita was stirring something in a pot on the top of the range; Ivy was ironing the clean washing; Sarah sat reading an airmail letter with Harvey stretched out over her feet; and Fran was setting Cordelia's freshly washed hair in large metal rollers.

'Hello, Aunt Peg. You've been gone for ages,' said Rita cheerfully, turning from the stove. 'We were beginning to think you'd left home.'

Peggy patted a welcoming Harvey and laughed nervously. 'As if I'd do that,' she said, hoisting Daisy from her hip to the floor and wrestling her out of her coat and bonnet.

'I saw Auntie Rosie,' Daisy told everyone in her

111

piping voice. 'We had cake, and she told me and Monty a story and Mummy got a job.'

There was stunned silence and Peggy slumped down into the nearest chair, the wind taken very firmly out of her sails. She regarded the shocked faces turned towards her and steeled herself for the outburst that would surely come.

They all started bombarding her with questions – except for Ron, who'd rescued the rabbits from Queenie's stealthy claws and was now standing by the sink with them in a bowl clutched to his chest as he stared at her in disbelief.

She gathered her determination and held up her hand for silence. 'Yes, it's true,' she said firmly. 'I start as a machinist at Goldman's eleven o'clock Monday morning. I've arranged to do six hours a day, Monday to Friday, which should give me plenty of time to organise the meals for the day, do the shopping and be back in time for tea.'

The barrage of questions came again and she tried to answer each one firmly so as to quell any argument.

'Well, it's all very commendable,' said Cordelia. 'But surely, if it's a matter of money making you do this, then we can all chip in more each week.'

Ron dumped the bowl of rabbit pieces in the larder and slammed the door on them as a chorus of agreement went up, and Harvey barked as if in support.

'Thank you – all of you – but it's not just the money. It's about me doing something for myself for a change, to have my own money to spend as I wish, and to find out what life is like outside Beach View. It will also be very good for Daisy to

112

have other little ones to play with and learn to share her toys.'

Her determination was strengthened by their nods of understanding. 'I've found something I can do, which will make me feel that at last I'm a useful part of the war effort – just as you girls are. There are opportunities at Goldman's for me and Daisy to learn new skills and make new friends and I'm excited by the thought.'

There was a chorus of murmurs and Harvey came to rest his nose on Peggy's lap, his soulful amber eyes looking up at her as if he understood.

'I do agree that Daisy would benefit by having other children around, but you already do a great deal, Auntie Peg,' said Rita. 'You've taken us in for a start, do stints at the WI and WVS, and help out endless numbers of neighbours when things get tough.'

She broke off to glance at the other girls to seek their approval before she went on. 'We're all just worried that it will prove too much and make you ill.'

'Then I'll have to pace myself, won't I?' Peggy replied. 'The WI can do without me, and I'm sure Doris won't mind if I don't continue with the WVS,' she said blithely – despite the fact that the thought of actually telling Doris made her stomach clench.

'Well, I think it's marvellous,' said Sarah. 'I'm sure I speak for the others when I say we'll help you all we can in your new enterprise.'

There were loud hear, hears, and a smattering of applause – broken by Ron's loud grunt. 'It would have been nice to have been told about this hare-brained scheme before you went off like that,' he said crossly, plumping into the chair next to her.

'You'd only have done your best to put me off,' Peggy retorted.

'Aye, maybe, but you never gave me the chance.'

Peggy reddened as he eyed her sternly. 'I'm sorry, Ron, but I needed to see if it was possible first.'

'And I'm sorry you didn't respect my position as head of this house by coming to talk it over with me.' He shifted in his chair and fiddled with his unlit pipe as Peggy's colour deepened, and Harvey scrambled under the table to avoid getting the blame for whatever was making Ron cross.

'I've never objected to women going out to work – the Lord knows my mother worked in a laundry for years. And these are extraordinary times which call for every hand on the tiller. I admire you for wanting to do more, but like the girls, I worry you'll do too much. And then there's your husband. Jim won't like you working, let alone in a factory.'

Peggy lifted her chin. 'I don't like him being sent to India,' she retorted. 'But I have to lump it. What he doesn't know won't hurt him, Ron.'

'Ach, Peggy girl, there are too many secrets already, and he deserves to know the truth of what you're up to while he's away.'

Peggy frowned. 'What do you mean? What secrets?'

Ron looked down and gave a heavy sigh. 'I was going to tell you in private later on this evening, but I suppose there's no time like the present.'

114

'What is it?' she said in sharp alarm. 'He hasn't been injured, has he?'

Ron shook his head and reached for her hand. 'No, wee girl. He's all in one piece so he is. But he has been keeping something from you, and I think it's time you knew where his letters really come from.'

She stared at him in confusion. 'Well, they come from India, obviously,' she stammered. 'They're all marked SEAC and stamped with Indian stamps and postmarked India – so I don't understand what you're trying to say.'

His grip tightened on her hand. 'All the service mail in that area is flown into Calcutta, and then sent on here, so you see no matter where the writers of those letters are based out in the East, they all bear the Indian postmark.'

A chill ran through her as she looked at him. 'He's not in India?' she managed, her voice reedy with anxiety.

Ron's gaze was steady as he continued to hold her hand. 'Not any longer, Peggy. He's in Burma, and has been since last October.'

'Burma?' She stared at him, her heart hammering painfully against her ribs as terrible visions raced through her head. She'd seen the newsreels at the cinema; had heard on the wireless about the Japanese incursion into India and Burma, and the brutal battles that had followed in the stifling heat of the jungle, and she couldn't absorb the fact that her darling, precious Jim was right at the heart of it.

'No,' she whispered. 'No, that can't be.'

The others swiftly gathered around Peggy to

115

give her their support as Ron explained. 'If you look at the earlier letters he's sent you, you'll see that they aren't marked SEAC, for that command wasn't formed until last August. SEAC stands for South East Asia Command, and is an alliance between Britain, America, China and parts of India – the men trained specifically in jungle warfare.'

Peggy's sob of fear broke the silence and the others drew closer as Ron continued. 'Jim is not out there to fight the Japs, Peggy,' he said firmly. 'He's been recruited to join the British 14th Army – known as the Chindits – to provide his mechanical know-how to the fighting men's machinery.'

'But he'll still be in danger of air attacks, Ron. The Japs are pouring into Burma and they're sneaky and vicious in the jungle – coming out of nowhere and setting booby traps.'

'I know it's hard to take in, wee girl,' he murmured, 'but he was under fire back in India, and actually got caught in a bit of fighting when the Japs first attacked. The danger is no greater in Burma, I'm sure of it.'

'But I've seen the newsreels – and why didn't he tell me about coming under fire in India, and that he's been sent to Burma?' she asked through her tears.

'He didn't want you to fret over him, Peg,' he soothed. 'As for where he is now, the MOD put a block on any information about the SEAC until the end of January, so he wasn't allowed to tell you anything.'

'But it's almost April,' she replied on a sob. 'Why has he left it so long?'

Ron gathered her in his arms and held her

close. 'His letter to me was delayed, and I only received it yesterday. He was unable to decide how best to tell you, because he didn't want you hearing about it from strangers,' he said softly. 'He wrote and asked if I would tell you in the comfort of your home and surrounded by those who love you, rather than reading it in a letter.'

When her tears finally subsided he smoothed back her hair and looked deeply into her eyes. 'I know you're frightened for him, Peggy – we all are – but he's doing what he knows best to help bring this terrible war to an end. And we have to be brave – to keep our faith and carry on as best we can until he comes home to us.'

Peggy nodded, determinedly pulling her emotions back under control, and hastily cleaned her face with her handkerchief. 'Yes,' she said, her tone belying the inner turmoil that made her heart thud. 'And for every shirt hem I sew I'll send a prayer for the man who will wear it, in the hope it will keep him safe.'

'That's my girl,' he murmured before kissing her forehead and releasing his grip on her shoulders. He looked at the others, a glint of mischief in his eyes. 'Now, as head of this household of women, I'm ordering you to stop crying and get on with the tea. To be sure, me stomach's sticking to me backbone, so it is – and it's making me shrapnel the very divil of a pain in the rear.'

'It's you who's the pain in the rear,' said Cordelia tartly. 'You should count yourself lucky you aren't wearing your supper after that show of male bossiness.'

'Now, Cordelia,' he replied, the twinkle growing in his eyes. ''Tis a terrible thing for an auld woman to be so hard-hearted to a man suffering still from his war wounds.'

'And it's even worse that you show no respect to your betters,' she fired back, her own eyes brightening with laughter.

Peggy listened to the lively banter, loving Ron for the tender way he'd told her about Jim, for giving her the courage to face the uncertain future, and bringing the laughter back into her kitchen.

As Cordelia and Ron continued to spar and the girls tended to the evening meal, Peggy knew she was blessed to be surrounded by so much love. From this moment on they would become even closer; stronger and united in the struggle to get through this war. Tears wouldn't bring their loved ones home, but courage and fortitude and the determination to never be beaten were to be her watchwords now, and she wouldn't falter – no matter what fate had in store.

And yet when she was alone in her bed that night the loneliness and fear became overwhelming, and she had to bury her face in her pillow to muffle her wracking sobs.

6

RAF Cliffe

Dawn was lightening the sky as Martin switched off the Spitfire's engine and sat for a long moment in deep anguish watching the other Allied bombers and fighters coming in to land. He knew the casualties would be high, for he'd already lost too many good men tonight, including the entire crew of two Lancasters as well as three fighter pilots, and there were bound to be more, for they'd dropped thousands of tons of bombs on Hamburg, reducing the city to rubble and ash, and had encountered heavy attacks from the Jerry fighters and even heavier bombardment from the enemy's anti-aircraft guns.

He pushed back the canopy and climbed wearily down from the cockpit, then stood easing his stiff limbs, chilled to the bone despite the thick layers of clothing and fur-lined flying boots, the tension of the long night's mission tightening the muscles in his shoulders and neck. Returning his engineer's salute, he made a concerted effort not to appear as weary and down-hearted as he was, and strode towards the admin block where some of his men were already gathered to count their comrades in.

'Well done, chaps,' he muttered, passing his brandy flask round, noting how their eyes were dulled by the loss of fellow airmen, their faces drawn by the stresses of the night's work and the sudden depletion of the adrenaline which had kept them going.

Martin drew his pipe from the pocket of his sheepskin-lined leather jacket and stood in silence with the others as he filled it and got it alight. The surviving bombers were roaring down the longest of the three runways in quick succession, their enormous tyres screeching as the pilots engaged the brakes and then taxied to their stands where the ground crew hurried to place the chocks once the rotors stopped spinning.

Spitfires, Hurricanes and Mosquitoes came in like small birds, landing with an almost delicate elegance before zipping over to their own part of the airfield to get out of the way.

'Smutty Smith's taken a battering,' muttered one of the rear gunners as a Spitfire landed on one wheel. 'He could use those wings as colanders.'

They all watched Smutty's plane tilt, its belly scraping along the ground as the bullet-ridden right wing snapped off and went spinning in a clatter across the runway right in the path of a Mosquito which was trying to land with its wheels still jammed up under it.

Martin held his breath as young Jack Newbury pulled hard on his joystick and climbed almost vertically out of the way with his engines screaming.

There was a general releasing of breath and some wag remarked that it was time Jugs learned where his bloody wheel release was.

Martin gave the ghost of a smile at this, for

giving the lad a nickname – albeit rather a cruel one considering the size of his ears – meant that he'd been accepted. He watched the Pilot Officer do an up-and-over turn to get back on course, marvelling at how much the lad had learned in his short time here.

The wheels were still up, so the fire trucks and ambulance were on standby and Martin silently applauded Jack's good sense when he chose a soft landing and belly-flopped onto the grass, shedding bits of wooden fuselage as the plane came to a skidding halt within feet of the control tower.

It was a moment before the canopy was pushed back, and Jack and his co-pilot – the equally young Bertie Goodall – climbed down with huge grins and a bit of a swagger. As a cheer went up from the WAAFs who'd poured out of the plotting room and offices to watch the boys come home, they executed flourishing bows before hurrying across to make the most of this chance to chat them up.

'Cheeky young beggars,' growled Roger Makepeace with a glint of pride in his eyes as he strolled over to Martin. 'But that's the second Mozzie those two have pranged in a month, so I'll have to have a word, unfortunately.'

'At least they made it home,' Martin murmured, searching the skies for sight of Freddy and Matthew.

Minutes later he saw Freddy bringing in his Spitfire with his usual flair for a dramatic entrance. He skimmed the control tower by inches, did a tight turn at the end of the runway and came down far too fast, slamming on his brakes to skid to a halt within inches of the tail of another Spitfire.

'It's time he grew up and stopped showing off to the gallery,' muttered Martin, watching him climb down to be immediately surrounded by admiring females.

'You have to admit, though, Pedro's an ace flyer.'

Martin bit down on the pipe-stem in annoyance. 'That he might be, but we're losing planes faster than they can build them, and stunts like that are unnecessary and dangerous.'

'Time you had a proper drink, old chap,' said Roger, laying a heavy hand on Martin's shoulder. 'My shout.'

'Not everyone's in yet, Tash. You go ahead. I'll wait for the stragglers.'

Roger frowned and quickly trawled the gathering. 'Where's Pinky? I thought I saw him trailing me back in. Isn't he back yet?'

Martin shook his head, concentrating on the few badly damaged planes that were limping home to make a messy but safe landing. He'd seen Matthew Champion too, but it had been much earlier during the ferocious dog fights over Hamburg – with a Jerry Heinkel on his tail, and a Messerschmitt closing in fast. There'd been nothing he could do to help, for he'd had his own problems with another Messerschmitt determined to blast him out of the sky.

Roger fell silent and they were soon joined by the other men in Pinky's wing as well as Freddy and young Jack. Brandy flasks were passed round, pipes and cigarettes lit as parachute packs were eased from shoulders and leather jackets unfastened.

Martin could feel the dark, steady trickle of dread begin to seep through him as the skies remained empty and the only sound he could hear was the distant, muffled clang of a hammer on metal coming from the repair hangar.

Time crawled past, but still there was no sign of Matthew, and with a heavy heart, Martin was about to suggest they go to the mess for a stiff drink when he heard the faint burps and rattles of a struggling engine. As one, the group of men searched the pale blue sky.

'There,' shouted Freddy. 'Coming in low at four o'clock.'

They moved out to the grass area that ran along the front of the admin building so they had a better view, the silent tension growing by the second as the Spitfire coughed and spluttered an uneven course towards them. Skimming the treetops, it jerked and juddered and tilted alarmingly as Matthew Champion fought to keep a straight flight path and get the wheels down.

But Martin could see that one of the wings was hanging by a thread of metal, the tail had been shot to pieces and the canopy was open. His heart was in his mouth, for the crippled wing could very easily catch on something and make the plane spin out of control or turn turtle. If he landed arse up, Matthew would be dead in an instant.

The Spitfire's propellers stopped turning as the engine cut out, leaving a terrible silence amongst those watching all over the airfield. Two fire trucks roared out towards the runway in readiness, swiftly followed by an ambulance and a posse of engineers carrying fire extinguishers.

Everyone held their breath as the Spitfire's wing scraped along the ground, sending sparks flying until it was ripped away to clatter harmlessly in its wake. The wheels were still not properly down, and as the plane landed with a series of jarring kangaroo hops, they collapsed and the belly of the plane thudded onto the ground.

The screech of tortured metal echoed over the airfield as the great shower of sparks burst into flames and billowing black smoke.

The fire engine raced alongside, waiting until it was safe to dowse the fire with the powerful jet hoses – for to do it now could send the plane into a spin and rip away any control the pilot might still have

The Spitfire finally came to a grinding halt, tilting abruptly to sink its nose into the muddy grass, its rear end pointing skyward.

The fire crew immediately opened the hoses as the engineers used their extinguishers and tried to find a way through the flames and smoke to get to the pilot.

Martin and the men around him began to run, desperate to help in any way they could to save their colleague and friend. As they were beaten back by the heat of the flames, the smoke was briefly shredded by the wind and they could see Matthew standing in the open cockpit, bracing himself against the powerful jets of water and shielding his face from the voracious flames that were being fed to greater intensity by the aviation fuel.

'Jump!' Martin yelled. 'For God's sake, jump!'

Matthew climbed onto the rim of the cockpit, the flames licking at his battledress. And then with a mighty yell, he dived out, over the flames and through the smoke, landing on the soft ground and immediately going into the tight roll they'd been taught during parachute training.

Martin and Roger were the first to get to him and drag him away from the burning plane. They beat out the few flames that were still licking at his battle-suit and then eased off the parachute pack and opened the collar of his jacket.

'All right, all right,' protested Matthew, batting them away. 'No need to fuss, chaps. I'm perfectly fine.'

He grinned up at them, his face blackened by smoke and streaked with sweat and engine oil. 'I got both Bogeys right between the eyes,' he said. 'That'll teach Jerry to bugger me about.'

'Jolly good show,' said Martin. 'I'll make sure they're marked up.'

But Matthew had fainted and didn't hear him.

Somerset

Tendrils of mist were caught in the treetops, the heavy dew sparkling in the muddy fields as the sky turned from grey to blue on the rising sun. It was Saturday morning and Anne could see the fog of her breath in the chill air as she finished feeding the chickens and went out into the fields to help Bob and the three land girls, Stella, Letty and Lucinda, bring in the cows for milking.

125

Sally was getting the younger children dressed, Vi was having a very rare lie-in to nurse her cold, and Charlie was bent beneath the tractor bonnet with old Fred and Bert, poking about with the engine which had suddenly decided to stop working. Despite the earliness of the hour, Owlet Farm was, as always, busy with people going about their daily chores.

Angus, the enormous, bad-tempered bull, eyed Anne sullenly from his field, lowering his head and pawing the ground as if preparing to charge. Vi rented him out to breed with other farmers' cows, and he brought in quite a bit of income to Owlet Farm, for his progeny had proved to be of excellent quality, which meant they could sell the beef and veal to the forces, and had more good milkers.

Anne kept a wary eye on him, for he was quite terrifying, and even the youngest children knew better than to bait him or go anywhere near him, for they'd witnessed him charging Bob one day, and he'd only just managed to vault over the fence before Angus's fearsome horns crashed into the railings.

The mud and soggy cowpats squelched beneath her wellingtons as she and the others coaxed the slow-moving, complaining cows out of their field, through the gate and across the cobbled yard into the milking parlour. The herd had increased over the past couple of years, and were grazed over several different pastures, but the milking parlour could only take a dozen at a time, so the process was strung out over half the morning before they could all be milked. And then it all had to be done

126

again at the end of the day, regardless of the weather.

Anne had become used to the pungent smell of cow-shit, as Letty insisted upon calling it, and had learned very quickly to avoid getting her feet trampled by heavy hooves as the cows bumped and jostled their way out of the field. The first and only time it had happened, she'd been bruised for days and had lost two toenails in the process, so she was very careful to keep the younger children well away from them, fearing for their delicate bones.

Cows could be very protective and quite dangerous when they had calves, but usually they were gentle, and although Anne didn't like it when they put their wet snouts close to her face and tried to lick her with their long black tongues, she no longer feared them. When she'd first arrived, she'd been cornered in a field by several beasts and had been terrified they'd attack her. Thankfully, Vi had come to her rescue, and explained that they were merely being curious, and that she'd done the best thing by standing absolutely still and silent until they lost interest. To run or scream would have frightened them into a charge, and she could have been trampled.

With a clatter of hooves on the concrete floor, the cattle went into the stalls and stood patiently as their udders and teats were hosed down and checked for tears or infection before the rubber tubes were attached and the milking machines began to hum.

As the steady stream of warm, sweet-smelling milk poured through the tubes and into the

127

collecting tank, Anne worked alongside the other girls, checking there were no injuries that might need dealing with before the cows were released back into the field. Most cuts and gouges were made by kicks or during the cows' overenthusiastic attempts to mount each other, which Anne still thought was bizarre behaviour.

As each animal was unhitched from the machine and shooed out of the parlour, she was replaced by the next – and then the next. By nine o'clock the last of them were back in their fields and Anne hosed down the cobbles to get rid of the mess they'd left behind as Bob and the girls washed and scrubbed out the parlour and then sterilised every part of the milking machine until it shone. The cream was skimmed from the top and put into a special chilling container, while the rest was poured from the tap in the tank into freshly scrubbed and sterilised metal churns.

It took two of them to hoist the heavy churns into the trailer behind the tractor, which was running again. Then the churns would be taken to the main gate to await collection by the wholesale dairy, who would bottle the milk and deliver it by carthorse and dray to the doorsteps of the surrounding villages and towns.

Despite the cold day, Anne was sweltering beneath her thick coat, woolly hat and scarf, and her back was aching after having swept the wide expanse of cobbles, but she felt energised by the exercise and a job well done.

She was beaming as she followed the land girls towards the farmhouse, where a hearty breakfast awaited them. The most exercise she'd had back in Cliffehaven was riding her bicycle back and forth to the junior school in Camden Road, and perhaps playing the occasional game of tennis at the local club – now she was slimmer, fitter and stronger than ever before, her bedroom mirror telling her that her skin glowed from the fresh air and healthy diet, her eyes were bright, and her dark hair was thick and lustrous now it was free at last from nits and DDT powder.

Martin would get a shock if he could see me now, she thought as she toed off her wellingtons in the porch and shed her outdoor clothes. Not that he was likely to get the chance. His latest letter hadn't even hinted at the possibility of his getting any leave, and she'd learned enough from the newspapers and wireless reports to know that it was unlikely to happen for a very long time yet.

She padded into the warm kitchen in her socks to find everyone seated at the enormous scrubbed table, tucking into eggs, fried bread and thick rashers of bacon that had come from the pig Bob had slaughtered the week before. It was quite a crush, for there were fourteen of them if you counted Emily who was ensconced in her high chair. Vi had made it a rule that everyone ate together, including the old farmhands, for this was what her parents had done, and it made for a harmonious atmosphere and a chance to air any grievances before they became a problem.

Anne kissed Rose and Emily, noting that they both seemed to be in a good mood, and sat down. 'Thanks, Aunt Vi,' she said. 'I'm definitely ready for this, but I hope you didn't get out of bed especially to feed all of us.'

Violet continued to cut Emily's food into manageable pieces so she could scoop it up with her spoon, or eat it with her fingers. 'I got horribly bored lying in bed,' she said. 'And as my cold seems better today, I thought we'd get on with clearing that last field.'

She drank some tea and regarded everyone around the table. 'The Food, Fish and Agriculture people are making noises about increasing our output, and with so many cows now in calf it makes sense to separate them from the rest of the herd. But that field has lain fallow for years and is covered in all sorts of weeds and wildflowers, so it's vital we rid it of everything that's harmful to the livestock.'

'I didn't know weeds and flowers could hurt them,' said Sally with the innocence of a girl born and raised in Bow.

'There are lots of plants that are deadly to cattle,' Vi explained. 'I've written out a list for each of you, and found a book of wild flowers so you know what to look for. A lot of them won't be in flower yet, so you'll be needing to check the leaves.'

She fetched the book from the dresser and placed it on the table alongside a large piece of paper covered in writing.

'Blimey,' breathed Sally as the others craned their necks to see what she'd written. 'That's one heck of a list. It'll take us a month of Sundays to find that lot.'

'Which is why we need to get on with it today while the weather's holding fair,' said Vi. 'Fred and Bert will come with us as their eyesight is keen, and they know more about wild plants and their properties than all of us put together. So heed what they say, and don't let your concentration flag. Every last bit of monkshood, wild onion, celandine and so on has to be cleared before we can put those cows in there – otherwise well end up with dead beasts and not meet the government quota.'

Anne read through the seemingly endless list of things that could poison cattle and kill their calves. It had taken her a while to become inured to the way of things on a farm – to accept that chickens and pigs had to be slaughtered, calves lived for just nine months before they became veal meat, unproductive cows were sent to the abattoir and sick beasts put down, but she hadn't realised the complexities of doing something so simple as moving them from one field to another.

'I propose we make a start after breakfast, and keep at it until it's time for the evening milking,' said Vi. 'I've prepared a picnic which we can eat out there, and of course the children can muck in as well.'

Her sweet, round face broke into a nostalgic smile. 'It will be like the old days, when my parents ran the farm. We'd work in the fields all day, especially at harvest time, and eat chunks of bread and cheese washed down with home-made lemonade while the grown-ups had jugs of strong ale.'

She regarded the faces turned towards her around the table. 'It's funny, isn't it, how memories are selective? I've forgotten how hard we worked, how we got bitten and stung and burnt by the sun, falling into bed exhausted every night to do the same thing all over again the next day. I just remember it being sunny, with us kids racing about, competing with each other to make the neatest stacks of sheaves, glad to be outside and doing something useful.'

'You make it all sound very romantic,' said Stella in her carefully modulated voice. 'But since joining the Land Army, I've experienced nothing but cold and muck and back-breaking work – most of it done even before sensible people are awake, let alone out of bed. I can't honestly say I'm enamoured with farming, and it's absolutely ruined my lovely nails.'

'That's because you married some toff who earned enough so you never 'ad to lift a finger before the war, so you don't know what 'ard work is,' said Letty, who'd worked in a canning factory in the East End before the war. 'I reckon we're lucky to be out in the fresh air, where Jerry don't bother us, and we get the best food.' She clattered her knife and fork together on her empty plate and then reached for the toast.

'Actually, I think it's all terrific fun,' piped up Lucinda Pearson-Ivory who, despite her illustrious and noble bloodline, had proved to be a tireless and very cheerful worker who wasn't at all afraid of breaking a nail or getting her hands dirty. 'I much prefer doing this to being stuck in some stuffy office at the Admiralty with Daddy.'

Letty rolled her eyes at this and began to slather butter on her toast. 'Blimey, Luce, you are a card. I'd never 'ave thought you'd fit in 'ere, but I reckon you was born to it, mate.'

'Well, the family did have a place in Sussex

132

before the Luftwaffe flattened it,' said Lucinda, 'so I am rather used to mucking out stables first thing.'

Anne and Vi exchanged amused glances as the banter went round the table. The three land girls were in their twenties and came from very different backgrounds, but despite the odd spat, they got on surprisingly well. And yet Stella was showing all the signs of restlessness they'd seen in other girls who'd found that life on a farm didn't suit them, and had gone off to find something else. Anne could only hope that she'd stay until the calving was over.

The five-acre field was surrounded by drystone walls and sloped quite steeply towards the shallow river, which raced over a stony bed to fall in frothy cascades over the larger rocks as it headed towards the broad valley. Parts of the field were sheltered from the winds by oak, ash and elm, and on the northern boundary stood the crumbling ruin of an old building which had once housed the oxen who'd been too slow and lumbering to bring all the way back to the farm every night.

The oxen were long gone, replaced at first by Shires, and now machinery, but the ruin had become a wonderful place for the children to use their imaginations in endless play. Anne glanced across from the far end of the field, noting that today the old place had become a cowboy fort, besieged by Indians, which meant a great deal of whooping and dashing about, and the firing of pretend guns and bows and arrows.

She rested back on her elbows and turned her

attention to the view. The sky was a duck egg blue, the valley a palette of greens and browns with the glint of the stream running like a silver ribbon through it. The wind had dropped and the sun felt quite warm on her face, so she slipped off her coat and woolly hat and basked in it, glad to rest for a while until they had to start all over again.

They'd spent the morning in search of the poisonous plants they had to dig up, gradually getting to know what to look for as Bert and Fred patiently followed them and pointed them out. The younger children had joined in at first but had soon grown bored, so they'd run off to find something more interesting to do until it was lunchtime. Once fed, their energy had been stoked, and everyone had been relieved when they'd left the picnic for further adventures.

Anne felt sated from the delicious lunch of home-made cheese and chutney and buttery fresh bread, cold elderberry cordial and sweet, rosy apples which had been stored away in a dark corner of the barn over the winter. Nothing tasted better than food eaten in the fresh air, but it did make her feel drowsy.

She rested her head on her folded coat and listened in to the murmur of conversation going on around her. Stella, Letty and Lucinda were discussing the terrible lack of decent make-up and clothes; Bob was discussing the price of milk with Vi; and Fred and Bert were having a loud conversation about the poor quality of the beer at the local pub, their deafness making it rather comical as they misheard one another which reminded Anne of Cordelia, who quite often forgot to turn up her hearing aid.

As for Charlie and Ernie, they were in a huddle plotting some sort of mischief which involved the large pond. She tuned in for a while and then interrupted sharply. 'You will not make a raft and play pirates on that pond,' she said. 'It's deep and full of weed, and those poor ducks have been, tormented enough by the pair of you.'

'We just wanted to see if we could make a raft that would float,' said Charlie crossly. 'You always spoil our fun.' He got to his feet and pulled Ernie up with him. 'Come on, Ern. Let's do a surprise attack on the fort and take the girls prisoner.'

'We'll be going back to work in ten minutes,' warned Bob. 'So don't leave the field.'

Charlie and Ernie rolled their eyes, gave great sighs of exasperation and ran off. 'Got to catch us first,' yelled Charlie over his shoulder.

'Cheeky beggars,' Bob muttered, flopping back onto the ground.

Silence fell amongst them as the boys tired of playing with the little ones and decided to see if they could walk along the top of the stone wall instead, and explore the possibility of making a rope swing from one of the overhanging tree branches.

Anne slowly became aware of a noise that sounded like the drone of a bee – which was very odd, for they were still hibernating in the hives Bert had constructed many years before the war. She shielded her eyes from the sun and looked around, realising that the others had heard it too – and that it definitely wasn't a bee, for it was

135

getting louder.

Everyone sat up and scoured the sky, realising now that it could only be the drone of a plane. 'It could be one of our fighters returning to Bristol,' murmured Bob. 'Or someone delivering a Spitfire – it's definitely not a bomber. The sound's not deep enough.'

'Whatever it is, it's moving with speed,' said Anne, getting to her feet.

And then it came out of the sun like a camouflaged bullet; so low that the downdraught of its jet engines flattened the grass, bent the trees and terrified the grazing cattle. It roared across the field, the pilot visible in the cockpit – the swastika glinting blackly on its tail.

'Run!' They screamed in unison as they moved to make a dash for the children who were frozen in play, their terrified gazes fixed on the enemy jet fighter which was now turning tightly to make another pass over the field.

Time seemed to stand still and Anne felt as if the world had slowed to a crawl and she was wading through deep mud. 'Run,' she yelled again. 'Hide in the ruin.'

But Emily, Rose and Harry were still frozen – Charlie and Ernie were shocked to a standstill in their run across the field to search for rope – and the ruin was at the very top of the steep hill – too far away to get the little ones there before the enemy plane began its second pass.

'Bastard's coming back,' gasped Sally as she caught up with Anne and they stumbled and slithered in desperation to get to their children.

Anne ran as fast as she could to keep up with

her, careless of the brambles ripping at her legs, her breath a sob as Bob came tearing past. She dared to look towards the enemy plane, saw it was bearing down on them and began to scream once more to the children to run and hide.

But the roar of the jet engine drowned out her cries and as it swooped low, flames shot from the guns as the pilot opened fire.

Anne and Sally were knocked off their feet by the downdraught, but Anne just caught a glimpse of Bob dodging the bullets as he scooped up the three little ones into his arms and carried them up the hill and shoved them into the ruined ox-barn. Her pulse was racing, the fear a living thing squirming inside her as she dared to watch him run back down and grab Ernie and Charlie by the arms and drag them into the ruins as well.

The relief made her weak and she sank onto the ground, her face buried in the long grass. Bullets thudded all around her and she felt the sting of something graze her leg, and the punch of another hitting her shoulder, but she was so terrified for her children that she took no notice. They were well hidden, but had the German seen them – was he going to make a third pass?

She became aware of Sally's sobbing breath beside her and grabbed her hand as she dared to look up again. 'I can't see them, Sal,' she said. 'They must be safe with Bob.'

'If I 'ad a bleedin' gun, I'd shoot the bastard,' Sally snarled. 'D'you reckon he'll come back for another go at us?'

'I don't know,' she managed, gripping Sally's hand tightly.

The bullets stopped thudding around them and the blast of the jet engines faded as the plane roared towards the Channel – trees bending and birds scattering in alarm in its wake. Everyone stayed where they were, fearful that he hadn't been alone – or might return.

'Has he gone?' Stella asked tremulously some while later.

Anne and Sally cautiously sat up and searched the sky. They couldn't hear anything but the thunder of their hearts. They glanced at each other and moved as one in a hectic dash for the hilltop ruin where they fell to their knees and gathered up their terrified children.

'Oh, thank God,' breathed Anne, holding the hysterical little girls to her heart and trying to kiss away their fears as she checked feverishly for any sign of injury to them.

'They're all right,' said Bob, rubbing his bruised elbows where he'd hit the rough floor as he'd thrown himself into the ruin.

Anne held on to her girls and grabbed hold of her brother's neck, pulling him towards her so she could repeatedly kiss his dirty face. 'Thank you, thank you for saving their lives,' she said through her tears.

'Gerroff,' he muttered, wiping away her kisses in disgust. 'There's no need to go all soppy on me.'

'You're a hero, Bob,' sobbed Sally, clutching Harry to her chest. 'A real, right, blooming hero, and if it were up to me, you'd get a medal for what you done today.'

Bob went bright red beneath the dirt and shrugged off her praise as Charlie and Ernie came scrabbling out of the corner of the ruin, their faces alight with excitement.

'Did you see that?' shouted Ernie as he and Charlie rubbed at their bruises and scrapes. 'It was a Messerschmitt Me-163 single seater jet fighter – the fastest plane Jerry's got. I read about 'em, but I ain't never seen one before.'

'Let's hope we never see another one,' panted Vi as she arrived with the land girls. 'Is everyone all right? No one hurt?'

'We're fine,' said Sally grimly, 'though it's more by luck than anything. I can't believe he opened fire on women and kids like that. We weren't doing no 'arm.' She turned to Anne. 'I hope your Martin shoots 'im down. Then he won't feel so bleedin' clever.'

Anne's teeth had begun to chatter from shock and the aftermath of an overwhelming fear, and her whole body began to tremble as she held her little ones close. But the slight pressure of Emily's head against her shoulder shouldn't have hurt so much, and there was a dull, throbbing ache in her leg.

'Mummy, you got jam on you, and it's making Emmy's hair all sticky,' said an ashen-faced Rose Margaret.

'Cor,' breathed Ernie. 'That's bl–'

'Hush,' snapped Vi, reaching for Emily and Rose. 'Bob, take Anne home and telephone the doctor. And you two,' she said sternly to Charlie and Ernie who were suddenly more sober, 'go and help Fred and Bert burn those weeds. I don't want to see either of you until it's done.'

'But Anne's–' Charlie protested.

139

'I said be quiet,' hissed Vi. 'I don't want the little ones any more frightened than they already are. Now do as I say and clear off. Your sister will be fine once the doctor's seen to her. I promise.'

Anne could see he was about to argue. 'Just do it, Charlie,' she said, feeling strangely weak and light-headed all of a sudden.

As the boys reluctantly rejoined the land girls and the old men at the bottom of the field, Vi shepherded the wide-eyed little ones out of the ruin. Anne saw the dark red stain on her sweater and felt the deep throb of pain coursing through her shoulder, then realised she was also bleeding from a wound in her leg.

'Don't try to walk,' said Bob. 'I'll carry you.'

'I can manage,' she protested. 'Don't make a fuss.'

He took no notice and lifted her up as if she weighed nothing. His expression was grim as he strode towards the farmhouse.

She closed her eyes and bit her lip as each step jolted her shoulder and sent a knife of pain right through her. Her children were safe, that was all that mattered – but she did feel very strange.

She slowly emerged from the darkness to the sound of the children singing a nursery rhyme along with Vi, who could barely hold even the simplest tune. Opening her eyes she wondered for a moment where she was, for the room was deeply shadowed, the only light coming from the low wattage bulb of the bedside lamp.

Confused as to why she was in bed when her children were still up and about, she lifted her head from the pillow to see what the time was, and then sank back with a gasp of pain.

She remained there as memory slowly returned and then, with tremulous fingers, explored the heavy strapping on her shoulder and the sling holding her arm tightly to her chest. She could feel another bandage around her calf, but lifting her head sent shock waves through her injured shoulder, making her feel dizzy and nauseous, so she explored it with her other foot and discovered it was just padding and sticking plaster – which meant the bullet must have merely grazed the flesh.

The relief that they'd all escaped far worse was immense, and her eyelids fluttered as sleep once more claimed her, and when she next woke, she discovered it was broad daylight, the church bell was ringing for Sunday Matins and Sally was sitting at her bedside.

'Keep still,' Sally urged when she tried to sit up. 'The doctor said you've got to stay in bed and not move until that wound heals. The bullet went quite deep in your shoulder, you know, and he had a bit of a job getting it out. He injected you with a strong sedative and a painkiller, which is why you've been asleep for so long.'

'But I can't lie about in bed. The children need to get dressed for Sunday school and there's work to do on the farm.'

'Vi's already taken them to Sunday school, and we can manage without you until you're better,' said Sally. She placed her hand gently behind Anne's head and helped her to drink some water. 'There's nothing for you to do but lie there like

Lady Muck while we look after you. So you might as well enjoy it.'

'How are the children coping with what happened?'

'Harry had a nightmare so I took 'im into bed with me – something I won't do again, 'cos 'e kicked me all through the bloomin' night. But Vi slept in with your two last night and said they went right through without a murmur once they were allowed to come in and see you and knew you were all right.'

'But there's no reaction to it all this morning?'

Sally shook her head. 'Not really. They're all three of them a bit quieter than usual, but eating well and quite happy to go with Vi to church, so you've no need to worry.'

Anne would worry until she'd actually seen her children and been reassured. She thought for a moment. 'I think it's best if we don't write home about this,' she said. 'Mum worries enough, and Martin has too much on his plate already. He can't afford to get distracted by what happened here yesterday.'

'I've already warned Charlie and Ernie about that – the little devils are planning to tell everyone at school how brave your Bob was and how they hadn't been frightened one little bit.' Sally smiled. 'I'll get a bowl of water and help you wash, then I'll bring you some breakfast.'

Anne closed her eyes as Sally bustled out. She was incredibly lucky to have such good friends around her, but oh, how she yearned for her mother right now.

7

Cliffehaven

Peggy had barely slept at all on the Friday night, but had managed to keep up appearances throughout Saturday and carry on as if nothing had changed. The effort this had taken meant that she'd been exhausted by the end of the day, but at least she'd slept right through, and this morning she felt slightly more composed.

Once Ivy, Rita and Fran had left for work – Sundays didn't count as a day off when there was a war on – and Sarah had gone upstairs to write to her sister, Peggy washed Daisy's sticky face and left her to play with a colouring book and crayons while she cleared the last few dishes from the table.

'You look better this morning,' said Cordelia, setting the Sunday paper aside and regarding her evenly over her reading glasses. 'I was worried about you yesterday. We all were.'

Peggy carried the dirty crockery to the sink. 'It was just such a shock,' she admitted, 'but please don't fret, Cordelia. I'm perfectly all right, really I am.'

'If you say so,' murmured Cordelia. 'But you don't fool me, Peggy. And should you need a shoulder to cry on, you know where I am.'

Peggy's knuckles were white as she gripped the

rim of the stone sink and determinedly blinked back her ready tears. 'Bless you, Cordelia. That's a lovely offer, but tears won't protect him or bring this war to a swifter end, and life has to go on here – no matter how difficult it might be.'

'But you don't have to struggle alone, dear,' said Cordelia, coming to her side and putting her arm about her waist.

Peggy turned and embraced her. 'I know,' she said quietly. 'And I count myself very lucky to have you.' She kissed the soft cheek, swallowed the lump in her throat and swiftly turned back to the sink.

Cordelia made no reply, and fetched the tea towel to dry the dishes.

Peggy had her emotions under control again, and as she glanced out of the window, she came to a decision. 'It's one of those lovely cold, crisp, sunny days – perfect for a walk along the front. Do you fancy coming with me?'

'I'm sorry, dear, I wish I could but I can't today. Bertie is taking me out for coffee at the golf club and then for lunch at the Briar Cottage restaurant. Should I cancel him?'

'No, no, of course you mustn't cancel. Goodness, what a treat. I've heard the food is very good there, although it's supposed to be expensive.'

Cordelia nodded. 'He's splashing out a bit because he's going away for a couple of weeks – a courtesy visit to some ancient relative who hasn't been well, evidently.'

'That doesn't sound much fun.'

'He doesn't have any other family and feels he ought to make the effort,' said Cordelia on a sigh.

'He's a dear man, Peggy. I'm fortunate to have him as a friend.'

Peggy had a fleeting memory of how badly Bertie had behaved the previous year when he'd joined some strange gentlemen's club, but as he seemed to have come to his senses and there had been no repeat of his rotten manners, she'd almost forgiven him. At the time Ron had hinted that there might have been more behind Bertie's discourtesy than met the eye, and Peggy supposed Ron had been right. 'He's the fortunate one,' she said firmly. 'And I hope he never forgets it.'

Cordelia chuckled. 'Anyone would think you were my mother, the way you jump to my defence.'

Peggy finished the washing-up and took the bowl outside to empty into the special butt Ron kept for watering the vegetable garden. She looked up at the sky, noting how clear and blue it was, then hurried back inside to finish her morning chores so she could enjoy the day.

Daisy soon became bored with her colouring book and was now piling wooden bricks onto a kitchen chair and then knocking them to the floor with a great clatter and squeals of delight. Cordelia switched off her hearing aid so she could read the paper in peace, and Peggy went to fetch their coats and hats.

It was a bit of a struggle to get Daisy dressed as she wanted to continue her game, but she was eventually ready, and Peggy swiftly put on her own scarf and coat and reached for her handbag and gas-mask box. Catching Cordelia's attention by tapping her hand, she waited for her to adjust her hearing aid before speaking.

'We're going for our walk now,' she said. 'Have a lovely lunch and I'll see you later.'

Cordelia smiled and waved before returning to her newspaper, and Peggy carried Daisy down the concrete steps to the scullery and strapped her into the pushchair.

'Wanna walk,' said Daisy grumpily.

'When we get down to the seafront you can walk all you want,' replied Peggy, firmly pushing the pram out of the back door and along the path before she could argue.

Daisy was soon distracted by a squirrel scampering up a tree, and they watched it for a while before Peggy continued down the hill to the promenade. The sea looked lovely despite the shipping traps strung along the bay. Although there was a tempting stretch of golden sand beyond the pebbles, it had long been out of bounds – the beach cut off from the promenade by rolls of barbed wire, the pebbles thickly laid with mines.

Peggy unfastened the straps and Daisy scrambled out of the pram to run ahead in pursuit of a gull which was exploring the contents of a discarded fag packet. Peggy kept a wary eye on her in case she went too close to the barbed wire, and walked along enjoying the sun on her face and the light, crisp wind that tugged at her headscarf.

She exchanged greetings with the soldiers manning the gun emplacements which were dotted all along the seafront, and stopped to chat for a little while with other locals who were out enjoying this lovely day. She preferred not to let her gaze dwell too long on the ugly bomb sites which had once been the two grandest hotels in the town, for they were grim reminders that nothing and no one was safe any more.

Peggy saw a young woman settle down on one of the stone benches, her little girl scrambling over the low brick wall behind it to play with her doll on the grassy bank that fronted the line of small private hotels. Daisy spotted the other child at the same moment and made a dash towards her, so Peggy went over to introduce herself.

'Hello,' she said, taking in the fact that the woman was probably a decade younger, well dressed, slim and very attractive, with tawny hair and a creamy skin. 'I hope you don't mind us barging in, but Daisy saw your little girl and wanted to play.' She stuck out her hand. 'I'm Peggy Reilly, by the way.'

The girl smiled as they shook hands. 'Delighted to meet you, Peggy. I'm Gracie Armitage, and that's my little Chloe. Do sit down. It's lovely for Chloe to have a playmate on a Sunday – she can get horribly bored with just me to amuse her, and at almost three, she still goes into frightful tantrums.'

'Daisy's just over two, so I know what you mean,' said Peggy. 'But that'll soon change once I start work and she goes into the crèche.'

The girl's hazel eyes widened. 'Goodness. You must have a job at Goldman's.' At Peggy's nod she chuckled. 'What a coincidence. I've been there for almost three years now, and Chloe absolutely loves Nanny Pringle – even though I suspect she's quite strict.'

Peggy smiled and nodded. 'Yes, I got that impression too.' She offered her packet of Park Drive to Gracie and when their cigarettes were lit, they checked on the little girls who were playing quite amicably, then sat back and enjoyed the sunshine.

Peggy was full of curiosity about this friendly girl, but decided it was a bit early to start pumping her for information. She didn't recognise her at all, so she wasn't local, and she had no accent, so it was difficult to place where she might have come from.

'So, Peggy, what are you doing in Cliffehaven?'

'I've been here all my life and my parents before me,' she replied. 'We used to run Beach View as a boarding house, but now I take in evacuees.' She smiled, glad to have the opportunity to get to know the other woman better. 'What about you, Gracie?'

'I moved down here from Surrey when my husband joined the RAF and was posted to Cliffe back in 1940.' She gave a sigh. 'And then, after a year, he was seconded to another squadron in a different county, just as I'd found out I was expecting Chloe.'

'That's typical of the services,' muttered Peggy. 'You never know what they'll do next to interrupt your life.'

Gracie's smile was sympathetic. 'That sounds like the voice of experience.'

'My Jim was supposed to be in India, but I've just learned he's been sent somewhere else. Hitler, the Japs and the army have a great deal to answer for,' Peggy said briskly.

'And don't I know it,' Gracie said wryly. 'My

148

dad's out in the Pacific somewhere, my brother's been in North Africa and is now down in Italy, and two of my uncles are with the Atlantic convoys. My poor mother is in a constant state of worry, and if she hadn't got so heavily involved in the Red Cross, I seriously believe she'd have had a nervous breakdown by now.'

'I'm surprised any of us left behind have remained sane,' said Peggy. 'But that's the way things are, and we just have to get on with it, don't we?'

Gracie grinned and reached into the shopping basket at her feet to draw out a thermos flask. 'Fancy a cuppa?'

'Always,' replied Peggy. 'Things look so much better after a brew and a good chat.' She watched as Gracie poured strong, dark tea into the little cups. 'So, why didn't you follow your husband when he left Cliffehaven?'

'I did think about it, but I was expecting Chloe and had a good job at Goldman's – and of course he could have been seconded anywhere else at a moment's notice.' She sipped her tea. 'Clive was a bit po-faced about me working at all, let alone in a factory. He's a bit old-fashioned like that – much like his father,' she confided with an impish grin. 'But I told him straight that I wasn't prepared to sit out the war and do nothing while he was having the time of his life flying Hurricanes, and I think he realises now how important it's been for me to do my bit and have the companionship of other women.'

'Good for him – and good for you,' said Peggy stoutly. 'Everyone needs friends at a time like

149

this. So, what job do you do at Goldman's?'

'Solly took me on as an apprentice cutter, and I had an excellent teacher in old Brian Howland, who's sadly since passed away. Now I'm in charge of my own table, doing officers' uniform jackets, with two apprentices under me. What about you?'

'A very new and inexperienced machinist – and the thought of starting tomorrow morning gives me the collywobbles.'

Gracie laughed. 'We all feel like that at first, but it'll pass, and most of the other girls are very helpful should you get in a pickle.'

Their conversation was interrupted by the sound of squabbling, and they discovered the two little girls were throwing a tantrum over one of Chloe's dolls. Peggy picked up a furious Daisy and Gracie balanced a bawling Chloe on her hip.

'Well, it was fun while it lasted but I'm no Nanny Pringle,' Gracie shouted over her daughter's bellows. 'So I'll take this one home, I think.'

Peggy helped her stow away the thermos and then strapped the struggling, screaming Daisy firmly into the pushchair. 'Do you have far to walk?'

'My place is just off the High Street in Warren Lane,' Gracie replied above the racket. 'I'll see you tomorrow, and we can have a proper chat during our break. It's been lovely meeting you, Peggy.'

Peggy ignored Daisy's tantrum and watched as Gracie bore her own screaming daughter away. 'What a lovely girl,' she murmured, hoping that the majority of the women at Goldman's were just as pleasant.

The talk of Goldman's reminded her that she

150

had an unpleasant task to fulfil before the day got any older, so she grasped the pushchair handle and, with Daisy yelling fit to bust, walked purposefully down the promenade and turned off at the junction with the High Street into Havelock Road. She couldn't put off facing Doris any longer.

Daisy's yells echoed in the quiet, tree-lined cul-de-sac and Peggy came to an abrupt halt. 'Stop it,' she ordered. 'Stop this minute, or I shall take you home and put you to bed.'

'Don't wanna go to bed,' Daisy snivelled.

'Then give me a smile and let me dry those tears.'

Daisy squeezed out a couple more tears and a sobbing hiccup. 'Wanna play with Chloe,' she pouted.

'You can play with Chloe at school tomorrow,' said Peggy, wiping her face with her handkerchief and getting her to blow her nose. 'Now where's that lovely smile, Daisy?'

Daisy obliged somewhat reluctantly, and Peggy gave her a kiss then quickly steered the pushchair down the uneven pavement where the tree roots had lifted the slabs.

Havelock Road was regarded as one of the posh areas of town, for the houses were detached and stood in large plots, their back gardens sloping down towards the promenade, their fronts facing Havelock Gardens – a small but very pleasant park which had been turned into a public allotment at the beginning of the war. Now, Peggy noted, there was litter and weeds in the gutters, and the grass needed cutting on the verge – a very different state of affairs to the way it had once been.

She passed the large bomb site where a fine old house had been completely demolished by a bomb, and noted how many of the once mani-cured front gardens had been turned into vege-table patches or left to the weeds and brambles. Peggy could see boarded-up windows, bullet holes stitched across garden walls and the evidence of lack of care in the flaking paint and dull door knockers, and reflected sadly that it didn't matter how posh or rich you were, this war got to everyone in the end.

She arrived at the last house but one and took a deep breath as she surveyed the pristine gravel driveway, the neat lawn and freshly dug earth in the beds where green shoots of spring flowers were already pushing their way to sunlight. Doris was obviously working hard to keep up appear-ances as usual, she realised, taking in the shining brass knocker, the clean windows behind the heavy taping and the fresh paint on all the wood-work. But then she didn't have much to do all day, and left most of the cooking and cleaning to the poor girls who'd been billeted with her.

'Wanna play on the swings,' Daisy announced. 'Don't like Dor-Dor.'

'I'll take you to the swings later. Just be a good girl for a little while, please.'

Daisy humphed and stuck her thumb in her mouth.

Grateful she hadn't gone into another tantrum, Peggy pushed the pram across the gravel, rapped on the door and waited, hoping to goodness that

Daisy didn't misbehave before she'd said her piece and escaped.

The door opened and Doris stood there in a well-cut tweed suit, silk blouse and highly polished shoes. There were pearls round her neck and in her ears, and her make-up and hair were immaculate. 'Margaret,' she said coolly. 'What on earth are you doing here on a Sunday morning?'

'I was out for a walk on this glorious day and thought I'd pop in to see how you're doing,' Peggy replied with determined cheerfulness.

'You'd better come in then,' Doris said grudgingly. 'Leave the pushchair outside. The wheels aren't too clean and I don't want it scratching the new paint on the skirting boards.'

'It's nice to see you too,' Peggy muttered as she got Daisy out of the harness and indoors. She slipped off their shoes, knowing how fussy her sister was, and padded after Doris who was already heading for her sitting room at the back of the house. On entering, she took a moment to drink in the magnificent panorama from the enormous bay window.

'You are lucky, Doris,' she sighed. 'If I lived here, I'd spend all day just looking at that glorious view.'

'I barely notice it,' her sister replied dismissively. 'I suppose you expect coffee,' she said with a sniff. 'I'll call the girl down and get her to make it.'

'Please don't bother,' Peggy said hastily. 'A glass of water would do.'

Doris raised a severely plucked eyebrow. 'Well, you know where the kitchen is – and while you're at it, that child needs the lavatory and to have her hands washed. They look very grubby, and I don't want my expensive furnishings ruined.'

Peggy bit down on a retort, took a fidgeting Daisy into the downstairs cloakroom, sat her on the toilet and then washed both their hands with the bar of lovely scented soap which didn't appear to have been used before. Having found some cordial in the kitchen, she gave Daisy a drink and then carried their glasses into the drawing room.

'Make sure she doesn't spill that,' cried Doris in alarm.

'Doris, for goodness' sake stop fussing, and tell me how you're getting on.'

Doris quickly put coasters on the coffee table to combat glass rings, and warily kept an eye on Daisy who was now climbing onto the window seat to look at the garden and the sea. 'I'm perfectly fine,' she said stiffly. 'Why shouldn't I be?'

'Well that's good,' murmured Peggy, forced to accept that Doris wasn't about to break the habit of a lifetime by telling her how she really felt about anything. 'Have you heard from Anthony and Suzy lately?'

'My Anthony is missing me most dreadfully, so he writes regularly and has sent some lovely photographs of baby Teddy. I'm hoping to go and visit them in the summer to make sure Susan is looking after him and that baby properly.' Doris plucked a silver framed photograph from the top of the piano and handed it to her sister, with a flush of pride.

Peggy smiled at the handsome couple with their gurgling little boy. Suzy had been one of her evacuees and had married Doris's son some time

154

ago. He'd been transferred to a new posting by the MOD shortly after the wedding, and they now lived miles away – probably extremely relieved not to have bossy, disapproving Doris on their doorstep.

'It's lovely that they called him Edward, isn't it? Ted must be delighted.'

Doris snatched the photograph back. 'It was her idea,' she snapped, 'and I find it most tactless in the circumstances.'

Peggy admitted silently that it probably was rather insensitive to name their baby after Anthony's father, but she knew Ted was over the moon about his grandson, and unbeknownst to Doris, had actually travelled up to spend a weekend with them. It was unfortunate that Doris had taken against Suzy right from the start, thinking she wasn't good enough for her one and only son. Thankfully, Anthony had a mind of his own and had stuck to his guns, and, from Suzy's letters, it seemed they were blissfully happy.

Following her nephew's example, Peggy decided to stick to her own guns and come clean about her job. 'Doris, there is another reason why I came to see you this morning,' she said. 'You see, I've got a job and won't be able to do volunteer shifts at the Town Hall any more.'

Doris looked at her with astonishment. 'A *job?* What sort of job?'

'As a machinist at Goldman's.' She lifted her chin, steeling herself for Doris's snooty reaction.

'Good grief,' Doris breathed. 'I never thought you'd stoop so low. What on *earth* am I supposed to tell Lady Chumley?'

'I don't see why you have to tell that woman anything,' Peggy retorted. 'It's none of her business what I do.'

'It is when you disrupt the smooth running of my branch of the WVS,' said Doris. 'How *dare* you put me in such an awkward position when you know full well that Lady Chumley is our chairwoman?'

'There are plenty of others who can take my place. I only did three afternoons, anyway, so I doubt you'll miss me.'

'But I rely on you to stand in when I have to go to meetings and so on. Really, Margaret, you can be so irresponsible and thoughtless at times.'

Peggy got to her feet. 'It must run in the family, then,' she retorted. 'Come on, Daisy, we're going to the park.'

'Now just a minute,' Doris stormed. 'You can't come round here and drop a bombshell like that and then leave.'

Peggy hoisted Daisy onto her hip. 'I'm a grown woman, Doris, and I can do whatever the hell I want.' She turned and walked out into the hall.

Doris followed her. 'But a factory?' she gasped. 'Surely you could have found something more respectable to do than work for Goldman?'

'It's honest work and it pays well,' said Peggy flatly, wrestling to get Daisy's shoes back on.

'But my two evacuees work there,' Doris hissed, darting a glance up the stairs. 'It would be too shaming.'

Peggy had had enough of this. 'What are their names?' she goaded. 'I'll make sure I introduce myself.'

156

'Don't you *dare* do anything of the sort!'

Peggy opened the door and settled Daisy in the pushchair before replying. 'You know, Doris, I actually felt sorry for you when Ted went off and had an affair, but now I understand exactly why he prefers living alone above the shop – anything has to be better than living with you.'

'I might have known you'd side with *him*,' Doris snapped. 'You always were inclined towards the lower orders and to turn a blind eye to disgraceful behaviour. I don't know why I'm surprised that you choose to work in a factory and mix with those ghastly common women.'

'Put a sock in it, Doris, and remember where you came from before you got ideas above your station.'

Peggy shoved the pushchair through the thick gravel and heard the slam of the front door behind her as she stormed off down the pavement. Doris could wind her up like a clock and no mistake, and one of these days she'd give that snooty nose of hers a right good thump.

The thought made her feel better, and by the time she'd reached the children's playground, she was quite cheerful again.

Somerset

Whatever was in the pills the doctor had given her had made her sleep for most of the morning, and Anne woke to the lovely smell of roasting meat and the creak of the bedroom door opening. She shifted on the pillow, wincing at the stab

157

of pain in her shoulder, and then broke into a broad smile.

'Rose, Emily. Oh, how lovely, Sally. Thank you for bringing them in.'

'Are you all right, Mummy?' Rose ran from Sally to lean against the high bed. 'You've been asleep for ages and ages.'

Anne tenderly stroked the dark curls and cupped the worried little face. 'Mummy's very tired and needs to stay in bed for a while. But I'm fine, really.'

She reached down to caress Emily's cheek as she joined her sister at the bedside. 'Did you both enjoy Sunday school?' she asked, regarding them closely for any sign that they might still be traumatised by what had happened.

'I drawed a picture for you,' said Rose, handing her a piece of paper with something indefinable scribbled on it. 'It's a plane,' she said excitedly.

'Me too,' piped Emily, shoving a scrap of paper with scribbles on it into her hand. 'Moo cow.'

'They're both lovely. Thank you.' Anne propped the drawings carefully against the bedside lamp and then patted the bed. 'Come and give Mummy a cuddle before you have your lunch.'

Sally lifted Emily and sat her on the bed before helping Rose to clamber up. 'Be careful, girls,' she warned. 'Mummy's arm's a bit sore.'

Anne let the children snuggle into her side, revelling in their warmth, and solidity, and reassured that despite what had happened, her children seemed to be over it. And then Emily shifted on the bed, her kicking feet catching the wound on her leg. The involuntary gasp of pain

158

was quickly swallowed, but Sally reacted immediately.

'Come on, girls,' she said briskly. 'Lunch is ready and you don't want Harry and the other boys to eat all the roast potatoes, do you?'

They quickly slid from the bed and raced out of the door. Anne and Sally shared a knowing grin. 'It seems the lure of roast spuds is far stronger than a cuddle with Mum,' Sally said jokingly. 'But it shows they're fine and back to their usual selves. You rest, and I'll bring your dinner in.'

The delicious roast pork was accompanied by salty crackling, apple sauce, three vegetables, golden roast potatoes and thick onion gravy, but Anne managed only a few mouthfuls before she nodded off again. When she woke, it was to find that the tray had been cleared away, there was a bunch of wilting wildflowers crammed in a jam jar on the bedside table with a note signed by Bob and Charlie, and the sun was much lower in the sky.

Her shoulder was throbbing again, so she took another pill and tried to read her book in the hope it would take her mind off the pain until the painkiller began to do its work. But the words were a blur and her mind was elsewhere, so she abandoned the book and watched the activity outside the window instead.

Two of the land girls were still hoeing the harmful weeds out of the northern field, Bob was tending a bonfire with more hindrance than help from Charlie and Ernie, and Fred was helping Vi with some repairs to one of the paddock fences. She couldn't see the others, but heard the piping

159

voices of the younger children playing on the lawn at the back of the house.

As the pain began to ease, the fog cleared in her brain and she suddenly wondered why Vi was fixing that fence when it had been perfectly all right two days ago. Had the terrified cattle stampeded? In which case, how had the cows in calf fared – and had any of them been hit when the Jerry pilot opened fire?

She shuddered at the memory of those terrifying moments when time had seemed to stand still, and the air had been filled with noise and dark, swift menace. The guilt of realising she hadn't asked about the beasts when Vi had come in earlier made her feel utterly ashamed. She'd been too taken up with her injuries and the safety of her children to think about anything else, and now Vi would think she didn't care.

Anne pulled back the bedclothes and gritted her teeth as a pulse of pain ran through her shoulder. Doing her best to breathe through it like she'd done when giving birth to the girls, she shoved her feet into her slippers and reached for her dressing gown.

It was one heck of a struggle to get it over her injured shoulder with one hand, but she managed eventually and tied the cord about her waist. She sat for a moment and waited for the pain to ease, and then limped unsteadily to the door, her head feeling as if it was stuffed with cotton wool.

Sally turned sharply from the sink as Anne tottered in and sank into a chair. 'What on earth do you think you're doing?' she gasped. 'The doctor said–'

'It doesn't matter what he said,' Anne replied. 'I can't be that seriously hurt or I'd be in hospital.' She regarded Sally through eyes that didn't seem to want to focus. 'I need to know what happened to the cows when that dreadful plane came over.'

'You aren't well enough to be worrying about anything but getting yourself better,' Sally told her. 'Come on. Back to bed.'

Anne resisted the gentle tug on her good arm. 'I saw Vi and Fred mending the fence. Did they stampede?'

Sally gave an exasperated sigh and sat down next to her. 'They bolted all right, and it took the rest of the day to round them all up. They must have pushed their way through that fence, because some of them were cut quite badly and it took ages to check them all over and get the splinters out.'

'What about the cows in calf?'

Sally's gaze shifted and she fiddled with a tea towel. 'We lost three. Vi and Bob tried to save the calves, but they weren't ready to be born.'

She blinked back her tears and tightened her fist around the tea towel. 'It were 'orrible, Anne,' she said with a hitch in her voice, the Cockney accent stronger in her distress. 'Them poor little things never even took a breath. I swear to God, if I could get me 'ands on that bastard, I'd throttle 'im.'

Anne reached for her hand and stilled it. 'I know exactly how you feel,' she murmured. 'How's Vi taken it all?'

'She's upset, of course, but as she said, life on a farm ain't ever easy and she's used to animals

161

dying.' Sally sniffed back her tears. 'Vi's a real diamond, Anne – just like your mum. She won't let something like this stop her, even if certain people let her down right when she needs them the most.'

Anne frowned, still battling to keep Sally in focus and her head from spinning. 'Who's let her down?'

'Bloody Stella, that's who,' Sally said crossly. 'Packed her bags and did a flit sometime last night.'

'She left without telling anyone?' gasped Anne in disgust.

'Not a word, nothing.' Sally sniffed again. 'Good riddance to bad rubbish is what I say. We can do without 'er sort round 'ere, anyway.'

'But with me out of action that means Vi's short of two pairs of hands,' said Anne worriedly. 'How on earth will she cope?'

'She rang through to the land office this morning, and they've promised to send two girls as soon as they can, but not to 'old 'er breath, 'cos they're short of recruits.'

'So what's she going to do?'

Sally grinned. 'She went over to the POW camp and spoke to the army officer in charge. Two Germans and an Austrian are starting tomorrow and will be under curfew at night in the empty cottage next to Fred and Bert's.'

'But is that safe with women and children about?' gasped Anne. 'We could all be murdered in our beds.'

'POWs are being used all over England to help on farms, and Vi chose those three because they've

162

had experience of farming and speak good English. They were pilots in the Luftwaffe, and Vi reckons they don't have the stomach for escape, and they'll be quite happy to stay here and work on the farm where at least they'll get well fed.'

'I still don't like the idea,' said Anne, chilled by the thought of having any German anywhere near her and the children after what had happened the day before.

'We ain't got much choice in the matter,' said Sally with a shrug. 'Vi has to meet the government quotas, and she can't do that without more help.'

'What do the others think about all this?'

'Fred and Bert aren't too keen,' she said, pursing her lips. 'They still have long memories of fighting Jerry in the trenches. And the rest of us are wary. I reckon I'll keep a gun handy just in case – better to be safe than sorry.'

Anne bit her lip, remembering the service revolver Martin had left with her on his one and only visit down here. She'd never fired it, but if her children were put in danger she wouldn't hesitate to use it – especially after what had happened to her.

'You look all in, love,' said Sally, holding out her hand. 'Come on, let's get you back to bed.'

Anne got to her feet and hobbled painfully out of the kitchen, her sluggish brain trying to accept that Vi was bringing the enemy right into the heart of their home. She could only pray that the pilot who'd used them as target practice was a lone renegade; acting outside the strict rules of engagement which, Martin had assured her, both

163

the Luftwaffe and the RAF abided by despite the fact they were at war. Only time would tell if that code of honour was upheld.

8

Cliffehaven

Peggy had returned home to Beach View after spending over an hour in the playground with Daisy. It had been deserted, and Peggy supposed this was because it was lunchtime.

She soon realised the house was deserted as well. Sarah must have gone out, and goodness only knew where Ron had got to. Queenie came to wind round her legs to welcome her, so Peggy made a fuss of her and topped up her bowl before preparing lunch for herself and Daisy.

Ron's pheasant was providing a stew for tonight, but there wasn't much in the larder at all. She'd have to go shopping early tomorrow to stock up, she decided. She cut thin slices of spam and laid them on thick slices of the gritty wheatmeal bread the government insisted they eat now that white flour was in such short supply. Adding a liberal splash of what passed as tomato sauce these days, she cut Daisy's sandwich into fingers and her own into four small squares to fool herself into thinking it might last longer and fill her up. Pouring a little of the vegetable soup she'd heated up into a mug and Daisy's special cup, she placed the unappetising lunch on the table and sat down.

Daisy tucked in with relish, and Peggy gave a sigh. Gone were the days of Sunday roasts with lashings of onion gravy and gorgeous crisp, golden potatoes, followed by trifle or apple pie. The thought of flaky sweet pastry and heavenly thick custard or cream put her off the sandwich, and she pushed her plate to one side and sipped the cooling soup. It didn't feel right to have an empty house with no aroma of roasting meat wafting enticingly through the kitchen, but then hers wasn't the only household in England going without this lovely Sunday ritual, so she should pull herself together and stop mithering.

While Daisy was occupied with her lunch, Peggy found a scrap of paper in the dresser drawer and began to plan the meals for the following five days. She'd have to prepare each one the night before so it could be put in the slow oven while she was out, but they were all getting heartily sick of stews and rabbit. Maybe if she could get some mince or sausages from Alf the butcher, she could make rissoles and toad-in-the-hole which she could cook when she got home. And if Fred was feeling obliging, he might get her some fish to fry with chips. At least they still had a good supply of spuds, and they were a godsend when it came to filling up hungry people.

The shopping list had lengthened considerably by the time Daisy had finished eating and was demanding to be got down from her high chair. There were so many things she needed, and she doubted she'd get half of them, but she'd do her best.

The butterflies were gathering in her stomach again at the thought of going to the factory the following morning, and so to keep her mind occupied, she decided to do the washing. Her routine would necessarily have to be changed, but that was all right. As long as everyone pulled together, they'd get through.

Daisy clattered her wooden trolley up and down the concrete floor of the scullery as Peggy worked at the sink, the steam swirling about her and the hot water making her hands go red. If she earned enough at Goldman's, perhaps she might even be able to put a deposit down for a proper washing machine like her sister's, she thought dreamily as she ran the wet laundry through the wringer and dumped it in the basket. She could also do with one of those electric irons instead of the old things she'd inherited from her mother which had to be heated on the hob. Such luxuries would make her life so much easier, but the repairs to the house had to come first, so there was little point in dreaming.

Daisy spied Queenie dozing in the corner of the garden and startled her awake with a shriek of delight. Queenie shot over the garden wall and disappeared and Daisy burst into tears. To placate her, Peggy found her dolls and spent a few minutes wrapping them in a blanket and placing them in the trolley. 'Take them for a walk while I hang out the washing,' she coaxed.

Daisy's expression was stormy as she folded her arms and refused to budge.

The moment was rescued by Ron and Harvey coming through the gate, and Daisy was immediately all smiles as she hugged Harvey and put her arms up for Ron to give her a ride on his shoulders.

'Thanks, Ron. You've come at just the right time. Keep her amused, will you, while I get the washing out?'

Ron frowned. 'Since when do you do the laundry on a Sunday?'

'Since I got a job,' she replied. 'Things are going to change around here, Ron, so you'd better get used to it.'

Ron muttered something about women making his life a misery, and then stomped off carrying Daisy on his shoulders to inspect his spring vegetables.

Somerset

Anne had lain in bed, thinking long and hard about the POWs who were going to arrive the following day. She wondered what her mother would do in the circumstances, and came to the conclusion that Peggy would be necessarily cautious, but give them a chance to prove themselves before she condemned them out of hand as an enemy not to be trusted. Ultimately, they were men who were no longer involved in the fighting and now bearing the stigma of being prisoners, far from home and family. No doubt they were just as keen as everyone else to have this awful war over and done with.

And going by the reports on the wireless and in the newspapers, it sounded very much as if the

Allies were making huge advances, for although Jerry had counter-attacked on the Anzio beach-head, the second attempt by the Allies to capture Monte Cassino was thought to be a sure victory. The Russians had begun an offensive on the Belorussian front, Berlin was being bombed day and night, and the massive air raid on Hamburg had left the city in ruins.

Anne shivered with dread as she closed her eyes and thought about Martin and the men who flew with him. Bomber Command had sent out a thousand planes the other night, with the loss of twenty-two over Frankfurt, and the Americans had also suffered severe losses when they'd attacked the industrial areas of Berlin. But the enemy death toll was even higher, and the thought of so many young men dying on both sides made her fear for Martin even greater.

Deciding she couldn't lie here getting morbid, she managed to get her slippers and dressing gown on and limped towards the kitchen where she'd recently heard the chink of china and the clatter of cooking pots.

Vi looked up from the government forms she had to fill in each week. 'You should be in bed.'

'I got bored,' Anne replied simply, 'and as I'm feeling much better, I thought I'd see if there was anything I can do.'

Vi smiled. 'It's all in hand, dear. We're only having cold cuts, parsnip and potato mash and sliced beetroot for supper.' She poured tea from the large brown pot, added a dash of milk and pushed the cup towards her. 'Drink that and relax while you can. The others will be back soon enough, no doubt, making their usual racket.'

'Where are the children?'

'Sally took them to a tea party in the village hall. It's a last-minute thing organised by Agatha, who thought the children needed something to take their mind off that Jerry attack.'

'Did he strafe the village too?' Anne asked in horror.

'He flew very low and frightened the life out of everyone, but he didn't open fire. The talk in the village is that he must have run out of ammunition by that point, thank God.' Vi looked up sharply as someone knocked on the door. 'Who the heck is that on a Sunday evening?' she muttered crossly on her way to opening it.

'Hello, Vi,' said Belinda. 'I hope you don't mind us calling so late on a Sunday, but George and I wanted to see how Anne's getting on.'

Anne smiled with pleasure at seeing them as Vi bustled about the kitchen to refresh the teapot and find some home-made biscuits. As they sat down and tried to avoid staring at her sling and the heavy bandaging beneath her dressing gown, she fended off their concern. 'It probably looks worse than it is,' she said lightly. 'The doctor gave me some knock-out pills, so I hardly feel a thing.'

'Are you sure?' asked Belinda with a frown. 'Only I heard he had to dig about to get that bullet out it was so deeply buried.'

'I wouldn't know,' she replied with a grin. 'I'd passed out.'

'You must take as long as you need to get better,' said George firmly. 'The shock alone will take time to get over.'

169

'I'm sure I'll be absolutely fine by tomorrow, George. After all, I can still teach with just one hand.'

'You're doing no such thing,' he said. 'I've arranged for Agatha to come in and take over your class until we break for Easter in two weeks.'

'But what about the nursery?'

'Sal's taking over with the help of one of the mothers,' Belinda told her. 'So you see, everybody's rallying round, and all you have to do is get better.' She grinned impishly. 'I'd make the most of it, if I were you. Extra time off is a luxury most of us can only dream about.'

Anne squeezed her hand and smiled at George who was still looking rather solemn. 'I'll write notes of thanks to both of them and send them in with Sally tomorrow. I do appreciate all you've done, but I feel an awful fraud.'

'Not at all,' said George, his damaged hand clattering the cup into the saucer. 'We just want you well again in time for the Easter Saturday dance. Belinda's helping me perfect the foxtrot and quickstep, she really is an excellent teacher, and a fantastic dancer. I promise not to stamp on your toes.' He had a soppy look in his eye.

Anne laughed. 'My toes were never in danger, George. You dance as well as Martin, and he's quite the whizz on the floor given half the chance.'

'How's he doing with all the raids going on over Germany?'

'He's fine as far as I know. No doubt there'll be a letter from him this week.' Her light tone belied the sadness she suddenly felt at not having heard from him for so long.

'You look tired, Anne,' said Belinda, pushing back from the table. 'We'll leave you to rest and I'll pop in sometime during the week to let you know how the children are coping with Agatha.' She grinned, a glint of naughtiness in her eyes. 'They all thought they'd escaped her once they'd gone into the juniors – so it'll be quite interesting to see their reaction when she comes in tomorrow morning like a battleship.' She bent to kiss Anne's cheek. 'Take care, Anne. I'll see you soon.'

George looked a bit uncertain and then stuck out his hand. 'We'll miss you about the place,' he said gruffly.

When it seemed the handshake was lasting rather longer than it should, Anne gently withdrew her hand from his warm, firm grip. 'I think you'll find you won't have time to do anything much once Agatha gets a toehold in the school. Don't let her steamroller you, George. She's a forceful character.'

George smiled. 'I'm fully aware of that, but she's met her match in me, I can assure you.'

They said their goodbyes to Vi and she closed the door behind them. 'He's a lovely man, isn't he?' she said quietly. 'It's sad he's been so injured, but he and Belinda seem to be getting on well, which is a good thing. Far too flighty for her own good, that one. She needs a man like George to steady her.'

Anne giggled. 'You're as bad as my mother with your matchmaking.'

Vi grinned back. 'I like a good romance, and nothing gives me more pleasure than to see a couple's friendship blossom into something else.'

171

Anne thought about the way George had looked at Belinda, and how well they seemed to be getting on together. Perhaps she'd got entirely the wrong end of the stick, and as she hadn't had the opportunity to speak privately to him, it was best to just let fate take a hand in things. 'Then we must hope Belinda's dancing lessons do the trick.'

Cliffehaven

Peggy was all of a fluster as she wheeled the pushchair along Camden Road towards the factory. She'd been up since dawn, panicking that she hadn't prepared properly for the week ahead. Having done her housework and left notes of things to do for the others, she'd posted her long letter to Jim and then managed to be first in the queue at the butcher's shop.

Alf had sneaked some extra mince and sausage-meat in with her order, and Fred the Fish had come up with enough haddock fillets to satisfy anyone. They'd both wished her well in her new enterprise, and as she passed their shops she returned their waves of encouragement and tried to quell the butterflies that seemed to be permanently lodged in her midriff.

The crèche was on the ground floor at the back of the factory, the doors opening onto a freshly laid square of lawn surrounded by a high fence to keep the little ones safe. Rachel Goldman had taken Nanny Pringle's advice and provided a swing and slide and a small sandpit to keep the children occupied on a fine day, and there was direct access to the vast underground shelter which had once been used for storage, packing and old machinery.

It was fifteen minutes to eleven when Peggy approached the door which had been painted fire-engine red. She adjusted Daisy's woolly hat, brushed down her coat with the velvet collar and pulled up her white socks before nuzzling her sweet cheek and giving her a kiss. It was important her baby made a good impression on her first day, but she was already dreading having to leave her.

At her tentative knock, the door was opened by Nanny Pringle who was the shape of a cottage loaf and dressed in a dark brown frock which was almost covered by a starched white apron. Beneath a stiff white cap, her grey hair was neatly combed into a bun at the back of her head, and between the sturdy laced shoes and skirt hem, her legs were encased in black stockings. She would have looked as formidable as the hospital matron if it wasn't for her lively blue eyes and bright smile.

'Good morning, Mrs Reilly,' she said before turning her beaming smile on Daisy. 'Hello, Daisy. Are you looking forward to coming to school?'

Daisy returned her smile. 'Wanna play with Chloe.'

'Chloe is inside, so let's get you out of here and go and see her, shall we?'

Peggy moved to help, but the older woman was already unfastening the straps and helping Daisy out of the pushchair. 'I'll take over from here,' she said, parking the pram next to a line of others.

'Oh, but I thought I'd come in and help her settle,' said a fretful Peggy.

'Mothers are inclined to have the opposite effect in my experience,' said Nanny Pringle firmly. 'Daisy will be fine.' As if to prove the point, Daisy took Nanny Pringle's hand, eager to get inside where she could see toys and hear other children's piping voices.

'Bye-bye, then, Daisy,' said Peggy forlornly. 'Be good for Nanny, and I'll see you later.'

Daisy ignored her and didn't look back as she stepped inside, and Peggy was left staring at the door which had been shut very quietly, but firmly, in her face.

She stood there feeling lost and close to tears. Daisy was still so young, just a baby, really. What sort of mother was she to leave her in the care of other people when she was barely out of the cradle? She felt the ache that had become so familiar when her other children had first gone to school, and had to fight hard not to burst into tears and bang on the door to demand Daisy back.

'It's horrid, isn't it?' said Gracie, emerging from the side door to the factory dressed in khaki dungarees, shirt and sweater, her hair covered by a knotted scarf. 'I cried buckets the first morning I left Chloe.'

Peggy nodded, unable to speak. She fished her string bag out of the pram to check that she'd remembered her apron and her sandwich lunch.

'At least she didn't howl the place down and refuse to go in like some,' said Gracie, taking

174

Peggy's arm and steering her towards a low boundary wall. 'That would have been far worse for you.'

She gave the girl a watery smile, as they both perched on the sun-warmed brick wall. 'She didn't even say goodbye – just went off with Nanny as if I didn't exist.'

Gracie slipped her hand into her pocket and drew out a packet of Park Drive. 'Have one of these while you gather your wits, Peggy. There's still time before you have to clock on.'

'Won't you get into trouble, coming outside when it's not your break?'

Gracie shook her head and plucked a strand of tobacco from her lip. 'As long as I do my quota, Solly's very good about the number of breaks I take, and I've already spoken to Loretta about easing you in on your first day, so you don't have to worry about me.'

While Gracie chatted about the various characters among the women working in the factory, Peggy smoked her cigarette and grew calmer. Minutes later she ground it out beneath her heel and followed the younger woman into the factory. She was given a time card which she slotted into the machine before placing it in the special board beside it.

Pushing through the swing door into the main body of the factory, she was once again stunned by the noise. 'You'll soon get used to it,' shouted Gracie above the blaring wireless and the whirr of machines.

She led Peggy over to a short row of four machines which had been set up in one corner.

'This is Lily, Flo and Nancy,' she said, introducing the three middle-aged women who looked up momentarily to smile before they returned to work. 'They only started last week, so you're all new. This is your machine. Loretta will be over in a minute to settle you in with your first batch of shirts.'

'Thanks, Gracie.'

'I'll see you later,' she said and hurried off towards the large cutting table on the far side of the factory floor.

Peggy shrugged off her coat and pulled her wrap-round apron out of her string bag and tied it firmly round her waist. Tucking the bag under her chair, she gave a tentative smile to Lily who sat to her left and then eyed her machine with some misgiving. She'd rather hoped it would already be threaded for her. Her fingers weren't very nimble as she fiddled about, trying to remember how she'd done it three days ago, but by taking a long, hard look at Lily's machine, she finally got the hang of it.

Loretta appeared with an armful of air force shirts and placed them on the ledge beside the machine. 'Well done for remembering how to thread it,' she said. 'Now, don't try and rush to get lots done on your first day, Peggy. I'd rather have half a dozen well-sewn shirts at the end of it than something which would have to be unpicked and done all over again.'

Peggy nodded and picked up the shirt on top of the pile, nervously folding back the hem and holding it down with the foot surrounding the needle.

'I'll leave you to it,' said Loretta, clearly under-standing that she was making things worse by looking over Peggy's shoulder. 'Your lunch break will be at the same time as Gracie's, so she can introduce you round. From twelve-thirty, you'll have forty-five minutes to eat and so on.' Her gaze dropped to the flask and packet of sandwiches in Peggy's bag. 'The food in the canteen is good and cheap, so if you get bored with sandwiches...' She smiled and turned away to speak to another woman who was trying to get her attention from the middle of the factory floor.

Peggy blew out the breath she'd been holding and began to sew, concentrating so hard she was no longer aware of the noise or the people around her. And with every hem she finished, her confidence grew.

And then disaster struck. The material slipped from beneath her guiding finger, the needle clattered on, the thread tangled and she had a nasty mess. In rising panic she cut the thread and examined the crooked stitching and where the hem had missed the needle entirely to become puckered up in a knot of cotton.

'It's all right, ducks,' said Lily. 'There's a little unpicker in that compartment. You'll soon have it right again.'

'Thanks, Lily.' Peggy scrabbled in the small compartment amongst the spare needles and spools. Working carefully, wary that if she tugged too hard it would tear the material, she managed to unpick everything and start again. Eyeing the finished hem, she gave a sigh of relief. There was no sign of her mistake.

'That was lucky,' she said to Lily.

'We've all done it, ducks,' she replied. 'And no doubt will do it again. It's the first time that's the worst.'

Peggy nodded, made a mental note to concentrate harder and started on another shirt. When she'd finished it, she realised with a sudden pang of remorse that she'd been so preoccupied in the last hour that she hadn't given any thought to how Daisy was getting on. She quickly came to the conclusion that should any emergency arise she'd be the first to know. Nanny Pringle was obviously adept at dealing with tantrums and spats, so there was no need for her to feel guilty.

Somerset

Anne's shoulder felt stiff and sore, but at least the pills were keeping the pain at bay. However, it had been impossible to bathe with her injuries and the heavy bandaging, so she'd had a lick and a promise with a flannel before struggling to get dressed. Vi had come to the rescue, and now she was wearing a sweater pulled down over her arm which was still protected by the sling, and her dungarees were held up by one strap and covered with a buttoned-up cardigan which had the empty sleeve tucked into the pocket.

The vacant cottage had been cleared of all the junk the previous day, and having rid it of mice, cobwebs and spiders, Sally and Vi had set to and cleaned it from top to bottom. Now Anne was carrying a large shopping basket over her good arm, filled with cutlery and spare crockery, while Vi carried the blackout curtains, a tin kettle, frying pan and a box of basics including tea, coffee, milk, eggs and bread.

'I thought it would be more tactful to have them collect their meals at the kitchen door and eat in here instead of with us,' said Vi as she entered the tiny kitchen and dumped the box on the battered old table. 'I know Fred and Bert aren't too happy with me taking them on, and I don't want to make them more uncomfortable, but I really had no choice with all those cows about to drop their calves.'

Anne placed the utensils in the dresser drawer and stacked the crockery on one of the shelves. 'When are they due to arrive?'

'Later this morning,' said Vi, unpacking the foodstuff into the larder. 'Luckily we found three old iron bedsteads in one of the barns, and I asked the chap in charge of the POW camp to send them with their own mattresses and bedding. So it's really just a case of getting these curtains up now, and making sure there's enough wood for the fire. With the Welsh miners on strike, I really can't spare more coal.'

Anne nodded, still unsure of how she'd feel once they were here.

Vi regarded the tiny kitchen with its flagstone floor, stone sink stained with rust from the dripping tap, and the battered old furniture. 'It's all very shabby, isn't it?' she sighed. 'Still, I'm sure anything's better than being in barracks under guard.' She pulled out a rickety kitchen chair and clambered up to fix the blackout over the window.

Anne put the pots and pans on the dresser shelves, frustrated that she was unable to do anything much to help while the older Vi was teetering on an unsteady chair, reaching for the curtain rail.

Vi got down and gathered up the rest of the blackout curtains she'd run up on her sewing machine the previous evening. 'We'll get these done and then...' She frowned. 'What's the matter, Anne? Are you in pain?'

'No,' she said quickly. 'I just feel so utterly useless, that's all.'

'Then don't,' Vi replied firmly. 'It's not your fault you got hurt, and I'm just thankful nothing worse happened.'

'And now we're taking in Germans to help on the farm,' said Anne.

'Is that what's really bothering you, Anne?'

'It is a bit,' she admitted. 'After being attacked like that it will feel very odd playing host to the enemy.'

Vi leaned against the corner of the table. 'They're not guests,' she said, 'but men brought in to help on the farm. I've spoken to other farmers who've been forced to do the same thing, and they all said they found the men to be polite and hard-working, and very little trouble at all. It seems they don't mind taking orders from women or working alongside them, but I've warned Letty and Lucinda there's to be no fraternising – it's happened on other farms and can cause no end of trouble.'

She patted Anne's good arm. 'You still don't look convinced, but our three have gone through

180

rigorous screening and have been classified as non-political or especially partisan, which is why you'll see they have a white letter P on their clothes. They have no allegiance to Hitler, and are certainly nothing to do with the SS military.'

Anne shivered and Vi gave her a swift hug. 'I think you'll find they're as wary as we are, and just relieved not to have to fight any more for a cause they don't really believe in.'

'But the Geneva Convention states that no officer should be made to work,' said Anne. 'I don't understand why it's different for these three.'

Vi smiled. 'They actually volunteered and got clearance from their senior officer in the camp to do so. No one's breaking any rules.' She picked up the blackout curtains again. 'Let's get on, dear. The day's wasting, and they'll be here before we know it.'

They were walking back to the farmhouse half an hour later when they heard a heavy vehicle coming down the track, and as it rounded the bend, they saw it was an army truck. Lucinda and Letty came out of the barn, Bob strode across the field and came to stand beside his sister, and the two old men stopped work in the vegetable patch and leaned on their hoes. Anne discovered that her mouth had gone dry at the thought of having to face someone who might very well have tried to shoot her darling Martin out of the sky.

The truck rumbled its way into the cobbled courtyard, and an armed soldier jumped down, sketched a salute and went round to the back to unfasten the tailgate. 'Look lively,' he barked. 'And bring them mattresses with you, chop-chop.'

The silence was tangible amongst them as the three men came into sight, each with a rolled-up mattress under his arm that seemed to also contain his belongings. They were tall and had the dignified bearing of men who still had some pride, even though they were bare-headed and dressed in working clothes, the rough trousers and jackets marked with a large white letter P.

To a man they stood to attention as the officious soldier continued his harangue about behaving themselves and reminding them they would be back in the camp quicker than they could blink if they didn't.

Fred and Bert glowered from beneath their flat caps, Anne, Letty and Lucinda stared, surprised at how young and good-looking they were with their short fair hair and blue eyes; while Bob grimaced. Vi gave an impatient cluck of her tongue before she stepped forward.

'Thank you, Sergeant,' she said briskly. 'I'll take it from here. Make sure you shut the gate behind you.'

It was a strange tableau, thought Anne. The three prisoners still standing to attention, the rest of them transfixed and silent as the lorry headed back down the track.

Vi broke the spell. 'Welcome to Owlet Farm,' she said warmly to counteract the bullying sergeant. 'This is the cottage where you'll sleep, so keep it clean. There are washing facilities, albeit rather basic, and you may bring your laundry in to me once a week. This is not a camp, it's my home where I am responsible for everyone living here, and I expect you to abide by my rules. All

182

meals will be collected at the kitchen door over there and eaten in the cottage. You will not leave the farm unless you have my permission, and curfew begins immediately after the evening milking session, when I expect you to stay within the boundaries of this yard.'

All three nodded, still stiffly at attention, their expressions giving nothing away.

'Stand at ease, for goodness' sake,' said Vi impatiently. 'This isn't a parade ground. Take your things inside, sort yourselves out, and then come back and I'll introduce you to everyone before you start work.'

The two old men turned away and bent their backs again to weeding the vegetable garden, clearly determined to have nothing to do with the new arrivals. Vi went after them, had a quiet word, and after a good deal of grumbling, they reluctantly came back, their expressions still reflecting their contempt.

As the three men emerged from the cottage a few moments later, Vi made the introductions. 'This is Maximilian,' she said, indicating the tallest of the three, 'Hans,' who was of a sturdier build, 'and Claus.' Claus was slighter, and possibly the youngest, but it was difficult to tell.

The three men clicked their heels and bowed stiffly towards each person in turn as Vi introduced them and explained their role on the farm. Despite their outward show of dignity, the men's expressions were wary as they scanned the suspicious faces turned towards them.

Anne followed the example of the others and gave a sharp nod in reply, rather disconcerted

183

that they looked like perfectly normal, fit young men. They certainly didn't resemble the demonic cartoons of the enemy that were so prevalent in the cheaper newspapers, and the very fact that they were prisoners of war and here to work as farm labourers couldn't have sat easily with them, even if they had volunteered.

'Bob,' said Vi, 'would you show them where the tools are kept, and then take them into the field to clear those brambles? They take up at least an acre and if we simply burn them back they'll grow even stronger next year.'

Maximilian stepped forward. 'Please, first, I vould like to say something.' His accent wasn't harsh as they'd expected, but soft and rather attractive.

At Vi's nod of encouragement, he glanced at the silent gathering and cleared his throat. 'Ve vould like to thank you for this opportunity, and to assure you that ve vill vork hard and not break the curfew. And please do not be afraid of us,' he added, his gaze taking in the four women. 'We have families at home, wives, mothers, sisters and daughters. Not all Germans are savages.'

'Thank you, Maximilian. We will bear that in mind,' said Vi.

Bob led the way to the shed where the tools were kept. The old men returned to their weeding and hoeing, Letty and Lucinda went back into the milking parlour and Anne limped into the kitchen after Vi.

'They seem to be quite ordinary, don't they?' Anne murmured. 'And very polite. But I dread to think how Martin would react if he knew they

184

were living here.'

Vi shrugged. 'We all have to make adjustments in life, and I'm sure he'll come to understand that they're of far more use to the war effort working here than stuck in a camp twiddling their thumbs.'

9

Cliffehaven

Peggy's slight misgivings that she wouldn't be able to cope with her home duties as well as going to work had proved unfounded, and although she'd felt a bit like a duck out of water to begin with, she'd soon made friends amongst the other women, and had come to accept that Daisy was perfectly at home in the crèche.

Most of the other women were closer to Gracie's age, but Peggy was happy to listen to their stories about their families, their worries over absent husbands and their moans about the struggle to cope with the lack of everything. She delighted in being able to share her own moans and worries, and give advice when asked, for it seemed the young ones felt drawn to her, and she could only suppose that was because they were missing their mums. In a way, the factory had become an extension of Beach View, and she'd begun to regard some of the much younger ones as her chicks.

The two weeks had sped past, and now it was early April and Good Friday afternoon. When Peggy glanced up at the clock, she was amazed at how swiftly the day had gone. She finished the hem, snipped off the cotton and folded the shirt on top of the large pile she'd completed that day.

'That's me done,' she said cheerfully to Lily, Flo and Nancy, who'd become quite pally as they'd worked alongside one another and gossiped during their tea break. 'I'll see you all on Monday.'

Gathering up her coat and string bag, she hurried over to the cutting table where Gracie was showing one of her apprentices how to chalk the pattern on the material with clean, neat strokes. 'I'm off home now,' she said. 'When are you finishing?'

'Not for another hour yet,' she replied, glancing at her watch. 'Will I see you over the Easter weekend?'

'I can't promise cake and chocolate eggs, unfortunately, but why don't you come over for tea on Sunday and then you can meet everyone?'

'That would be lovely, Peggy. I look forward to it.'

Their conversation was interrupted by her spotting a costly error the apprentice was about to make on the navy serge, and she turned away sharply to deal with it, so Peggy left her to it. She clocked off, collected her wages and hurried to the nursery to pick up Daisy.

The scarlet door, was opened by the young assistant to Nanny who didn't look as if she should have left school yet. 'Hello, Amy,' said Peggy with a warm smile. 'How's your gran?'

'She's feeling a lot better, thanks, Peggy,' the girl replied with a weary smile.

'You look tired, dear.'

'It's been a long, rather noisy day, and I shan't be sorry to get home.' Amy smiled. 'Daisy's been very good. She's through there.'

Peggy walked into the playroom where the children were quietly absorbed in puzzles or toys, or sat listening to a story; and the small babies lay gurgling on the thick floor mats. Peggy still found it a marvel that one woman and her assistant could control eighteen toddlers and four babies when she had a hard time of it coping with just Daisy.

Daisy was sitting at a tiny table, busy with crayons and talking nineteen to the dozen to Chloe. She looked up and grinned in delight. 'Mummy!' she yelled. 'Mummy, look what I drawed! It's Granda.'

Peggy regarded the scrawl on the paper which was supposed to be Ron, noting that she'd actually captured his wild hair perfectly – even though it was squiggles of green and yellow. 'That's wonderful,' she praised. 'Come on, then, let's get you home and show it to Granda.'

'Don't wanna go home,' she grumbled.

'Chloe's coming to tea on Sunday, so you can play with her then,' said Peggy, trying unsuccessfully to coax her into her coat.

'Come along now, Daisy,' said a bustling Nanny Pringle. 'Coat, hat and gloves. We mustn't keep Mummy waiting now, must we?'

Daisy meekly pulled on her coat and hat and

allowed the woman to fasten the buttons and pull on the mittens. Peggy watched with silent admiration and some chagrin that Nanny Pringle seemed to have worked wonders with her small, wilful daughter in such a short time.

'Now, Daisy, what do you say when you're leaving somewhere?' Nanny asked.

'Goodbye. T'ank you, Nanny.'

Peggy raised an eyebrow at this but didn't comment.

Nanny escorted them to the door and the minute it was closed behind them, Daisy reasserted her independence. 'Wanna walk,' she said grumpily.

To avoid a full-blown tantrum, Peggy held her hand and slowly pushed the pram out of the entranceway into Camden Road while Daisy prattled on about Chloe and her little friends, and how they'd had jelly and bread and butter for their tea. From previous experience, Peggy knew it wouldn't be long before Daisy changed her mind about walking, and they'd only just reached the hospital when she stopped and said she wanted to ride now.

Happy to oblige, Peggy strapped her in and hurried towards home, eager to see if there were any letters for her in the second post. Jim might have got hers by now, telling him she knew he was in Burma, and that although it had been a terrible shock, she'd come to terms with the fact and could only pray that he stayed safe and well away from any fighting. She'd also told him about her job at the factory, but was unsure what kind of reaction that would get.

With the pushchair parked in the scullery, she wrestled Daisy's coat and hat off and helped her up the concrete steps to the kitchen. Everyone was gathered to listen to the news on the wireless, so she patted a welcoming Harvey, checked on the saucepans and the spam hash in the slow oven and sat down for a well-earned fag.

The announcer's voice was solemn as he informed them that the government had been defeated by one vote on the question of equal pay for women teachers, and that now the Yorkshire miners had gone on strike.

There was no change on the Italian front where the fighting was still raging, and the Allied planes were continuing to bomb Essen, Hannover and the airfields in Northern France, but on their return from a bitter three-hour battle over Nuremberg, ninety-four planes had been lost. It was a terrific boost to learn that 150 German aircraft had been destroyed by the US forces. The Russians had now arrived on the Czech border, and Odessa was on fire.

Peggy couldn't bear to listen any longer, so she went to her room to change into her old house dress and slippers, and brush out her hair which, despite the knotted headscarf she'd taken to wearing, still caught the lint that floated about the factory and settled on everything. And then she saw the two letters on the bed, recognised Anne's writing and immediately changed her plans.

Anne was surprised that her stay-at-home mother had the time to go out to work, and shared the concerns of the others that she might be doing too much, but she was proud of her and wanted to

189

hear all about the new friends she'd made, and how Daisy was getting on at the nursery.

She was now on the Easter break from school, and coming to terms with the fact that Vi had found it necessary to employ German prisoners of war to help on the farm. She'd been very unsure of the wisdom of this, but over the past two weeks they'd proved to be pleasant men who were worried sick about their families back at home, two of them being unsure where their families were following Allied attacks on their home towns.

However, they seemed to find great comfort in the fact there were so many children on the farm and had made lovely little wooden dolls for the girls, and a super wooden train for Harry in their long and, she suspected, rather lonely evenings in the cottage. Charlie and Ernie were constantly plying them with questions that they answered patiently and tactfully with no mention of dog fights or lost comrades, and the people in the village had slowly become used to seeing them working in the fields or going into the local shop for their tobacco and matches.

Bob was still a bit stand-offish and Sal was as undecided as the land girls, but the two old men who'd been so against their arrival had been charmed by their manners and their genuine respect for their age and war record – and Anne suspected that the tobacco and cigarettes the Germans shared with them helped to thaw the old boys out. It was quite usual, now the evenings were lighter and the weather more clement, to see the five of them sitting outside the cottages deep in conversation as Charlie and Ernie listened in, and Bob pretended not to.

Anne had made sure the little ones were always supervised when they were with the men, but Hans was a brilliant storyteller and the children were entranced by his soft accent and the way he acted out each character, so it had become an after-tea ritual which both she and Sal enjoyed as much as the children.

Vi too had lost her initial wariness, for she'd been delighted when they'd gone into the woods the previous Sunday and returned with a trailer full of logs which they'd then split for the fires. She had confided in Anne that she was considering asking them to share breakfast and supper in the farmhouse instead of eating in that cold cottage.

They were rarely idle, Anne continued, for they'd applied a rough plaster to the walls inside the shabby cottage, fixed the windows and doors and even repaired the leaking tap and some of the roofs about the place. They'd also cleaned all the chimneys, which meant they no longer smoked quite so badly every time someone opened an outside door; and Claus had proved invaluable when it had come to helping with a difficult calving which could have seen the loss of both beasts if he hadn't acted so quickly and expertly.

He'd been a farmer in Austria, and had been forced to leave his home which had been in his family for several generations to enlist in the Luftwaffe. The other two were also flyers, and Anne had had several interesting conversations with them during their meal break at lunchtime,

191

and she'd soon come to realise that they shared the same fearful experiences as the Allied pilots and longed for the war to be over and Hitler vanquished so they could go home.

She hadn't told Martin yet about the new arrivals, but as it was highly unlikely he'd get down to Somerset, she thought she'd wait a bit and see how things went.

Peggy remembered the conversation she'd had with Martin and didn't think this was at all wise, for if he did suddenly turn up down there it would be an awful shock, and could even cause trouble. It crossed Peggy's mind that she seemed to be communicating with her daughter and her son-in-law more than they did with each other. Deciding to write back this evening and tell her daughter not to keep secrets, she turned to the second letter.

She didn't recognise the handwriting, for it seemed to have been scrawled in haste, but the postmark was London. She tore it open and, in delight, discovered it was from Danuta, the Polish girl who'd come to Beach View at the beginning of the war looking for her brother Aleksy – who'd sadly been shot down and killed only weeks before her arrival.

Dear Aunt Peggy,

I am sorry I have not written for so long, but since leaving Cliffehaven I have been very busy. I cannot say what I have been doing, or even where I am, but I just wanted you to know that I am well and think of you and everyone at Beach View all the time, and wish that I could be with you again.

I write this letter to thank you for being my family during my stay, and for looking after the graves of my brother and my little girl – I know they are not alone with you and Ron to watch over them.

You are in my heart, Peggy, and always will be.

I kiss you, and wish you well,

Danuta x

Peggy had tears in her eyes as she held the letter, for she remembered that night when Danuta's little baby had come into this troubled world for such a short, tragic time. It hadn't been long after that she'd left Cliffehaven with a determination to use the skills she'd learned in Poland to help defeat the Nazis who had slaughtered her family and brought her country to its knees.

Ron had hinted that she might be working for the secret services, since she was fluent in several languages and had experience of covert action with the underground back in Warsaw – now this letter made Peggy shiver, for although the words were lovely and clearly heartfelt, it was almost as if Danuta had been saying a last goodbye.

'No,' she breathed. 'No, I mustn't think like that.'

But the letter had affected her deeply, and she carried it into the kitchen and handed it to Ron. 'It's from Danuta,' she explained.

Ron scanned the letter quickly before giving a sigh and handing it back. 'To be sure, I worry about that wee girl, Peggy. I have a bad feeling about that letter. It's as if she's tying up the loose ends and not expecting to see us again.'

'My sentiments exactly,' Peggy murmured beneath the general hubbub of conversation. 'Do you really think she's working undercover somewhere abroad? Did she send this in case something happens to her?'

'Aye,' he said solemnly. 'It's a fair assumption.'

'Then I can only pray she comes back from wherever it is, safe and well and all in one piece,' Peggy said tremulously.

'Ach, 'tis all we can do. But I'll tend the graves on Sunday for her as usual. The spring bulbs I planted are looking a picture,' he sighed. ''Tis a great pity she couldn't have come down and seen them for herself. I think she'd have been pleased.'

Peggy blinked back her tears as she took off her headscarf and shook out her dusty hair. 'I'm sure she'd love them.'

Ron brightened visibly as Sarah placed a large bowl of onion and potato soup in front of him. 'Now, that's a sight for sore eyes,' he said, breathing in the aroma. 'Talking of which, I saw you had a letter from Anne as well. How are she and the wains?'

Peggy told him about the German POWs and Ron grunted. 'Better they plough our fields than blow them up,' he rumbled. 'They've brought in some over at Whitlock Farm to help out after Andy Walsh fell off his tractor and bust his leg. Nice enough fellers by all accounts, and don't seem to mind Annie bossing 'em about.'

'I was hoping to hear from Jim,' Peggy admitted as Sarah placed the soup in front of her. 'I don't suppose you've had a letter you're not telling me about, have you?' she asked, watching him keenly.

He shook his head and then slurped the hot soup. 'I expect he'll reply soon enough.' He eyed her from beneath his flyaway brows. 'I hope you weren't too rough on the boy,' he muttered. 'He's got enough to contend with without you giving him earache.'

'I do not give him earache,' she protested.

'Tell that to the marines, as the Yanks would say,' he rumbled, then applied himself to clearing his bowl of soup.

Sarah went round the table replacing the empty bowls with plates of steaming spam hash. 'When do you think Kitty will come down?' she asked Peggy. 'She wrote to you a while ago and you haven't had any word since, have you?'

'Probably fairly soon,' Peggy replied, adding some Worcester sauce to the potato, onion and spam. 'She must be nearly four months along by now, and her job is dangerous enough without risking her baby's life as well as her own in those planes.'

'How are you going to cope, Auntie Peg?' Rita piped up. 'Now you're working, it'll make things even more difficult once she's had the baby.'

'She's a very capable girl who I'm sure will quite happily muck in with everyone else,' Peggy said firmly. 'Besides, there's always room for one or two more under this roof, so everything will be just fine – especially once the man comes to sort out the damp under the sink and on the bath-room ceiling.'

'Oh aye?' Ron's eyebrows lifted. 'And who's that, then?'

'Billy Wilmott. He's coming after Easter to

make a start.'

'He better not be overcharging you, or I'll have something to say about it.'

'I wouldn't have to pay him at all if you'd seen to the damp when it first appeared,' Peggy retorted. She relented and smiled. 'Don't let's argue, Ron. I have the weekend off, Gracie and her little girl are coming to tea on Sunday, and the weather forecast is good. Besides, I get double pay for working today and Monday, so let's celebrate with a fresh pot of tea.'

'I've got a better idea,' he replied. 'I happen to have come across a bottle of whisky or two last night, so let's have a couple of nips of that instead. Put hairs on our chests, that will.'

'You've got more than enough for everyone put together,' said Cordelia, eyeing his chest where the buttons on his shirt had come undone. 'But I wouldn't mind a drop or two to wet my whistle. It helps me to sleep soundly, you know.'

There was a general chuckle, for Cordelia could sleep for England, especially after a session down at the Anchor.

'And it will only be a drop,' Ron grumbled. 'I know what you're like when you get the taste of a good whisky. There's nothing stopping you, and then I have to carry you up the stairs.'

'I am perfectly capable of making my own way upstairs,' she retorted. 'You just enjoy the chance to show off and prove how strong you think you are.'

The banter went back and forth in mutual delight, so the girls left them to it and discussed where they were going for the evening, and what

196

they could possibly find to wear in their much depleted wardrobes. Harvey began to snore, stretched in front of the meagre fire, and Queenie softly leapt down from her perch above the sink and curled up contentedly against his belly.

Peggy sat back in her chair and was warmed by the reminder of how blessed she was to have this home, this refuge – and to be surrounded by the people she loved, even if some of them were absent – when brave young girls like Danuta were risking their lives so these blessings could continue.

RAF Cliffe

Martin paced anxiously back and forth, awaiting the return of the Mosquito bombers who'd joined a mass raid on targets in Hamburg and on the Ruhr and the Rhine. He jammed the pipe-stem between his teeth even though the tobacco had gone out some time ago, and tried not to speculate on how many of his brave boys would make it back. This was a relatively small raid, but there had been others with over a thousand aircraft going into combat – and the losses had been soul-destroying.

'Sir, could I have a word, please?'

Drawn from his dark thoughts, Martin turned and saw his sister-in-law standing in the doorway. With a strained smile, he returned her smart salute. 'What can I do for you, Cissy?'

She looked at him in silence, the muscles in her face working to control the emotions she was

197

clearly battling with. 'It's Randy,' she managed. 'He was... I got...' She fell silent, unable to speak as the tears rolled down her face.

Martin took her arm and steered her into his office, then sat her down and handed her one of the clean handkerchiefs he always kept in a drawer for such occasions. He waited until she was a little calmer before speaking, aware of the sound of the returning Mosquitoes. 'Was the First Lieutenant on the Americans' raid over France at the beginning of the week?'

She nodded, still not trusting herself to speak.

'Would you like me to ring the station commander at Biggin Hill and find out what's happened to him?'

'I already know,' she replied, her voice ragged. 'One of his crew saw him shot down, but couldn't confirm if he'd managed to parachute to safety. He was posted as missing in action – and this afternoon I received a visit from one of his friends who said his body had been found and identified.' She covered her face and curled into herself as she sobbed.

Martin moved around his desk and awkwardly put his arm about her shoulders. The commanding officer of the WAAFs usually dealt with such things, but as Martin was Cissy's family, she'd turned to him instead, and he'd never found it easy to deal with crying girls.

'I'm so sorry, Cissy,' he murmured, knowing that whatever he said couldn't possibly ease her pain. 'I'll arrange for a car to take you home to Beach View. It's at times like this that we need our mothers, and Peggy will look after you.'

Cissy shook her head. 'It's a lovely idea, Martin, but I need to keep busy.' She made a sterling effort to contain her tears and pull herself together. 'Other girls have lost their chaps, and they haven't caved in and rushed home to Mother.'

'Their mothers probably don't live just down the road,' Martin pointed out, mentally counting in the Mosquitoes as they landed. 'I really do think it would be best if you took twenty-four hours' leave, Cissy.'

She shot him a watery smile, then got to her feet and gave him a hug. 'I just needed to tell you, Martin,' she said, her voice muffled by his uniform jacket. 'And to get a hug.' She burst into tears again. 'Randy used to hug me a lot when we could get time together. Oh, Martin, I'm going to miss him so much.'

He held her close, his chin resting on the top of her head as she sobbed into his chest, and silently prayed that Anne would never have to go through this torment.

Eventually Cissy stopped crying. She mopped up her tears and smiled up at him bashfully. 'Sorry about that, but I've been holding it in all afternoon.'

She brushed ineffectually at the dampness on his jacket and gave up. 'I'll tell Mum when I'm feeling a bit steadier, so if you could keep it to yourself should you see her, I'd be grateful. She has enough to worry about with Dad over in Burma, and there's nothing she can really do to change things, is there?'

'She can comfort you and look after you for a bit,' said Martin. 'Peggy's very good at that.'

Cissy nodded. 'Yes, I know, but actually I think I'm better off staying here with the other girls. They understand what I'm going through having lost boys themselves, and I don't think Mum fussing over me will help me get over it. Thanks for everything, Martin. I do appreciate you taking the time when you're so occupied with much more important things.'

'I'll always have time for you, Cissy,' he said firmly. 'You're as important to me as any of my chaps.'

She bit her lip, executed a ragged salute and dashed out of the office.

Martin followed slowly and stood in the doorway watching her run towards the women's barracks, the sorrow welling from deep within him. There were no words to say that could bring real comfort or ease the pain. The letters he'd had to write over these past years had been filled with platitudes and praise for the young men who'd died so bravely but so needlessly in this terrible war – but had they really consoled? How could words replace a son, a brother, a husband, when the void they'd left behind remained like an open wound to remind their families of their loss?

He reached for his tobacco pouch and slumped into one of the deckchairs that had been placed outside the officers' barracks. Filling his pipe, he watched the Mosquito bombers land and taxi off the runway, their pilots climbing wearily out to make their reports to their wing commanders before they headed for the mess bar and the welcome oblivion at the bottom of a beer glass before they had to do it all again the next day.

Realising he'd lost count of the numbers coming in, he dragged himself out of the deckchair and headed for the Ops Office. He was saluted smartly as he entered, but he could tell immediately that the mood amongst the Mozzie pilots was gloomy, and as he turned to look at the blackboard where each set of pilots were listed, his low spirits plummeted further.

There was a blank space where two crews had once been – and as he watched, the corporal solemnly and irrevocably erased the names of Jack 'Jugs' Newbury and Bertie 'Burlington' Goodall.

Martin turned on his heel, went back to his office and sat for a long moment fighting his emotions. He'd instigated their transfer from the Mozzie Pathfinders to the bombers, thinking they were experienced enough to handle the responsibility – and now they were dead.

He hung his head in defeat, acknowledging that the loss of those two young boys had brought him to breaking point, and if he continued as Station Commander without taking leave he'd become a liability, not only to himself, but to those who trusted his judgement. He couldn't afford to fail again and have more deaths on his conscience.

Martin picked up the telephone and ordered the switchboard to put him through to his superior officer.

10

Cliffehaven

Every night was Saturday night at the Anchor, for the weekends no longer counted with the factories working day and night and the servicemen and women constantly on duty. An evening off was to be celebrated, for life was tenuous, the future uncertain, and not a moment could be wasted.

This evening happened to be a Friday and Ron was helping Rosie and her middle-aged barmaid to serve the customers who were clamouring for another round of drinks. Someone was crashing out a tune on the old piano, there was a loud and not very harmonious sing-song accompanying it, and the chatter and laughter rose in pitch as the stock of beer went down.

Ron pulled on the beer pump and it spluttered out a few drops and then stopped. The barrel had clearly run dry and wouldn't be replaced until the brewery drayman came on Monday. 'I'll go and fetch the last few crates from the cellar,' he shouted to Rosie.

'No need,' Rosie yelled back. 'I got an extra barrel of bitter this afternoon. Change it over, and we'll keep the bottled beers for tomorrow.'

Ron raised an eyebrow. 'How did you get an extra barrel on a Friday afternoon?'

'Ah,' she replied, tapping her nose and giving

him a naughty wink. 'That would be telling.'

Ron glared at her from beneath his brows, but she merely laughed and turned away to serve another customer.

He stomped off down to the cellar, his happy mood wiped away at the thought of the brewery man who only delivered on Mondays, and clearly fancied Rosie something rotten. Rosie wasn't averse to a bit of flirting, she did it all the time with her customers, although it never went any further. Had she used her feminine wiles to get that barrel – and if so, what had she promised in return?

Tony 'Leg-over' Langborne was a randy little beggar with a questionable reputation when it came to women – married or otherwise – and Ron silently vowed that if there was something going on he didn't like the look of, he'd be having a word with the pair of them.

He was so preoccupied with these dark thoughts that he banged his head on the low beam at the bottom of the cellar steps, and then hit his thumb with the mallet as he was banging in the bung to attach the tap. Beer slopped over his feet and he swore loudly as he wrestled to get the fitment in so the beer could be pumped up to the bar.

Deciding he was in no mood to face the racket upstairs just yet, he plumped down on one of the couches that had been brought into the cellar when they'd turned it into a makeshift bomb shelter, and filled his pipe. If Rosie was clever enough to find beer on a Friday, then she could manage the bar without him. It was a bit mean and childish to feel that way, he knew, but the thought of Rosie getting entangled with Leg-over had shocked him to the core, and he wasn't quite sure how to deal with it.

'Ron? Ron, what the hell are you doing down there?' yelled Rosie from the top of the steps.

'Smoking me pipe,' he called back.

'But I need you up here,' she wailed.

'Then I suggest you ask Leg-over Langborne to help you.'

Rosie clattered down the steps in her high heels, her expression stormy. 'For heaven's sake, Ron,' she snapped. 'I've got a full pub and you're down here playing silly beggars. What *has* got into you?'

He regarded her through his pipe smoke. 'How did you get the extra barrel, Rosie?'

She expelled a breath of exasperation. 'So that's what all this is about. Honestly, you men can be so childish.'

He stood and faced her. 'You haven't answered my question, Rosie.'

Her blue eyes sparked fury. 'If you must know I managed to persuade Gloria Stevens at the Crown to sell me one of hers,' she exploded. 'Satisfied?' She didn't wait for him to reply, but ran up the steps and disappeared back into the bar.

'Well, to be sure I made a mess of that,' Ron sighed. 'Blasted women. Why can't they just come straight out with things and not make a blooming mystery out of it?'

He slowly went up the steps, realising he'd have to apologise, and that she would no doubt make his life very difficult until she was ready to forgive him.

Cliffehaven

Cordelia had felt tired so she'd gone to bed earlier than usual with a hot water bottle and her new library hook. Ivy was out with Andy who had an evening off from the fire station; Fran and Robert were at the pictures with a couple of pals; and Rita and Sarah were at a fund-raising dance with a group of land girls from the Cliffe Estate. As for Ron, he was at the Anchor helping Rosie, and probably wouldn't be back with Harvey until very late.

Peggy sat at the table with the cat curled on her lap as she finished writing her long letter to Anne and sealed it in an envelope. The wireless was providing soft background music to compensate for the unusual silence of the deserted kitchen and she found it rather soothing after the noise and clatter in the factory.

Sitting back in the chair, she lit a cigarette and stroked the purring Queenie, trying to decide on whether or not to make a fresh pot of tea. It would be wasteful really, she thought, for there was no one else to share it with her and she'd have to open the last packet of tea. The last lot of leaves had been used so many times they'd had to be chucked on Ron's compost heap.

She regarded the meagre range fire and the empty coal scuttle, glad that she'd thought to put on an extra cardigan after tea. It might be April, but the nights were cold, and with the miners still on strike every bit of coal had to be used sparingly. Her gaze drifted up to the mantelpiece where the studio photograph of Jim smiled back at her, and she thought how strange it was that while she shivered, he was probably sweating in the uncomfortable, damp heat of a jungle, and being eaten alive by mosquitoes.

Her thoughts were scattered by the sound of swiftly approaching aircraft coming from over the hills at the back of the house. Martin and his men were leaving for yet another raid, but this sounded as if it was a big one.

Queenie scooted off her lap and sought refuge in the scullery, so Peggy switched off the light and followed her down, not wanting to miss the spectacle of so many planes. The cat shot out through the back door and disappeared into the darkness, while Peggy stood on the doorstep and looked up at the enormous number of aircraft which roared overhead and blotted out the moon and stars.

She could see the huge American Flying Fortresses, the Lancasters, Halifaxes and Typhoon fighter-bombers that were now thundering above the rooftops, making the windows rattle and the ground vibrate beneath her feet. The heavy-bellied bombers were accompanied as usual by the smaller, swifter fighter planes like the Spitfires and Mosquitoes, and as Peggy watched, she felt an almost overwhelming surge of pride for the brave, determined men who flew them.

She wrapped her cardigan more tightly around her to keep out the chill as the display of awe-some power continued, the town echoed and trembled with the noise, and the roosting birds flapped and shrieked in panic.

'It's quite a sight, isn't it?'

Peggy gasped, peering into the darkness at the little figure approaching her with a swinging gait that was deeply familiar. 'Kitty? Is that really you?' She headed for the girl, her arms outstretched.

Kitty dropped her overnight bag and they embraced for a long moment, each revelling in being together again after so long. 'I should have rung to warn you I was coming,' she shouted above the overhead racket. 'But things didn't quite go to plan, and I had to just hope you wouldn't mind me turning up like this.'

Peggy was close to tears as she brushed back the girl's fair hair and cupped her lovely face. 'This is your home,' she managed. 'You can turn up whenever you like – and for as long as you like.' She grabbed Kitty's bag and linked arms with her. 'Come on in out of the cold and noise so we can talk properly. I want to hear all your news.'

She closed the back door and switched on the light so she could see the girl properly. 'You look very well,' she said, taking in the healthy glow of her skin, her bright eyes and the swell of her pregnancy beneath the short jacket.

Kitty grinned and patted her stomach. 'Cooking nicely, as Roger will persist in saying, but the added weight isn't doing my prosthetic leg much good – the stump is quite painful at times if I walk too far.'

Peggy nodded, unable to speak through the lump in her throat and the huge wave of admiration and affection she felt for this brave young woman. She forced herself not to offer help as Kitty went slowly up the cellar steps, knowing that she was fiercely independent and wouldn't appreciate it. Her determination to carry on regardless of losing her leg had meant she'd returned to the ATA immediately after her wedding to Roger Makepeace, and had been delivering the much-needed planes straight from the factories to the airfields ever since.

'Oh, good,' breathed Kitty as she looked around the kitchen. 'It hasn't changed a bit. Now I know I really am home again.' She shed her jacket, rolled up the sleeves of her thick sweater and dug her hands into her trouser pockets. 'Where is everyone?'

Peggy placed the kettle on the hob and reached for the new packet of tea. 'They're all out except for Cordelia, who's upstairs and probably asleep by now.' She turned from the range, her eyes blurred with happy tears. 'Oh, Kitty, it's so lovely to have you back.'

Kitty hugged her. 'It's wonderful to be back,' she murmured in the sudden silence left by the departing bombing raiders. 'But I'm afraid it's only for the weekend, Peggy.'

The disappointment was like a knife to the heart. 'But I thought...'

'I know, and I'm sorry, but my plans have changed.' She took Peggy's hand and gently drew her down to the chair beside her. 'I'm not down here on my own, you see.'

Peggy frowned. 'But Roger and Freddy are up at Cliffe and all leave has been cancelled.'

'I'm down here with Freddy's wife, Charlotte,' Kitty explained before breaking into a wide smile. 'She's pregnant too, and rather than go back home to her parents, she suggested we both came down to Cliffehaven and found somewhere to live so we could keep in touch with our men.'

'Oh, but you didn't need to spend money on renting a place all the while I've got plenty of room here,' Peggy protested.

'Bless you, Peggy,' she replied softly, 'but we're used to being independent, and now the ATA have chucked us out, we wanted to set up our own place here so Roger and Freddy could come and visit and feel relaxed in their own home.'

She squeezed Peggy's fingers. 'And you've no need to worry about our finances. We've all been saving hard since we discovered our babies were on the way, and Roger has found a sweet little cottage we could buy just on the northern fringes of the town in Briar Lane.'

Peggy knew exactly which cottage she was talking about, for she'd often daydreamed about owning it herself. It was a bit dilapidated and the thatch was rotten, but it was a charming example of a quintessential English country cottage. Set within what had once been a lovely garden, it was dark red brick with ribs of black oak threading across it. There were climbing roses and wisteria trailing above the door and diamond-paned windows, and the back gate opened right onto the hills behind it.

'It's a lovely place, but it's been empty for ages and needs a lot of work doing to it,' she said. 'Why don't you and Charlotte stay with me until it's habitable?'

Kitty giggled. 'You just don't give up, do you, Peggy?'

'Well, you can't blame me for trying,' she replied with a tearful smile.

'Of course I don't, which is why I'm here for the weekend, if that's all right. I couldn't sleep easily without seeing you and explaining everything before I settle in. I didn't want you to find out from someone else, or bump into me in the street – it would have been too cruel after everything you've done for me.'

Peggy nodded and squeezed her arm. 'I do understand, really I do, and it warms my heart to know that you feel that way.' She pushed back her chair and busied herself making the tea to give herself time to settle her mixed emotions. 'So you'll be moving in there after the weekend?'

'Charlotte's already there, fussing over curtains and where to put the second-hand furniture we managed to bring down with us in the Oxford we were transporting to Cliffe. Roger arranged for a lorry to cart it all to the cottage this afternoon.'

'But what about all the repairs that need doing to the place?' Peggy set the teapot on the table. 'Builders and thatchers are hard to find these days, and it must be very damp after being empty for so long.'

'Roger and Freddy managed to find the right men eventually – retired, of course, but very efficient – so now we have a new thatched roof, a safe chimney, new damp course and repaired windows. The place smells of paint which unfortunately makes me feel a bit sick, but as it doesn't affect Charlotte, she's promised to keep the doors and windows open so it should all be fine by Monday.'

'My goodness, you do sound very organised.'

Kitty chuckled. 'That's what happens when you've spent time in the services. You get used to the discipline of making lists and sorting out the best way to get things done. I doubt either of us could have managed without Roger and Freddy doing their bit.'

Peggy poured out the tea, added extra milk for Kitty as she was pregnant and spooned in some sugar. 'Have you managed to see either of them yet?'

'We saw them briefly when we flew in, but they were busy preparing for tonight's raid, so once we had the lorry we left them to it.' She gave a sigh as she stirred her tea. 'They both looked utterly drained, and even my brother seems to have lost the spring in his step.'

'Martin's the same,' said Peggy. 'There have been too many losses, and I know how deeply they've affected him.'

Kitty sipped her tea. 'The awful pressure is getting to all of us,' she said sadly, 'and there are times when Charlotte and I almost wish we weren't expecting – which makes us both feel very guilty. But what sort of world are we bringing our babies into when their fathers are risking their lives every day, and there's no certainty about anything?'

Peggy saw the tears glistening in the girl's eyes and quickly rounded the table to gather her into her arms. 'We all have to be strong, Kitty,' she murmured into her hair. 'And believe that we will win in the end so the world will be a better place for our children.'

211

She drew back and gently brushed away the girl's tears. 'I know how hard it is to be brave and positive at a time like this, but you must never feel guilty when it seems as if there's no end to this war and you begin to falter. It will end, Kitty. Because of brave men like your brother and husband and the thousands upon thousands of others who are scattered across the world – and the women who wait for them as they work in factories or in the forces to keep the home fires burning. None of us walk alone, Kitty, but each one of us is part of an enormous united army fighting the battle for freedom and a world where children can live without fear.'

Kitty smiled tearfully. 'Lovely, sweet, wise Peggy,' she murmured. 'My goodness, how I've missed you.'

Peggy had missed her too, and although she was disappointed her stay would be so short, she wasn't about to spoil it through her selfish tears. 'So when are these babies due?' she asked brightly. 'I want to hear what the doctor says, and how you're feeling – and have you written to your mother? She must be thrilled to have two grandchildren on the way.'

Kitty laughed. 'Three, actually, Peggy. Charlotte's expecting twins.'

'Good heavens,' Peggy breathed in delight. 'How on earth will Freddy cope?'

'I have no idea,' she giggled. 'But he'll certainly have to stop being Jack-the-lad and knuckle down to fatherhood.'

Several hours later Peggy was once more alone in

the kitchen with the cat purring on her lap. She and Kitty had caught up on their news, the girls had squealed with delight on arriving home to find Kitty once more in their midst, and even Ron's grumpy mood had fled when he'd stomped up the steps and seen what all the noise was about.

Harvey, of course, had got thoroughly over-excited, leaping up and trying to lick everyone until Ron had told him very firmly to sit down and behave. He'd sulked for a while, regarding the assembly with mournful eyes, and had then set about washing Queenie, who purred and stretched and dug her claws into the fireside rug in absolute ecstasy.

Ron refused to reveal where he'd got those bottles of whisky, but having opened them, they were soon drained, and now he was snoring in his basement bedroom with Harvey for company. The girls were still chattering and giggling up-stairs long after they should have been asleep, and it was as if her home had been invaded by a flock of parrots. Luckily, Cordelia always took her hearing aid out when she went to bed, so there was no danger whatsoever of waking her.

Peggy smiled at the thought of how thrilled the old lady would be when she saw Kitty in the morning. She eased the cat onto the floor so she could shut the door on the range fire. It was lovely to hear their laughter and scampering about up there, and to have Kitty home again – even if it was only for a couple of nights. She would still be in Cliffehaven, close enough to Beach View to visit, and when the time came for her baby to arrive, Peggy would be there to hold her hand and do all she could to help.

Still smiling, she turned out the light and closed the kitchen door. It would be like having another grandchild to love and care for, and with three babies in that tiny cottage, the girls might soon find they needed all the help they could get.

11

Somerset

It was Easter Saturday morning, with heavy dew still glittering on the grass where the sun had yet to reach it. Mist lingered in a veil amid the treetops, but the sky was clear, the rising sun promising a lovely day. The scar on Anne's leg had faded, and although her shoulder still hurt if she tried to lift anything heavy, the wound was almost healed and she could discard the sling and the heavy bandaging. The doctor had been very pleased with her progress, and she was looking forward to the dance tonight before going back to the classroom after the Easter break.

The long grass swished against her wellington boots as she followed the three youngest children who were racing across the fallow field to where the calves were being kept with their mothers. They had been tremendously excited by the arrival of so many small animals, for not only had the cows calved, but the sows had produced forty piglets between them, fluffy yellow chicks ran about the pen, and there were ducklings on the pond.

Rose and Harry climbed up onto the five-bar gate as Emily peered through the bottom railings to watch Maximilian fill the trough with a feed supplement that would boost their growth. Anne finally caught up with them and leaned against the sturdy fence. 'The calves are doing well, Max,' she said.

'They are good stock,' he replied, coming towards her with a smile.

Anne noted that, like his comrades, he was looking much fitter and stronger than when he'd first arrived. After hours spent working out of doors, his skin was a healthy colour and his figure was filling out from the good food Vi provided, and where his shirtsleeves had been rolled up, she could see that he was becoming quite muscular.

'You are going to the dance tonight vith the schoolmaster?' he asked almost casually as he rolled a cigarette and kept an eye on the children who were trying to reach through the bars of the gate to stroke the inquisitive calves.

'I shall be going with the other girls,' she replied. 'But I expect I shall see him there.'

Max regarded her with his pale blue eyes. 'He is liking you, I think.'

'We're just friends,' she said briskly. 'I'm a married woman, Max.'

He smiled. '*Ja*, you have said. But that does not stop a man from liking you,' he murmured. He lit the cigarette. 'Vill you dance vith him tonight?'

Anne was getting a bit uncomfortable with this conversation. 'I will dance with anyone who asks

215

me,' she replied shortly. 'As there are so few men about, I expect I'll end up partnering Sally or one of the other girls.'

'It is a shame that ve are not allowed to attend,' he said. 'Then you could dance vith me.' He grinned, his blue eyes bright with humour. 'But perhaps is a good thing. I have the two left feet, and my vife tell me I am a danger to her toes.'

Anne laughed and picked up Emily who was whining that she couldn't see anything. Perching her on her hip, she was about to ask what the country dances were like back in Germany when Rose got too adventurous and slipped from the top rail.

Max moved swiftly, catching the child before she hit the ground, and swinging her up into his arms and twirling her round.

'Do it again,' shouted Rose.

Max duly obliged and Rose screamed in delight as he lifted her high and swung her round. Carrying her on his shoulders, he closed the gate behind him and then gently set her on her feet.

'Me too,' shouted Harry, grabbing hold of Max's leg and almost falling over as he leaned right back to look up at him.

'Me too,' echoed Emily, reaching out to him.

Anne met his gaze and they both laughed. 'It seems I have new job,' he said cheerfully, picking up Harry.

'You'll be at it for the rest of the day if you're not careful,' Anne warned.

'It is good job,' he said and swung Harry about by a leg and arm until he was roaring with laughter and quite giddy. Max reached for little

Emily and grinned back at Anne before whirling her round like an aeroplane. 'Remind me of my sister's children. They love this game.'

All three children were now tugging at his trouser legs and he gave a roar like a lion and they fled in screaming delight as he chased them about the empty field. Anne was in fits of laughter as he caught each one and spun them round so they couldn't run in a straight line. It was wonderful to see the children's joy in the fun a man could bring to their lives.

She saw Hans and Claus pause in clearing the river bank to shout encouragement and her smile broadened. Their arrival had been good for them all – each learning about their not-so-different cultures – becoming friends instead of enemies, and bringing a much-needed male presence for the children.

Martin's telephone conversation with the Air Vice-Marshall had been tricky to say the least, for the timing was all wrong and he'd felt like a traitor asking for time off while others were still risking their lives. Thankfully the man had understood and granted him forty-eight hours' leave.

He'd had to wait another twenty-four hours for his replacement to arrive from an airfield in Yorkshire, in which time he'd completed another op, lost three more crews and returned to the airfield in his badly damaged Spitfire, stiff with tension. But the moment he'd set out for Somerset, he'd begun to feel the great weight of his responsibilities lift from his shoulders.

He'd managed to hitch an overnight lift in a

Mosquito Pathfinder that was being delivered to RAF Church Stanton, and had gone straight to the station commander's office and persuaded his old school chum to lend him the little roadster he knew he kept at the aerodrome. As it was the man's pride and joy, he'd had to promise faithfully not to prang it, and bring it back, with a full tank of petrol.

The sun was just coming up over the hills as he left the base, and so, with the canvas roof folded back and his uniform hat discarded so he could feel the wind in his hair, he kept an eye on the road map his pal had lent him and drove carefully along the narrow, winding lanes towards Barnham Green and Owlet Farm.

The countryside was beautiful on this April morning, the hedgerows and trees bursting with birdsong and blossom, the fields gloriously green with young wheat, the grassy banks on the side of the road dotted with wild flowers that seemed to bob their heads in welcome as he went past. He could smell rich, damp earth and the musty scent of cow parsley mingling with wild onion, and felt the sun on his face, which made him relax even more. This was England at its best, and he was lucky to be alive to enjoy it.

He drove slowly into the village where children were playing hopscotch on the pavement and football in the lane. It was a lovely little place, with thatch-roofed cottages, an ancient church, a general store, post office and the school where Anne taught. Deciding to keep his arrival secret for as long as he could, he parked by the church to be immediately surrounded by excited small boys plying him with numerous questions about the car.

Martin climbed out and answered as best he could, realising that in fact he knew very little about the workings of the roadster apart from where to put the petrol. When the questions turned to what plane he flew and how many Jerries he'd shot down, he judged it was time to move on. He promised sixpence to one of the older boys if he would look after the car and make sure no one scratched it. Fastening the roof back into place, he pocketed the key, tilted the peak of his hat rakishly over one eye and whistled a happy tune as he set off down the lane.

As the roof of the farmhouse came into view, his anticipation and excitement rose at the thought of seeing Anne and his children and the rapturous welcome they were bound to give him. He paused for a moment by the gate to fasten the top button of his shirt and adjust his tie, then vaulted over it and headed down the track towards the cobbled yard that fronted the farmhouse.

He could see no one about, and when he knocked on the door there was no reply. Realising that at this time of day they'd probably be out in the fields, he left the yard and headed off towards where he could see a couple of men leaning on a fence, clearly enjoying the sight of something he couldn't yet see.

As he approached them he heard the unmistakable guttural German as they laughed and pointed and shouted some sort of encouragement. He slowed his pace momentarily, for Anne had said nothing about Violet taking on Jerry

219

prisoners of war. Then he saw what the men were watching and froze.

Anne was laughing up at a tall, fair-haired man who was holding Rose in one arm and Emily in the other, while a small boy clung to his trouser legs, begging him to give him another spin. A cold chill ran down his spine and he felt sick as he watched his beautiful wife say something which had the man tilt back his head and roar with laughter.

Rage galvanised him and he pushed the watching men aside, vaulted over the fence and strode furiously across the field. 'Get your hands off my children,' he roared.

Anne, Max and the children froze, their eyes widening as Martin stormed towards them. 'You heard what I said,' Martin barked. 'Put my children down and step away from my wife.'

Max gently put the children on their feet and they immediately ran screaming to Anne, hiding behind her legs in fear of this stranger who was clearly very angry.

'Martin, please don't shout,' Anne called, holding on to the sobbing children as he drew near. 'You're frightening them.'

'How *dare* you fraternise so shamelessly,' snapped Martin, his fists curled at his sides. He glared down what he considered to be an impertinent stare from the German who had now been joined by his two compatriots.

'Max was just playing with the children,' Anne said, struggling to draw them from behind her. 'We were doing no harm, just having a bit of fun.'

'I saw the way you were looking at each other,'

he retorted. 'What's really going on here?'

'Ve go, I think,' muttered Max. 'You vill be safe vith this man?'

'Of course she'll be safe. I'm her bloody husband,' Martin roared.

'Just go, Max,' said Anne. 'I'll deal with this.'

'Oh, so it's Max, is it?' Martin snarled. 'How very cosy.'

'Don't be like that, Martin,' she fired back. 'We all have to work together, so of course we're on first-name terms. They miss their families just as we do, and the children enjoy the rough and tumble of having men about the place.'

'You certainly seem to enjoy their company,' he said bitterly.

Anne blinked as if his words had hit her, and then reached down to draw a sobbing Emily into her arms. 'I've been waiting so long for you to come down,' she said. 'Please don't spoil things by being cross.'

'I have every right to be cross,' he retorted. 'I've always trusted you, Anne, but it seems I should have warned you that I was on my way, instead of planning a surprise.'

'It is a surprise – a wonderful surprise, but you really have got hold of entirely the wrong end of the stick.'

He still felt sick with rage and could barely look at her. 'Is that Emily?' he asked gruffly.

Anne tried to persuade the little girl to turn to look at him, but she clung to her neck, her tiny legs gripping hard against Anne's ribs as she buried her face in her shoulder. 'I'm so sorry, Martin,' she said fretfully. 'She'll be all right once

221

she calms down and gets to know you.'

Martin regarded the sobbing, fearful child he'd last seen as a tiny baby and his rage dwindled into terrible sadness.

In equal despair, Anne tried to coax Rose from behind her. 'Come on, Rose. This is Daddy. He didn't mean to frighten you, darling, and I'm sure he'd love a hug.'

Rose shook her head and backed away. 'Don't want to,' she muttered.

'Oh, dear,' sighed Anne, close to tears. 'I'm sorry, Martin, but it's been so long since she's seen you, and she hates it when people raise their voices.'

Martin regarded the little girl clinging to her mother, and his small Rose who was watching him fearfully from behind her legs. And then he looked at Anne and knew he'd made a terrible mistake by coming here unannounced. 'It's all right,' he said stiffly. 'I can't expect my children to remember me when they are clearly encouraged to play with enemy prisoners. I'm disappointed in you, Anne. I never thought you'd stoop so low.'

'And I'm disappointed in you,' she said, her voice flat with anger and bitter regret for what should have been a wonderful moment. 'Instead of your homecoming being the joyful thing it should have been, you've jumped to conclusions, terrified the life out of your children and been insufferably rude.'

'Perhaps it would be best if I left you to it, then,' he replied sourly. 'You clearly don't need me here ruining your fun.'

'That's enough, the pair of you,' called Vi,

222

hurrying towards them with Sally just behind. Vi stepped between Anne and Martin, and Sally gathered up little Harry. 'Sally, take the children back to the house. They've seen more than they should for one day.'

As Sally coaxed the little ones away, Vi turned to Martin. 'I can only guess what this was all about, but let me tell you straight, Martin, I'll have no more of it. Oberst Maximilian Schultz was a Group Captain and the same rank as you in the Luftwaffe, and the others were Oberstleutnants – Wing Commanders – and as such they deserve some respect for their ranks from a fellow officer. You lot bang on about the honour between the airmen on both sides, but I've seen little of it today.'

He looked down at her coldly. 'So you approve of my wife and children carrying on with those men, do you?'

'Carrying on is not what I'd call it,' she replied with equal coolness. 'Those men have become a part of the family of people who are keeping this farm going. As such, they have earned our respect as well as friendship, and in return they have the company of women and children who remind them of their families back home.'

Martin thought of all the boy pilots who'd died – of all the mothers and wives whose lives had been changed because of German bombs and German tanks and German fighter pilots. 'I can't stay,' he said. 'Not while they're here.'

'But you've only just arrived,' protested Anne.

'It feels much longer,' he muttered, turning on his heel.

'Just a minute,' snapped Vi, grabbing the sleeve of his uniform jacket. 'You're going nowhere until you and Anne have settled things.'

'So, Violet, what do you expect me to do? Stay here and share meals with them? Watch as they play with my children, who clearly prefer their company to mine? Or have to witness my wife laughing and joking with them as if they're all best friends on holiday?'

'I'll telephone the pub and see if they have a spare room for you both,' said Vi. She looked back at Anne, who was looking very upset at Martin's diatribe. 'Would that suit you, Anne?'

Anne bit her lip. 'Fine,' she said shortly. 'But what about the children?'

'They'll stay with me.' Vi turned back to Martin. 'When do you have to go back?'

'Tomorrow afternoon. But I really think it would be better if—'

'Stop being awkward, Martin,' Vi snapped. 'You and Anne need time alone to iron this out, and if you can't see that, then I fear for the future of your marriage.' With those few harsh words she stomped off in her wellington boots, every inch of her plump figure quivering with anger.

'Do you want to come to the house and see the children?' asked Anne. 'I'm sure they've calmed down by now and will be more willing to get to know you.'

Martin shook his head. 'I'll take a walk until Violet's made the arrangements at the pub.'

'Would you like me to come with you?'

'I'd prefer to be alone,' he replied stiffly.

'Then I'll meet you by the entry gate in an hour.'

He nodded tersely and Anne watched him walk away to the river's edge and follow the narrow, twisting path that ran alongside it. He didn't look back, didn't acknowledge her at all, and she turned and ran towards the farmhouse, blinded with tears.

'Where is everyone?' she asked tearfully as she entered the kitchen.

Vi put down the telephone receiver. 'Bob isn't back from the farmers' market yet with Charlie and Ernie. Sally decided to take the little ones into the woods to repair the camp they set up last summer, so they couldn't see how upset you were.' She rubbed Anne's arm affectionately. 'I managed to book a room,' she said softly. 'You can move into the Shepherd's Arms whenever you're ready.'

'I don't know that I ever will be,' Anne admitted. 'He's like a stranger, Vi. And I can't just pretend everything's all right when it's clearly not.'

'That's why you need some time alone to talk and try to find that spark again,' Vi soothed. 'I know it's been a long time, and that forty-eight hours isn't nearly enough, but it's more than many other couples have, and it would be a terrible shame if you couldn't kiss and make up before he leaves for Cliffehaven.'

Anne nodded. 'It's all such bad timing,' she sighed. 'If only he'd telephoned first, none of this would have happened.'

'It's no good thinking like that,' said Vi. 'What's done is done, and it's up to both of you to put it right.'

'Thanks, Vi,' she said, kissing her cheek. 'I'll do my best.'

She went into her bedroom and closed the door. Resting against it, she took a shuddering breath in an attempt to steady her racing pulse. She'd been shocked to the core by Martin's outburst – had actually been quite frightened of him when he'd bunched his fists and shouted at her – and the thought of having to share a bed with him made her stomach clench. Eighteen months was indeed a long time apart, and all her worst fears had been realised, for he had become a stranger – a cold, angry stranger who'd looked at her with such contempt that it had made her skin crawl.

She pushed away from the door and reluctantly pulled an overnight bag out of the wardrobe. Reason returned as she packed, and she began to think about how he must have felt coming upon that little scene in the field. He was the father of her children – a brave and patriotic man who cared deeply about his men and his family. He'd meant his arrival to be a surprise – had wanted so much to hold his children – but how profoundly it must have hurt to be rejected by them, when they'd so clearly been at ease with Max.

She closed the small bag and sat down on the side of the bed. In hindsight, she could see how Martin had got the wrong impression, for she had been laughing and joking with Max, enjoying his company perhaps a little too much – for she couldn't deny that he was a handsome young man, and his rapport with the children had drawn her to him.

'Oh, Martin, I'm so sorry,' she sighed, tears

pricking her eyes. 'But I'll make it up to you, I promise.'

Dashing away the tears, she quickly plastered on a bit of lipstick and changed into her prettiest sprigged cotton frock and best shoes, then pulled on a thick cardigan and brushed her hair. A swift glance in the mirror showed that she was rather pale and drawn and that her eyelids were still a bit puffy from crying, but a brisk walk down to the pub would soon bring the colour back to her cheeks – and hopefully, higher spirits.

She picked up her case, fetched her coat from the boot-room and went into the kitchen. 'Thanks for looking after the children, Vi. Tell them I'll see them tomorrow afternoon. If things go well we might even come back earlier, but don't say anything, just in case.'

'You look very pretty, dear,' said Vi. 'I do so hope the two of you manage to put things right between you.'

'So do I.' Anne kissed her cheek and left the farmhouse, thankful the yard was deserted, for surely everyone must know what had happened by now, and she really didn't want to have to stop and talk about it.

The track was rough underfoot and she had to zigzag down it to avoid the puddles and sharp stones damaging her best shoes. She should have kept her wellies on, she thought, and packed the shoes. But her mind was all over the place, and just as she saw Martin standing by the gate, she remembered she was supposed to be taking Vi's scones to the dance tonight.

His expression was still stony as he held the

gate open for her.

'I'm sorry, Martin,' she said nervously. 'But would you mind waiting a few more minutes? I forgot Vi's scones for the dance this evening.'

'I'm sure they'll manage without them,' he said, firmly closing the gate.

Anne realised it wouldn't be wise to argue, so she let him take her bag and they walked in silence down the lane to the village. As they approached the church, Martin stopped by a smart, bright red roadster and opened the boot.

'Goodness, how thrilling,' she breathed. 'Is it yours?'

'It belongs to an old school chum,' he replied, grabbing his bag and slamming the boot shut. 'He lent it to me so I could spend as much of my leave with my wife and children as possible.'

His words were like a knife, but she forced herself to smile. 'How very generous of him. Perhaps we could all go for a drive tomorrow if the weather stays fair?'

'Perhaps,' he muttered, flicking a sixpence into young Wally White's hand and thanking him for taking such good care of the car.

She had to almost run to keep up with him as he strode towards the pub, and at every step her pulse rate quickened and her mouth grew drier. She looked up at the weathered sign creaking above the studded oak door, and then beyond it to the diamond-paned windows of the bedrooms above, and shivered, for despite her determination to make things better between them, she didn't know how she'd cope with the intimacy of a double bed.

Martin was clearly feeling uneasy too, for after speaking to the cheerful landlord who kept winking at them both suggestively, he ordered drinks instead of going straight upstairs and then led the way through the pub into the back garden.

Sheltered from the elements by a high garden wall, the rustic wooden tables were set beneath a trellis covered in burgeoning roses and clematis. There were tubs of daffodils nodding their heads in the light breeze, and the lawn had been turned into a vegetable patch where butterflies were dancing above the border of lavender.

'Mrs McCormack is a terrific gardener,' said Anne, desperately trying to make conversation. 'She wins all the prizes at the local show.'

Martin regarded the garden and took a long drink from his glass of beer. 'It's very nice,' he murmured before starting to fill his pipe. When he got it alight, he looked across at her, his expression unreadable. 'I'm sorry I shouted,' he said stiffly.

'I know you are,' she said quickly. 'And I quite understand why you did.'

'Do you?' he murmured, his gaze steady.

'Well of course I do.' She babbled on about prisoners of war, and the need to keep things harmonious on the farm, and the men were no longer really seen as the enemy, and the children had been merely shocked by his shouting but would soon get over it. And then she stopped mid-sentence, realising he wasn't really listening.

'I'm trying to do my best, Martin,' she said tremulously. 'But really, you are making it very hard.'

'It's not easy for me, either,' he said flatly. 'This is not how I envisaged spending my leave.'

She felt a flutter in her stomach as she broached the subject she'd been dreading. 'Then why don't we go upstairs and see if we can't make things better?'

He slowly shook his head. 'That's not the answer, Anne – and you know it.'

Anne sat back from the table feeling a mixture of relief, and a terrible sense of failure. 'But we can't spend the rest of your leave like this. We have to do something, Martin.'

He looked at his watch and got to his feet. 'I need to bring the car round to the back of the pub, then, as I haven't eaten since leaving Cliffe last night, we'll have lunch,' he said. 'And while we're eating, you can tell me what else you've been doing to entertain yourself while I've been fighting a war.'

Stung by his words, Anne knew then that it would be an uphill struggle to make him see how damaging his attitude was, for he'd become as cold and detached as his awful mother.

Martin knew he was being unreasonable, but he simply couldn't get the image of Anne and that man out of his head. With the roadster safely parked behind the pub, he ordered a second beer and ate silently as she tried to make conversation; prattling on about the farm, the children and school, her work with the WI, the friends she'd made in the village and the fund-raising dance this evening.

He didn't care about any of it, and could barely

force himself to do justice to the magnificent vegetable pie the landlady had set in front of him. His wife had become a stranger – albeit a very attractive one – and because he'd been shocked to see her so at ease with that blasted German, he'd acted without thinking, and been insufferably rude to everyone. Now his children were frightened of him, and his wife's nervousness showed in her eyes as she babbled on. He certainly had no interest in the people she was talking about, or the day-to-day routine of the farm. He just wanted silence, a darkened bedroom and the chance to sleep until it was time to return to Cliffe.

Anne finally gave up on her food and pushed away the barely touched plate. Her smile was hesitant, her eyes wary as she regarded him. 'Why don't we go for a drive somewhere? It will do us both good to get out of the village, and you might find it easier to talk to me when there's no one about.'

'Petrol's too precious to waste on a drive in the country,' he said before draining his glass. He placed it carefully on the table and gave a deep sigh. 'I'm tired, Anne. Tired to the very bone, weighed down by responsibilities and the awful pressure of having to go on ops night after night and see my boys – my very young boys – not come home because of men like those. I had hoped to rest and recuperate with you and the children – had been longing to see you all, to hold you and know that what I was doing was worth all the horror. But seeing you with him – seeing my children laughing in his arms... It was too much.'

'Oh, Martin, darling.'

231

He moved his hand away as she reached for him. 'I need to sleep,' he murmured.

'Then I'll come up with you,' she replied.

He looked at her, his vision blurred with the onset of a headache. 'I'd rather you didn't,' he said gruffly. 'Perhaps when I've rested I'll be more amenable and ready to listen, but for now, I'm afraid, I need to be alone.'

Martin saw her stricken expression and strode out of the dining room before she could cause a scene in front of the other diners. He ran up the rickety stairs, slammed the bedroom door and leaned against it for a moment, his heart pounding. He was being cruel to her – so cold and unfeeling when she was simply trying her best to appease him. What *was* the matter with him, for God's sake?

Stripping off his clothes, he flung them onto a nearby chair, drew the curtains and climbed into bed, the clean sheets cool against his feverish skin. He still loved her, of course he did; she was his wife, after all. But she'd changed, become more self-assured and careless of the company she kept – careless too of their children's welfare, for what did she really know about those men – and just how friendly had she become with Max?

He'd seen the attraction between them immediately and could almost understand it, for he was a handsome bastard, and she was still young and pretty, abandoned by her husband for too many months and enjoying the attentions of a man again. But he'd been on his own too, battling with the pressures of his job and his responsibilities – it would have been easy to stray, for women seemed to be drawn to men in uniform, and the rule book on fidelity had been discarded the minute the war had begun. Yet he'd hardly noticed other women, and had certainly never taken up the opportunities to break his wedding vows, for he believed in the sanctity of marriage and had thought Anne felt the same way.

He pulled the soft eiderdown over his head and buried his face in the pillow, trying to blot out the scene in the field; the laughter, Anne's glowing response to the man with the fair hair and blue eyes, and the children's free and easy acceptance of him. The tensions of the past months returned to weigh him down; the anguish of losing so many men, of doubting his wife's faithfulness, and the rejection of his children became too much to bear and, overwhelmed by it all, he curled up like a child and began to cry.

Anne didn't know what to do when Martin left the dining room. She was aware of the other diners watching her, noticed the raised eyebrows and knowing looks exchanged by the McCormacks, and realised her difficult reunion with Martin was far from private – and would probably soon be the main topic of gossip around the village.

She could feel her cheeks burning with embarrassment as she gathered up her handbag and gas-mask box and did her best to make a dignified exit. Having reached the narrow, dimly lit hall, she dithered for a moment, wondering whether to go for a walk and leave Martin to it for a bit – or defy him by going up and confronting him.

Realising she couldn't let this situation go on any longer, she took a deep breath and slowly went up the stairs. Standing outside the bedroom door, she wondered how best to approach him after his rejection, for he might start shouting again and they'd end up having a furious row. And then she heard the unmistakable sound of wracking sobs.

It was like a knife to her heart, and without further thought, she softly turned the handle and slipped inside.

The room was dark, the heartbreaking sobs muffled by his pillow. Her doubts and fears were swept away, and she trembled with love and concern as she stripped off her shoes and clothes and padded across to the bed. Without saying a word, she climbed in beside him and curled herself around him, holding him gently, feeling his whole body shuddering with anguish.

'Go away,' he rasped.

Anne ran her hand over his hot chest and pressed herself harder against his back, longing to comfort and console him because she loved him and couldn't bear to witness his pain. 'Not this time,' she whispered. 'I love you, Martin, and can't bear to see you like this.'

He turned with a deep groan and pulled her roughly to his chest, his lips seeking hers – hard and demanding – his hands moving over her curves and hollows as if needing to explore every inch of her and repossess her.

Anne yielded to his touch, the familiar scent and feel of him wiping away the months of separation and worry, to bring a swelling, sweet and increasingly urgent need for him to make love to her.

But as she ran her fingers lightly over his hip and between his thighs, he clamped a hand over her fingers and pulled away. 'I can't, Anne,' he said hoarsely. 'I'm sorry.'

'If you'll let me...'

He lay on his back, one arm across his eyes as if ashamed to face her. 'It won't do any good,' he replied, the sharp edge of frustration in his voice. 'It's not that I don't want to, but...'

Anne felt a profound ache of sorrow for this troubled man whom she loved so dearly. She curved into his side and softly kissed the pulse that was beating in his neck. 'It's all right,' she murmured. 'Really it is. And a cuddle is just as lovely.'

Martin gathered her into his side, kissed the top of her head and gave a deep sigh. 'I do love you, you know, and I'm sorry for earlier.'

Anne smiled in the darkness as she snuggled into him, soothed by the knowledge that they'd be all right – that once he'd slept and rested, they could really enjoy the short time they had together. She closed her eyes, exhausted from the emotional rollercoaster of the past few hours and on the brink of sleep when his next words brought her sharply awake.

'I want you and the children to go back home to Peggy's as soon as it can be arranged. You can't stay here.'

'But what about my teaching job? I can't leave everyone in the lurch.'

'I'm sure they can find someone else to take your place. I want you home where I can see you more often – where we can spend more time together, and I don't have to worry about you.'

Anne was so stunned by this she couldn't reply, but lay unmoving next to him as he drifted off into sleep.

When she was sure he wouldn't wake, she eased herself carefully from the bed, and with trembling hands began to dress. What he was asking was not impossible, and of course it would be wonderful to be back home again with her mother – but she had responsibilities here, and her children's safety was paramount.

She sat down in the easy chair by the window and listened to his soft snores as her mind raced and she tried desperately to think of a way to persuade him against the idea without causing further friction between them.

12

Cliffehaven

Ron had walked the two dogs a bit further than usual, and because Queenie had insisted upon coming too, he'd had to put her in his coat pocket when she'd grown tired of racing about on her three legs. Now he was tramping down the country lane which ran through the valley and the farm estate belonging to Lord Cliffe, his thoughts troubled.

Rosie was barely speaking to him after he'd

accused her of shenanigans with Leg-over – and although it bothered him, he knew from past experience that she'd forgive him eventually. It was the letter from Jim which he'd managed to hide from Peggy this morning that truly worried him, and had driven him to walk further than usual so he could absorb the reality of what his son was facing.

Ron crossed the small stone bridge arching over the fast-flowing river and then began the long trek up the hill between the fields of burgeoning wheat to the plateau that would give him a clear view of the aerodrome, which spread across several hundred acres.

As the dogs raced ahead of him, disappearing now and again into the hedgerows and stands of trees on the scent of something interesting, Ron could only thank his lucky stars that he'd got to the letter box first and retrieved the letter before Peggy could see it. She too had received something from Jim, but when she'd read it out, it had been clear to Ron that it was written to keep her from worrying and to deflect her from lighting on the real facts. It was filled with lots of guff about him and Ernie having a great time, although they missed the stray dog, Patch, who'd been taken on by an Indian Private since they no longer had time to look after him.

His own letter had been very different, with graphic accounts of lightning strikes by the Japs creeping out of the jungle – of bombing raids, deadly booby traps, piles of stinking bodies which attracted black clouds of flies, and native villages where even the children and animals had not been spared. Of having to have hundreds of tons of food and supplies airlifted in each day because everything edible went off within hours and they were so deep in the jungle valley, the only way in or out was by plane.

Jim was with a mobile mechanical workshop, and now fully armed for combat. He and his team were being flown in to where they were needed to repair the trucks and tanks being used by the Chindits and the Americans. They were in constant danger of being shot down, and had in fact had several close calls, but the sights and sounds he'd had to face were beginning to prey on his mind. There were lighter moments when they'd been flown into what he called safe areas for R&R, but they were few and far between.

Jim had written about the constant damp of sweat and humidity that had fungus growing in the creases and crevices of their skin, their clothes simply rotting into rags, while their boots became so soaked in the mud and swamp they were all going down with trench foot, just as they had in the trenches during the first shout. It had become impossible to keep dry and clean, and with every minute spent keeping an eye out for poisonous spiders and snakes it was difficult to concentrate on his work, let alone sleep peacefully at night.

Ron reached the summit and sat down on a hillock of grass to lift the cat out of his pocket and light his pipe. While Harvey and Monty raced about like idiots, Queenie arched her back in a luxurious stretch before sprawling beside him and keeping a wary eye open on Monty, who was a bit inclined to take liberties with her.

Ron stroked her fur once he'd got his pipe going, and gazed out over the flat landscape to the aerodrome where he could see row upon row of different aircraft lined up in readiness for their next sortie. There had been another big raid the previous night, and Jerry had retaliated swiftly by bombing the two towns just along the coast from Cliffehaven. They'd all spent several hours crowded in the damp Anderson shelter before the all-clear went, but at least it was more comfortable than the conditions Jim was enduring.

He gave a deep, sad sigh for his younger son, whose happy-go-lucky outlook on life had been such a huge part of Beach View, and whose youth had acted as a shield against the horrors of trench warfare the first time around. But Jim was older now, settled and softened by a good life, and Ron knew from bitter experience that he would be a changed man when he finally came home. A man who'd find it hard to sleep for the nightmares – a man of shifting moods who would laugh too loudly and talk too much – who'd go into dark depression, but wait until he was alone to shed tears for lost comrades and lost innocence. It was what happened to men who'd faced the horrors of war head on – seen sights that no one should ever witness – and borne the stresses and strains of just trying to stay alive while all around you were being slaughtered.

His thoughts turned to Peggy, who was being so brave throughout it all, determined to hold her head high and keep the home fires burning in the belief that everything would be all right once Jim came home – and that family life would continue as it had before the war. But Ron knew they could never go back to how they'd been, for each of them had been changed by this war – his grand-daughters Anne and Cissy maturing and becoming independent, his grandsons growing into young men who might yet be dragged into it – and Peggy, now used to being without her husband, making important decisions and finding her own independence in her work at the factory.

It would take time for Jim to adjust to life at home, the tedium of routine after the adrenaline rush of being a soldier in dangerous territory, and the fact that he'd be a stranger to Daisy, Rose Margaret and little Emily. That was assuming Jim returned home, and Ron prayed to God he would.

The distant thunder of plane engines broke the stillness, and as Ron watched, three squadrons of American B-25s took off to be quickly followed by two squadrons of Lancasters and a swarm of Spitfires, Hurricanes and Mosquitoes.

Queenie darted beneath his coat as they roared towards them, so he dumped her in his pocket, got to his feet and stood to attention, snapping off a salute as they flew overhead. His whole being was filled with pride and patriotism as he stood there silhouetted against the clear blue sky, an old soldier, honouring the new generation of heroes.

Peggy hadn't had to lift a finger all morning since Kitty and the other girls had taken charge of Daisy, made breakfast, cleared it away and then gone through the house like a dose of salts, cleaning, scrubbing and polishing until the place looked almost respectable. Sheets, towels and pillowcases had been changed and now there was a line of washing flapping outside; Ivy had gone out early with the ration books to do the shopping so the larder was stocked for the week ahead; and Sarah had worked with Cordelia to put together a lovely fish pie for tea.

Peggy had enjoyed going to see the little cottage and meet Charlotte for the first time, and had been delighted to see how lovely they'd made it. Freddy and Roger would take great comfort in having their own private little place to visit when time allowed, and she had felt rather guilty about resenting the brevity of Kitty's visit to Beach View. Kitty was a married woman now with a baby on the way – and although she still needed mothering, she also needed time and space to plan her own future with Roger.

The house was quiet as she sat in her kitchen re-reading her letter from Jim. Fran was on duty at the hospital, Ivy had a late shift at the factory, Sarah was upstairs writing letters, and Rita had taken Kitty on the back of her motorbike to the old track where she was organising another of her fundraising bike races. They'd proved incredibly popular, and the money she'd raised had provided a Spitfire and a Mosquito to the war effort, both of them emblazoned with the name of the town on the sides.

Cordelia was making the most of the spring sunshine by sitting in a deckchair in a sheltered corner of the garden to keep an eye on Daisy, who was playing in the makeshift sandpit Ron had constructed from an abandoned cattle trough he'd found up in the hills. Peggy was just putting the letter away when she heard a bit of a kerfuffle outside and went to investigate.

'Hello, Mam,' said a beaming Cissy, picking up a demanding Daisy and hooking her onto her hip.

Peggy shot out of the door and threw her arms about them both. 'Oh, darling,' she breathed, on the brink of tears. 'How lovely.'

'I can't stay very long, I'm afraid,' Cissy said, jiggling Daisy up and down to make her giggle. 'I'm not really supposed to even be here, but I had to come. I've got such marvellous news.'

Peggy saw how her skin glowed and her eyes shone, and wondered if her young American airman had finally proposed. 'Go on then,' she urged. 'What's happened?'

'Randy isn't dead at all,' Cissy said, her voice ragged with emotion.

Peggy's heart missed a beat and she frowned. 'I don't understand...'

Cissy carefully put Daisy down, encouraging her to wheel her trolley along the path before she turned back to Peggy. 'I asked Martin not to say anything as I needed to come to terms with things before I told you. You see, he was shot down two weeks ago and posted as missing in action. And then someone identified the body of another airman as his.' She took a quavering breath. 'I was in pieces, Mam. Absolute pieces.'

Peggy's heart broke at the thought of her daughter suffering so much, and she also felt rather hurt that she hadn't been able to tell her but had preferred to deal with it on her own for two whole weeks.

Cissy's tears brimmed and fell, then a radiant smile broke through. 'But he's alive, Mam. He's alive and a prisoner of war somewhere in France.'

Peggy took her into her arms as she sobbed, holding her tightly and rejoicing in the fact that Cissy's lovely young man had beaten the odds. 'Thank God,' she murmured.

'Oh, I do,' said Cissy firmly as she drew from the embrace and got her emotions under control again. 'And because he's a prisoner he won't have to go risking his life night after night on bombing raids. I know it's selfish to think that way, and he's probably champing at the bit to escape and get back here to continue the fight – but he's safe, and that's all that really matters.'

Peggy's heart swelled with love. 'That's the most wonderful news, darling,' she said through her own tears. 'But you're to promise me you'll always tell me the things that are truly worrying you. These shoulders might be narrow, but they're very strong.'

'I know they are, Mam,' she said softly. 'But sometimes a girl needs to deal with things on her own until she's ready to share them.' She kissed Peggy's cheek. 'Now I have to get back. With Martin on leave I'm driving the new station commander, and he's the most frightful old grouch.'

Peggy experienced a stab of alarm. 'Martin's on leave?'

Cissy frowned. 'He left for Somerset late last night. Why? What's the matter?'

'Nothing,' she replied hastily. 'I'm just surprised, that's all.'

Cissy giggled. 'I suspect he's hoping it will be a

243

surprise to Anne as well. He was so excited at the thought of seeing her and the children again.'

Before Peggy had a chance to reply, Cissy had kissed Cordelia and Daisy and was hurrying towards the gate. 'I'll call in again as soon as possible,' she said with a wave, and then was gone.

Peggy turned to Cordelia. 'I just hope she got my letter in time and wrote to warn Martin about those POWs.'

Cordelia took her hand and smiled up at her. 'Stop fretting about everyone and go and put that kettle on. Anne's not a girl to keep things like that to herself. Of course she wrote to him.'

Somerset

Anne had begun to feel stifled in that darkened room, her thoughts going in circles as Martin continued to snore and move restlessly in the bed. Eventually she could stand it no longer, so she wrote a quick note and left it on top of his clothes so he wouldn't miss it, then hurried downstairs and out into the fresh air of the back garden.

It was late afternoon and although the sun was still bright there was little warmth in it, and she felt chilled in her cotton dress and cardigan. Reluctant to disturb Martin by going back to fetch her overcoat, she found the most sheltered spot and sat down. Yet it wasn't long until she became restless again, wishing she had a book or paper to read, or somewhere to walk where she wouldn't encounter other people who would no doubt question her about Martin's homecoming.

244

She began to pace about the garden, stopping now and again to pull a few weeds or tie something back more firmly. Having found the outside tap, she watered the window boxes and pots, and then swept up a few leaves that were still lingering in various corners.

'If you keep going at that rate, it'll soon be me paying you,' said Mrs McCormack, appearing at the back door laden with a tray of tea.

Anne blushed and couldn't look her in the eye.

'I'm sorry,' she murmured. 'I hope you don't mind.'

'Not at all,' she replied cheerfully, putting the tray on the weathered table. 'I can always do with a hand in the garden. Patrick's not a one for such things.' She patted the nearby chair. 'Come and sit down, dear. You look all in, if you don't mind me saying so.'

'I'm fine, really,' Anne said firmly, even though she wasn't. 'But a cup of tea would go down a treat.'

'I made a couple of cakes for this evening, but I'm sure they won't mind if we have a slice each out of one.' She poured the tea and passed it to Anne along with a large slab of Victoria sponge.

'Goodness. How did you manage to get the ingredients for this?'

'I get a bit extra on the ration because of running this place, and I saved it up special because of the dance tonight.' Her kind brown eyes regarded Anne. 'Will you and your husband be going?'

'I was planning to,' she admitted, 'but Martin arrived unexpectedly, so...' She let the words hang between them, reluctant to go into any further detail.

'Asleep, is he?' the older woman asked gently. At Anne's nod, she gave a sigh. 'Poor lamb. They're all the same, you know. My friend has a hotel in Taunton, and she told me how they come in full of the joys of spring, drink themselves into a stupor, and then crash out for hours. I suppose it's the stress they're under.'

Anne bit into the delicious cake, reminded that she'd had very little to eat today, and that although there had been endless upset, she was very hungry. 'He's certainly sleeping well,' she said eventually. 'Which is why I thought I'd leave him to it and get some fresh air.'

Mrs McCormack nodded sagely. 'He'll come and find you when he's ready. And I shouldn't worry, dear, these leaves are always difficult, especially when you've been apart for a long while.' She cocked her head. 'How long since the last one?'

'He came down just after Emily was born,' Anne replied reluctantly. She finished the cake and washed it down with the good strong tea. 'That was lovely,' she said, and smiled. 'Thank you so much.'

'You're very welcome, dear.' Mrs McCormack reached across the table and took Anne's hand. 'You know, Anne, you've become very much a part of this village, and although you might think we're being nosy, it's only because we care. If you want to talk about anything then you know where I am. And I promise it won't go any further.'

Anne was warmed by her kindness and had to

clear her throat before she could reply. 'That's very kind of you, Mrs McCormack, but I suspect Aggie Fuller has already told the rest of the village that this reunion is not as happy as it could be.'

'Yes, it was a shame she chose today to come in for her lunch, but never you mind. I had a word and warned her on pain of death not to say anything,' said the other woman grimly. 'She knows better than to cross me.'

'Bless you. That was kind.' Anne gently withdrew her hand and pushed back from the table. 'I think I'll go up and sit with him for a while. I don't really like the thought of him waking up to find me gone.'

'You do that, dear, and I'll get my baking down to the hall before starting tonight's dinner.'

Martin was still asleep, and as the light began to fade, she opened the curtains and looked rather wistfully down to the street. People were walking past laden with baskets of food and drink, their happy chatter drifting up to her as they headed for the church hall, which now wore a permanent and rather tattered string of bunting across the eaves. The vicar would be sorting through his collection of records to play for the dancing, George Mayhew was no doubt doing a last-minute practice with Belinda to refine his quickstep, and Sally and the land girls would be dressing up in anticipation of having a good evening out while Vi, bless her, babysat.

For the first time since coming to Barnham Green, Anne felt isolated and very much alone with her dilemma, and the thought that she might soon have to leave made her feel quite tearful. If

247

Martin didn't change his mind about her and the children leaving, then she had no choice in the matter, but every part of her rebelled against it.

'Anne? Anne, are you there?'

She turned towards the bed where Martin was groggily pulling himself up against the pillows. 'Yes, I'm here,' she replied softly. 'Do you feel better for your sleep?'

'How long have I been out?'

'Five hours,' she said with a smile in her voice. 'It's almost time for dinner.'

He threw back the covers and grinned as he patted the bed. 'Bugger dinner,' he said roguishly. 'I've got a much better idea.'

She knew there was a lot to discuss, but for now she was just thankful that Martin seemed to be his old self again. With a frisson of anticipation, she shed her clothes once more and slid in beside him.

It was a very sheepish couple who came down rather late for breakfast, for they'd missed dinner entirely, forgotten about the village dance and had eventually fallen asleep in one another's arms at around midnight.

Mrs McCormack was wreathed in knowing smiles as she served more toast to the ravenous pair, and they had to stifle their giggles as they caught one another's eye. Once the last crumb had been eaten and the teapot was drained dry, Martin paid the bill while Anne telephoned Vi to warn her they were coming to see the children.

With their bags packed in the boot of the road-ster, she sat next to Martin as he drove to Owlet

Farm, the nerves jangling once again. She could only hope that Vi had sent the men off to a distant part of the farm, and that she'd prepared the children for a visit from their father. She certainly didn't want a repeat of yesterday – and yet the thorny subject of where she'd spend the rest of the war still loomed.

Vi was waiting for them in the farmhouse kitchen where the table was littered with flour, apple peelings and cores. 'It's good to see you've both come to your senses,' she said after a single glance at their happy faces. 'The girls and I have just finished making apple pie, and as they seem to be wearing most of it, Sally's taken them off to get washed and changed.'

'Thank you for looking after them, Aunt Vi,' said Anne. 'Have they been all right?'

'Absolutely fine,' said Vi. She took off her apron and reached for her handbag, hat and coat. 'You won't be disturbed,' she said. 'Bob's out with the other men to top the fallow field, Charlie's gone off with Ernie and one of his pals on their bicycles with a picnic, and little Harry's at Sunday school. Sally and I are off to church now with the land girls, and the way the vicar's sermons seem to be getting longer by the day, I doubt we'll be back for at least an hour and a half.'

Just as Anne was about to go in search of her children, Vi stopped her. 'I almost forgot,' she said. 'Your mother telephoned. Nothing to be alarmed about; she just wanted Martin to know that Cissy's young American has been posted as a POW in some French prison.'

'That's jolly good news,' said Martin. 'We'd

been told he was dead.' He gave a deep sigh. 'It just goes to show that miracles do still happen.'

Their conversation was interrupted by squeals of excitement as Rose and Emily rushed into the room and threw themselves at their mother, both talking at once, not even noticing their father standing there.

Anne acknowledged the smiles and nods from Vi and Sally as they left, and then squatted down to gather the little girls into her arms. 'I've missed you very much too,' she assured them, 'and look, I have a lovely surprise for you. It's Daddy, and he's here to say sorry for shouting yesterday.'

The little girls eyed him warily; Emily with her thumb plugged in her mouth, Rose wide-eyed and poised to run away.

Martin sat down on the flagstone floor, heedless of the fact it was still dusted with flour. 'Hello, girls,' he said softly. 'I am very sorry I was so cross yesterday. Will you forgive Daddy?'

Emily looked to her mother, and then nodded, though she didn't quite understand what he was asking her. Rose stood her ground and folded her arms, her expression stormy. 'Are you going to shout again?' she asked. ''Cos I don't like it, and you made Mummy cry.'

'I know I did,' he said sadly, glancing across at Anne. 'But I won't do it again, I promise.'

'Cross your heart?' demanded Rose, who most definitely had a way of her own when it came to making people keep their promises.

Martin crossed his heart and tentatively reached for Emily who'd toddled towards him. He didn't pick her up immediately, but waited until she felt comfortable enough with him to come and lean against his side. Then, with tears glinting, he picked her up and nuzzled her cheek. 'Hello, little Emily,' he murmured. 'It's wonderful to hold you again. My goodness, how you've grown.'

'I've grown too,' shouted Rose, put out that her sister was getting all the attention.

'Indeed you have,' he replied, getting to his feet and settling more comfortably in a chair. 'Come and sit on my other knee and tell me all the exciting things you've been doing since yesterday.'

Anne sat with tears in her eyes as Rose prattled on about how she was going to marry Harry one day and they'd go and live in the camp they'd made in the woods – and Emily showed him the tiny graze on her arm where she'd fallen in the yard and old Fred had put a plaster on it. It was going to be all right, she thought with huge relief, for now Martin could have the leave he'd been dreaming about – and perhaps, if he realised how very happy they all were here, he'd change his mind about their leaving.

Martin had wanted the day to last forever, but time had flown as they'd gone for a ride in the roadster with the children, eaten a delicious lunch at a riverside restaurant and then ambled through tiny hamlets on their reluctant way back to the farm.

'It's been a perfect day,' he said after the children had kissed him goodbye and run off to tell the others about their adventures. 'And we can have so many more once you come back to Cliffe-haven.'

251

'It might take a while before that happens,' she replied carefully. 'I'll have to give at least a term's notice at the school so they can find another teacher, and of course restrictions on travel could make it even more difficult to get home.'

He frowned at the reluctance in her tone. 'You seem to be putting up a lot of objections, Anne,' he said. 'Don't you want to come home?'

'Well, I am rather reluctant to leave here,' she confessed carefully. 'You've seen for yourself how much we love it on the farm with Vi and the girls. The children are flourishing and happy with my brothers and Harry, and all their little friends at the nursery school, and it will be a bit of a wrench for all of us.'

'But I thought we'd agreed it was for the best?' he replied, tamping down on his exasperation.

Anne bit her lip, her gaze drifting to somewhere over his shoulder. 'I've had time to think about it,' she said, 'and really, Martin, Cliffehaven isn't the safest place to take our children. It's too near the aerodrome and right in the middle of Bomb Alley.'

He felt a cold tingle of uncertainty run down his spine at her continued reluctance. 'It's not exactly safe here,' he pointed out. 'You were incredibly lucky that sniper didn't kill one of you.'

Anne touched the spot on her shoulder that he'd questioned her about the previous night. 'It was a one-off thing,' she said lightly. 'It's the first time we've even seen an enemy plane, and it's not like poor Mam who's constantly under attack.'

Martin didn't want to argue with her, or pressurise her now they'd managed to rekindle the feelings between them, but he certainly didn't want her staying here longer than necessary. He glanced over her shoulder, saw the three German prisoners loitering down by the river and was reminded of Vi's words about the code of honour between airmen the previous day. He knew what he had to do, but every part of him mutinied against it, and he played for time by turning his attention once more to Anne.

'I love you very much, Anne,' he said quietly, 'and although I don't wish to be heavy-handed about this, I'm not happy with the situation here and want you to come home.'

Anne looked up at him and then, with clear reluctance, nodded. 'I'll do my best,' she promised. 'But you'll have to be patient, Martin. Organising it might prove difficult.'

'I understand that,' he said. 'Just do what you can as quickly as you can, and I'll warn Peggy to expect you.'

Anne frowned. 'But surely we'd be moving back into our cottage?'

'Not until the tenants' lease is up, I'm afraid. But you'll be fine with Peggy, and she'll relish the chance to spoil you and the girls.'

He glanced across at the distant figures standing by the fence. 'There's something I have to do before I leave,' he murmured, placing his highly decorated hat on his head. 'Stay here. I won't be long.'

He walked purposefully towards the three men, steeling himself for what he had to do, aware that they too were now stiffening at his approach, and that Anne was watching in some trepidation – no

253

doubt wondering if he was about to punch one of them on the nose and cause a fracas.

He came to a halt, stood to attention and saluted.

The three men snapped to attention and saluted back – thankfully not with a stiff right arm and a shout of *'Heil Hitler!'*

'Oberst Schultz,' Martin said to Maximilian. 'I wish to apologise for my rudeness yesterday.'

Max dipped his chin sharply in acknowledgement. 'Vill you, as a fellow flying officer, shake my hand?'

Martin had no choice but to do so, and met the man's steady gaze without flinching.

'Thank you, Group Captain Black. It is an honour to meet you.'

Martin certainly wouldn't go that far, but he acknowledged the compliment, nodded to the other two and turned swiftly away to head back to Anne.

She was waiting for him in the yard, her eyes shining with pride as well as tears. 'Thank you, Martin,' she breathed. 'I know how hard that must have been for you.'

He put his arm around her shoulders and walked her towards the car which he'd parked to one side of the barn. 'Honour had to be restored,' he said gruffly. 'I couldn't leave things as they were.'

He drew her into a close embrace and kissed her deeply. 'I don't want to go,' he murmured against her cheek. 'But there might be a long wait at Church Stanton before I can get a lift back to Cliffe.' He stroked the hair back from her face and looked down into her eyes. 'I love you very much, Anne. Thank you for being so understanding and sweet.'

He kissed her again, tasting the salt of her tears, and then quickly turned away and leapt into the car.

'I love you too,' she called after him as he drove slowly out of the yard. 'Take care of yourself, my darling.'

He tooted the horn and gave one last wave before he set the little car roaring through the gate and out into the country lane. His leave might have begun inauspiciously, but because of Anne's stalwart refusal to be cowed by his appalling behaviour, he'd reacquainted himself with his children, eventually managed to make love to her, and restored his honour as an RAF officer by apologising to that bloody Kraut. All he could do now was trust that she would abide by his wishes and do everything in her power to return to Cliffehaven, where she belonged.

13

Cliffehaven

Peggy had been enormously relieved when she'd finally managed to get through to the farm on the telephone. She'd felt even better when Vi told her that, although there'd been a tricky confrontation between Martin and the prisoners when he'd first arrived, it had all quietened down, and Anne was now out for the day with him and the children.

'At least I managed to get Cissy's news to him,' she said, clearing up the last of the toys after a hectic afternoon. 'There are so few happy stories these days, and something like that is bound to give him a bit of a boost.'

'I don't know that he'll be particularly safe, even in prison, now our lot are bombing France,' said Kitty, retrieving a wooden building block from beneath Cordelia's chair. 'The way this war is going, there won't be anywhere in Europe that's not a target for our bombers.'

'Oh dear,' said Peggy fretfully. 'Do you really think so?'

Kitty put an arm around her shoulders. 'I'm just making an educated guess, Peggy. Don't take it as gospel.' She smiled and tilted her head towards Ron, who'd come in looking quite smart for a change. 'Someone's trying to make an impression,' she murmured. 'Are you in the doghouse with Rosie, Ron?'

'To be sure, I'm not,' he protested, grimacing as he ran his finger inside the stiff shirt collar and adjusted his tie.

'It's probably why he's been so grumpy lately,' said Cordelia, eyeing the suit, clean shirt and neatly brushed hair over her reading spectacles. 'Rosie was bound to discover sooner or later that he's nothing but a scoundrel.'

'She has not,' he growled. 'That woman loves me, so she does.'

'Well, you must have done something pretty serious to warrant such a transformation from

256

your usual lack of sartorial splendour,' teased Kitty.

'Aye, well, Rosie's got a bee in her bonnet about something, so I thought I'd make a bit of an effort.' He again eased his finger inside the stiff collar with a grunt of annoyance. 'Though why a man has to half strangle himself to make an impression, I don't know.'

'So what did you do to make Rosie cross?' asked Peggy, trying very hard not to laugh.

'Ach, it was a misunderstanding, that's all. You women are such complicated and awkward creatures, it's no wonder a man can't get through a single day without making some mistake or other.'

'Then you'd better go and do your best to put things right,' said Cordelia. 'Although what she sees in you is a mystery.' She gave a sniff of disapproval which belied the light of humour in her eyes.

'Well, now, Cordelia, 'tis a mystery to me why Bertie Double-Barrelled keeps hanging about you – but as a gentleman, I have refrained from making the point before.'

Cordelia snorted in a most unladylike manner. 'I think the word *gentleman* is an unfortunate choice when it comes to you,' she said, her lips twitching with laughter. 'Rogue would be far more appropriate.'

Peggy rolled her eyes at Kitty. 'Here we go again,' she giggled. 'You see, nothing changes in this house.'

'There's too many women about, that's the problem,' muttered Ron. 'It's enough to turn a man to the drink, so it is.'

257

'Then you'd better get yourself to the Anchor,' said Cordelia dryly. 'I'm sure Rosie's waiting for you with bated breath.'

'Sarcasm doesn't suit you, Cordelia.' Ron glared at her from beneath his heavy brows. 'Why not just stick the knife in like you always do?' He stomped off with Harvey at his heels, the sound of their laughter following him down the cellar steps.

Peggy sat down and had a cigarette with the last of the tea in the pot. It had been a chaotic afternoon, with Gracie and Chloe coming to tea, and Ron getting the children overexcited by chasing them about the house. Gracie had taken a sleepy Chloe home half an hour ago and the girls had helped to clear everything away before preparing for the new week and an evening at the Anchor.

Peggy eyed the two large bunches of daffodils Ron had brought home from his morning walk on the hills. 'I think I'll take some of those to the cemetery,' she said. 'It's been a while since I visited Aleksy and Danuta's poor little baby.' She saw the frown of incomprehension on Kitty's face and explained about the girl whose latest letter had disturbed her so deeply.

'Would you like me to come with you?' Kitty asked.

'That would be lovely, but I thought you were going to the Anchor with the others?'

'I can catch them up. I'm sure they won't mind if I'm a bit late.'

'Thank you, dear, I'll enjoy your company.' Peggy wrapped a few of the daffodils in a sheet of newspaper and tucked them into her shopping basket. She waited for Kitty to write a note to the other girls who were upstairs getting ready, then they both left the house.

They walked arm in arm along the streets, content in one another's company and not really needing words to fill the silence. The pubs were busy, there were far more Americans than usual in the town, and the amount of army trucks roaring about made it quite dangerous to cross the road.

'There's a sense of something in the air, isn't there?' Kitty said.

Peggy nodded. 'Yes, I feel it too. A sort of pent-up excitement as if something tremendous is about to happen.'

'Rumours are flying about an Allied invasion,' said Kitty. 'If the whispers about travelling restrictions coming in next week are to be believed, then it's very possible those rumours are true.'

Peggy sighed. 'There have been rumours before, Kitty. I'm almost afraid to hope that this time they could have some substance. This war has gone on for so long, and the entire world is in such turmoil that we're all exhausted by it and clutching at straws.'

They reached the tiny church perched on the edge of the town in a quiet, tree-shaded plot overlooking the distant coastline, and took turns to push through the lych-gate. The church was the oldest one for many miles, and had, so far, escaped the attentions of the Luftwaffe. Built during Norman times, it had survived the Reformation, the ancient stone walls as solid now as they'd ever been, the cool sanctuary echoing with history and a sense of great peace. It had become a haven for

259

those who sought solace during these troubled times, and a few moments of contemplation in the churchyard refreshed the soul.

The cemetery had been cared for by old Bill Wheatley these past fifty years, and was a testament to his love of order and beauty. The grass was as smooth as a bowling green, the trees pruned back so they didn't overshadow the graves, the wooden benches had been freshly varnished, and he'd planted a small rose bush by the newer headstones – his way of honouring the fallen of both wars.

There were birds singing in the trees as the sun slowly made its way towards the western hills, and as they walked along the neat stone path, they could feel the light breeze drift over them, carrying the scents of early roses and freshly cut grass.

'I never knew this was here,' breathed Kitty. 'What a lovely, peaceful place it is.'

Peggy nodded, feeling the chaos and stress of the past day slip away to be replaced by a profound sense of calm. 'I don't come here very often,' she replied softly, 'but perhaps I should.'

She approached the two graves that were set at the far end of the cemetery with a magnificent view of the sea in the distance. Bill Wheatley had planted a white rose for the baby, and a deep crimson one for Aleksy, and the tiny buds were just beginning to open, their fragrance barely perceptible. Peggy knelt and separated the bunch of daffodils into two while Kitty went off to fill the small watering can from the tap outside the vestry door. The flowers Ron had left last week were still quite fresh, so she arranged the daffs with them in the stone pots, and then sat back on her heels.

'Keep watch over Danuta,' she murmured. 'I fear for her, Aleksy. And if it's at all possible, could you please have a word with God and ask him not to take her yet? She still has so much life to live.'

Peggy read the epitaphs and ran her fingers over the black lettering on the baby's memorial which had a stone cherub carved in marble sitting on top. The cherub had been Ron's idea, and every time she saw it, it made her cry. Blinking back her tears, she got to her feet and gave Kitty a watery smile. 'Don't mind me,' she said. 'That little cherub always affects me.'

Kitty hugged her. 'You are a soppy date,' she said fondly. 'But that's why I love you so. Don't ever change, Peggy. You're perfect just the way you are.'

'Get away with you,' she said in pleasure and embarrassment. 'Now who's being a soppy date?'

'I have the excuse of being pregnant,' Kitty said with a giggle. They linked arms and walked back down the path and through the gate. 'I catch myself crying over the least little thing – but they're happy tears,' Kitty added on a little sigh.

Ron was all too aware of the girls from Beach View sitting at their favourite table by the inglenook, and wasn't best pleased that Kitty had brought Cordelia along with her. He loved and admired the old girl even though they were always having spats, but tonight she was watching the interaction between him and Rosie like a hawk as she sipped her second glass of sherry, and it made him feel uncomfortable.

He tried to put a brave face on things and pretend that everything was all right between him and Rosie, but he could feel the arctic frost emanating from her even at the far end of the bar. He was at his wits' end to know what to do to turn things around. He'd apologised profusely, made an effort to look smart for her – had even tried flirting and flattering her. None of it had worked.

Rosie sashayed past him in her tight skirt and high heels as he was serving a customer and pointedly ignored him. She bent down to retrieve fresh glasses from beneath the bar, the tight skirt stretched temptingly over her pert bottom, the hem rising just enough to reveal a flash of luscious pale thigh above her stocking tops.

It was too much for Ron, and without thinking he gave her bottom a loving pat.

Rosie whirled round furiously and slapped his hand away before stabbing an angry finger at him. 'Do that again, Ronan Reilly, and I'll slap your face.'

Ron was struck dumb and could only stare at her as she stormed back to the other end of the bar. Rosie had never complained about a bit of slap and tickle before – but now, he realised, he really was in trouble. He turned, red-faced, to serve the next customer and was met by the grinning, ugly mug of Leg-over Langborne.

'It looks like you're out of favour with our lovely Rosie,' he said superciliously. He gave a sly wink. 'Perhaps it's time for a younger man to take her on.' Ron gritted his teeth, poured the half-pint and placed the foaming glass carefully on the bar. He took the man's money and then leaned towards him. 'You lay one finger on *my* Rosie, and I'll have your guts for garters,' he growled.

Leg-over just grinned and flexed his bulging shoulder muscles beneath the tweed jacket. 'I'd like to see you try, old man,' he replied, aware that the other people standing at the bar were watching this exchange in anticipatory silence.

'No, you wouldn't,' retorted Ron. 'You might be younger than me, but I could have you help-less on the floor before you could blink.'

'Oh yeah?' Langborne stood tall, the smirk wiped from his face by a flush of belligerence as the crowd around him backed away and a sudden hush fell over the rest of the room.

'Aye.' Ron clenched his fists at his sides and met the other man's challenging glare with his own. 'Fancy your luck, do you? Because we can take this outside now and settle things once and for all.'

Langborne drank his beer down in two swal-lows and slammed the glass on the bar. 'You're on, old man.'

Ron was about to charge round to the other side of the bar when Rosie grabbed his arm in a steely grip and positioned herself across his escape route. 'What's going on here?'

'Private business,' snapped Ron, yanking his arm free. 'Get out of the way, Rosie.'

Rosie didn't budge an inch, her blue eyes cold and furious as she glanced at both men. 'As you've finished your drink, Langborne, I suggest you leave,' she said sternly.

The drayman raised his hands and looked around for support from the other customers. 'He started it,' he protested. 'And I want another beer.'

'I don't care who started it,' said Rosie. 'This is my pub, and I won't stand for that sort of behaviour. Now get out, Langborne, before I throw you out.'

He tilted back his head and roared with laughter. 'Now that I'd like to see,' he spluttered.

Rosie moved so quickly he hardly had time to blink before she had his arm twisted high up his back, the collar of his jacket gripped in her other hand as she propelled him towards the door.

The customers parted like the Red Sea, a helpful sailor opened the door and Rosie gave Langborne a hard shove that sent him sprawling headlong into the gutter. She walked back into the bar, the sailor closed the door and everyone cheered and gave her a round of applause.

'The show's over,' said Rosie, dusting her hands as she returned to the other side of the bar. 'You've got ten minutes before closing time.'

Ron had seen her deal with drunks and fist fights before, and really, she was quite the most magnificent woman he'd ever met. 'I could have handled him,' he said quietly.

'I know,' she replied. 'But I'm so out of sorts with everything that I needed to let off steam.'

'Rather him than me,' he said with a nervous smile.

The blue eyes were turned on him without a hint of warmth. 'Oh, I haven't even started yet,

Ron. I'll deal with you later.'

Ron swallowed. Rosie was fire and ice, and when she was in this kind of mood anything could happen. He busied himself collecting the empty glasses from the bar and mopping up the spills, not daring to look over to the Beach View table, but profoundly grateful that they'd had more sense than to come over and make silly remarks.

Rosie clanged the bell to call time, and the customers began to leave, slowly at first and then in a great tide. Ron saw Kitty and the girls helping Cordelia to her feet and steering a rather ragged path to the door – the old lady had clearly had one too many sherries. He didn't miss the wink Cordelia gave him, or the silly grins on the girls' faces, so he ducked his chin and concentrated on filling the crates below the bar with empty bottles.

With the pub empty and the door locked behind the last customer, the three of them set to work. An hour later the glasses had been washed, the long oak counter and brass beer pumps polished to a shine and the floor swept and mopped. Tables and chairs had been tidied, pewter tankards returned to their hooks above the bar, empties carried down to the cellar, the barmaid paid and sent home.

Ron was coming up the cellar steps with Harvey as Rosie bolted the back door behind the barmaid. 'I'll be off then,' he said warily.

'You're not going anywhere until I've had my say,' she replied sternly.

Ron stood there in the narrow hallway, twisting his cap in his hands, and Harvey sat by his feet, both of them looking hangdog as Rosie let rip.

'How *dare* you question my fidelity?' she stormed. 'We've been together for more years than I can count, and still you don't trust me. Whereas *you* – you give me the run-around all the damned time; not telling me where you are or who you're with – disappearing for hours with no explanation.'

She paused for breath. 'And as for accusing me of messing about with Leg-over – that really is the limit. Don't you know *anything* about me after all this time?'

Her voice had risen in pitch and volume, but still she wasn't finished. 'I wouldn't touch that man with a bargepole – other than to chuck him out of my pub. And as for you,' she yelled. 'What the *hell* do you think you were doing picking a fight with him?'

Harvey buried his nose under a paw and Ron swallowed. 'I was only–'

'I don't want to hear it,' she snapped. 'I'm fed up with your blarney and the way you think you can take liberties by touching my bum in front of a bar full of bloody people.'

'Ach, to be sure it's a very nice bum,' he muttered, daring to look at her from beneath his brows. 'And it looked so very tempting, wriggling right there in front of me.'

'It doesn't mean you can touch it whenever the mood takes you,' she retorted. 'Especially after you've accused me of messing about with other men. I'm not your plaything, Ron, and I'm bitterly disappointed that you think so little of me.'

'It's sorry I am that I've upset you, Rosie,' he murmured with heartfelt sorrow. 'I got the wrong

266

end of the stick, and am at me wits' end to know what to do about it.'

She expelled a breath of exasperation. 'You really are the bloody limit, Ron,' she said, a smile tweaking the corner of her lips, her eyes defrosting from arctic to warm sapphire. 'But I suppose I'll just have to put up with it.'

'So I'm forgiven, then?' he asked hopefully.

'Until the next time,' she replied. She took his face in her hands and kissed him deeply. 'How about coming upstairs for a nightcap?' she said softly.

'That would be grand, so it would.' He raised an eyebrow in forlorn hope. 'I don't suppose that would include a bit more than a kiss and cuddle?'

'You supposed right,' she giggled.

'Ach, well, no harm in asking. I'll settle for the cuddle.' He swept her off her feet and carried her upstairs, leaving a very confused Harvey in the hallway.

Somerset

Anne had been very well aware that the subject of Martin's leave had been carefully avoided by everyone around the table while they'd eaten the evening meal. The three POWs had collected theirs from the kitchen and taken it back to their cottage, clearly feeling awkward in Anne's company after what had happened the day before. The land girls had chattered to Sally about how much fun they'd all had at the village dance, for George Mayhew had lost his shyness and shown off his prowess on the dance floor, not only with Belinda, but with just about every other woman there. He had, apparently, kept returning to Belinda, which had set tongues wagging in the hall. And Belinda hadn't seemed too displeased to be dancing with George half the night. Anne had told the girls to stop gossiping, but she secretly wondered if romance could be in the air.

Everyone had finally gone to their own cottages, Bob and Charlie were engrossed in a game of chess in the sitting room, and the kitchen was quiet as Anne and Vi had a last cup of tea. Rose and Emily, who were usually very chatty at the table, had been overtired and whining after their exciting day, and Anne had been relieved to get them both to bed a little earlier than usual.

'I'm glad things turned round for you and Martin,' said Vi. 'I was a bit worried at first that he'd simply turn tail and go back to Cliffe, leaving you high and dry at the Shepherd's Arms.'

'He was very tired,' said Anne. 'And extremely stressed and disappointed that his lovely surprise had gone so horribly wrong. But I'm proud of the way he made amends with Max and the others. It couldn't have been easy.'

Vi sipped her tea. 'Max told me he thought Martin was about to punch him, and was perfectly prepared to take it without retaliating. So when he saluted and shook his hand, he was delighted to accept that although they were enemies, they did indeed belong to the same brotherhood of airmen. I think he felt quite honoured by that.'

'I'm glad,' sighed Anne. 'Because, when all's said and done, they're just ordinary men caught up in something they can't control – and who knows what the future might bring? I just hope that the code of honour still exists should Martin find himself taken as a prisoner of war.'

'We can only pray he never finds himself in that position,' said Vi. She sipped her tea and then fiddled with the little spoon sitting in the saucer. 'Max and I had a bit of a chat on Saturday after you'd left with Martin. He's a surprisingly sensitive man, you know, and can see how their presence here might continue to cause friction between you and Martin.'

'Surely you're not sending them back to that awful prison camp, Vi? That would be most unfair.'

'He came up with a much better idea. He'd discussed it with the other two, and they've agreed to clear out the shepherd's cottage down by Rectory Field, sort out the ancient cooking range and move in there to fend for themselves.'

'But that's been abandoned for years and it's in a terrible state.'

'They've already started work on it, and it will probably be habitable within the week, knowing how quickly and efficiently they get things done. Until then, they've said they'd prefer to eat in their place.'

'That's extremely thoughtful of them, and I feel horribly guilty about putting them to so much inconvenience. They've no need to feel awkward with me or the children – and besides, I might not even be here for much longer.'

Vi's eyes widened. 'What do you mean? Where are you going?'

'Martin wants me and the children back in Cliffehaven as soon as possible. I really don't want to leave here, but he has enough to cope with without worrying about us.'

'I'm sure that if you wrote and told him about the new arrangements, he'd see sense,' Violet said. 'It's utterly ridiculous to expect you to go back there while it's still being attacked.'

'I can try writing to him, but I don't think even the new arrangements will change his mind. He's really set on it, Vi, and as his wife, I have no other choice but to do as he asked.'

'When it comes to the safety of your children you have every choice,' Violet said emphatically. 'Just because he's got a bee in his bonnet about Max and the others, doesn't mean you have to turn your life upside down. What about your teaching post? You can't just chuck that up at a moment's notice.'

'I have warned him it could take time,' Anne sighed. 'Oh Vi, I hate being in such an appalling situation. He won't forgive me if I stay, but if I go back I doubt I'll see anything of him, and our little cottage has been rented out so I'll have to live with Mam at Beach View, and the house is already overcrowded.'

Vi smiled at this. 'Peggy would move heaven and earth to have you home again, and of course her house is crowded – she's always taking in waifs and strays by the sound of it.'

'Yes, and I'd just be one more,' Anne said fretfully. 'It's not that I don't love Mam or want to be with her, but I'm too old to be living at home again. I'm used to doing things my way and making my own decisions.'

'Well, Anne, this is a decision only you can make. And I wish you luck, my dear, because it won't be easy.'

Anne hadn't slept well, for her mind refused to be still, reaching decisions and then rejecting them repeatedly, until she lost patience and got out of bed to prepare for her first day back at school.

The girls were noisy, refusing to sit still at the table, making a mess with their breakfast porridge and generally being a nuisance to everyone, so it was impossible to hear the news on the wireless.

Anne just about managed to hold on to her patience as she bundled them into their coats and boots, picked up her bag of shoes and packed lunches and went out to meet Sally in the yard.

'Are you all right, Anne?' the younger girl asked as the three little ones raced off to join Charlie and Ernie, who were swinging on the gate down the lane. 'You look a bit peaky, if you don't mind me saying so.'

'I didn't sleep too well,' she confessed, 'but that's probably because I'm overtired.'

Sally grinned knowingly. 'It must have been a good leave after all. Lucky you. I'd swap a good night's sleep for a couple of days tucked up with my John and no mistake.'

They walked in amicable silence as the boys raced ahead and the little ones tried to keep up with them. Emily soon became fractious because the others were leaving her behind, so Anne picked her up and carried her until they reached the nursery school. There was no sight of Charlie – he must have already caught the bus, because Ernie was now running back to the school.

Anne went through the usual routine of kissing the girls, telling them to be good and handing over their indoor shoes and lunches to Sally, but she wasn't really concentrating, for she could see George waiting for her in the school playground. 'I'll see you later,' she said to Sally.

'Are you sure you're all right, Anne? You look as if you're suffering from more than a sleepless night.'

'I'll tell you about it this evening,' she murmured. She turned away quickly and headed for the smiling figure waiting at the school gate, knowing that by the end of the day his smile would probably not be in evidence.

George's grin broadened as she approached. 'It's good to have you back,' he said, closing the gate behind her. 'The children will be delighted to see you after their two weeks with Agatha Booth.'

She returned his smile. 'It's good to be back,' she said truthfully. 'And I was sorry to miss the dance. I heard you were quite the show-stopper.'

He blushed and couldn't quite meet her gaze. 'Well, you had other things on your mind, I'm sure – and I hardly think my dancing was anything special.'

'But the girls said you were marvellous and partnered everyone.' Her smile was teasing. 'I understand you even had the nerve to take Agatha for a turn on the floor. Now that's what I call brave.'

He chuckled. 'It was more foolhardy than brave,' he said. 'I felt I was in the clutches of an armoured tank, being steered across the floor pressed tightly against that enormous, corseted bosom. But she was surprisingly light on her feet for such a big woman.'

Anne knew she couldn't put things off any longer. 'George,' she began hesitantly, 'do you think I could come and discuss something with you during break time?'

'Of course. My door is always open, you know that, Anne.'

'We'll talk later then,' she murmured. She hurried inside and found Belinda in the cloakroom repairing her lipstick.

'I say, who's a lucky girl then?' she said, giving Anne a hug. 'Goodness, what a wonderful surprise for you to have Martin home on leave. No wonder you didn't show at the dance. They say the beds at the Shepherd's Arms are very comfortable.'

Anne listened to her prattling on about what fun the dance had been, and how she'd been amazed at how quickly George had learnt all the steps and had proved to be quite the thing on the floor. As she nodded and smiled and made the appropriate noises, all Anne could think about was the fact that soon she would have to leave, and she'd probably never see George or Belinda again.

'I say, Anne, have you heard a word I said? You've been miles away. Is something bothering you?'

She was saved from answering by the loud clanging of the bell and the great surge of small children jostling their way through the doors into the main classroom for assembly. Promising to catch up with Belinda's news at lunchtime, she followed the mad skirmish, her emotions in turmoil.

'But you can't leave,' protested George two hours later. 'There's absolutely no possibility of finding another qualified teacher before the end of term – and besides–'

'I understand,' she interrupted, 'but he's my husband, George, and he wants me and the children to go back home.'

He sat forward in his leather chair and rested his withered hand on the desk between them. 'But why now, Anne? What's happened to make him ask such a thing of you? You're settled here, the children are happy, and it's much safer than back on the coast.'

She bit her lip. 'The reasons are complicated, George, and I'm sorry, but I'm not willing to explain them.'

He regarded her levelly as the noise from the playground drifted into the small office. 'Do you want to leave?' he asked finally. 'Or are you just doing this out of loyalty to your husband?'

The dilemma of wanting to be loyal to Martin and the opposition she felt to leaving this safe haven had plagued her throughout the night and she still had no real answer. 'I don't really want to leave,' she admitted softly. 'But–'

'But you love him enough to sacrifice every-thing you've built here – even your children's safety – to do as he asks,' he said flatly.

'Don't condemn me, George,' she said, strug-gling not to cry. 'It's a hard enough thing to do as it is. And without the support of my friends, it will just make it even harder.'

'I'm sorry,' he replied. 'That was harsh. I hope Martin realises what a very lucky man he is to have a wife like you. But I'm afraid he's going to have a long wait before his wishes are granted.'

'I know it will take time to find someone to take my place. But I would appreciate it if you could do your best.'

'It's not really up to me, Anne. You see, things have changed over the past couple of days, and I'm sorry, but you won't be going anywhere.'

She frowned. 'What on earth are you talking about?'

'You haven't heard the news on the wireless this morning?' She shook her head and he carried on. 'As you know, there have been rumours flying around for weeks about something big about to happen, and it looks as if finally they might actually be true.'

'But what's that got to do with me going back to Cliffehaven?'

'All travel along the south coast has been cancelled until further notice, except for members of the armed forces. There will be no permits issued, no county borders crossed and certainly no way back to Cliffehaven.'

Anne didn't know how she felt as she slumped back into the chair. She was elated she now had a valid reason for not leaving, but also saddened by the fact she hadn't been totally honest with Martin and told him she really hadn't wanted to leave in the first place. The relief that the decision had been taken out of her hands was like a great weight being lifted from her shoulders. She just hoped that Martin wouldn't be too upset by it. If there was an invasion – and it looked most likely now the travel ban was in place – then there would be retaliations, and Cliffehaven would become a prime target.

'I'm sorry this has come as a bit of a shock,' George continued. 'I did try to tell you earlier, but you were so set on doing the right thing by your husband you didn't let me get a word in edge-ways.'

Anne took a deep, tremulous breath. 'I have to admit, I feel much easier knowing it's no longer possible. Thank you, George, for being so under-standing. You really are a very good friend, and I'm sorry I snapped earlier.'

'I'm just glad we're not losing you,' he said with a shy smile. 'Now let's go and help Belinda with those children. It sounds as if they're running wild out there.'

14

RAF Cliffe, 29th April

Martin tossed and turned in bed, unable to dispel his sense of unease, until eventually he gave up on the idea of sleep. Turning on the light, he looked at his watch: three-thirty. He decided to read Anne's letters again. He'd been back at the aero-drome for almost two weeks and she had written several times since, giving him all her news.

Carefully folding her latest one back into its envelope, he placed it between the pages of the book he'd been meaning to start the previous day, then, with a heavy heart, got dressed. The combined forces briefing was scheduled for four o'clock.

He'd known about the plans for an Allied invasion on the French beaches for some time, so he hadn't been surprised when it was announced that all civilian travel was to be strictly curtailed until further notice. Yet it had felt as if fate was working against him, keeping Anne and the children down there with those Germans. And although it seemed that Violet's new arrangements for the men meant they had fewer opportunities to fraternise, the mere fact that they were there, and Anne couldn't leave, niggled away at him.

He donned the prickly woollen flying suit over his long combinations and thick vest, fastened the buttons and sat down to pull on the fleece-lined boots. After slipping on his uniform jacket and cap, he grabbed his leather flying jacket and parachute pack then made his way out of the officers' sleeping quarters along with the others.

It was still dark outside, but the USAAF 8th had already arrived from Biggin Hill. Their B-17s were vast black shadows lined up on the main runway, the propellers spinning as the engines were fired up by the ground crew carrying out last-minute checks. This would be his third op – or mission, as the Yanks called them – since returning from leave, and he felt the usual tension in his shoulders and butterflies in his stomach.

He went into the crowded briefing room and

returned the men's salutes before sitting to listen to the American in charge go through his instructions. The raid was being led by the USAAF, with the RAF providing extra fighter defence. There would be two main groups, the 392nd and the 44th – the latter responsible for the raid on Berlin. Martin and his fellow officers would be escorting the 44th.

The American Lieutenant General pointed out the three targets and the flight paths they would take on the large map pinned to the wall and told the fighter pilots under his command how they should make their formations, timing each wing in synchronisation so that every beehive fully protected the bombers. Martin knew he was preaching to the converted. These men were experienced veterans now, and even the youngest sprog had become battle-hardened. But the senior officer was right to attend to every detail, for things had to be done correctly – this was not the time for showing off and going rogue. Too many lives were at stake.

He listened as the man went through his instructions for his huge bomber force of eighteen crews – ten men to every B-17, and another ten for the B-24s – and Martin surveyed the serious faces of the young men who sat before him. By the end of the day there would more than likely be more names scrubbed from the blackboard. Martin felt his stomach clench. He had a nagging feeling that this op would not go well.

He silently berated himself for this negative thinking and tuned back in to what the American was saying. As he came to the end of his briefing everyone stood and saluted before tramping out of the room in search of breakfast, the thud of their boots echoing on the wooden floor, their voices and laughter a little too loud and forced. They were all feeling the tension.

Martin wasn't hungry, so he settled for a large mug of black coffee and escaped the noise of the canteen for the cold damp air outside. The pale grey light of pre-dawn spread slowly across the horizon, making the sky above it seem darker and deeper. He watched as the grey became iridescent pearl tinged with pink and tangerine, leaching through the night velvet to reveal the curve of the landscape. It would be good flying weather, and if it was the same over Germany, then their targets would be clearly visible.

He glanced across at the squadrons of Bristol Blenheims, Lancasters, B-24s and B-17s, and then at the mass gathering of Mosquitoes, Spitfires, Mustangs, Thunderbolts, Typhoons and Hurricanes. They would be joined by several squadrons of Lightning fighters coming from an American base further west just before they reached the other side of the Channel. This was going to be one hell of a big raid, and if all went well – which he had to believe it would – then Berlin would be smashed to smithereens.

He took the mug of coffee into his office and made sure that all his paperwork was in order: his mess bills paid and his will up to date – every man had to write a will the minute he joined the RAF – for it was important to avoid any extra distress to the bereaved families by not having one. Then he sat smoking his pipe, deep in thought,

279

preparing himself for what was to come.

Almost two hours later he propped his cold pipe in the ashtray, pulled on his fleece-lined leather jacket and wrestled his arms through the straps of his parachute pack. He was just reaching for his hat when his concentration was broken by 'Pinky' Champion coming in.

Pinky saluted. 'Sorry, sir, but I meant to drop these off to you last night.'

Martin took the three envelopes and raised a brow in query.

'It's my will, and letters for my mother and Rita in case I don't make it, sir.' His youthful face was solemn.

'But you've already written a will,' Martin objected, placing the envelopes on the desk blotter for his adjutant to deal with.

'I know, sir, but I've given it a lot of thought and made a new one. I hope you don't mind, sir?'

Martin shook his head then followed Champion outside, thinking how wrong it was for boys of his age to have to think about such things, when they should be enjoying life and the company of their girls. Little Rita and Matthew Champion were very well suited, and he suspected it wouldn't be long before he popped the question – which of course would delight Peggy and Cordelia, for they liked nothing better than having a good cry at a wedding.

He was smiling at the thought as he checked the time. It was seven-twenty. Only another five minutes before they were ordered to scramble.

'Here we go again,' said Roger Makepeace,

shrugging into his parachute pack. 'I'm rather hoping to get back early enough to pop down and join Kitty for supper, so I hope Jerry won't hold us up as long as they did the other day.'

He stroked his moustache and twirled the ends, looking up at the sky and then across to the gathering of Flying Fortresses, each fuselage emblazoned with a nickname, and a picture of a half-naked girl. 'Noisy damned things,' he muttered without rancour. 'But that's the Yanks all over. I've never known men to make such a racket. But they're jolly good chaps for all that, and I don't know what we'd have done without them.'

'I say, Tash,' said Freddy, joining them with his usual bright smile. 'It's a jolly good show this morning. I don't think I've seen this many crates all in one place before.'

'It's one of the biggest raids yet,' said Martin, emerging from his thoughts about Matthew and Rita. 'If you'd been listening at the briefing instead of mooning about Charlotte and the babies, you'd know there'll be two thousand planes going in. The rest are joining us later.'

Freddy clamped a heavy hand on his shoulder. 'Don't worry, I was listening. But you have to admit, Martin, twins are definitely something to be proud of.'

Martin's smile was affectionate, for the man from Argentina never lost his joy in life, never suffered from lack of confidence or got down in the dumps, no matter what happened. 'Of course they are – and I dread to think how insufferable you'll be once they're born – especially if they're boys. You're bad enough now, strutting about like an old rooster,' he teased.

Freddy threw back his head and crowed several times, which made the others turn and grin. He then roared with laughter. 'The strut has been perfected, but I think the crowing needs a bit of work. I'll practise during the flight to Berlin.'

'Nothing you do up there would surprise me,' said Roger. 'I hear all sorts of rubbish from you through my earpiece – and I do rather wish you wouldn't sing. You sound like a crow with constipation.'

'You're only jealous, old chum,' said Freddy, his handsome face wreathed in a smile, his dark eyes bright with humour.

Martin realised the time was fast approaching for them to leave, so he shook their hands. 'Good luck and Godspeed,' he said just as the bell began to clang.

The hundreds of men were galvanised into action and moved as one towards their planes.

Freddy slapped his two best pals on the back. 'The drinks are on you when we get back,' he shouted over the increasing thunder of engines before running athletically towards his Spitfire to join his co-pilot.

'Keep your end up old chap,' shouted Roger, breaking into an ungainly trot towards his Hurricane.

Martin ran over to his one-man Spitfire and clambered in, hampered by his bulky clothes and the parachute pack. He strapped himself in, pulled on his gloves and goggles and then adjusted the headphones and mouthpiece so he could hear the orders from the tower and speak to the men on his wing.

As the engineer fastened down the canopy and removed the chocks, Martin could already see the enormous B-17s lumbering down runway three and then lifting slowly into the air, the four powerful engines screaming with the strain. The accompanying Mosquitoes, Spitfires, Halifaxes and Typhoon fighter bombers sailed lightly into the air from runway four, and before the next wave of aircraft took off, they were already mere dots in the sky.

Martin checked that all his men were present and correct, and then informed the control tower his squadron was ready for take-off. The Spitfire's Rolls-Royce Merlin engine burbled smoothly beneath him and he patted her instrument panel fondly before settling back into the seat to await his turn, his gaze flitting momentarily to the small photograph of Anne and the children that he'd stuck beneath the ignition switch. He would try and telephone her tonight, he decided.

Now it was the turn of the 44th Group, and the next squadron of heavy-bellied American bombers thundered down runway two to be followed by a squadron of Lancasters. Martin and the men around him began their own progress down runway one in pursuit.

The Spitfire was light to handle and quick to respond, and as Martin throttled up to its full 1,175 horsepower, it lifted from the runway into the clear blue sky like a bird. Keeping an eye on his instruments, he climbed to 16,000 feet, where he and his men formed a protective shield around the B-17s and B-24. Roger, who was on

Martin's wing, gave him a thumbs up and Martin returned the gesture, the adrenaline rush of being part of such a huge attacking force wiping away all thoughts but the task in hand.

The primary target was Berlin, but the orders from the USAAF Command also included two large industrial installations outside the city. If things went to schedule, they should be landing back in Blighty by 16:00 hours, and in plenty of time for afternoon tea.

Cissy Reilly folded her arms tightly across her chest and stood with the other WAAFs by the administration block to watch the hundreds of planes taking off. She'd hoped to speak to Martin and the others to wish them luck before they'd left, but with so many men wandering about the aerodrome, she'd missed them all, except for Matthew Champion. He'd given her the most terrific hug, and she'd been quite emotional as she'd seen him fly away.

'Hey, what's with the tears, Cissy?' asked her friend Emma. 'At least your chap's not up there,' she said with a consoling squeeze on her arm.

'I know, and I'm very grateful. But some of my best friends are, and it was such a huge show I couldn't help but get emotional.'

'Silly girl,' Emma teased. 'Come on, we've got office work to clear, and I know for a fact that you're way behind with your reports.'

Cissy took one last lingering look at the busy runways and then reluctantly headed for the office and the dreaded paperwork she never seemed able to clear.

Cliffehaven

Peggy had been inexplicably restless throughout the night. Eventually she wrapped her dressing gown around herself and went into the kitchen to make a pot of tea. On hearing the first wave of aircraft going over, she took her cup outside into the clear early morning and stood on the front step to watch as they came over the house and out towards the Channel.

She wasn't alone, for her neighbours had also come out to watch, so she nodded a greeting to them before turning her attention back to the overhead display of awesome power.

The Flying Fortresses and Lancaster engines were deep and throbbing, sending their vibrations right through her and making the ground shudder. The sound of the lighter fighter planes was almost lost within that thunder, and her tears of pride and patriotism blurred her vision as she waved and cheered them on.

'I don't think they can see you, Auntie Peg,' shouted Rita above the almost deafening noise as she and the rest of the household came out to join Peggy on the steps.

'It's silly, I know,' she admitted, 'but I couldn't help it.'

They stood together, the residents of Beach View, looking skyward as squadron after squadron roared overhead, their vast number spread across the sky as far as the eye could see, their shadows chasing over the rooftops and gardens and then on the water, which was becoming ruffled by the huge downdraught.

Ron brought out a chair for Cordelia as the seemingly endless show continued, and held an excited Daisy in his arms, pointing out the different planes.

Peggy folded her arms tightly about her waist, knowing that Martin was probably up there along with Kitty's husband and brother, and Rita's lovely Matthew. 'Bring them home,' she prayed. 'Please God, bring them home.'

Allied Raid on Berlin

They had crossed the Channel at 20,000 feet and were now at 24,000 feet above the Netherlands with about an hour and-a half to go before they were flying across Germany towards Berlin. There had been a bit of flak sent up as they'd reached the occupied Dutch and Belgian coastline, but so far there had been nothing much to worry about – although by now the Germans would know they were coming, so there wasn't much point in maintaining radio silence.

The pack of Thunderbolts and Lightnings had joined them right on schedule, and his Spit was performing beautifully as usual. Everyone sounded relaxed, if the chatter in his headphones was anything to go by, and thankfully, Freddy had stopped singing and crowing.

Martin patted his jacket pocket in search of his pipe. It didn't seem to be there, but he was sure he'd picked it up before leaving the office. With a cluck of annoyance, he tried the other pocket, and then the ones in his uniform jacket. In rising panic he then searched for it in the deep map pocket of his trouser leg, but it wasn't there either.

'It's got to be,' he muttered, furiously searching every pocket again. 'I never leave it behind.'

'Something up over there?' said the voice in his ear.

Martin looked across at Roger, who was watching him from his Hurricane cockpit, a broad grin on his face. 'Nothing's up,' he replied. 'I've just got an itch, that's all.'

'It's a bugger, isn't it? Especially with all this kit on.'

Martin nodded and surreptitiously did another search. But it became horribly obvious that he'd left his pipe behind – and as he'd carried it on every op since joining the RAF, it had become something of a talisman, and he felt quite naked without it.

Determined not to let stupid superstition unsettle him or get in the way of the task ahead, he checked his instruments and flight path, and then called for updates by the rest of his group. They were about to cross the border into Germany.

He could see the huge attacking force sprawled across the sky, their shadows racing across the landscape far below, the sun glinting on metal wings and tail fins. It would be a matter of minutes before the smaller 392nd Group peeled away to bomb the secondary targets before joining up again with the 44th to attack Berlin.

Martin watched as the squadrons in front of him peeled off left and right for their targets. His

287

squadron was now leading, and as they approached Hannover, he knew they were less than an hour away from their prime target.

They came from nowhere, wing to wing in two long parallel lines of Messerschmitt 109s and Focke-Wulf 190s, guns blazing as they made a level pass right through the formation.

Martin's reaction was swift, plunging the Spitfire beneath their flight path and turning tightly to fire at them as they raced back for a second attack. He was aware of the other fighter pilots doing the same, attacking, evading, twisting, turning, firing at will as the 190s and 109s kept coming back. It was vital to keep the enemy fighters fully occupied so the heavy bombers could proceed unmolested – for should they take a hit, the bombs they carried would explode and the large crews would stand little chance of survival.

He chased a Messerschmitt across the skies, hauling on the joystick to send the Spitfire soaring, and then yanked it back down again so he rolled into a backward dive in an attempt to get behind the enemy – always aware of what was going on around him in the skirmishing dogfights. The g-force was terrific, pressing him back into his seat, the blood rushing to his head until he straightened out, only to find the other pilot had done the same thing, and now it was a deadly game of chase played out amid the swirling chaos of dozens of other dogfights and heavy flak.

He glimpsed a B-17 take evasive action, veering sharply to the right only to collide with another B-17, losing its entire tail section and going out of control into a steep, spinning dive, ending in a massive explosion as it hit the ground. On making a second overhead loop in an effort to shake off the 109 which was still shooting at him, he saw the second B-17 had lost part of its wing, and there were only two parachutes floating down.

He pressed the firing button, stitching a line along the fuselage and shattering the 109's windscreen. From the corner of his eye he saw the plane plunge out of control, black smoke rising from its engines, then became fully occupied by another attack from a Focke-Wulf.

Heavy flak was hitting them from all sides now as they continued to battle against the enemy fighters who were making it impossible to defend the American bombers. The Thunderbolts and Mustangs wheeled and swirled, tracer fire zipping too close for comfort as a Lightning was hit and went down in a billow of smoke.

Despite the cold, the sweat was pouring down Martin's face and soaking through his flight-suit. This sort of dogfight was hell, for one moment he was thrust back into his seat on a tight turn, the next he was upside down, hanging in the safety harness, his head almost banging against the canopy, his insides rebelling. Every second felt like a lifetime.

He dispatched the Focke and went to help Roger, who had two of the bastards on his tail.

As he swerved left and right and fired salvo after salvo, he saw Roger's Hurricane taking a hit in the flanks by the heavy flak of 22mm shells. Flames shot from the fuselage, thick black smoke pluming beneath it. He saw Roger struggling to take control, realised the Hurricane was about to veer towards him and quickly got out of the way before they collided.

'Get out, 421,' he yelled. 'Your arse is on fire.'

Martin didn't have time to see if Roger had made it out, or if his parachute had opened, for there was a warning shout from Matthew. 'Bogies at twelve o'clock.'

His heart almost stopped as he looked up to see at least sixty enemy fighters zooming down towards them. He opened fire and made a steep climb, closely followed by eight Allied Thunderbolts. The op was compromised, men and aircraft being slaughtered, or forced to turn tail and limp home, and now it was just a question of staying alive long enough to take as many of the enemy down with him as he could.

The ensuing battle for survival seemed to go on for ever as the enemy fighters came to attack again and again. He saw numerous B-17s take direct hits, Spitfires blown to smithereens, Lightnings hammered by shells and spun into death spirals, and numerous, explosive collisions.

Martin had lost count of the enemy planes he'd shot down, but he heard through the headphones that the bombing of the secondary targets had been successful, and the 44th Group were closing in on Berlin.

A B-24 plunged past him, narrowly missing his wing as it rocketed to earth and crashed with a series of massive explosions, the updraught rocking his Spitfire. He got it back under control and went after a pair of Focke 190s that were giving Matthew a hard time.

But Matthew was already in trouble. His Spitfire was belching thick black smoke and the canopy was shattered.

There wasn't time for Martin to see if he'd managed to get out – he was too busy trying to get rid of the three Messerschmitt fighters on his own tail. The fuel indicator needle was close to zero, the red light flickering, warning him the tank was dangerously close to being empty.

He managed to cripple one Messerschmitt, but then another took its place, followed by five more.

All eight opened fire. Their bullets rammed into the Spitfire and his left wing burst into flames.

Martin tried to take her up in a tight, fast climb in an attempt to put the fire out, but it had too strong a hold. The Spitfire was so damaged it couldn't maintain height and speed, and the enemy planes were still on his tail.

He ducked automatically as another salvo of bullets zipped past his head and thudded into the fuselage, cutting the fuel-line. The Spitfire coughed and spluttered, then the engine died, the propellers grinding to a halt as the flames spread along the wing. It was time to get out

The enemy fighters peeled away to become embroiled with a pack of Thunderbolts, and Martin shoved open the canopy. The Spitfire executed a lazy dip towards what looked like a large forest below, and he knew it would only be seconds before she spiralled out of control – taking him with her.

He released the safety harness and struggled to get out, the Spitfire's plunge already speeding up; the g-force so strong it made any movement almost impossible. He clung to the rim of the

291

cockpit, placing a foot on the undamaged wing for balance, desperately trying to combat the downdraught and keep some sense of spatial awareness as the plane spun even faster and the ground came up to meet him.

Then his boot slipped on the fuel-slicked wing, his hand was ripped from the lip of the cockpit and he was tossed helplessly backwards into the spinning tail. It thudded into him, taking his breath and knocking him senseless before he had time to pull the rip-cord on his parachute.

RAF Cliffe

Cissy had finally managed to get through the paperwork, and since she had a couple of hours off duty, she'd slipped into the plotting room to watch the unfolding battle being marked out by the girls moving miniature replicas of planes about on the vast table map as the reports came in from the observers and pilots.

The raid had been a disaster for the Americans, with men and planes annihilated before they'd even reached Berlin. Even so, the two minor targets and the primary target of Berlin had been successfully bombed, along with what was called a 'target of opportunity', although the result of that one had not been recorded. The damage suffered by the rest of the bombers had been too great to fulfil the mission, and there were reports of many being shot down, and very few sightings of parachutes recorded.

Cissy felt quite sick as she watched squadrons

of Allied fighters and bombers being removed from the chart. Hearing the drone of incoming aircraft approaching the aerodrome, she quietly went outside to watch them land. It was four o'clock in the afternoon but felt much later, for the hours had dragged very slowly since they'd taken off this morning.

Six battle-damaged B-24s came in coughing and spluttering to rattle their way towards their positions near the vast hangars. They were followed by two Flying Fortresses, both making emergency landings which brought the fire crews running. Bullet-ridden Lightnings and Thunderbolts streaked in, some on one wheel, others belly-flopping and skidding onto the grass at the side of the runway.

As Cissy watched the first of the Spitfires, Hurricanes and Mosquitoes arrive, hope began to blossom that Martin, Freddy, Roger and Matt would be amongst them. But the numbers on the tail-fins didn't tally with her hopes, and she had to tamp down on the awful, sick dread that was slowly growing with each plane that came in.

She watched more fighters and B-17s limp home, battle-scarred by their encounter with the enemy on the other side of the Channel. Still there was no sign of Martin and the others.

Hearing the heavy-bellied thunder of a Flying Fortress approaching, she watched as it performed a wide circle above the perimeter of the aerodrome in an attempt to lose height before landing. The undercarriage was down and it didn't seem to be at all damaged, and Cissy gave a sigh of relief that at least that ten-man crew had made it back safely.

The enormous explosion sent her stumbling, shattering windows and rocking the ground beneath her feet. She instinctively curled up tightly, hands over her head, back pressed against the wall of the ops room, as bits of the Fortress spun in all directions, scything through metal as easily as a hot knife through butter.

She watched through trembling fingers as splinters of glass spat viciously through the air and part of a heavy engine plunged straight through the roof of the ablutions block. A propeller went winging off to become embedded in the side of a B-24, and ammunition from the gunners' store of weapons whistled through the air and thudded within inches of her head.

She crawled beneath the hut, careless of ripping her stockings and getting her uniform dirty, as the huge wheels spun like burning Catherine wheels across all four runways, one of them crashing into a Mosquito that had just landed and turning it instantly into a fireball. She gave a cry of distress, covered her ears and curled once again into a tight ball, her eyes squeezed tightly shut. She simply couldn't watch any more.

Fire bells clanged, alarms went off. Shouts rang across the aerodrome and she could hear the sound of running feet and racing engines, the heavy hiss of water being pumped and flames being extinguished. She could smell burning as the sky rained flaming parachute packs, bits of seating and shards of lethal metal, and was frozen with terror.

Cliffehaven

Peggy had continued to be restless throughout the day waiting for the pilots to return safe and sound to Cliffe Aerodrome. Ron had finally become so impatient with her endless sweeping, dusting, washing and cleaning that he ordered her to fetch her coat. He was taking her and Daisy for a walk into the hills so they could watch the planes come back in.

Peggy didn't really want to go, but as Ron had already dressed Daisy and perched her on his shoulders, she didn't have much choice. Walking hills wasn't her idea of fun, but she needed to do something to keep her mind off her worries, for unknown to Ron, she'd found the letter from Jim in his trouser pocket when she'd been sorting through the laundry – and having read it, knew without a doubt that Jim was in a very dangerous situation. But she'd said nothing to anyone about this, knowing that Ron had only been trying to protect her from the truth, and it was her own curiosity that had brought about her anguish.

She tramped up the hill behind him, wheezing fit to bust as she reached the top. Ron was striding ahead, Daisy still perched on his shoulders singing along with him in her piping voice as Harvey dashed back and forth, when the first of the American planes appeared above the cliffs.

'Hold on a minute, Ron,' she gasped, bent double and fighting for breath. 'You're going too fast.'

'Ach, you're out of condition, wee girl,' he replied. 'Do this every day and you might even get as fit as me.'

'If I did this every day I'd be dead,' she panted, pressing her hand to the stitch in her side. She looked towards the Channel as more planes began to appear, and as they roared and whined and hiccupped their way towards Cliffe Aerodrome, she got her breath back and followed Ron to where they'd get the best view of them all landing.

'To be sure, there's a lot of damage,' Ron muttered around the stem of his pipe. 'Look at that one; it can barely maintain enough height to get over the control tower.'

'Daisy, don't go too far,' Peggy warned fretfully as the little girl wandered off to see what Harvey had found in the long grass. She turned back to watch a Flying Fortress make slow, ever-descending turns around the perimeter of the airfield. 'At least that one doesn't look damaged.'

The explosion made them all jump and Peggy ran to gather up Daisy, who was screaming with fright. 'It's all right,' she soothed. 'You're all right. Mummy's here.'

Daisy nestled into her neck, clinging tightly to her, and Peggy turned her horrified gaze back to the airfield. She could just make out the flying debris from the plane, could see the secondary fires which had sprung up in the wake of the burning wheels, and saw with sickening horror the ball of flame that had once been a Mosquito.

'Cissy's down there,' she breathed. And then her voice rose in pitch as the realisation took hold. 'Oh, my God, Ron, our Cissy's down there.'

Ron put his arm about her shoulder. 'She'll be

fine,' he said. 'Look, Peg, none of the buildings are alight – she'll have found somewhere safe to shelter.' He took Daisy from her and hugged them both to his heart. 'I can see the fire crews and crash teams going to work. They'll have the fires out and all of it cleared away before the rest of the boys come home, You'll see.'

Peggy looked over his shoulder fearfully as the buzz of fighter aircraft grew louder, accompanied by the heavy-bellied B-24 and more Flying Fortresses. They all looked battered, with bullet holes stitched along their sides, bits of tail-fin and wing missing. Some were flying on one engine when there should have been two or four; others had their gear still up even as they swooped low in preparation for landing.

'I've seen enough,' she murmured. 'I want to go home and wait for Cissy to telephone me.'

Ron nodded his understanding and they turned away from the airfield and headed back to Beach View, their thoughts focused on Cissy and Martin and the boys who'd become such an intrinsic part of their family.

RAF Cliffe

Cissy emerged from her hiding place, rather shamefaced, to find that all the fires were out and the debris had been cleared from the runways. She looked down at her shredded stockings and the smears of dirt on her uniform jacket and skirt. She'd also torn her jacket sleeve, probably from a nail sticking out from beneath the hut, but in the circumstances, none of it really mattered.

She was still shaking as she headed for the WAAF accommodation to sponge down her uniform and find a fresh pair of stockings. The planes were still coming in, but there was no sight yet of Matt and the others. It was going to be a long, anxious night of waiting.

Cliffehaven

The blackout curtains had been drawn, supper was over and Daisy was soundly asleep. Fran was on duty at the local hospital and Ivy was working the night shift at the armaments factory, but Sarah and Rita sat close together at the kitchen table, while Cordelia tried to concentrate on the evening news and Ron polished his boots. Peggy sat by the fire opposite Cordelia smoking one cigarette after another.

The report of the raid was good, for they'd hit their targets, and the number of downed German fighter planes meant that the enemy force had been greatly weakened. There was no mention of how many planes the Allies had lost, and the reporter went on to talk about the unfortunate refusal of Sweden to relinquish their neutrality and co-operate with the Allies – and the arrival in London of the Premiers of New Zealand, Rhodesia, South Africa and Canada to attend the Imperial Conference.

'What the heck's an Imperial Conference when it's at home?' asked Rita, whose nerves were as stretched as everyone else's.

'It's probably just an excuse to stay in a posh hotel and eat food we haven't seen for years,' Ron muttered. 'I'd like to know where Churchill gets his big fat cigars, because there's no shop around here that sells 'em.'

'You're just being grumpy as usual,' Cordelia retorted.

Ron ignored the snipe and looked at Peggy, who was twisting the hem of her apron in nerveless fingers. 'You'd think that girl would phone and put us out of our misery,' he grumbled. 'What on earth is she doing up there?'

Peggy shrugged. 'I don't know, Ron. But I do wish you wouldn't keep going on about it. She'll telephone when she gets permission.'

Ron was about to reply when there was a knock at the front door. Everyone froze, and when it came again, louder this time, it was Ron who went into the hall.

Everyone got to their feet, their eyes fixed on the door to the hallway, their, hands reaching for one another as the conversation continued, too low to carry as far as the kitchen. Peggy could feel Rita trembling beside her, could hear the thud of her own heart and the rapid pulse beating in her neck as she held her breath – waiting – waiting – waiting.

Ron was grim-faced when he returned to the kitchen, but he wasn't alone, for his arm was about a tear-streaked Cissy, and behind them was a man in the uniform of the USAAF, the weak kitchen light catching on his medals and the gold decoration of his cap.

Peggy let out the breath she'd been holding as

her daughter flew sobbing into her arms. She clasped her close, her fearful gaze on the man standing in her kitchen – the man who would only have come if there was really bad news.

'Sit down, Peggy, love,' said Ron. 'First Lieutenant Grant has something he has to tell us.'

Peggy's legs were shaking so badly she almost fell into the chair. She kept a tight hold on Cissy's hand and reached for Rita, who was wide-eyed with fear. 'Where's Martin?' she asked, her voice high with anxiety. 'Why didn't he come?'

The American officer looked at Peggy. 'I'm sorry, ma'am, but I have witness reports that Group Captain Black was shot down. We have no further reports, but someone thought they saw his parachute open in time, so there is hope that he landed safely.'

Peggy burst into tears. 'Does Anne, his wife, know? And what about the others? Roger and Freddy and Matthew?'

'An officer will be visiting Mrs Black this evening,' he replied, clearly uncomfortable at being the focus of such terrified attention. 'And the same applies to the wives of Wing Commander Makepeace and Squadron Leader Pargeter,' he added softly.

The gasp echoed through the room and Cordelia burst into tears. 'All of them?' asked Peggy hysterically. 'Are you telling me that all of them are dead?'

'No, ma'am,' he said hastily. 'Parachutes were reported in each case, so we are hopeful they have survived.'

'Dear God,' breathed Peggy, the terrible images

of military figures knocking on the farmhouse door – and at the little cottage in Briar Lane – flashing through her head. 'Those poor girls – those poor, dear girls.'

The American was clearly finding it very difficult to bring such devastating news to this house of women, and his expression was deeply solemn as he turned his gaze regretfully to Rita, who immediately went ashen and had to sit down. 'I regret to inform you, Miss Smith, that–'

'No,' she screamed. 'No, no, no.' Tears streamed down her face as she covered her ears.

Peggy wrapped her arms about the sobbing girl, her heart breaking with the terrible sadness that had befallen all of them. 'Go on,' she said quietly to the man who was struggling to keep his composure.

'Squadron Leader Matthew Champion's Spitfire was shot down just north of Hannover,' he continued reluctantly. 'Witness reports coming in are that there was no sign that either of the crew managed to parachute to safety.'

Peggy's tears increased as she hugged the sobbing girl to her heart, not wanting to believe that such a terrible thing had happened to dear young Matthew, with his cheeky smile, his winning manners and his deep and abiding love for her little Rita. And what of Martin, Roger and Freddy? Had they survived? Were they even now being taken prisoner – or were they lying injured or dead somewhere in a German field?

The American cleared his throat as he clutched at his decorated cap. 'His family will be informed tonight,' he said gruffly. 'I'm so sorry for your

301

loss.' He snapped off a salute, nodded to Ron and made a quick exit, closing the front door behind him softly.

As Rita and Cissy clung to Peggy, her heart was heavy with sorrow for all the girls who'd lost their men tonight. Their pain was like a knife already opening a chasm in their lives which Peggy knew could never be filled.

It was a night of tears, of profound sorrow mixed with moments of agonising hope that despite all evidence to the contrary, their men had survived against the odds.

After the local vicar had departed from Owlet Farm, and she'd assured Vi that she preferred to be alone to absorb the terrifying news, Anne sat at her sleeping children's bedsides in silent, tearful prayer. She was tortured with guilt that she should have wanted to go home when he'd asked; and filled with longing for her mother's comfort.

In the tiny cottage in Briar Lane, Kitty and Charlotte lay curled together on Kitty's bed, their unborn babies moving between them as their tears mingled, and they clung to each other as fiercely as they held on to their hopes and dreams for the future – for without hope, they were lost.

Ron had sat with Cordelia for what felt like hours as the old lady wept, not just for the lost boys, but for the girls and the babies they'd left behind. When she'd finally fallen into an exhausted sleep, he'd kissed her forehead, turned out the light and softly closed the door.

In the darkness of his basement bedroom, he silently shed his own tears, finding comfort in the warmth of the animals lying beside him, and in the tiny glimmer of hope that Martin and the boys *had* survived and would come home.

Sarah had tried to console Rita, but it seemed she preferred to deal with her anguish on her own, so she'd gone to the room she shared with Fran and lain awake staring into the long hours of darkness.

Rita had thought she wanted to cry alone, but was swept into a vortex of such pain that she could barely breathe. Needing the comfort of a mother, she crept down in the night to Peggy's bedroom, and within minutes was wrapped in her loving arms.

Cissy sat in the darkness of her childhood bedroom, staring out of the window as the moon slowly sailed across the sky. The fear and horror of the day had drained her to the point where she was almost numb and could shed no more tears. She'd lost too many friends over these past years, and although she thanked God that Randy was relatively safe in that French prison, this was the first time the war had really touched her family, and she could almost feel the terrible grief emanating from the walls of Beach View.

It was so very hard to keep strong, to take each blow on the chin and prepare for the next, when inside she was being torn apart.

The night was an agony for Peggy. It was vital she

303

stay in control of her emotions for her girls and offer comfort and solace – but how was that possible when every time she thought of those boys her heart broke all over again, and her spirits dwindled that little bit more? Was her lovely son-in-law lost to them? Was Anne a young widow – her babies never really getting the chance to know their father?

And then there was Jim. How long would it be before a telegram arrived at Beach View – or a grim-faced army officer came knocking at the door? She held Rita close, the fear for them all rising with every beat of her heart.

15

Somewhere in Germany

Martin drifted in and out of consciousness, only vaguely aware that his head hurt and every part of him felt bruised; that a strangely familiar voice was whispering to him to keep quiet; and of being carried over someone's shoulder through a forest.

When he finally opened his eyes he was utterly confused, and it was a moment before his vision cleared and the fog in his brain dissipated so he could absorb the unfamiliar surroundings. He could smell straw and cattle, dimly see high wooden rafters above him in shafts of light emanating through weathered timbers, and feel the warmth of the beasts as they shifted uneasily in the pen next to him. He was in a cattle byre or a barn. But where? And how did he get here? The memory returned of being flung from the Spit, his parachute still unopened as he was slammed into her tail-fin. He should be dead. So what miracle had saved him?

Upon hearing whispers from nearby, he tried to sit up, but his head hurt so badly he collapsed back with a groan.

'Jolly good, sir,' whispered the voice. 'Glad to see you're awake at last.'

He looked blearily at the figure kneeling beside him 'Forbes? Pilot Officer Forbes, is that really you?' he asked in a daze.

'Yes, sir. And, sir, you have to keep your voice down,' he whispered urgently. 'We're still in Germany, and we don't know if we can really trust this farmer.'

Martin gingerly sat up and took the proffered water canteen from the younger man. As he drank thirstily, he peered into the darkness but could see nothing. 'How many of us made it here?'

'Just you and me and a woman from the Resistance,' he whispered back. 'She's gone to see if it's safe for us to move on.'

Martin felt better now he'd had the water, but his head was pounding like the very devil. 'I don't suppose you've got an aspirin, Forbes?'

'Sorry, sir.'

A shaft of moonlight shone through the gaps in the weathered timbers, enabling Martin to see the young man more clearly. Allan Forbes was nineteen and one of Freddy's sprogs – a gifted pilot who, like his mentor, was inclined to be a bit gung-ho at times. 'The last thing I remember is being flung out of the plane with my parachute still in its pack. How come I'm still alive?'

'Well, sir, it was a bit of luck really, because I too had to bail out and happened to be passing at the time.'

'It was more than luck,' said a woman's soft voice. 'It was sheer bloody lunatic brilliance.'

Martin frowned; he recognised that voice. And as she emerged from the gloom into the splinters of light he saw a slight, dark-haired girl in peasant's rough clothing and could hardly believe it. 'Danuta?' he gasped.

'Shh, Martin.'

'But what ... how...?'

'I knew the raid was coming and waited with some of my colleagues to try and rescue as many of the downed pilots as we could.' She glanced across at Allan Forbes and grinned. 'You have him to thank for being alive, Martin. I've never seen such a thing in my life.'

'What did you do?'

Allan Forbes shrugged. 'It was a trick I'd seen at one of the flying club exhibitions. I wasn't awfully sure it would work, because you were out cold and a deadweight. But I knew I had to give it a go, sir.'

'He is too modest,' whispered Danuta, her dark eyes flashing with humour. 'I watched him go almost into free fall as he parachuted down to you – then he grabbed you by the parachute harness. He held on all the way down, and only dropped you when he hit the trees.'

Forbes reddened. 'I lost my grip. Sorry, sir.'

Martin squeezed his shoulder. 'Saying thank you seems inadequate, but I'll make sure you get a medal for that the minute we get home, Forbes.'

'You must get home first,' said Danuta, packing things away in a hessian bag. 'For now we must leave here before the farmer comes to milk the cows.'

Forbes took Martin's hand and helped him to his feet. 'Can you walk, sir?'

Martin nodded, even though his left ankle felt decidedly painful and every movement made his head thud, blurring his sight and sending stabs of pain down his neck. He grabbed the younger man's arm. 'What about the others? Do you know what happened to them?'

'Sorry, sir. I was too busy staying alive to see much.'

'Enough talk,' hissed Danuta. 'It will be sunrise soon.' She slung the hessian bag over her shoulder and tucked her Luger pistol into the thick leather belt holding up her trousers, then adjusted her sheepskin-lined coat so it covered it. 'From now on you must be silent,' she whispered.

At their nod she led them through the darkness of the byre into the pale moonlight.

They pressed against the old byre wall, looking out onto a clearing and a ramshackle cottage set some distance away. All was still but for a barn owl hooting close by, and at her signal, they moved swiftly across the open space to plunge into the safety of the dark, silent forest.

Cliffehaven

Cissy had barely slept, and was up and dressed and drinking tea in the kitchen with Ron by six o'clock. 'I have to go back on duty, Granda,' she said. 'There's nothing I can do here, and I'll be able to pick up more information at the airfield. Reports and witness statements will still be coming in, and you never know, someone might have seen something to give us a bit of hope.'

'Aye, let's pray that's the case,' he rumbled.

'Well, anything's better than seeing so many people upset and not being able to do anything about it. And besides, it's not fair on the other WAAFs to leave them with all my paperwork.'

'Ye're a brave young woman, Cissy. And it's proud of you I am.' He rubbed his rough hand gently against her powdered cheek. 'Will you walk with me over the hills? Or will you arrange transport?'

'I'd rather walk with you,' she murmured, stroking Harvey's head which was resting on her knee. 'It's been a long time since we went up there together.'

'Aye, you were just a wee wain with pigtails, all coltish limbs and boundless energy – and then you decided you were destined to become a star of stage and screen and abandoned your walks with your granda for tutus and ballet shoes,' he teased.

'They were happy days, though,' she said wistfully. 'It almost feels now that it was another world, and that young girl was simply a figment of my imagination.'

He patted her hand. 'Hold on to those memories, Cissy. They'll keep you going.'

He drained his cup of tea and reached for his stained old cap. Setting it firmly over his wayward hair, he shrugged into his equally filthy poaching coat and fastened the laces on his sturdy boots.

Harvey knew it was time for their walk and began to dance and whine excitedly.

Cissy eased the straps of her handbag and gas-mask box over her shoulder, thankful that she hadn't thought to bring more than a change of underwear and a bit of make-up with her.

'Are you ready for this, wee girl?' he asked. 'I set a fine pace, and your Mammy couldn't keep up with me yesterday.'

'As ready as I'll ever be,' she replied, placing the note to her mother on the table so she wouldn't miss it. 'And I think you'll find I'm quite fit after running about the aerodrome all day delivering messages.'

Ron locked the cat-flap he'd recently installed in the scullery door so Queenie couldn't follow them, and headed down the garden path.

Harvey jumped over the gate in his eagerness to gallop across the hill in search of interesting smells, and as he shot up the twitten between the backs of the houses, Cissy smiled. This was bringing back so many happy memories that she was feeling better already, despite the lack of sleep and the awful experiences of the previous day.

They set off at a brisk pace, following Harvey up the hill and along the relatively flatter ground at the top. They paused for a moment to look at the sea glittering in the rising sun, and then over the sprawling town that was just waking up on this early Sunday morning. Then they turned away towards the spot where they could look down over the fields to the airfield.

Cissy felt refreshed, the cobwebs of the night blown away in the light, cold breeze and the unaccustomed exercise. 'Thanks, Granda,' she said, giving him a hug. 'I needed to be reminded of what it is we're fighting for. And you're right. Those memories have given me heart.'

She kissed his bristly cheek. 'I'll go on alone from here,' she said. 'Look after Mam and Rita for me, won't you?'

'Aye,' he said gruffly. 'To be sure, I always will. Take care, Cissy.'

Ron watched the small, solitary figure going down the hill to cross the country lane and eventually disappear from sight as she rounded the bend on her way to the main entrance gate of the aerodrome.

He gave a deep sigh of longing for the golden days when he'd carried her on his shoulders, just as he'd carried his sons and all his other grandchildren. They were growing up – growing away from him as this war continued, but deep in his heart he knew that when it was over they would return to this place to be refreshed and renewed in the landscape of home and childhood.

He tramped the hills for another hour, and then set off for home. The bells were ringing now for early service, and so he changed course and headed for the old Norman church.

He ordered Harvey to sit and stay on the path and approached the two graves where Peggy had placed the daffodils. He stood for a long moment in deep contemplation before looking around him. There were other graves now, of young men and women who'd lost their lives in the battle against Hitler, and as he wandered past them to read the epitaphs, his thoughts turned to Jim and the ferocious fighting all across the Far East against the Japanese emperor's armies. Hirohito was as fanatical as Hitler, and Ron had felt quite sickened when he'd learnt that the man's name translated as 'boundless benevolence'.

With a snort of disgust, he turned away and went to sit on a bench to smoke his pipe and gather his thoughts. He had contacts in the Secret Services that he'd kept up since the last shout, and a few from more recent involvements; perhaps he could find out more about Martin and the others through them. Although it was less than twenty-four hours since the raid, so if they had been found by either the Germans or members of the Resistance, it was unlikely that any news would have filtered through yet.

He gave a deep sigh. He knew from past experience that escaping men had to be got far away from where they'd been found; they had to be hidden; put their trust in the people around them and at all costs keep their uniforms, for without them they ran the risk of being classed as spies, interrogated for hours and then shot. But at least the Germans observed the conventions and reported prisoners of war as well as the dead, giving them a proper burial – which was more than the Japs did, for there had been absolutely no news coming out of the Far East, and poor Sarah and

311

Jane had no idea what had happened to their men.

He looked out over the graveyard to the distant sea as the night raiders returned from yet another mission. It just went on and on – and there seemed to be no end in sight. Yet, if the rumours of a landing in France were to be believed, perhaps this really was the beginning of the end. He knocked the dottle from his pipe and stroked Harvey's head. 'We can only pray that's the case,' he muttered. 'Come on, ye heathen beast, let's go home and see what we can do to help those girls.'

Somerset

Anne kept up a brave face for the children's sake, but they seemed to pick up on the heavy atmosphere in Violet's kitchen, and for once ate their breakfast quietly and did as they were told. She'd asked the others not to say anything in front of them, for they were too young to understand all the implications of what missing in action really meant. But each time she thought about Martin going down in his Spitfire, the nausea rose and the tears came unbidden so she had to leave the table and pretend to be doing something at the range.

She prepared the children for Sunday school and tried to concentrate on their chatter, but she felt numb, empty and very much alone despite all the people around her. 'I won't come with you this morning,' she said to Sally and Violet. 'I think I'd rather take a walk.'

'And why not?' said Violet. 'God can hear your prayers wherever you are, and I often find it easier to hear his answer out there than in that cold, damp church with the vicar piously droning on.'

Anne gave her a hug. 'I'll see you later, then.'

'Take your time, Anne,' said Sally. 'You know where we are should you get sick of your own company.'

Once they'd left, Anne went into her bedroom, determined not to collapse in a storm of tears and self-recrimination. She picked up the photograph of Martin which she kept by her bedside and touched his smiling face with a gentle finger, then put it back. If she kept busy she wouldn't have time to think, so she tidied her room and then went into the children's bedroom and tidied that. Returning to the kitchen, she finished the washing-up, prepared the vegetables and large chicken for lunch and then reached for her coat.

Just as she was about to go outside, the telephone began to ring, and she dashed back into the kitchen, hope giving her wings that it would be good news. 'Hello?'

'Anne, it's me,' said Peggy at the other end. 'I'm so sorry, darling. How are you coping?'

'But how did you know?' Anne listened as her mother told her haltingly about Matthew, Freddy and Roger. She began to shiver as if with a fever and had to sink into a nearby chair. 'Dear God,' she breathed. 'The vicar only told me about Martin. I didn't realise...'

'Poor little Rita is in a terrible state, so I sent Ron to the fire station to tell John she wouldn't be on duty today.' Peggy gave a tremulous sigh.

313

'Kitty and Charlotte arrived here earlier, and Charlotte managed to get through to her mother on our telephone, but of course with the travel restrictions no one can get here.'

There was a pause in which Anne thought she could hear her mother trying to keep her emotions under control. 'Cissy has gone back to Cliffe to see if any more information has come through, and Ron has promised to keep his ear to the ground, regarding some of his old contacts. Though I suspect they're too old and past it to know anything after all these years.'

Anne was battling with her own emotions as she sat there in the silent kitchen gripping the receiver. 'You might be surprised, Mam. You know what Granda's like – he has a lot of fingers in many pies.'

'I suppose so.' Peggy sounded unconvinced. 'But how are you and the children coping?'

'I haven't told the girls, and I'm coping – just. But I wish we could be with you, Mam.' Her voice broke and she struggled to contain her tears.

'And I wish I was with you. But there's nothing we can do about it, except keep our hopes up that things aren't as bad as we fear. So we have to cling on to the fact that they're just missing, not reported as anything else. Martin and the others will come through, I'm sure of it.'

'Bless you, Mam. I wish I could be so optimistic.'

'We both have to be,' Peggy replied firmly. 'Otherwise we won't cope.'

'I love you, Mam.'

'And I love you. I'm sending hugs and kisses to

you and the little ones, and I'll try to ring again as soon as possible.'

The telephone exchange cut the call before Anne could reply, and she replaced the receiver, determined not to break down again – determined to believe that her mother was right and that Martin and his men would come through. The thought that they might not was just too awful.

She tucked her hands in the pockets and dipped her chin into the coat collar. She set off for her walk with no real plan as to where she'd go, but the simple act of walking seemed to ease the pain inside her, and as the sun's warmth fell on her face and the cool fresh air ruffled her hair, she knew she'd made the right decision. This glorious countryside was God's real church, for here she could see his glory in the patchwork of fields, and in the cloudless canopy of blue that encompassed the rolling hills and deeply shadowed valleys.

She remembered the walks she'd taken with her grandfather from her very earliest years when he'd carried her on his shoulder or against his heart in an old army satchel. Ron had taught her how to see things differently as they'd explored the hills and woods behind Beach View. He'd shown her rabbit warrens and badger's setts; had taken her to the deep, dark pool where the eels slithered over one another into his nets, and revealed the tiny hatchlings of a sparrow or blue tit's nest. She could remember lying beside him on the river bank to watch the salmon, and how silent she'd had to be as he put his hand in the water and, with a flick of the wrist, landed a fish on the grass.

She'd soon learned that most of his activities were unlawful, but the excitement of the moment far outweighed the possibility of getting caught.

Finding a sheltered spot beneath a tree, she sat down and leaned against the rough bark of the trunk. She surveyed the vista spread out before her, watching a flock of white gulls following the tractor as Bob cleared a neighbouring farmer's fallow field, and saw the distant figures of the German POWs working alongside Letty and Lucinda as they dug up the new crop of potatoes.

Anne shivered and hugged her knees. She had nothing personal against Max and the others, but was nowhere near able to face them in the light of what had happened to Martin, and she was glad they no longer came into the farmhouse for their meals and kept themselves to themselves.

But their presence had spoilt Martin's home-coming, and although it had turned out all right in the end, it was possible that upset had caused a momentary lapse in his concentration. Were his thoughts still on the sight of her and his children playing so happily with the enemy, which had made him careless? She didn't know – but the possibility was too awful to bear.

She sank her head to her knees as the tears came again, and because she was alone she let all the anguish she'd been holding in pour out in an endless flow of heartbroken sobs.

Somewhere in Germany

They had walked through what remained of the

night, and as dawn lightened the sky, they had moved more carefully. Avoiding isolated farms and keeping within the shadows of trees, hedges and ditches, they made their way westward. Absolute silence was maintained, and at the sound of a distant motor or the clank of a bicycle, they lay flat and still, scarcely breathing until it had passed.

They reached a small village tucked away in a valley at about ten in the morning. 'I'm going to that house over there,' said Danuta, pointing towards the largest building in the village which was of grey stone and set at the bottom of the hill in an untended plot. 'You must stay here until I signal that it's safe for you to come.'

Martin and Allan lay on their bellies in the long grass beneath a tangle of bushes and brambles, watching her follow a rough track down the hill towards the house. She was such a slight figure in those mannish clothes, and incredibly vulnerable – as they all were.

Martin's heart was thudding so hard he was sure it could be heard, but Allan seemed oblivious, and almost too calm under the circumstances. Perhaps his youth protected him – or perhaps he was simply far braver – whatever it was, Martin knew his status as his commanding officer meant he must never show just how frightened he was.

He looked down at the village which was made up of a sprawling community of less than three dozen houses, a church and a cobbled main street lined on either side with shops and cafes. The two-storey houses were mostly built of weathered grey stone, with dull red tiled roofs and smoking chimneys. The street was deserted but for a scavenging dog, and in one of the distant fields he could see a farmer with a large horse pulling an old-fashioned plough. The wooden shutters on the windows had been thrown open and bedding was being aired over the sills.

It had clearly once been a prosperous place and looked so peaceful, one could hardly believe there was a war raging all round. Yet there were signs of it in the broken shutters and roof tiles, the large bomb crater he could see beyond the farmer with his horse and plough, and the damage to the church windows. The Allies had passed this way, and he felt a momentary pang that it might have been him who'd caused the damage.

He shook off that ridiculous thought and regarded the house where Danuta had gone. It was quite imposing, built on three or four floors, with a round tower to one side, and what might have been servants' quarters behind the windows in the steeply sloping roof. However, it had all the signs of neglect in the long grass studded with unpicked fruit and weeds in the orchard, the broken fence and damaged back wall. But some-one had planted vegetables in between the roses which had gone wild through inattention.

Danuta appeared from the shadows of a back door and began to beckon them with some urgency.

Martin and Allan slithered on their bellies over the brow of the hill and then used the bushes and trees as cover as they ran down towards the house. On closer inspection the apples littering the grass were rotten, which explained why they

318

hadn't been picked.

'In here, quickly,' said Danuta.

They slipped into a dark room with a stone slab floor, which could have been a kitchen or a scullery. But there was no time for more than a glance, for Danuta closed the door and was chivvying them along a narrow corridor and up several flights of wooden stairs.

They passed closed doors at every turn, and the silence of the house was like a heavy blanket, which made their footsteps echo. And yet in that silence, Martin could sense people behind those closed doors, listening, watching through key-holes, and he wondered who they might be, and why they'd risked their lives by hiding them.

They came to the fourth floor where each wall was covered in ornate paper decorated with birds and flowers. Danuta took them to the very end of the long, silent corridor and stood on a nearby chair to press the centre of one of the plaster roses which decorated the coving.

Martin and Allan looked on in amazement as a secret door in the fussy wallpaper opened on silent hinges to reveal a narrow, winding stone staircase.

'Go up there and wait for me,' murmured Danuta. 'There's food, water and bedding. But whatever you do, don't walk about or talk above a whisper, and don't smoke.'

'What is this place?' Martin asked.

'It was the home of the village Mayor before the Gestapo took him,' she replied, her eyes darting along the deserted corridor. 'Now only his mother and daughter live here. Go up quickly and

I'll shut the door behind you. I don't know how long I'll be, but I will be back.'

Martin's unasked question must have been clear in his expression, for Danuta smiled. 'If I don't make it, others will come. There will be one tap, followed by two swift ones. Now go.'

He wanted to thank her, but she shoved him through the door and it closed behind him with a click of finality. It was gloomy on the stone stairs, but as they climbed, light filtered in through the heavily taped tower windows, making it easier to find their way. They halted when they reached another door.

'Boots off, I think, Forbes,' he muttered. They pulled them off and held them to their chest as they opened the door and tiptoed inside.

It was a circular room, as they'd expected, with thick stone walls, deep slits for windows and a solid wooden floor. There was no furniture, but straw-filled mattresses, blankets and pillows were piled on one side, and next to them was a large jug of water and a plate of black bread, sausage and cheese. On the other side of the tower room was a tin bucket with a wooden lid – their lavatory.

'Home sweet home,' Allan whispered. 'I wonder how long we'll have to stay here?'

'That's up to Danuta,' Martin replied, inspecting the bedding. He caught sight of something scratched into the stone wall. 'Hello,' he breathed, 'it looks like we aren't the first to be here.'

He shifted the mattress away from the wall and they inspected the initials and dates the previous occupants had left behind, hoping they might recognise Freddy's or Roger's – or any one of the pilots who'd flown with them that fateful day. But none of them rang a bell, so he shoved the mattress back and they began to sort out their sleeping arrangements.

Once everything was to their satisfaction, they tucked into the unappetising black bread, spicy sausage and rather bland cheese, washing it down with water from the jug.

'What do you think happened to the others, sir?' whispered Forbes after they'd taken it in turns to use the bucket and were stretched out on the surprisingly comfortable palliasses.

'I really have no idea,' Martin whispered back. 'We can only hope that Danuta's colleagues managed to rescue them if they made it down in one piece.' He stared up at the thin streams of light coming through the narrow window slits. The food and water had gone some way to ease his headache, but his body still felt battered and bruised and he was exhausted.

'Do you think our families will have been informed by now, sir?'

'I expect so,' he murmured, his heart twisting as he pictured Anne being told the news by some stranger in a uniform. 'Though what they've been told is anyone's guess.'

'I suppose it will depend on eyewitness reports – in which case we're probably down as MIA. I do wish I could get word to my mother, sir. Only my brother was killed last year during the Dambuster raid and she will be fearfully upset.' His voice was uneven. 'I'm all she's got left, you see, sir.'

Martin heard the youthfulness in his voice and

the quaver of tightly held emotions. For all his bravery and daredevil stunts in the air, he was just a boy. A boy who looked to him for answers he couldn't provide – a boy who simply wanted his mother to know he'd come through.

He reached across and squeezed Allan's arm. 'Chin up, lad,' he whispered gruffly. 'Danuta will probably send a message to London and they'll know soon enough that we're all right.'

'Do you think so, sir?'

There was such hope in his eyes that Martin couldn't bear to be truthful to him. 'I'm sure of it,' he said firmly. 'Now close your eyes and try to get some sleep. We might have to move on again tonight, and will need to be rested.'

The boy fell asleep almost immediately, but Martin lay there wide awake, his scrambled thoughts refusing to let him sleep despite his exhaustion.

Danuta was putting her life at risk by helping them; the women in this house could be shot for sheltering them, and even now the Germans might be searching for them. He had no idea how far they'd come since young Forbes had saved him from certain death, but his instruments and flight manual had indicated that he'd been only a few miles south of Hannover when he was shot down.

Which meant they were too far north from neutral Switzerland to risk seeking shelter there, which was probably why Danuta was leading them west – to the borders of either the Netherlands or Belgium. Both of which were enemy occupied.

And then there was Anne, his darling Anne and

his precious little girls. How was she coping with the news that he'd been shot down? He couldn't bear to think of her in tears, of her losing hope and envisioning a life without him. He closed his eyes and dismissed these images, turning towards the stone wall and curling beneath the blanket.

He would think of her as she'd been on his last leave – warm and soft and fragrant, yielding in his arms and smiling with such love into his eyes. He vowed then that he would hold that memory close until he could once more feel her arms around him, for it would be sustaining, no matter what befell him on this perilous journey to freedom and home.

16

Cliffehaven

The planes had been taking off from Cliffe all day and throughout the night to bombard the main railway lines and ammunition dumps in France and Belgium, as well as the military installations in the Pas-de-Calais area. Soldiers and sailors from all the Allied countries seemed to have converged on Cliffehaven, with many more troop trains running on to Portsmouth and Southampton. The rumours of an Allied invasion into France were growing ever louder, and every household, shop and factory in the town was glued to their wirelesses in the hope they'd get the news that it had begun.

Ron had changed the route of his usual late afternoon walk, for he could no longer bear to watch the planes land at Cliffe, some coming in with broken wings, others crashing into the sea or belly-flopping on the concrete runways. He'd had enough of fire and carnage – enough of seeing brave men die.

He sat on the top of the hill looking down on the bombed ruins of the old asylum that stood to the west of the town, and regarded the phalanx of American bombers heading over the Channel in a great thunder of noise that vibrated right through him. There was no escaping the racket, day or night, and with the Germans making counter-attacks, and the air-raid sirens going off repeatedly, no one was getting much sleep and already frayed nerves were now in tatters.

It was the fourth day of May and Martin and the others had been missing for five days. Despite his best efforts, Ron had been unable to get any information out of anyone, and it didn't bode well; for if they'd survived being shot down and had been taken prisoner, the authorities would have been told – the Germans were very efficient about that – and usually, if the Resistance had managed to rescue them, someone would have informed London.

Ron's mind churned with logical explanations for that lack of information. Perhaps the expected invasion had forced radio silence; perhaps the cell of Resistance people had been compromised – or taken prisoner themselves? And then of course there was the awful possibility that the lack of any news meant that none of them had come through. It was like living on a knife's edge.

The stem of his unlit pipe clenched between his teeth, he surveyed the Channel with the army issue binoculars he'd managed to keep on his demob back in 1919. There was a convoy of Allied ships steaming past, and he could hear the distant booms and thuds of their big guns now that the Allied bombers had gone, and see dark plumes of smoke rising on the horizon. He could only guess that more German military installations along the French coast were on the receiving end of that heavy mortar fire.

He tucked the binoculars back in their case and put it into one of his deep inside pockets. They weren't the thing to carry about in public, and as there had been an identity card check only this morning, security was clearly being tightened.

He idly watched Harvey and Monty charge about, noses to the ground, tails windmilling as they sniffed out scents of rabbit, badger or fox. How simple life was for a dog, he thought wistfully. If only it was the same for humans.

'Ah, Ron. I thought I might catch you here.'

Bertie Double-Barrelled came up the hill towards him, looking quite dapper as usual, even though he'd exchanged the three-piece suit for twill trousers, sturdy brogues, peaked cap and a sweater beneath a tweed jacket. If he'd been carrying a gun, Ron would have thought he'd just returned from a shoot on some country estate.

'Hello, Bertie.' Ron was surprised to see him, and couldn't suppress a dart of hope. 'This isn't your regular neck of the woods. Have you got something to tell me?'

'In a minute, old chap.' Bertie sank to the ground. 'Need to get my breath back, don't you know.' He patted his heaving chest with a pale, almost feminine hand. 'Not as fit as I was,' he said remorsefully. 'The years seem to be catching up on me.'

Ron grinned. 'To be sure, you're fitter than most men in their seventies. Even I find that hill a wee bit of a struggle.'

He waited impatiently until the other man had got his breath. He'd discovered a long time ago that Bertie couldn't be rushed – and as they were connected through their undercover work, he knew that whatever Bertie had to say was important enough for him to come and find him all the way up here.

Bertie took in the view with a sigh of appreciation as the distant bombardment shook the ground beneath them. 'Poor France is getting it again,' he muttered. 'Still, it's either that or occupation beneath the heel of the Boche.'

'So the invasion is coming?'

'Oh, yes, old chap. And quite soon. Just got to clear Jerry out of the way of those beaches and we'll be in as quick as you can blink to clear up the mess once and for all.'

'That's good to know,' Ron said. 'But I have the feeling that wasn't why you came all this way to talk to me.'

Bertie offered a cheroot to Ron, who couldn't stand the things, and then spent a moment to get it alight. 'I have someone in London,' he began. 'Good chap. Very trustworthy, and with strong contacts in a certain department which you and I are familiar with.'

Ron knew immediately he was talking about the Special Operations Executive, which deployed secret agents to enemy territory to sabotage and harvest information that could be sent back to London. The SOE had employed him several times during this war – although he was far too old to be sent abroad – and his knowledge of the town and the people in it had helped him pass on many a useful nugget. 'Go on,' he pressed.

'It seems there are two downed airmen in the safekeeping of one of their operatives,' said Bertie carefully. 'One of them is a young pilot officer; the other's your son-in-law.'

Ron let out his breath on a deep sigh of relief. 'Is he fit and well? Where are they?'

'They're still in Germany but approaching the Dutch border. Both fit and well, I'm glad to say.'

'And the others?'

'I'm sorry, old chap. Nothing reported at all. But that doesn't mean there's no hope,' Bertie added quickly. 'They could have been taken in by an Allied sympathiser and hidden, or still be on the run. It's just rather a nuisance that no one has reported sight of their parachutes – which would at least add to the hope that they made it down in one piece.'

'I expect the other pilots were too busy trying not to get shot down themselves,' Ron said. 'I've watched some of those dogfights, and it's a miracle anyone gets out alive.'

The scent of the cigar had him reaching in his pocket for his tin of tobacco. 'So, do you know if the person who's looking after them is reliable?'

'She's extremely reliable, so you should have no worries on that count. We just have to hope they don't run into the blasted Germans as they beat a retreat from the bombardment of the French coastline.'

'A woman's got them?' Ron looked at him sharply. 'I don't suppose you're allowed to tell me her name?'

'Sorry, old boy. Out of my remit. All I can say is that she's Polish by birth and still very young. Although this is her first operation in Germany, she's been behind enemy lines numerous times and has built quite a reputation for delivering vital information which has helped our side tremend-ously.'

Ron's pulse began to race. 'I'm about to ask you something, Bertie, that you might find rather strange,' he said quietly. 'It's a long shot, I know, but her name wouldn't happen to be Danuta Chmielewski, would it?'

Bertie's eyes widened. 'Good heavens, Ron, where … how did you dig that name up?'

'She and her brother were Peggy's lodgers back at the beginning of the war. After her brother was shot down during an RAF raid, I introduced her to someone we both know because she could speak several languages, had the experience and skills of fighting and sabotage with the under-ground back in Poland, and was determined to do her bit.'

Bertie regarded him impassively. 'I couldn't possibly confirm or deny it, old chap.'

That was when Ron knew it was Danuta, and

why she'd written that letter. She was behind enemy lines, working for the Resistance and helping stranded pilots like Martin escape the attentions of the SS and get back home – of course she'd had to prepare for the worst. 'Thanks, Bertie. That explains a lot,' he said.

'Explains what?' he replied with a frown.

Ron didn't have time to answer because the sirens began to wail through the town, growing in pitch and urgency. Both men looked out towards the horizon but could see nothing, and the dogs, who hated the sound of the sirens, sought shelter in the ruins of the asylum.

Ron was about to say that it was probably another false alarm when four Messerschmitt fighters shot over the valley behind them, all guns blazing as they spotted the two men.

Ron and Bertie reacted with the speed and agility of veterans used to being under attack. Rolling down the hill towards the ruins, they threw themselves beneath what was left of the tall hydrangea hedge which had once shaded the rear garden of the asylum and lay flat, breathing heavily.

'Whew,' puffed Bertie. 'Quite like old times, eh?'

'Aye, it is that,' Ron agreed, looking wildly round for sight of his beloved dogs.

The animals must have heard their voices, for Harvey and Monty crawled towards them from the other side of the hedge and lay between them.

The two men inched their way under the hedge and lay there on their stomachs to watch what the Messerschmitts were up to. They saw them make a sharp turn to the east of the Norman church

329

and head back to them, their guns still firing as they passed over the town and headed west.

Ron heard the bullets thud into the ground, and the twang and whine as they ricocheted off the stone rubble nearby. Neither man bothered to cover their heads, for they knew that a stray bullet could easily penetrate steel, let alone flesh – but they both wished they had a high-velocity rifle in their hands, or a bazooka to fire back and shoot them out of the sky.

When the Messerschmitts had gone they looked at each other and moved as one back up the hill as a posse of Spitfires and Mosquitoes took off from Cliffe after the Jerry fighters. From the top of the hill they could see the aerial combat in the distance, the planes turning, twisting and soaring like birds against the blue sky, and the stuttering rattle of gunfire echoing across the next valley and the tiny bay, as engines strained and the sun glinted on metal.

And then came the blast of an explosion which sent a ball of fire spinning out of control in a dive of death, followed by an awful crump as the burning Messerschmitt hit the stone shipping barrier which had been strung across the neighbouring bay.

There hadn't been time for the pilot to get out, and although he was an enemy, the sight of that terrible death affected both old soldiers, for it had come too swiftly after the April raid that had killed so many of their own boys.

The Germans realised they were vastly outnumbered and turned tail for home, but the one at the back was losing height as black smoke poured from beneath it. Within seconds, they saw the white blossoming of a parachute, and both men felt a strange sense of relief that they didn't have to see another death.

The Spitfires and Mosquitoes had done their job; now it was up to the coastguard services to rescue the downed pilot and cart him off for interrogation, and a nice cosy billet in a prisoner of war camp.

'Jolly good show,' shouted Bertie as they stood on the hill and saluted their returning airmen. He turned to Ron, his face alight. 'Jerry's losing fighter planes left, right and centre, and as we keep blowing up their factories and supply links, they don't have the resources to build more. We're going to win this damned war, Ron. We're going to beat them at their own bloody game.'

They slapped each other on the back and went down the hill towards town, their faces wreathed in smiles as the dogs raced ahead of them. The town was quiet, waiting for the all-clear to sound, but they could both see the damage caused by those bullets in the broken windows, chipped bricks and scarred pavements.

Upon reaching the outskirts of the large playing field which had been turned into a public shelter and allotment, Bertie came to a halt. 'I'll leave you to pass on the good news, old boy, and of course I don't need to tell you not to say word about where you got it. Besides, I can't have Cordelia seeing me like this,' he added ruefully, tweaking at his jacket and sweater.

'Well, you look respectable enough to me,' Ron replied, hitching up his sagging corduroy trousers and tightening the garden twine he was using as a belt. 'By the way, I thought you were supposed to be out of town visiting some ancient relative?'

Bertie tapped his nose and winked. 'Of course I was, dear boy. What else do you think I might have been up to?'

Ron had a fair idea it was probably something to do with the group of Fifth Columnists – Nazi sympathisers – that he'd been brought in to monitor the previous year. They'd moved on, but Ron suspected Bertie was still keeping tabs on them. Yet he said nothing and just shook his hand.

'Thanks, Bertie. Keep up the good work, and if you should need me again, you know where I am.'

'Will do,' said Bertie, heartily returning his handshake. 'I'll be popping in later to see Cordelia, if that's all right.' He leaned towards Ron. 'The ancient relative died, don't you know, so I could come home.'

Ron raised a brow. 'Really? Dead?'

'In a manner of speaking.' He grinned. 'We'll talk another time when the dust has settled on that one, Ron. I'm glad I could be of help to you on the other thing.'

Ron watched him stride away – a fit old man with a military bearing, regarded by the people of this town as something of an eccentric who spent his retirement years playing golf and bridge and driving Cordelia about in his car. But beneath that persona was a man as skilled at silent killing and sabotage as Ron was, and who could change like a chameleon into any character he wanted when on surveillance of a suspected Fifth Columnist. He should have been an actor really, but of course that wasn't half as exciting as working under cover.

'It's true what they say, Harvey, me boy,' he said. 'You can never tell a book by its cover. Come on, let's get home and tell everyone the news.'

Peggy had said goodbye to Gracie and Chloe and was on her way home from the factory with Daisy, having spent the last half-hour in the shelter waiting for the all-clear to sound. All the factory girls had been jolly about being down there on an unscheduled break, and they chattered like starlings, swapping dress and knitting patterns, discussing the lack of decent make-up and generally catching up on the local gossip.

Peggy usually joined in with alacrity, for she loved a good gossip, but she was tired after the long day and dispirited by yet another sleepless night of fretting over everyone – and to her chagrin, her concentration had faltered and she'd made several mistakes with her sewing, which had not gone down well with Loretta, who'd recently promoted her to bell-bottom trousers. But at least Rita had gone back to her own bed now, so she could worry in peace and let the tears flow freely.

Dear little Gracie had been a stalwart friend over these past few days, and although Peggy hadn't wanted to burden her with her troubles, she'd found it comforting to talk through things sensibly with someone who had a husband in the RAF and lived in constant fear that something similar might happen to him. Strangely enough, it had bolstered both their spirits and given hope to Peggy.

Upon reaching Beach View, she left Daisy in the kitchen with Rita and Cordelia and went into her bedroom to change into her house dress, slippers and pinafore. Brushing out her hair, which had been under a knotted scarf all day, she smiled at the photograph of Jim which she kept on the bedside table.

'You see, Jim,' she murmured, 'I'm fine, really I am. Coping with the house and Daisy and earning a lot of money too – certainly enough to pay for the repairs on the house and put down a deposit on that washing machine I've always hankered after.'

She picked up the photograph and kissed his face before holding it to her heart. 'I know it's a sign of madness to talk to a photograph, but it makes you feel nearer somehow,' she sighed. 'I wish you were here,' she continued, 'and I can't wait until you come home.'

Her monologue came to an abrupt halt at the sound of someone knocking on the front door. She hastily put Jim's photograph back and hurried out of the room, her heart thudding. 'I'll get it,' she called to the others in the kitchen.

On opening the front door her legs started shaking and she had to grab the jamb to stop from crumpling into a heap on the doormat. The young American officer was standing on her doorstep again.

'No,' she breathed. 'Not more bad news.'

'It's good news, ma'am. May I come in?'

'Yes, of course.' She opened the door wide then slammed it behind her, about to lead him into

334

the kitchen, when she realised he hadn't moved from the door. 'What is it? What's the matter?' she asked fearfully. 'I thought you said it was good news?'

He took off his uniform cap and placed it under his arm. 'It is, ma'am – for you. Are you alone in the house, ma'am?'

'No. Cordelia my lodger is in the kitchen with my youngest daughter and young Rita, who's still very upset about her Matthew.'

'Then perhaps it would be best if we have this conversation out here in private,' he said quietly, glancing across to the open kitchen door.

Peggy was at the end of her tether. 'For goodness' sake, young man, will you tell me why you're here; or do I have to shake it out of you?'

'I'm sorry, ma'am. A message arrived at the base from London. It seems that your son-in-law is alive, along with another officer. They have not been captured and are not injured, but they are still behind enemy lines.'

Peggy was trembling, the tears of joy running down her face as she absorbed the wonderful news that Martin had survived. 'But how does London know such a thing?'

'I am not in possession of that information, ma'am, but the Station Commander thought it was vital you and your daughter should be informed at once.'

'And who's Martin with?'

'I'm not at liberty to divulge that, ma'am, until his family has been informed.'

'What about Freddy Pargeter and Roger Makepeace?'

'I'm sorry, ma'am, I am not in possession of that information.'

He was talking like a mechanical toy, standing there to attention on her doormat, spouting out the same stupid thing repeatedly and looking extremely uncomfortable. Peggy could see that he was very young beneath that smart uniform – barely older than her Bob – and yet he'd been sent on a task that surely must be the most dreaded during wartime.

Her soft heart melted and she flung her arms about him, hugging him fiercely. She would have kissed his smooth young cheek if she could have reached, so she kissed his neck instead.

'Thank you,' she said through her tears as he remained stiffly to attention in her embrace. 'Thank you so much for coming to tell me, and for being so tactful about Rita. You've had to do an awful job, and I want you to know that I do appreciate how hard it must have been for you the other day.'

'It's my duty, ma'am,' he replied, his tone gruff, his gaze fixed to a point over her shoulder and his handsome face reddening.

'Do you know if Anne's already heard this wonderful news?'

He opened his mouth and her giggle cut off his reply. 'It's all right. I understand that you're not in possession of that information.' She was still chuckling as she opened the door.

He stepped outside, replaced his hat and executed a smart salute. 'Thank you, ma'am,' he said softly. 'It's been a while since my mom held me like that, and you'll never know how much that hug meant to me.' He reddened further and then ran down the steps to where a staff car was waiting for him at the kerb.

Peggy could barely hold back the tears as she closed the door. There were so many boys missing their mothers, and for all their swagger and smart uniforms, and regardless of their age and rank, there was nothing like a motherly hug to make them feel that all their sacrifices and stresses were worth it.

She blew her nose and mopped at her tears, trying to gather her wits so she could decide how best to tell everyone the wonderful news. And then she felt a cold wave of fear wash over her, and had to sit down rather abruptly on the hall chair. Martin might be alive, but he was behind enemy lines, and therefore in terrible danger.

Eventually she took the coward's way out, deciding to say nothing until Ron came home and she could ask his advice. She checked her appearance in the hall mirror, took a deep breath and went into the kitchen.

'Would anyone like a cup of tea?' she asked brightly.

'Who was that at the door?' asked Rita, looking up from the large jigsaw puzzle she was helping put together with Daisy. 'He sounded American.'

'You must have been mistaken, dear.' Peggy avoided her gaze. 'It was just someone looking for Ron.'

'Oh, right,' Rita said on a sigh. She pushed away from the table. 'I think I'll go back to the fire station and see if they need any extra help after those Jerry planes shot up the town. And then I might take my bike out for a run.'

'I'll keep your tea warm in the oven for when you get back,' said Peggy affectionately. 'A bit of fresh air might help you sleep better.'

Rita nodded, her dark curls bouncing. 'Maybe,' she said, her brown eyes liquid with sadness. She dragged her First World War flying jacket from the hook on the door, stuffed her feet into her boots, gave Daisy a quick hug, and then went down the concrete steps and out of the back door.

The Norton ES2 was kept beneath a sheet of tarpaulin, and Peggy watched from the kitchen window as Rita wheeled it down the path, through the gate and into the alleyway. It roared into life, and Rita steered it carefully over the rough track and then with a burble and backfire thundered away into the street.

'I do wish she'd be careful on that thing,' Peggy sighed. 'She's such a little dot, and that bike's far too powerful.'

'She's much stronger than you think, Peggy,' said Cordelia, who'd taken over helping with the puzzle. 'Strong enough physically to handle that motorbike – and certainly strong-minded enough to hear any news from the aerodrome.'

Peggy turned away to fill the kettle and placed it on the hob. 'I don't know what you mean,' she hedged.

'Peggy, dear, I might be old and a bit deaf, but even I can tell an American accent from a local one – although I admit I couldn't make out what he was saying.'

Peggy couldn't keep her news in any longer.

'Martin's alive, Cordelia,' she said, taking her hands.

'But that's marvellous news. Why on earth didn't you share it with Rita?'

'I didn't want to upset her with our good news while she's still mourning for Matthew.'

'That's very commendable, dear,' said Cordelia, 'but don't you think she'd be glad of something cheering at this dark time? She's as fond of Martin as the rest of us are, and, as I said before, she's tougher than you think.'

'I didn't want to give her false hope that Matthew might still be alive,' Peggy admitted.

'I do understand,' murmured Cordelia, 'but I think she knows very well that he won't be coming back.'

'What's all this gloomy talk?' Ron stomped up the back steps into the kitchen with the dogs, who both made a beeline for the cat's bowl.

Peggy attempted to rescue Queenie's food – but it was too late. They'd licked the bowl clean. 'I had some news today – really good news – but I didn't think it very tactful to share it with Rita around,' she said. 'Will you *please* keep these dogs under control, Ron?'

Ron grabbed the pair of them and ordered them to sit down and behave. He smiled at Daisy who was toddling towards him with a piece of jigsaw in her hand, and lifted her onto his knee for a cuddle. 'Well now, Peggy girl. I've had some good news today too.'

'Oh, are they serving free beer at the Anchor?' asked Cordelia cheekily.

'Better than that, Cordelia. Martin's still alive,'

he said in triumph.

'Yes, we know,' the two women chorused before breaking into chuckles at his sour expression. 'There's no need to look like that, Ron,' said Peggy. 'I realise you wanted to surprise us, but that sweet American boy came round only minutes ago to tell us the news.'

'I should have known there were no secrets in this place,' he muttered. And then his expression brightened. 'But I know something you don't.'

'We know he's behind enemy lines and is with another pilot,' said Peggy. 'And how come you're such a mine of information? Who told you – and when?'

'I have me sources,' he said grumpily. 'And I know he's behind enemy lines,' he paused for effect. 'But do you know who he's with?'

'The American boy said he was with another flyer.'

'Ach, to be sure, so he is, but who are they with?'

'Well, it can't be Roger or Freddy – the American lad said there was no news of either of them.'

Ron chuckled and shook his head as he ruffled Daisy's dark curls. 'Martin is with a member of the Resistance who is trying to get them out of Germany and across the border to the Netherlands or Belgium.' As the two women stared at him in confusion, his chuckle deepened. 'And do you know who that person is?'

'Oh, do get on with it, Ron,' said Peggy crossly. 'You're driving me round the bend with your silly games.'

'It's Danuta,' he replied. 'Our little Danuta.'

Peggy covered her mouth with her fingers and sank into the chair beside him. 'She's in the Resistance? She's the one helping Martin?'

'Aye, that she is. So now we can both understand why she wrote that letter.'

Peggy's tears began to fall again. 'Oh, my Lord,' she breathed. 'Where does it end, Ron?'

'I don't know, but you'll do none of them any good by wearing yourself to a frazzle and getting ill. We have to be thankful that Martin is alive – and that someone as clever and resourceful as Danuta is looking after him.'

Peggy frowned. 'How come you know so much about what she's doing and where she is? How can you be so certain that she's clever and resourceful and can get them out of Germany to safety?'

He regarded her levelly over Daisy's curly head. 'There are some things best kept a secret, Peggy, girl and that happens to be one of them. Now stop fretting and see to that kettle. It's in danger of boiling dry, and it's the divil's own job to get a new one these days.'

17

Somerset

Archibald Chisolm was nothing like the romantic notion of a country village vicar, for he didn't have the rotund figure of a friar, a jolly outlook on life, or the sort of character that drew people easily to him. Archibald's black suit hung off him and was worn to a rusty shine; the stiff white dog collar was too loose about his scrawny neck; and his bony hands were always cold regardless of the weather. He was tall, angular of face and whip-thin. Yet, despite all evidence to the contrary, Anne had discovered that he did care deeply for his mixed congregation of villagers, farmers and evacuees – he just didn't know how to express his concern.

Archibald had been the vicar at Barnham Green since Methuselah was born – or at least that was the opinion of the elder residents – and his long, dry sermons meant most of them nodded off while he was droning on with the sort of pious expression that irritated everyone. However, as Anne watched him walk back along the track towards the gate, she was warmed by his words of hope that Martin and the young pilot with him would make it through, and his promise that he would say a special prayer for all pilots at the Sunday morning service.

'He's really not such a bad old stick,' she said to Violet, accompanying her across the cobbled yard to check on the progress of the evening milking. 'I think he just has no experience of the real world, being a life-long bachelor. But he was genuinely touched by Martin's plight, and seemed to understand how difficult it is for me to have to wait for news of any sort.'

'Archibald's a funny cove. He should have retired years ago, but there's a shortage of vicars now they've all become padres in the services.' Violet grinned. 'I'll say this for him, though, he does have a marvellous record collection, and it's very generous of him to lend some of the more modern ones to us for our dances.'

'I think that could be George Mayhew's influence. The two of them have become quite pally just lately.'

They spent the next two hours finishing off the milking and getting the cows back to their fields while the children fed the chickens and pigs under Sally's supervision, and Bob went off to do a stint as an observer with his former schoolmaster. Charlie was tinkering with the farm truck's engine, and trying unsuccessfully to teach Ernie the finer points of engineering, and the German prisoners had finished hedging and decamped to their cottage in Rectory Field.

Anne went into the boot room, struggled out of her coat and slipped her feet into her slippers. The past five days had been torture, for nothing was certain, and she'd swung from hope to deepest despair as the days had gone on and she'd heard nothing from anyone. However, now she knew Martin was alive, it was as if a great weight had lifted from her shoulders, and although he was still in great danger behind enemy lines she could begin to believe that he was resourceful enough to make it home.

She walked into the kitchen and saw the flowers immediately. They were overflowing from one of Vi's decorative pottery jugs in a riot of cabbage roses, wisteria and twigs of apple and cherry blossom interspersed with the vibrant yellow of forsythia. At first she thought Vi must have put them there, but she'd been with her ever since the vicar had left. Then she saw the envelope leaning against the jug, her name written on it in black ink.

She smiled as she opened the envelope. George or Belinda must have brought them while she was out with the cows, for flowers like that could only have come from a village garden.

Opening the single sheet of folded paper, her hands began to tremble and she had to sit down.

Dear Mrs Black,

We don't wish to intrude, or cause offence in any way, but we wanted you to have these flowers as a token of our high esteem, and our thankfulness that Group Captain Black is alive.

We understand what you are experiencing at this difficult time, for some of our family members have gone through the same thing. We also know that this is probably no consolation to you, but we felt it was important you should know that whichever side you're on, the trauma for the families is the same.

344

The flowers were kindly given to us by Mrs Mc-Cormack at the Shepherd's Arms, who also sends her very best wishes.
Yours sincerely,
Max, Claus and Hans

'Goodness,' said Violet as she came bustling into the kitchen with Rose and Emily in tow. 'How lovely, Anne. Are they from a secret admirer?'

'Hardly,' she replied, 'but it was a very kind thought, and I feel I ought to reciprocate in some way.' She passed the letter over for Vi to read.

'It's a lovely letter,' said Violet, 'and also heart-felt, I think. Why don't you take one of those apple pies we made this morning over to them? They'd appreciate that.'

'You don't think it might be a bit forward?'

'Silly girl. Of course it's not. We all have to work on this farm, and they've taken the first step to try and heal the unfortunate break in the harmony. I think it's time we put all that behind us, don't you?'

'Well, if you're sure.'

'I wouldn't say it if I wasn't,' Vi said firmly. 'Besides, the children miss playing with them and hearing their stories. There's enough doom and gloom in the world today, and Owlet Farm has always been a happy place.'

Without waiting for a reply, Violet took one of the apple pies out of the enormous larder and put it into a basket with a jam jar of thick cream. Covering it all with a clean tea cloth, she held it out to Anne.

Anne realised she was being silly avoiding the

men, blaming them for what had happened to Martin simply because they were German. And it was clear that Vi wasn't happy with the atmosphere on her farm after Martin's aggressive behaviour – in fact, she admitted silently, she didn't like it either, for it soured everything.

She took the basket, exchanged slippers for wellington boots and headed out across the fields for the tiny cottage. Slowing down as she reached the gate leading into Rectory Field, she surveyed the cottage the men had worked so hard to make habitable.

There was a wisp of smoke coming from the refurbished chimney, the broken peg-tiles had been replaced from an old stock they'd found in an abandoned shed, the windows and door had been repaired and the narrow chalk path leading to the front door was clear of weeds. The old shepherd's hut only consisted of four rooms – two at the front and two at the back – it must be quite a squash with three large men vying for space.

She saw a figure move behind one of the windows and felt rather foolish standing there, so she gripped the basket a little tighter and walked purposefully down the path.

The door opened before she'd reached it, and she returned the man's smile. 'I wanted to thank you for the beautiful flowers and your lovely letter, Max,' she said. 'I did appreciate them both.' She held out the basket. 'Violet and I thought you might like a treat to make your rations a little more appetising.'

He managed not to click his heels together as he dipped his head in acknowledgment and took

346

the basket. 'That is very kind, but it is not necessary. Ve just vanted you to know that ve vould like to be friends again if you vould permit it,' he said rather stiffly.

'I would like that,' she replied with a shy smile. 'But how did you know Martin was alive? The vicar only came here a couple of hours ago.'

His broad grin lit up his handsome face as the other two crowded in the doorway behind him. 'It is easy in a small village,' he replied. 'We vent in to get our cigarettes and saw the vicar heading for the farm, and ve asked your schoolmaster friend who vas in the shop if it vas more bad news for you. He assured us it vasn't, for the vicar had confided in him.'

'But George is not a gossip,' she protested.

'No, of course not, but someone overheard vhat the vicar vas saying to him and of course they spread it to everyone else. It is the same, I think, in every village. People like to know vhat is happening.'

'And even if they don't, they're very good at making it up,' said Anne with a chuckle. 'Look, I'd better get back; it's almost the children's bedtime. Enjoy the apple pie, and I'll see you all tomorrow.'

She heard the door close behind her as she went through the gate and headed back to Owlet Farm. Despite all the upset of the past weeks and the continuing worry over Martin being on the run in Germany, she actually felt more positive about everything. The atmosphere at the farm would lighten, the children would have their playmates again, and harmony would be restored.

347

Somewhere in Germany

Danuta set a fast pace as they walked through the night, and although Martin had strapped his twisted ankle as tightly as he could, it was still giving him trouble, and he was in constant danger of lagging behind. So he gritted his teeth, tried to ignore the pain and kept up.

They had left the turret room before dawn the following day, and since then, they'd hidden in barns, cellars and haylofts during the day and walked through the night, crossing endless fields to avoid the roads and villages they passed, wary of barking dogs setting up an alarm, or the convoys of German troops which seemed to be everywhere. They had been very lucky so far, but none of them knew when that luck might run out.

It was cold tonight and they could see the fog of their breath as they headed west, but both Martin and young Forbes were sweating beneath the layers of clothes Danuta had made them wear. She'd explained on that first night that it was vital they keep their air force uniforms on, for without them they could be taken as spies by the SS. But since they would make them stand out, she'd provided rough trousers, shirts and coats to put over them, and ordered them to ditch the flying boots for the worn old boots she'd bought in a local flea market. They didn't fit properly, and let in water through the holes in the stitching and on the soles, but the leather was soft after many years of wear and tear, so they didn't suffer from too many blisters.

Danuta came to an abrupt halt and raised her hand, every inch of her sensing danger.

Martin and Allan stopped immediately and strained to hear whatever it was that had alerted her. And then, above the distant booms and crumps of heavy artillery, Martin heard the sound of trucks and tanks approaching, and as one, the three of them lay flat in the reeds and long grass that grew beside the river they'd been following. Hardly daring to breathe, they were barely aware of the chill of the water that reached their midriffs as they watched through the grasses.

The enormous convoy rumbled and rattled its way along the road. At its head was a series of large black staff cars with swastika flags fluttering from the bonnets and outriders on motorbikes and sidecars keeping pace with them. They were followed by numerous grey trucks carrying armed troops beneath their canvas awnings; and behind them were the tanks, the hatches open to reveal armed lookouts.

Martin caught Danuta's eye and realised their thoughts were similar, for this was a very large convoy, and if they'd had the ammunition and hardware to blow up the road now, it would settle a huge score. But as Danuta was the only one with a gun, they had to simply lie there and watch them pass.

It felt like an age until the rumble of the last tank faded into the distance, but still they lay there – just in case there was another motorcade of staff cars behind the convoy. When Danuta judged they'd waited long enough, they scrambled to their feet and tried to wring as

349

much water from their clothes as possible, and then, with their shoes squelching at every step, once again followed the river.

'They are retreating, I think,' she muttered. 'The Allies' bombardment on the coast is proving successful.'

'Where are we going?' asked Allan through chattering teeth.

'Across the border into Holland,' she replied softly. 'We have just passed Munster, and are now following the river to a place just north of Enschede.'

'But that's one of the first cities in Holland to be occupied,' said Martin, now chilled to the bone by his sodden clothes and unable to stop shivering. 'Eighth Bomber Command attacked it only a few months ago.'

'I know that,' she whispered. 'I was there. But it is also a city that has protected and hidden its Jewish citizens since the beginning of the war, and I have good contacts there who will take you north where a boat will be waiting for you.'

'But surely there'll be border guards,' whispered Allan. 'How do we get past them?'

'We will not go straight into the city,' she replied. 'There is another way, with no guards, dogs, guns, or even barbed wire.'

Martin looked across at Allan and saw that he too was getting somewhat jittery at the thought of such things – but it was important to keep the lad's spirits up. 'Danuta knows what she's doing, Forbes, and we can't expect her to give us information about an escape route. We could still be captured and interrogated, so the less we know the better it will be for everyone.'

'Yes, sir,' he said, his voice sounding very young, the earlier ebullience quashed by the seriousness of their situation.

They walked through what remained of the night, hearing the distant booms of heavy artillery, the explosions of bombs which they guessed were hitting railways, storage depots and arms dumps – and the drone of heavy planes delivering those bombs accompanied by the roar of fighter engines and the stutter of machine-gun bullets. It seemed the Allied forces were out again in another unrelenting attack on the northern beachheads, and they could only hope that their final destination would still be there when they arrived.

It was an hour before dawn when they saw the two gun-towers and the high fence of barbed wire. Still damp and aching with cold, they crouched down in a small copse of trees while Danuta took stock of where they were. Even from this distance, Martin could see the soldiers patrolling with their powerful-looking dogs, and the armed men standing at the guard post where a barrier had been erected across the road.

Danuta tucked her binoculars away in an inner pocket of her rather smelly old coat. 'We must move. Now. No more talking.'

Martin and Allan slithered on their bellies through the long grass, following Danuta as she led them northward. The high barbed-wire barricade seemed to be endless, and Martin's heart was thudding as they inched their way along, aware that within the hour the rising sun would give them away.

They finally came to another river which ran swiftly beneath a stone bridge which appeared to lead to the outskirts of the city. Danuta took her gun from her belt and held it high as she slid down the steep bank and into the water. She had to push against the strong flow, which was almost up to her chin, and finally reached the deep shadows beneath the bridge.

Martin and Allen followed suit, the chilly water swirling around their waists as they waded towards her. When they reached the stone pillar holding up the southern end of the bridge, Danuta grabbed their arms. 'It's very deep,' she breathed against Martin's ear. 'We will go across together.'

They went, arm in arm beneath the arch of the bridge, their feet slipping and sliding on the polished pebbles as they fought sideways on to the flow, the water almost level with their chins. Martin and Allan held on to Danuta as it soon became evident that she could no longer touch the bottom, and if she was torn from their grip, she'd be swept away.

Their thick layers of clothing impeded them, for the icy water made them heavy and dragged them down, but their determination to get to the other side was finally rewarded, and they crawled up the bank and lay gasping and shivering.

Danuta gave them only a minute, and then indicated they must move on.

Martin had always considered himself to be quite fit, but the past five days had drained him utterly – and the river crossing had left him numb with cold, each movement a terrible struggle. And yet they had no option but to follow her, for she was crawling up the bank to disappear into the thick undergrowth that grew beside the narrow road.

Shivering, with chattering teeth, they crawled towards her. She put her finger to her lips and then indicated they should follow.

Martin could no longer see the barbed wire, and while they moved as silently as they could through the tangle of scrub and brambles, he realised they were leaving the road and the city behind them and heading down into a shallow valley.

Danuta came to a halt and hid in the shadows of the surrounding vegetation, the binoculars tight to her eyes as she scanned the area before her.

Martin could see a high stone wall which had been roughly plastered and had once been painted white. Behind it there seemed to be an orchard and he could just make out the dull red of roof tiles and a broken chimney.

Danuta put the binoculars away, hitched her sodden hessian bag over her back and began to tentatively crawl forward. Every inch of her was poised for flight, and the tension emanated from her so strongly, the two men could almost feel it.

They reached the edge of the overgrown vegetation and Danuta stopped again, lying flat, sensing danger in the air.

Martin and Allan knew then that something was very wrong. They lay beside her as she drew the Luger from her belt and released the safety catch, the tiny click sounding very loud in the tense silence. And then Martin's heart missed a beat as

353

he saw a German officer come through a gate in the wall, the lightning bolt flashes of the SS clear on his uniform. He was swiftly followed by a group of heavily armed soldiers who were aiming their weapons right into their hiding place.

Danuta began to inch her way back, and the two men did the same.

'I know you are there,' said the SS officer in heavily accented English. 'The owner of this house told us you vere expected.'

Danuta went white and froze against the ground.

'I am not a patient man,' said the German more sharply. 'Come out, Englishmen, before I order my men to open fire.'

Martin realised that if he and Allan gave themselves up, they'd probably be thrown into some prison before being transported to a POW camp – whereas Danuta would more than likely be interrogated and then shot as a spy. 'Get away, Danuta,' he whispered urgently.

She shook her head.

'You have to live,' he insisted. 'Go – go now while you still can.'

'But–'

'We'll give ourselves up and keep them occupied while you get away,' he hissed. 'Now clear off.'

She shot him an apologetic grin, wished them good luck, and slithered deeper back into the shadows.

'English pilots, I am running out of patience. I can hear you vispering. Come out and show yourselves.'

Martin glanced behind him. There was no sign of Danuta, and he could only pray that she got away safely. He looked at Allan, who was as white as a sheet, and gripped his shoulder. 'It's the only way to save her,' he said.

They stripped off the peasant shirts and jackets to reveal their uniforms, and got to their feet, arms raised above their heads in surrender.

18

Cliffehaven

Peggy didn't know really how to feel. The days had gone on and there was no more news about Martin and the others. She had written to Jim telling him what had happened because she'd felt he had a right to know, but she was still very upset that he hadn't been quite as truthful to her about the situation he was in, for his latest letters had been in the same vein as all the others and had told her very little.

Since it was Saturday morning, she didn't have to go to the factory, so she wrapped herself and Daisy against the cold wind, picked up her ration books and identity card and left the house. Her spirits tumbled when she saw the long queue already waiting outside Alf's butcher's shop which was yet to open. It seemed a person had to be out earlier and earlier these days to get any chance of something decent.

Eyeing the queues at the other shops, she decided she needed meat and dripping more than anything else and joined the line of chattering women outside the butcher's. She knew most of them and, after their concerned enquiries about Martin, Freddy and Roger, was soon immersed in the usual exchange of local gossip, war news and general moans about the lack of everything. There seemed to be nothing new going on in Cliffehaven that warranted much interest, but it passed the time quite pleasantly as they waited for Alf to open his shop.

Two hours later she had a laden basket, although much of it was loaves of the unpalatable wheatmeal bread that always seemed to be in supply, but did go some way to fill hungry stomachs. She was on her way up the High Street to see her brother-in-law Ted at the Home and Colonial for her weekly ration of cheese and butter when she was stopped by the officious ARP warden.

'I need to see your identity card,' he barked.

'For heaven's sake, Wally, you've known me for years. You don't need to see anything.'

'It's the law,' he replied. 'Any refusal to prove your identity will lead to arrest.'

Peggy was very tempted to tell him to stick it up his jumper, but Wally had very little sense of humour, so it probably wasn't wise to bait him. She plucked the identity card out of her handbag and handed it over.

He took a long time reading every word on it and checking the photograph against the woman standing in front of him who'd once sat near him at school. 'All right,' he said grudgingly. 'You can move on.'

Peggy gritted her teeth and snatched back the little brown card. 'You really are the limit, Wally Hall,' she hissed.

'Warden Hall to you,' he said with a sniff before marching off to accost another local.

Peggy glared after him and then stomped off at a furious pace which had Daisy screeching with laughter and begging her to go faster. Men like Wally had grown too big for their boots, parading about in a uniform and ordering people about as if they were important, and Peggy was fed up with it. Things were difficult enough without men like him, and if Daisy hadn't been with her she'd have given him a piece of her mind and no mistake.

Still furious, she headed for the Home and Colonial general store and almost rammed the pushchair into Doris's ankles as she was coming out of the door.

'Do look where you're going, Margaret,' she said crossly. 'You could have ruined my nylons.'

'You're lucky to have nylons,' retorted Peggy, who, like most other women, had taken to staining her legs with tea. She moved the pushchair out of the way so Doris could come out of the store, in the hope that her sister would go on her way without any more sniping.

Doris stood firmly in the doorway. 'I thought you were working in the factory?'

'Monday to Friday. What of it?'

'In that case you'll have time to nip into the Town Hall and help out with the comfort boxes

357

this afternoon.'

'I don't have time,' said Peggy flatly. 'And in case you haven't noticed, I do have a home and family to organise.'

Doris dismissed this with a wave of her hand. 'They're all quite capable of looking after themselves, and no matter how much cleaning and polishing you do, that house will never be improved. I'm sure Daisy won't mind spending an hour or two in the crèche.'

Peggy tamped down on a sharp retort – all too aware of the interested audience of women waiting to get out of the shop. 'Do it yourself,' she snapped.

'But I can't,' Doris insisted. 'I have an important meeting this afternoon, and we're very short-handed now most of the women are employed in the factories.'

'That's really not my problem,' said Peggy. 'Now, are you going to move out of the way, or do you want this pushchair rammed into your legs?'

Doris clearly realised Peggy would do as she'd threatened and moved out onto the pavement. 'Really, Margaret,' she muttered. 'You can be very common at times.'

Peggy didn't retaliate, although she very much wanted to, and pushed the pram into the shop. Seeing Ted serving behind the counter, she caught his eye and gave an eloquent shrug. 'She doesn't change, does she?'

He shook his head. 'I doubt she ever will. It's a cross we all have to bear, Peggy.'

Having put the world to rights with Ted and purchased her measly rations of cheese, sugar and butter, Peggy hurried home. Rita was still in deep mourning for Matthew, and as Ivy was on shift at the factory, she didn't want her moping on her own.

She reached the garden gate and stared in amazement at the line of washing flapping in the breeze. 'Goodness,' she breathed. 'How very thoughtful.'

Arriving in the kitchen she found Cordelia sitting in her chair, Rita on the floor at her feet, her head resting on the old woman's knee as the arthritic fingers stroked her dark curls to soothe her.

Peggy's heart twisted. 'Oh, Rita,' she sighed, rushing to her. 'I wish there was something I could do to take away your pain.'

'I can't believe I'll never see him again,' she replied, her voice muffled with previously shed tears. She raised her head and kissed Cordelia's gnarled hand before getting to her feet.

'I got this today,' she said tremulously, pulling a crumpled envelope from her trouser pocket. 'It's a lovely letter Matt must have written just before he went on that raid. At least it shows he was thinking of me – but it makes it all seem so very final.' Her voice broke. 'It was as if he knew he wasn't coming back.'

Peggy took the letter, unsure if she should be reading such a personal thing, but Rita insisted, so she drew out the single sheet of notepaper and read the neat, looped handwriting.

My darling Rita,

I hope you never get to read this, but if you are, then I'm sorry I had to leave you, and my heart breaks at the thought of your tears. I want you to know that I love you – have loved you since the moment I set eyes on you at Kitty and Roger's wedding, and one day, I had hoped you would be my bride.

We had such dreams, didn't we, Rita? Such lovely dreams, and I can only hope that they will sustain you until you're ready to face the world again. Don't cry for me, my darling. I have gone to a better place, already halfway to heaven in my plane, forever soaring above the landscape of home and watching over you.

I have written to Mother, and if you could, please would you contact her? She knows all about you, and I think you would both find comfort in one another.

Should my body be found and repatriated, I have left you my signet ring as a lasting token of what we've been so very fortunate to share.

I carry you with me in my heart.
Goodbye my precious girl,
Matt

Peggy folded the letter back into the envelope, her soft heart breaking as the tears made it impossible to speak. Wordlessly, she gathered Rita into her arms and held her close, feeling the girl trembling, and knowing it would take a long time for her to get over the boy who'd loved her so well.

Somerset

Anne was sitting outside shelling peas while Claus told the children a German fairy tale that had them in thrall – mostly because it had witches and bad elves in it. There had still been no news about Martin, and hope was rising that he'd continued to escape capture and might, even now, be on his way home.

She smiled as she watched the children's faces, glad that things had settled down and the Germans were once more included in the family of people who ran the farm. Bob had loosened up a bit about them being here, the two land girls treated them like older brothers and the old men were happy to spend their evenings involved with them in games of chess or dominoes.

The story came to an end and all the children begged for another one in the hope their bedtime might be put back a while. 'That's enough for tonight,' said Sally, hoisting Harry up onto her hip. 'It's late and poor Claus needs to have a rest.'

Anne rounded up a moaning Emily and Rose, while Ernie sauntered off with his hands dug deep into his pockets, socks half-mast, to see what Charlie was doing in the barn.

'I don't want to go to bed,' whined Rose, folding her arms and refusing to budge. 'Wanna 'nother story.'

'If you don't come indoors now, there will be no story for you tomorrow,' said Anne firmly.

'Don't care,' she replied with a pout.

'Well, I'm not standing here arguing with you. Claus and the others have gone off for a game of

361

dominoes, so you can stay out here on your own if you want to. But I'm taking Emily in for her bath, and will probably let her have a biscuit with her warm milk.'

'I don't care,' she said again, looking furiously at Emily from beneath her lowered brows.

Anne was about to turn away towards the farm-house door when she saw the unmistakable figure of Archibald Chisolm walking up the track towards her. Her mouth dried and her pulse raced as she handed Emily to Violet, ignored Rose, and went to meet him.

She couldn't tell from his expression if the news was good or bad, and she had to steel herself against the possibility it could be the worst. 'Hello, Reverend,' she said nervously.

'Good evening, Mrs Black.' He took off his hat and wisps of his white hair ruffled in the light breeze. 'I have news of your husband – but I think you will feel a little easier knowing that although he has been caught, he and his junior officer are now in a prison somewhere near the borders of Holland.'

'Was he injured when they took him?'

'He is quite well, and he and his junior officer are expected to be transferred soon to a POW camp.'

The relief that he was all right was tremendous, and she burst into tears.

'I'm sorry you're distressed, Mrs Black,' said the elderly vicar quietly. 'But at least you know now that he'll be coming home once it's over.'

'I'm not really distressed, just hugely relieved that he's still alive. Thank you for coming all this way to tell me,' she said through her tears. 'You could have telephoned and saved yourself the walk.'

He twisted his hat in his bony hands. 'I always think that good news should be shared in person, Mrs Black. And I hope that you can feel easier now you know he's safe. I'm led to believe that their POW camps are not much different to ours, and of course the Germans do stick by the Geneva Convention, so I expect you'll soon get a letter from him once he's settled.'

'Thank you, Reverend. That's such a comfort.'

He nodded and put on his hat. 'I will leave you to pass on the good news, and hope I shall see you in church tomorrow morning for a special service of Thanksgiving.' Tipping the brim of his hat to her, he wished her a pleasant evening and then walked back down the track.

Anne turned towards the farmhouse, her tears almost blinding her. Everyone was gathered there and as she approached them, Violet broke away and came to meet her. 'What's happened, Anne?'

'He's been taken prisoner, Vi. His war's over,' Anne managed before collapsing against Vi in relief and with a fresh storm of tears.

Cliffehaven

Hearing the rattle of the letter box, Peggy dashed into the hall to see what the postman had brought today. She had received the news about Martin in an official letter two days after Anne was told, and although she was disappointed that Martin and his junior officer had not been able to

363

make it home, she could at least rest easy that they'd be out of harm's way in a POW camp until the end of the war.

However, there had of course been no mention of Danuta and that worried her deeply. She'd tried pumping Ron for information, but he was as much in the dark about her as Peggy. He had promised to try and find out what had happened to her, yet it seemed his source of information had dried up, and the anxious days passed with still no news.

Peggy had tried repeatedly to telephone Anne, but found out from April, her former evacuee who was working at the exchange, that only the most important official calls were going through now. April promised to try to get a message through, and in the meantime Peggy had resorted to writing a stream of letters, and had a quick response from Anne.

It was a bountiful delivery today, with letters for all the girls and Cordelia, and two from Jim – one of which was for Ron. And then there was an official-looking letter in a brown envelope which she didn't like the look of at all, so she carried it into the kitchen and handed it to Ron.

'It's addressed to you,' he said, glancing at it before tucking into his boiled egg and toast.

'I know, but I don't think I can take any more bad news.'

'If it was bad news, it would have been a telegram,' he replied. Dusting crumbs from his fingers, he opened the letter and began to laugh. 'Well, Peggy, I'd say that was very good news.'

She snatched it back and began to read. It was

an invitation to attend the makeshift cinema in the scout hall for the showing of a film that had been taken of the men of the SEAC British 14th Army while on leave in Calcutta. Warrant Officer James Reilly would feature in the film with a message for his wife and family. The special showing would be on the following Saturday at eight o'clock, and all at Beach View were invited to attend.

'Oh, Ron,' she gasped. 'I don't believe it! My Jim on film.' She quickly passed the letter to Cordelia.

'Aye, that will be grand – and no doubt he'll be full of himself, thinking he's Ronald Colman or suchlike.'

'Don't be such a grouch,' she said, playfully slapping his arm. 'I bet he's more handsome than any of those other fellows.' She picked up Daisy and gave her a hug. 'We're going to see Daddy at the pictures, Daisy. What do you think of that?'

Daisy looked at her as if she was making no sense and then wriggled to get back on the floor. 'Daddy gone away for a soldger,' she said solemnly. 'You are silly, Mummy.'

Peggy laughed. 'Let's refresh the teapot and discuss what we're going to wear,' she said to the others. 'I fancy dressing up for a change, and getting my hair done. It's going to be quite an occasion.'

It was now Saturday morning of the big day, and despite the early hour, Beach View was in chaos as everyone dashed about preparing. Ron had eaten breakfast with Rosie at the Anchor after he'd brought Monty back from the morning

365

walk, and having kissed her thoroughly and promised to return to help out during the lunch-time session, he was now strolling contentedly along Camden Road towards home.

He hadn't said much to Peggy, but he was quite excited by the thought of seeing his son on the cinema screen, and had surreptitiously sorted out something respectable to wear tonight. It was important to look smart on such an occasion, for he was proud of Jim and wanted to do his best for him.

As he reached the crossroads he saw a shadow shift in the bombed-out house on the corner and was immediately on alert. It had become a favourite place for some of the children to play, but whoever was in there clearly didn't want to be seen.

'Seek, Harvey,' he whispered.

Harvey shot into the rubble and, within sec-onds, shot out again, his tail wagging, a silly grin on his furry face. Ron gave a grunt of exasper-ation and stomped after the dog which had once again disappeared into the rubble. 'Who's playing silly buggers in here?' he demanded.

'Keep your voice down, Ron. I don't want the whole town to hear.'

'Bertie! What the divil are you playing at, man?'

'I needed to speak to you urgently, Ron. I've been waiting for you to come out of the Anchor.'

'It's a bit cloak and dagger, isn't it?' he said grumpily, settling down on a lump of masonry next to the other man. They were in deep shadow here, unseen by passing traffic on the road, or pedestrians on the pavement. 'You're lucky no wains spotted you lurking – this is a favourite place to play, you know, and they might have taken you for a dirty old man.'

Bertie waved away Ron's concern. 'I'm assuming you've had no notification yet of where the Germans are holding Martin and Forbes?'

'Not a dicky bird,' he replied. 'I assume they're still in prison.'

'Which is most unsettling,' said Bertie. 'Downed pilots are usually transferred immediately to POW camps, and the next of kin informed of the address so the Red Cross can pass on their letters and parcels. They've been under arrest for almost two weeks, Ron, and it's most unusual that you haven't heard what's happened to them.'

'Should I be worried about that?' he asked sharply.

Bertie nodded. 'I think we all should.' He edged nearer to Ron, his voice dropping to almost a whisper. 'You see, there are over 170 Allied airmen being held over there, and our contacts have informed us that they've been discharged from the prisons in France, Belgium and Germany. But what is really worrying is the fact that none of them have since been registered at a POW camp.'

Ron's pulse began to race. 'Are you saying they've been shot?'

'It's a possibility,' Bertie said grimly, 'although we've had no information coming through to confirm that. The execution of 170 men would not go unnoticed, Ron, and we'd have been notified – so we have to hope that isn't the case. The real problem is that there's been no information coming through at all. Those men have simply vanished.'

The dreadful possibilities of what could have happened to them flashed through Ron's mind. 'What about Danuta?' he asked, the dread making his voice gruff.

'We have no way of knowing, Ron. She's maintained radio silence ever since, and none of the other operatives have seen her.'

'It doesn't bode well, does it?'

Bertie shook his head and gave a deep sigh. 'I'm sorry to burden you with this, Ron, but if the worst news comes, I wanted you to be prepared to deal with the fallout at Beach View.'

'Aye, there's enough sadness there already. Something like this could break Cordelia and Peggy.'

Bertie patted his arm. 'They're strong women, Ron – more likely to bend than break. We can only hope that it doesn't come to that.'

They got to their feet and Bertie dusted down his immaculately pressed trousers. 'I'll walk with you the rest of the way,' he said. 'Promised Cordelia I'd pop in and exchange her library books before taking her out for lunch at the British Restaurant. I understand from Peggy that the food there is rather good and not at all expensive.'

Ron nodded, his thoughts still on the plight of Martin and his fellow airman. He marvelled at how easily Bertie had become chipper again after delivering such awful news – but then Bertie was far more involved in the darker side of this war than he was, and he could only suppose the man had his own way of dealing with it.

Fran was doing the finishing touches to Peggy's freshly washed and set hair when Cissy came running up the steps into the kitchen. 'Oh, darling, thank goodness you could come,' Peggy said in delight, giving her a hug.

Cissy grinned. 'Well, it was a bit of an invitation from on high, so I suppose the brass hats couldn't really refuse to let me attend. After all, this is my film star father we're going to see.'

Peggy rushed to put the kettle on while Cissy greeted the girls and kissed Cordelia. 'Where's Granda?'

'Downstairs making himself beautiful,' giggled Fran. 'To be sure, I'm thinking it will take a while. He still won't let me cut his hair.'

'I heard that, you cheeky wee girl.' Ron stomped up the stairs in his best suit, Jim's dark blue fedora and polished shoes. He gave them a twirl. 'So what d'ye think, then?'

'Very handsome,' said Peggy.

'You could have done with a haircut and those brows being tamed,' said Cordelia, who was sitting in her fireside chair looking very smart in her best coat, with a little straw hat perched on her head.

'Well, I think you look lovely,' said Rita, giving his freshly shaven cheek a kiss.

'Yeah, not bad for an old 'un,' Ivy giggled. 'Scrub up quite well.'

'It's a great pity he doesn't scrub up more often,' muttered Cordelia, scrabbling in her handbag. 'Oh dear, I seem to have lost my spectacles.'

Sarah found them stuck down the side of the chair. 'You're looking lovely, Aunt Cordelia,' she said fondly. 'Are you ready for our walk?'

'I've been ready ever since Bertie brought me back from lunch,' she replied. 'And if we don't get a move on, we shall be late.'

They left by the back door, the four girls looking very smart in the dresses and cardigans they'd managed to salvage between them, and Ron in his suit, with Harvey at his heels and Cordelia leaning on his arm. Peggy had resurrected her ancient fox fur wrap from the bottom of the wardrobe, and although it ponged a bit of mothballs, she thought it looked very well with her navy dress and jacket. She wheeled the pushchair with Daisy strapped in, all excited to be going out after tea and looking very sweet in the miniature dungarees and sweater Peggy had made, and her velvet collared coat.

Queenie sat on the kitchen windowsill and howled pathetically, which made everyone feel a bit mean for leaving her behind.

Since they could only go as fast as Cordelia, Peggy let Daisy out of the pram so she could walk too, and soon they were part of a flood of people all heading for the scout hall where the Americans, bless them, had provided a makeshift cinema after the old Odeon had been bombed. There were crowds waiting outside, milling about waiting for the door to open, and the excited chatter and laughter were rising as more friends and acquaintances arrived.

Peggy saw her sister-in-law, Pauline, and rushed to greet her, and then was swamped in a bear hug by Stan the stationmaster. His wife, Ethel, was there with her daughter Ruby, and Rosie Braithwaite was looking very glamorous in scarlet and black. Everyone hugged and kissed and chattered like starlings, and when the door was flung open there was an eager surge to try and get the best spot.

Peggy and the party from Beach View managed to get a whole row to themselves, with Ethel, Ruby and Stan sitting right behind them. They were settling in when Wally Hall strode down the aisle and came to a halt beside Ron.

'You can't bring that there 'ere,' he said, pointing to Harvey.

'Why not?'

'It's unhygienic,' he said with a sniff.

Ron could smell the stale sweat on the man from where he was sitting. He stood to his full height and squared his shoulders. A hush fell over the room as he surveyed the audience. 'Does anyone else object to Harvey being in here?'

A chorus of support for Harvey staying went up and people began a slow handclap, while some wag at the back suggested it should be Wally leaving as he'd never been known to wash properly.

Ron turned to the man, his demeanour calm but with an underlying menace. 'You have your answer, Wally. Probably best you leave if you don't want trouble.'

Wally went red and stomped out of the hall. One of the men from the Home Guard turned off the lights, another started the projector and everyone settled down to watch their loved ones.

There were lots of scenes shot in what looked like a mess hall with a bar and a piano, others where they were sitting outside under palm trees

371

on a beach, or messing about in the water. Peggy realised it must have been filmed at one of the 'Peace Stations' Jim had mentioned, which provided respite from the flies, the heat and the mosquitoes of the jungle.

One by one each man came to speak to the camera, clearly feeling very awkward and not at all sure what to say. There were excited gasps in the audience as someone recognised a husband or a son or a brother, and when the camera panned across the mess hall, Peggy caught sight of Jim.

'There he is,' she squeaked in excitement, shifting to the front of her chair and getting Daisy to stand on her lap so she could see him. 'Look, Daisy, that's Daddy.'

Harvey got to his feet and gave a yelp of welcome as Jim walked towards the camera in an open white shirt and khaki shorts, looking so brown and handsome it made Peggy want to reach out and touch him.

'Hello, Peg,' he said, his dark eyes looking straight at her. 'I expect you and the rest of the family at Beach View are watching this, so I send you all my love – especially to you, darlin' girl, Da and Frank. Oh, and special kisses for all our wains. I can't wait to see you all again, and hope it won't be too long until I come home.'

And then he walked away and another man came into shot to a cry of delighted recognition from someone towards the back of the hall.

Peggy slumped back in the seat and cuddled Daisy, who didn't really understand what was going on, so she kissed her curls and reached for Ron's hand. 'It was lovely to see him looking so fit and well,' she whispered, keeping one eye on the screen in case he came into shot again.

'Aye, he always was a bonny lad,' Ron replied gruffly.

Harvey was still looking at the screen, his head tilting one way and then the other as if he was trying to figure out where Jim had gone. Then he lay down on the floor with a deep sigh and rested his nose on his paws.

Peggy felt as if she was floating on air as they walked home again an hour later. Her Jim looked better than she'd ever remembered him, fit, muscular and deeply tanned – and although he was still on the other side of the world, she knew that tonight she could dream about him and feel closer to him.

19

Münster Prison

'I don't understand why they're keeping us here,' Allan said fretfully. 'It's been over two weeks since they arrested us. Surely they ought to be transferring us to a prisoner of war camp?'

'It's probably because it was the SS who captured us, and not regular soldiers.'

They sat opposite one another on the unforgiving metal beds, their knees almost touching in the confined space as they ate their stale black bread and over-spiced, glutinous sausage and washed it down with metallic-tasting water. The small window high up in the stone wall was so dirty the light could barely penetrate it. It was cold and dank in the cell, and once their clothes had dried, they were grateful for the warmth of the 'Hairy Marys' and the thick wool of their uniform jackets, for they'd been provided with only a single thin blanket, a straw-filled mattress and a pillow as hard and uncomfortable as a brick.

'Do you think our families will know where we are, sir?'

'I'm sure they've been informed,' Martin replied, weary from all the boy's questions. 'I suggest we try and get some shut-eye before one of us is taken back to the office for more questioning.'

He left the tin plate and mug on the stone floor and lay back on the lumpy mattress, cupping his hands behind his head as he closed his eyes. He hadn't wanted to say anything to young Forbes, but he was very worried. The German officer had questioned them individually and relentlessly, but they'd stuck to giving just their name, rank and number, refusing to say anything more, especially not revealing that Forbes spoke passable German – that really would have set the cat amongst the pigeons.

However, the man's line of questioning told Martin quite a lot about their status as prisoners and it worried him deeply – not only for himself, but for Forbes. The fact they hadn't turned themselves in immediately after they'd been shot down meant they were now suspected to be saboteurs and terrorists, deliberately parachuted into Germany and in league with the outlawed

Resistance – which could very likely lead to a firing squad.

He'd vehemently denied it, of course, but the man was immovable, refusing to believe him and continuing to question him about his Resistance contacts, shouting and banging his fist on the table, pacing back and forth and yelling in his ear. Martin had expected violence to follow these harangues and could only hope that he and Forbes were strong enough to withstand any torture and keep silent about Danuta.

And yet, for some reason, the man hadn't touched him, and Martin wondered if a specific order from his superiors had held him back, for he could feel the anger in the Nazi, the pent-up violence that emanated from him in waves as he strutted about in his pristine uniform; the swagger stick frequently slapped in frustration against his long, black, highly polished boots or crashed against the table. Were they simply being held here because someone of a much higher rank was coming to seriously interrogate them – or was there a demonic plan in store for them he had yet to know about?

Martin flinched as he heard a scream of agony coming from deep within the prison walls, and then the awful sound of gunshots from a nearby yard. He tried to close his mind to it all, for gunshots and screams had become a regular reminder of where they were and what could be awaiting them at the hands of their captors – and he had to remain positive that his uniform and status would protect them both. Yet he dreaded to think what that Nazi had done to the people in

375

that house to make them betray one of their own, and prayed that Danuta had escaped to fight another day.

He'd been a prisoner for two weeks and the not knowing what was ahead ate away at him, so he simply couldn't imagine how she coped with living on such a knife-edge day in and day out, year upon year – never really knowing whom she could trust, and what was waiting for her at the next safe house.

He silently saluted her courage and indomitable spirit, hoping that he might possess even a fraction of it to get him and Forbes through the following hours, or days, or even weeks.

The sound of rattling keys was followed by the crash of the steel cell door against the end of the metal bed. *'Raus, Raus,'* bellowed the guard.

Martin and Allan exchanged fearful glances, for they'd never been called out together before. Were they going to be interrogated again – or something worse? Both were dry-mouthed and unsteady as they got to their feet.

The guard pulled them out of the cell and jabbed them in the back with the butt of his rifle.

'Where are you taking us?' Martin demanded, stumbling in the narrow, echoing hallway which was lined with numerous other cells.

'Silence, English svine. Move, move.'

Martin could hear despairing voices calling to them from behind the cell doors they were passing – some in French, others in German, wishing them courage – but the guard was pushing them along so quickly it was impossible to exchange any words with them.

And then a door opened to admit a glare of almost blinding daylight, and as they were shoved through it, they shielded their eyes and saw they were in an enclosed yard. There were posts cemented into the ground, and a rusty stain of blood was splattered on the wall behind them, with fresher blood pooled on the ground.

So this is it, he thought. This is where it ends. He felt strangely calm and was about to take Forbes by the arm and wish him Godspeed when he was shoved forward towards a gateway in the wall that he hadn't noticed.

Stumbling to keep their footing, the two men were thrust towards a long line of trucks that were waiting, the engines emitting clouds of exhaust fumes. The soldiers were everywhere, armed with rifles and some even with machine guns and dogs, as Martin and Forbes were frog-marched towards the rear truck.

The tailgate was down, and he couldn't make out who was sitting in the gloomy interior because he was still dazzled by the sun. With an encouraging prod in the kidneys from the rifle-butt, he climbed up, swiftly followed by Forbes. They sat down on one of the narrow benches which ran along both sides of the truck's rear, the tailgate was slammed shut, and the convoy of lorries moved off, taking them through the high outer gates, beyond the barricade and out onto a country road.

'Welcome to the Kraut's idea of a Sunday drive in the country,' drawled a young American as they swayed with the movement of the truck along the rough road. 'First Lieutenant Andrew Pearce the

Third. USAAF.' He gave a sardonic salute. 'I guess we're all on our way to a POW camp, unless they're planning to shoot us along the way.'

Martin's eyes had finally adjusted to the gloom and he returned the salute, introducing himself and Forbes to the other six men. 'Where were you being held?'

'Me and my buddies have been in some rat-infested, stinking hole of a prison on the other side of the Belgian border,' Pearce, replied. 'It's taken us two days to get here already.'

He went on to introduce his friends, who it turned out were American, Canadian and Australian pilots that had been shot down and then hidden by the Resistance. 'I guess you're our senior officer, sir,' he said, sitting a little straighter.

Martin nodded and then turned to regard the plume of dust rising from beneath the wheels and the empty road behind them. The farmland seemed to stretch for miles in every direction, and in the distance, he could see a pine forest. There were no outriders and the armed soldiers were riding up front in the cabs, so it should be possible to jump out the back, lie still until the convoy had moved on and then head for the forest.

'I wouldn't contemplate it, sir,' said one of the Australians, reading his thoughts. 'A couple of blokes tried jumping out earlier, and they got shot to buggery before they'd taken more'n a few steps. Pardon my French, sir.'

Martin shrugged off the apology. He was used to Australians being forthright; he'd had several under his command in the early days of the war. 'But surely, if we just drop off the back...'

'Flaming wing mirrors, sir,' he replied laconically.

'What about the men in the other trucks? Are they from the same place as you?'

The American shook his head. 'They joined us just before we stopped for you, but I reckon most of them are civilians. There are prisons all over this darn country; they could have been kept anywhere.'

Martin did a quick count of heads and multiplied it by the number of trucks he'd seen waiting outside the prison. 'That means there are over a hundred of us,' he murmured. 'Surely that would be enough to overpower a few soldiers?'

'Maybe, but how do we get the message down the line?' the Australian replied. 'Don't get me wrong, sir, I ain't no bludger, but I reckon it's better to form an escape committee once we get to the camp – trying anything now is plain bloody suicidal.'

Martin realised the man was right and slumped back against the canvas cover, watching the miles slipping beneath him as the truck headed east.

About two hours later they saw the rest of the convoy turn off at a crossroads to head south. They were on their own, a solitary truck now closely guarded by armed soldiers riding shotgun on motorbikes with sidecars – still heading east – and with every mile the unease grew. Why had they been separated from the rest of the convoy? Was it because they were airmen – or because they were classed as saboteurs?

The truck kept moving, from rough tracks to

country roads and then onto smooth bitumen. The sun had executed a full arch across the sky and was beginning to dip towards the hills in the west. They'd had no food or water since they'd set out, and all of them were suffering from terrible thirst in the confined heat beneath the canvas.

Martin checked his watch. By his calculations, they'd been travelling at about thirty miles an hour for five hours – which meant they'd already covered about 150 miles. Where the hell were they being taken?

'Strewth, would you blokes look at that,' said the Australian, who'd managed to unfasten a bit of the canvas side and was peeking out.

Everyone fell silent as they began to pass between huge camps on either side of the road, which seemed to sprawl to every horizon behind acres of barbed-wire fencing. Watchtowers were regularly spaced along those fences, and they could see armed soldiers with guard dogs patrolling the perimeters. Martin could smell something strange in the air that was mingled with smoke, and his misgivings deepened. This didn't feel right at all – and he sensed that the other men were feeling just as uneasy.

As the truck slowed, every man went to the front and yanked a gap in the canvas so they could see over the roof of the cab. They were now slowly approaching a heavily guarded gate within the high fence of barbed wire, beyond which was another running parallel to it. In between the fences was a cleared strip of land patrolled by grim-faced guards – with snarling dogs straining at their leashes – and above it all were two watch-

380

towers. Beyond the lines of fencing they could see hundreds of wooden huts and people who appeared to be dressed in striped pyjamas.

'What the flaming hell *is* this place – and what does that mean?' asked the Australian, pointing to the wording embedded in the beam above the gate.

Allan Forbes went the colour of paper as he read the words out in flawless German: *'Jedem das Seine.'* He swallowed, and had to cling to the side of the truck to steady himself. 'It means "to each his own" – or "everyone gets what he deserves".'

He turned to Martin, his eyes dark with fear. 'This isn't a POW camp, sir. It's the SS labour concentration camp – Buchenwald.'

A stunned silence followed, and they all looked to Martin for guidance. He could feel the horror racing through him in icy shards, for he'd heard rumours about this place, and his scrambled thoughts couldn't absorb the fact that soon they'd be behind those fences. He realised the men were waiting for him to take charge, and as he was the senior officer, he knew he had to pull his thoughts together and not show his fear.

'We will all conduct ourselves as honourable members of the Allied flying forces,' he said. 'There has clearly been a grave administrative error, and I shall demand to see the camp commandant immediately to put things right.'

'And what if you can't?' asked the Australian.

'I'll do my best, Stokes. You can be assured of that.'

There was no time for further discussion, for

the lorry was now driving through the gate, across the clearing to the second gate and then into the barren clearing, where it came to a standstill.

The tailgate was lowered and they were faced with a line of armed soldiers and two snarling dogs. Martin went down first and was swiftly followed by the others. They stood in line, warily watching the dogs, the terror growing as they saw skeletal figures of boys and young and old men dressed in rags or striped pyjamas slowly and painfully lifting dead bodies onto wooden wagons. They'd arrived in hell – and it seemed there was to be no reprieve.

The SS officer strode up and down the line of men, tapping his riding whip against his polished boots, his grey eyes cold in his austere face. He came to a halt in front of Martin. 'Velcome to Buchenvald,' he said in remarkably good English. 'I am *Standartenführer* Pister of the SS. Death is your only escape from here,' he said coldly. 'I vould suggest you obey orders.'

Martin stepped forward. 'Sir,' he said. 'I object strongly to us being brought here and demand that you abide by the Geneva Convention and send us to a proper POW camp.'

The riding whip flashed, the thin leather strips scoring deeply into Martin's face. 'You do not object or demand,' the man roared. 'Such insolence vill be punished in future.' He turned to one of the guards. 'Process them, and then put them to vork.'

Martin was about to protest again when he felt the pressure of Forbes' elbow against his arm and caught the look of warning in his eyes. He realised then that the safety of his men was paramount, and should he complain again, he might endanger them all. So, very reluctantly, he said nothing.

Somerset

Anne had become deeply concerned that there had been no notification of the POW camp Martin had been sent to, and as three weeks had now passed, the fear for what might have happened to him had grown.

'It's unusual, isn't it?' she asked George Mayhew as they sat in his garden drinking tea at the end of the school day.

'It is rather,' he replied solemnly. 'Captured prisoners are usually kept in prison for a few days and then transferred to a Stalag – a German prisoner of war camp. I'm sorry, Anne, but I really don't know what to say to you that will ease your mind.'

Belinda grasped her hand. 'He might very well have escaped that prison and be on the run again. He sounds like a resourceful man.'

A tiny spark of hope ignited and Anne clung to it fiercely. 'It is a possibility, I suppose,' she murmured. 'And of course it would explain this awful silence.' She took a tremulous breath. 'I'm sorry I haven't been much help these past three weeks, but Martin's situation is all I can think about. I've hardly noticed a thing going on around me.'

'That's understandable,' said George. 'Poor Anne, you really are going through the mill, aren't you? I wish there was something Belinda and I could do to help.'

Through the foggy haze of anxiety, Anne suddenly noticed something: Belinda's other hand was resting lightly over George's fingers. The shock of realisation must have shown on Anne's face because Belinda moved her hand, embarrassed, and George flushed pink.

'Oh my goodness! It seems I haven't just been a useless colleague recently but a useless friend as well.' She grinned at them. 'So how long has this been going on, you two?'

'Well, I suppose the cat is out of the bag now, at least where you're concerned, Anne,' said George. 'Belinda and I have become ... very close friends over the last few months. And it's all thanks to you.' Anne couldn't see how this was possible, but before she had time to dwell on it George continued, 'I meant to ask your advice, Anne, but the moment didn't present itself, what with all that's happened lately. You see, I needed to find a way to see Belinda out of our day-to-day school environment. And then it seemed the only way would be to go to that blasted dance you were both so keen for me to attend.' He reddened further. 'And what a triumph that turned out to be.'

Anne found she was beaming despite herself, for this was wonderful news in an otherwise bleak time. She actually felt rather foolish that she'd got the wrong end of the stick quite so spectacularly with George's behaviour. She'd thought he'd been holding a candle for her, when really Belinda was the one he'd been interested in all along.

She took both their hands. 'I'm so happy for you, and I'm sorry for being so wrapped up in my own world. There's really no excuse. But it's good to know I have such good friends.'

'Anyway, that's enough about us,' said Belinda. 'Is there anything we can do to help?'

'No, thank you, really. I just have to deal with this myself and keep up my hopes that perhaps he has escaped and is on the run.' She smiled at them. 'Seeing Da on film the other night did give my spirits a tremendous boost. He's clearly making the best of things, out in Burma if his letters are anything to go by.'

George poured more tea and handed round the plate of home-made biscuits Mrs McCormack had brought over that morning from the Shepherd's Arms. 'From all I've heard from you about your father, I suspect that might be the case,' he said with a wry smile.

Anne thought of her big, handsome father, with his deep tan, twinkling eyes and the lilting Irish accent he'd inherited from his parents. 'He's got headquarters behind the front line, where he supervises his Indian mechanics, and he and his mate Ernie have certainly made their living quarters as comfortable as possible. He's acquired chickens and ducks and fish to supplement army supplies – and has somehow found another dog which has proved to be a tremendous ratcatcher as well as a good companion.'

She chuckled. 'He's managed to "borrow" a wireless from somewhere which he's running off a lorry battery, so he can keep up with the news and listen to *Forces Favourites*. There's also a SEAC newspaper, so it's almost like home from home.'

'How's your mother coping with him being so far away?' asked Belinda.

'Mam's not the sort of woman to weep and wail and make a fuss. She'll have rolled up her sleeves and got on with things, knowing that the others look to her for guidance and care. But although she always sounds cheerful when we manage to talk on the telephone, I suspect there's many a night when she lies awake in tears.'

Anne gripped Belinda's hand. 'The death of Rita's young pilot hit them all hard – and now, with Martin and the other men missing... She must be under the most awful strain.' She gave a sigh. 'I wish I could be with her. It would make things easier for both of us, I think.'

'With the travel ban in place, no one can get anywhere,' said Belinda. 'My poor mother's in hospital after that raid on London, and I desperately want to see her.'

'I'm sure that once this rumoured invasion takes place the ban will be lifted,' said George. 'Until then, we'll just have to carry on in the belief that the end of the war is finally in sight; and that before too long, we can all go home.'

Cliffehaven

They were all gathered in the kitchen to listen to the six o'clock news on the wireless, which they'd had to turn up so they could hear it over the roar and thunder of the Allied planes on their way across the Channel for another bombing raid.

Earlier in the month the Russian troops had

recaptured Sevastopol in the Crimea, and taken many German prisoners. The Fifth and Eighth Armies had attacked the Gustav Line south of Rome, making the Germans withdraw to the Adolf Hitler Line, and Monte Cassino had fallen to the Allies. Now they waited with bated breath to see if Rome had also fallen.

'The Allies have made a serious breakthrough of the Adolf Hitler Line,' said the newsreader solemnly, 'and over six thousand German prisoners have been taken. Meanwhile a new offensive has begun on the Anzio beachhead. It is hoped that soon we will hear even more heartening news from Italy that our courageous men have broken through to Rome itself.'

'It's really happening, isn't it?' breathed Peggy. 'The war's turning in our favour.'

'Aye,' murmured Ron. 'It can't turn quick enough in my opinion.'

'The news from India is also heartening,' said the newsreader, bringing Peggy's attention back immediately. 'The Japanese are retreating as fast as they can from the borders of India in a race to beat the British troops and the monsoon. The odds against them became hopeless after they were cut up by our British defences at Kohima and their supply lines were threatened by the monsoon. Kohima is now entirely under Allied control. In the Bishenpur area, south of Imphal, the process of mopping up isolated Japanese positions continues.'

Peggy shivered. Jim had mentioned Imphal in some of his letters, and she wondered if he was at this moment taking part in that clearing up.

'In the South West Pacific campaign,' the news-reader continued, 'Allied troops are now closing in from three directions on Mokmer Aerodrome, which is the key point of Biak Island off Dutch New Guinea.'

Peggy reached across for Sarah's hand and grasped it warmly. 'They're on the run, Sarah. They'll soon be pushed back into the sea and Singapore and the Far East will be liberated. We'll get news very soon about your father and Philip. I'm sure of it.'

'I'm almost afraid to learn what's happened to them,' Sarah confessed. 'It's been so long, and there have been so many horror stories coming out of that region.'

'We have to stay positive, dear, or we'll all go mad with worry,' Peggy replied, trying not to think of Martin and Freddy and Roger.

Sarah's anguish for her father and her fiancé Philip plagued her, for it had been over two years since she'd seen them on the dockside in Singapore, and she'd heard nothing since. There had been awful rumours of death camps; of starving prisoners made to work at breaking rocks and building railway bridges; of enforced marches, beatings and executions – and if they were true, then it was almost impossible to keep faith that they had survived. Yet she knew she had to maintain that faith, no matter what.

Peggy got to her feet as the broadcast ended and set about dishing out the tea, which tonight was a spam, onion and potato hash – more spud than anything, but at least it would be filling. She looked up in surprise as Ron got up from the table and began to pull on his coat and cap. 'Where do you think you're going?'

'I have to be somewhere,' he replied, tying the garden twine laces on his boots. 'Keep my tea warm. I won't be long.'

'But I'm about to dish up,' she protested. 'Can't it wait for ten minutes?'

He shook his head. Donning his filthy cap, he went down the cellar steps and out into the garden, with Harvey racing ahead of him.

Peggy peeked round the edge of the blackout, but he'd moved swiftly and was already out of sight. 'Honestly, Ron,' she sighed crossly, 'you really are the absolute limit.'

Ron and Bertie had arranged the meeting earlier in the day. Bertie had taken Cordelia out for lunch again at the British Restaurant, and when he'd returned, he'd tipped Ron the wink that he needed to speak to him. A hastily whispered few words in the hall had followed, and now Ron was on his way to see what it was that had got Bertie so fired up.

He avoided his usual route and headed into the maze of streets and alleyways that lay between Camden Road and the High Street. Emerging into the alley directly behind the Crown, he saw that the gate in the high fence had been left ajar, so he stepped into the yard, closed it behind him and gave three light taps on the back door.

Gloria Stevens smiled at him as she let him in. 'Hello, 'andsome,' she said. 'I can't say I'm that happy with you, though. You're late and I've 'ad to keep the pub shut until you got 'ere.'

'Sorry, Gloria, lost track of time. Where is he?'

'In the back function room. I've left a window open in the little kitchen, so you'll have to use that to get out again.' She rolled her eyes. 'I dunno,' she giggled, 'all this bleedin' cloak and dagger stuff can't be good for me 'ealth.'

'You look healthy enough to me, Gloria,' he replied with a grin, taking in her generous curves and the plunging neckline on her blouse. 'To be sure, girl, you're built for sin, so you are,' he added with a sigh, and then stomped off to find Bertie.

He was sitting at the far end of the large room with two pints of beer and two whisky chasers on the table in front of him. 'I thought you weren't coming,' he said as Ron sat down and Harvey sprawled beneath the table.

Ron took a deep draught of his beer. 'This better be good, Bertie, because I haven't had me tea yet.'

'The whisky was Gloria's idea, and on the house,' said Bertie, sipping at it to savour every drop.

'Good for her. Get on with it, Bertie, for goodness' sake.'

'There has been a series of very short communications from Danuta,' he said, leaning his arms on the table. 'It's not from her usual location, and my contact suspects she's moving around a lot, and that the brevity of her messages means she's aware of being either watched or closely tracked.'

Ron gave a deep sigh of relief. 'I'm just thankful she's still alive,' he said. 'Do you know where she is?'

Bertie's expression was very serious. 'I know

390

where she was two days ago. The signal was coming from Weimar in Germany.'

'But what the divil's she doing still in Germany? Why didn't she get out after Martin and the boy were arrested?'

'She clearly decided to keep watch and find out what had happened to them. Using her most reliable people in the Resistance, she followed the convoy that took them to Weimar.'

'What's in Weimar? A Stalag?'

Bertie's hand was shaking as he raised the whisky glass to his lips. 'Unfortunately, not a Stalag, but Buchenwald concentration camp.'

An icy shiver ran down Ron's spine. 'Holy Mother of God and all the saints,' he breathed as he crossed himself. 'But why, Bertie? Allied prisoners of war are supposed to be in proper Stalags.'

'I think it's as we feared, Ron. They didn't give themselves up, were aided by the Resistance and therefore have been classed as spies or saboteurs. The rule book has been thrown out the window along with the Geneva Convention.'

'So what can Danuta do to get them out of there?' Ron asked, his heart racing with fear.

'I don't think she can do anything, old boy,' said Bertie. 'She's one girl working virtually alone in enemy territory and way out of her usual area. Unless she has contacts within the SS hierarchy and can persuade someone to liberate them, I'm afraid there's very little hope.'

Ron downed the whisky in one before holding his head in his hands. 'I wish you'd said nothing, Bertie. How the hell am I going to face Peggy knowing what I do now?'

'You'll manage, Ron, you're good at keeping secrets. And who knows, Danuta might have a plan. She's a very resourceful girl, and has resolved many a difficult situation before.'

'She'd have to be a miracle worker to resolve this one,' muttered Ron.

20

Buchenwald

Their first impressions had been correct; they *had* arrived in hell.

Martin had done his best to bolster the spirits of the younger men, but as his own were so low, he knew he was unconvincing. And now even the chirpy Australian wasn't quite so ready with his quips, for they'd been forced to give up all their valuables as well as their uniforms and boots the moment they'd arrived and exchange them for the striped pyjamas, both halves marked clearly with a red triangle so they'd be recognised immediately by the guards as *Sonderhäftlinge* – enemy servicemen and spies. Then had come the humiliation of having their heads shaved – these two acts had swiftly brought them down to the same helpless and hopeless state as the poor skeletal figures that surrounded them.

Their hut was large, narrow and draughty, letting in the cold night air and the stench of their surroundings. It was made of wood with a corrugated iron roof, and on both sides there were three parallel lines of wooden shelves which served as bunks. Stinking straw-filled and bug-ridden mattresses were the only bedding. There was no heating or lighting, nothing to cover the windows, so the ever-present sweep of the searchlights and tower lights had at first kept them awake – now they were so exhausted they hardly noticed the discomfort any more.

During the past two weeks they'd been sent to work in a munitions factory that had been built deeper within the vast complex, which they learned consisted of over 140 satellite camps. Each one had been built for a specific purpose and a specific type of prisoner – what those were none of them wanted to know, but they could guess, for the smell of death and chimney smoke was everywhere.

They also learned that the slightest lapse in effort at work, or infringement of the bewildering and conflicting rules earned a beating – or long, isolated hours in an underground pit barely big enough for a child, let alone a man. They'd all lost weight, and most of them were suffering terrible diarrhoea, which wasn't helped by the thin gruel and weevil-infested rice they were given once a day, and the vermin in the filthy straw mattresses that bit them throughout the night. Martin knew that the things he'd witnessed here would never leave him, and even if he was lucky enough to be liberated, he could never speak of them.

They were lying exhausted in the half-empty hut after another gruelling day of being bullied and shouted at in the factory when the Australian, Billy Stokes, came hobbling back from his fifth visit in the last hour to the latrines.

'Listen up, you blokes,' he said breathlessly. 'A train's just arrived, and you'll never guess, it's full of Yanks and Poms.'

'How the hell do you know that?' asked one of the Americans.

'Because I can hear them talking,' he replied, 'and you Yanks never could talk without flaming shouting.'

'That's rich coming from you, Stokes,' the American replied without rancour. 'Your voice is like a foghorn.'

They trooped outside, their bare feet scuffing the dry earth, and went to look through the wire fencing behind the latrines to the railway line which ran right through the centre of the camp.

'See, what did I tell you?' said Billy. 'Flaming hell,' he breathed. 'There must be near two hundred of 'em.'

They edged closer to the wire, hearing the hum of the electricity running through it as they watched the men being pulled out of the cattle trucks and complaining loudly at the rough handling. Not all of them were in uniform, and Martin guessed that they'd used the peasant clothing as a disguise while on the run. They looked a sorry lot, even though they were doing their best to retain their dignity but they were clearly disorientated by the bright sulphur lights, the shouting, bullying guards and the snarling, ferocious dogs straining on their leashes to get to them.

They were roughly pushed into a ragged line and jostled towards the gate which would take them straight into the showers, where they'd have to forego their clothes and personal treasures for prison attire – the roughest treatment meted out to the dark-skinned airmen.

'I say, sir. Isn't that Wing Commander Makepeace?' Forbes said excitedly. 'And look, Sir. There's Squadron Leader Pargeter right behind him.'

Martin followed his pointing finger and couldn't believe his eyes. They were barely recognisable in the rough shirts and trousers and broken boots, their faces almost hidden by thick beards. 'Good grief. So it is, and I could have sworn I saw Roger's plane go down with no parachute in sight. It's a miracle, Forbes. An absolute, bloody miracle.'

'I don't know why you blokes are so excited about seeing your mates,' drawled Billy Stokes. 'They'd've been better off dead in a burning plane than in this flaming place.'

'They've survived to fight another day,' said Forbes, with all the bravura of youth.

'They'll have to survive old Pisser first,' replied the Australian. 'And they look half-dead already, especially those black fellas.' Then his expression changed to one of deep shock. 'Strike a light and burn me tail feathers,' he breathed. 'If it ain't old Jock Cannon. I thought he'd bought it when our kite went down.'

'Was he your co-pilot, then?' asked Forbes, trying to work out which man he was talking about.

'Na, mate, I was his,' he replied, his haggard face alight with pride. 'That old bastard used to fly us all over Australia when we were on the shearing runs – toughest, meanest old bugger you're likely to meet – but a bonzer bloke for all that. He could drink me under the table and still fly us on to the next job. Jeez, I hate to think of him here.'

They stood in silent despair and watched the line of shambling men being pushed and shoved into the ablutions block, and waited until they emerged a short while later in the hated prison garb, each carrying a tin mug and bowl, their shaved heads bowed in defeat.

'Pisser' – Commandant Pister – gave them the usual harangue and then they were shuffling through the last gate and into the compound.

Moving as one, they went to meet them, but there was very little joy in the reunion, for Martin knew they must look as half-dead as the other inmates, and he could see the new arrivals were so stunned by where they were and what was happening to them, they moved like sleepwalkers.

They still stank despite the shower, for it would have been brief with very little soap to go round, and Martin could see that beneath the stubble their skin was grey, their eyes dull and sunken with exhaustion and dread.

Martin headed straight for Roger and Freddy, with Forbes right beside him. 'Hello, chaps,' he said quietly as he took their arms. 'Come into the hut and rest. You look all in.'

They both stared at him and Forbes in bewilderment. 'Martin? Allan? We thought you'd bought it.' Roger swayed on his feet. 'Sorry, old bean, a bit wobbly on the pins. Never did like travelling by train.'

'We'll catch up on your news once you've rested.' Martin and Forbes steered the two shambling men towards the hut, and they'd just reached the wooden steps leading up to it when Martin heard someone calling out his name.

He turned and saw Cissy's American boyfriend hobbling towards him, and his spirits plummeted even further. 'Randy? I thought you were safely tucked up in a French prison. What on earth are you doing *here?*'

'The same as the others,' he replied, following them into the hut. 'I was picked up with Roger, Freddy and ten others, and we were taken to some station near Paris where the rest were already being forced into those cattle trucks.'

He sank down on the nearest makeshift bunk as if his legs could no longer bear his weight. 'We've been packed in there for five days, having to stand most of the way, with barely anything to eat or drink and having to defecate on the floor. We were all terrified, because we somehow knew we weren't going to arrive at some civilised Stalag.'

He was wide-eyed with fear as he looked up at Martin. 'But this is beyond our worst nightmare.'

'We don't have any food,' said Martin apologetically, 'but we do have water. We'll fetch some for you all from the tap outside.'

The other men had had the same idea and soon there was a procession of tin cups and bowls being handed in and then out again to be replenished, until the exhausted arrivals had had their fill and felt a little more able to talk.

Billy's mate Jock Cannon turned out to be a whip-thin individual in his forties, with a

397

weathered face, the nose of a serious drinker, a stubble of bristled sandy hair, and eyes of the brightest blue. He was definitely a character, for once he'd recovered, he'd broken the solemn atmosphere by asking where the flaming bar was, because he could really do with a long, cold beer and the company of a nice hot Sheila.

This elicited a few chuckles and then quiet conversations broke out amongst the men as acquaintances were renewed and failed escape stories swapped. Martin was deep in conversation with Roger and Freddy when a loud voice broke through the hum of talk.

'Who's the senior officer here?'

Martin heard the clipped, rather nasal twang of New Zealand and turned towards the burly man making his way from the far end of the hut. Despite the bald head, bare feet and sagging pyjamas, he still retained the regal dignity of a man used to being in charge.

'I am for the moment, sir,' he replied, getting to his feet.

'Rank?' he boomed.

'Group Captain Martin Black of the RAF, sir,' he replied.

'Colonel Fuller, ANZAC Royal Marines, Airborne Division.' He approached Martin and, shook his hand. 'It seems we are the same rank sir, but I don't reckon that counts for much in this place.'

'Unfortunately not, sir,' Martin agreed. 'But perhaps it would be wise to check that there isn't an American amongst the new arrivals who might outrank both of us? They do seem to be here in the greatest number.'

The New Zealander looked round. 'Well, speak up, you Yanks. Who's your top man?'

'I guess that would be me, sir.' The drawling Texan voice came from one of the top bunks and belonged to a lengthy, supine figure that didn't bother to move – whether through inertia, or sheer despair, they couldn't tell. 'Group Captain William Hurst the Third, USAAF.'

'Well, that seems clear enough,' said the Colonel. 'It looks, men, as if we're the three to come to if you have any problems.' He turned back to Martin. 'Now, how do we get out of here?'

'We don't,' said Martin. 'The fences are electrified and lit up all night, with searchlights sweeping across the compounds and a constant patrol of all-too-efficient guards. Their dogs would make minced-meat out of you given half the chance, and it's the guards' favourite game to let them get within a hair's breadth of your legs as you walk past.'

He took a breath and continued, aware that a shocked silence had fallen within the hut. 'We can't dig tunnels because the ground is too hard, and we're miles from anywhere that has cover. This place is the size of a small city isolated in the middle of nowhere. Apart from all that, we've been weakened by the runs, countless beatings, long hours working in a factory, lice, bedbugs and the lack of even the most basic of decent food. We've tried very hard to work out a way to escape, but...'

He held out his hands and shrugged. 'You've seen what this place is, Colonel. The only way out is in a wooden box or up one of the chimneys, unless by some miracle the war is about to be over and the Allies find us.'

'Thank you for being so honest. Better to know what we're up against right at the start.' The Colonel gave a deep sigh. 'It looks as if we're in a bit of a tight spot, doesn't it?'

Martin smiled for the first time in weeks. 'And here's me thinking it was only the British who were the masters of understatement.'

'Ah, yes, but we're all colonials under the skin. It's in the blood, you know.'

North of Weimar

Danuta's German and French were flawless. This had helped her to find several jobs working in bars and restaurants favoured by the German soldiers and airmen, which meant that she could pick up information to pass on to London.

As Marie-Claire Rousseau, she'd overheard a great many things over the last few years, but what had surprised her the most was the talk amongst the Luftwaffe pilots, who despite their joy at having downed their opponents could still praise them for their bravery and skill and regard them as part of the band of brothers who ruled the skies.

She hadn't quite believed her SOE instructor back in England that there was a kinship between fliers of all nations, regardless of politics or war, and had to hope now that the bond remained unbroken.

She'd been horrified to learn from her friends in the Resistance that Martin and over a hundred other airmen had been sent to Buchenwald, for she knew what went on there and how the lives of the inmates counted for less than the dirt beneath the jackboots of those SS thugs who ran it.

As time was of the essence, she had to act swiftly – which meant coming into the open where she might be recognised. The SS had been after Marie-Claire Rousseau for months – had even nicknamed her 'The Vixen', and she'd seen the wanted posters that bore a sketch of her face which was much too close to reality for comfort. Someone had betrayed her, and she had yet to discover who it was, but if she was to save those men, she had no other choice but to do her job and forget about her own safety.

The Luftwaffe base was located a few kilometres out of the small German town which lay to the north of Weimar, which was, in turn, five or so kilometres from the concentration camp. It was the middle of the night when she'd reached the outskirts, but before entering the town she'd buried the radio, which had been her lifeline to England but was now a liability, deep beneath an overgrown hedgerow, along with the peasant clothing, which she might need again if she was lucky.

She bathed in the chilly waters of a nearby stream to rid herself of the stink of that awful coat, and then dressed in a dun-coloured frock and brown cardigan she'd stolen from a washing line three days before. Her sturdy boots had finally fallen to pieces and now they'd been replaced by a rather down-at-heel pair of walking shoes she'd found on the doorstep of an isolated cottage. With her hair and body clean, she'd gone over her plan again before snatching half an hour's sleep. She was now ready to face whatever was to come.

Hiding her hair beneath the ubiquitous headscarf worn by most women now, she put on a pair of wire-framed spectacles with slightly tinted lenses, to disguise the colour of her eyes. The idea was to be as unremarkable as possible, to be able to move about unnoticed – and as this ruse had worked countless times, she could only hope it would prove successful tonight.

The town was still asleep as she cycled through it, but she'd been informed that there was no curfew in place, so was reasonably certain there would be no roving police patrols. Yet caution was her byword and she remained alert.

Having reached the northern edges of the town, she proceeded even more cautiously towards the airfield and the great mass of buildings that sprawled across the flat valley. She got off her bicycle and stayed within the deep shadows of the nearby trees to take stock. It was three o'clock in the morning – the most vulnerable hour for someone on night-watch – and in the gloom she could see the guard at the delivery gate yawning as he sneaked an illicit cigarette. It was time to move.

She patted the cardigan pocket again to ensure that the carefully written letter she'd penned the day before was still there, and then slowly cycled towards the guard, taking him almost unawares as he stamped out his cigarette.

'Excuse me,' she said quietly as the startled youth stared at her guiltily. 'But I have an urgent letter for *Generalmajor* Franz Baumann.'

She thrust it at him before he could reply, and he automatically took it as she'd known he would. 'It must be delivered to him personally, for it is most important and could bring him much praise from our revered leader.' She executed a Nazi salute. 'Heil Hitler.'

Before the boy could respond, she'd turned the bicycle around and was cycling away.

Within the hour she'd changed back into the smelly coat and rough trousers, the wireless buried deep in her canvas bag along with her water canister, dress, cardigan and change of underwear. Taking the back roads she cycled south-west, and as dawn began to lighten the sky, she ditched the bike and waited amid the ruins of a house for the farm truck that would take her into Luxembourg.

Once there, she'd disappear across the border into France to join her Resistance group.

Luftwaffe Air Base

Generalmajor Franz Baumann was a vigorous man in his thirties and an early riser. He enjoyed the solitude of dawn and liked to run and stretch in the quiet time before others had risen to break the peace.

He'd completed his exercise and had showered, shaved and was about to go into the officers' mess for his breakfast when a young soldier approached him at a run.

'Sir,' he panted, clicking his heels and giving a salute. 'I have an urgent letter for you, sir.'

Franz took the letter and studied the handwriting – it was not familiar. 'Where did you get this?'

'I was on guard duty sir, and a woman gave it to me.'

Franz raised a quizzical brow. 'What woman?'

'I don't know, sir,' he stammered, suddenly not looking at all sure of himself. 'She wasn't much to look at,' he went on, avoiding Franz's piercing gaze. 'Probably in her forties, and wearing glasses.'

'So. You didn't think to question her, or ask for her identification?'

'She'd gone before I could do that,' he admitted shamefacedly.

Franz regarded the letter again and slapped it gently against his palm. 'I think an hour of cleaning out the latrines should sharpen your wits,' he said brusquely. 'See to that before you go off duty – and then,' he added with a sharp prod of his finger against the corporal's shoulder blade – 'perhaps you will remember the rules of guard duty. Dismissed.'

He watched the youth scurry away towards the latrines and gave a deep sigh. The quality of servicemen was going downhill by the day now they had to recruit pimply boys who were barely out of school and as thick as a plank of wood.

He regarded the letter, which intrigued him, even though he was wary of it, for he didn't trust mysterious missives arriving in the middle of the night – and urgent communications usually came from Luftwaffe Headquarters.

He carried it into his office, closed the door and

sat down at his desk. Placing the letter on the pristine blotter, he turned it this way and that and then held it up to the bright light of his desk lamp. The envelope was of good quality and seemed to contain a single sheet of paper. Impatient with his inability to make up his mind about it, he tore it open.

The single sheet was again of good quality paper, and the writing was educated and easy to read.

Generalmajor *Baumann, greetings.*

I believe strongly that the officers of the elite Luftwaffe are honourable and just-minded men, and that there is an unspoken code amongst you that, regardless of nationality, all pilots belong to the same noble brotherhood.

To this end, I wish to inform you that over 150 British and Allied pilots have been falsely imprisoned in Buchenwald, rather than taken to prisoner of war Stalags. If, as I hope, that bond still exists between the different air services, would you consider visiting them to find out why they have been sent there? I'm sure your presence would be much appreciated.

With kindest of regards,
S. Schmidt

Franz read the letter through again. Whoever S. Schmidt was, she seemed to be more fully informed than he, which led him to believe that she might be working for the Resistance – or even within the Wehrmacht itself, concerned by the breaking of the Geneva Convention regarding

405

such prisoners. Either way, the letter disturbed him, for the bond between the air services certainly did still exist, and if those men were being held at that labour camp for no good reason, then he had to do something about it.

He tucked the letter into his trouser pocket and then picked up the telephone. 'I need to speak to the Commandant of Buchenwald,' he told the operator. 'What's his name?'

There was a moment of silence and then, 'SS *Standartenführer* Hermann Pister, sir.'

'An unfortunate name,' muttered Franz, who had enough English to understand what the Brits and Yanks would make of that. 'Put me through to him, will you?'

'It's still very early, sir. He may not be available.'

'Then keep ringing until he is,' snapped Franz.

Buchenwald

Martin and the seven men who'd travelled with him felt strangely comforted by the arrival of so many others. There was an odd sense of safety in numbers – a brotherhood of men withstanding all the beatings and hunger and fear together – and as the fourth day after their arrival began, the mood in the hut was remarkably relaxed considering they'd already lost two of their comrades who'd been too weakened after that train journey to withstand the conditions.

They were a varied bunch, mostly American, with some Canadians, Aussies and Kiwis – and even a Jamaican who'd joined up with the RAF. It had immediately become clear that the Jamaican and the other black men were being singled out for punishment by the sadistic guards, and although they'd tried to shield them, there was nothing really that they could do.

With the hut now full to bursting and with some of the men having to share the narrow sleeping spaces, it was much warmer at night, and they exchanged stories of how they'd ended up in this place.

There was the same thread going through most of them – although a small number had dropped out of the sky and found themselves faced by grim-faced armed soldiers and placed under immediate arrest, only to be mixed up in the chaos of the Allied bombing raid and the Germans' hurried retreat, with those the Germans regarded as saboteurs and spies.

The general story was that they'd been shot down and hidden by farmers or villagers, and then passed on to members of the underground or the Resistance. Many had discarded their uniforms in favour of trying to get back across the Channel as peasants or labourers. Upon capture, they'd been found to have false identity papers on them and so were thrown into prisons throughout France and Belgium, interrogated and then brought here.

'It was rather different for us,' said Roger as he washed the sleep from his infected eyes with water from his tin mug. 'Freddy and I fell out of the sky almost at the same time. Our parachutes were rather reluctant to open, so we came down hard right in the middle of a blasted forest. Hadn't a clue where we were, of course, and I'd broken my compass.'

'Luckily, I hadn't broken mine,' said Freddy. 'We headed north as that seemed the best idea, planning to get in sight of the Channel and find someone willing to take us across.'

'It took us weeks,' said Roger dolefully, 'and then we had the worst luck. The fisherman we approached immediately alerted the local Gestapo. The man in charge was a sadist and gave us both a damned good kicking just for the fun of it. Then we were hauled all the way back to bloody France, just in time to share the delights of that hellish train ride.'

'I suppose we've been classed as missing in action back home,' said Freddy, who'd lost all of his spark. 'And having heard nothing, my poor wife and sister must be going through agonies.'

'We can only hope that Pisser has informed the authorities that we're here,' said Roger, scratching at the bristles on his chin. 'But this place is so far removed from anything humane and civilised, I doubt he's bothered.'

The klaxon sounded for them to go into the compound to be counted, and they rose stiffly from their bunks with groans and moans and helped the weaker ones hobble outside.

Pisser was there, marching up and down self-importantly as the men shuffled into ragged lines before him, the armed guards prodding them with their rifles, and other guards with machine guns watching them from the high towers.

They stood there in the chill grey light of morning as the count went endlessly on, and then were force-marched through the camp to their various work sites. Another day had begun, and none of them knew if it was to be their last.

As Station Commander, Franz Baumann ordered three of his most senior officers to accompany him. He'd explained the reason for the visit to the camp, which they'd all heard about in vague terms but had never visited before, and now their staff car was slowing down at the gate.

'Keep your eyes peeled,' Franz murmured to his colleagues as the stench drifted through the open windows. 'We need to know exactly what sort of place this is.'

They were saluted through both sets of gates by the guards and the car drew to a smooth halt within a metre of the waiting Commandant. As the driver opened the door, Franz regarded the Commandant for a long moment before stepping out. First impressions weren't good.

He clicked his heels and gave the Nazi salute before coming straight to the point.

'I understand you have a number of British and American pilots here. Would you care to explain why that is?'

Pister stood even more stiffly than before. 'They are traitors and saboteurs, *Generalmajor*. I am waiting for orders from Herr Hitler himself as to what I should do with them.'

Franz was surprised to hear this, for Hitler didn't usually meddle with such things – he preferred to leave matters concerning pilots to Goring. 'And what are your thoughts on the matter?'

he asked smoothly.

'It is not for me to even dare guess our beloved Führer's thoughts, *Generalmajor*,' Pister replied nervously.

'I'm sure you could if you tried hard enough,' said Franz coldly.

'I have reason to believe that the order will be to have them shot.'

Which explained why that letter had been so urgent, he thought. The woman was obviously extremely well informed. 'I would like to interview their senior officers,' he said.

'It isn't possible, *Generalmajor*,' the man replied, not quite daring to meet his eye.

'And why is that?'

'They are at work.'

'Where?'

Pister swallowed, clearly discomforted by the hard stares of the four very imposing Luftwaffe officers standing in front of him. 'At our armaments factory, *Generalmajor*. It's situated in the centre of the camp about three kilometres from here.'

Franz turned to his three officers. 'What do you say to a bit of exercise? We can have a good look at what's going on here before we do the interview.'

They nodded, and Franz turned back to Pister. 'Lead on, *Standartenführer*,' he said briskly.

'I am Commandant of this camp and I'm sorry, *Generalmajor*, but I cannot permit you to go any further without the necessary documentation.'

Franz felt the chill of loathing for this pompous excuse of a Wehrmacht officer. He glared down his nose at him. 'You might be Commandant but I outrank you, Pister. You'll do as I order, or be arrested just as your predecessor was.'

The man paled visibly then stood rigidly to attention and clicked his heels. 'Of course, *Generalmajor*. It will be an honour to escort you through the camp. Perhaps you would like to take coffee first? It's quite a way.'

'Now, Pister. Stop wasting my time.'

As they walked through the camp Franz was sickened by what he saw, and so disgusted at what was going on here, he could barely bring himself to speak. He could see that his men felt the same, and by the time they reached the enormous armaments factory they had the stench of death in their nostrils and a deep and abiding loathing for the man in charge and his sadistic acolytes.

He ordered Pister to find a quiet room nearby where he could interview the men, and then pushed past him with his officers and entered the building.

Guards hastily saluted and stood to attention, overseers stopped to stare, but the men working at the enormous vats and on the production lines never looked up or paused.

'Stop vork immediately,' shouted Franz in English, his order echoing to the rafters of the high corrugated iron roof. Once he saw he had everyone's attention, he took a pace forward. 'I vish to speak to the officers in charge of the British and American airmen,' he rapped out.

Three men came forward, their filthy prison clothes hanging off them and dragging over their bare feet so they had to hold up the trousers. All three stood to attention and saluted.

He looked at each in turn. There was a tall one, an average-sized one and one with the stubble of a white beard who looked to be the eldest. They were clearly half-starved and bore the bruises and scars of beatings – but he noted there was still a spark of pride in their eyes.

'Would you please introduce yourselves?' he asked politely.

'Group Captain Martin Black, RAF, sir,' said the average-sized one. 'I apologise for being un-suitably dressed, sir, but my Number Ones are at the cleaner's.'

'Group Captain William Hurst the Third, USAAF,' said the lanky one. 'Good to meet you, sir. Though I'd advise you didn't come too near. It's been a while since we washed.'

'Colonel Fuller, ANZAC Royal Marines, Air-borne Division.' The white-bearded man snapped off another salute as he held onto his pyjama bottoms with his free hand. 'It's a pleasure to meet you, *Generalmajor*. Sorry about the mess, but it's the maid's day off.'

Franz acknowledged these pleasantries with a nod and bit down on a smile, for even in this hell on earth they'd retained their humour, and he felt a strange sort of pride in that, for it showed the grit of true airmen. 'Come vith me,' he said pleasantly, 'Ve need to talk.'

21

Buchenwald

The following six days were spent in an agony of not knowing if their interview with the Luftwaffe officer had borne fruit – or if he'd decided to leave them to rot in here. But Air Commodore Baumann had clearly put old Pisser in his place, and ordered a new regime, for they hadn't had to work since his visit; the quality of their food had improved – not by much, but enough to help them get some of their strength back – and there had been no more beatings.

'It'll be just our flaming luck to go down with typhoid before that bloke gets us out of here,' drawled Billy as they stretched on their beds that seventh morning. 'It's run amok through some of the smaller camps.'

'Ever the flaming pessimist,' rumbled Jock Cannon. 'Put a sock in it, mate. I'm trying to get some beauty sleep.'

'It'd take years for you to get beautiful, you old bastard,' retorted Billy fondly. 'I wouldn't bother, mate.'

Martin exchanged glances with Forbes, Roger and Freddy. The two Aussies had become quite a cabaret act since the *Generalmajor's* visit.

The klaxon went and they all trooped out, hope that they might soon be out of this place giving

413

them a spring in their step. And when a furious-looking Pister emerged from his office closely followed by Baumann and his Group Captains, there was a sharp intake of breath.

'Strewth, now that's what I call pissed off,' muttered Billy on a snigger. 'Look at Pisser's ugly mug – it would sour milk.'

Baumann stepped forward, immaculate in his grey uniform, his highly polished boots gleaming in the sun along with the Iron Cross pinned to his lapel. 'As I call out your names, you are to reply and then make your vay to that hut over there,' he said, indicating a storage hut next to the ablutions block the other side of the wire fencing. 'You vill find the clothes and possessions you arrived with vaiting for you. Change into them and then proceed to the trucks outside.'

Martin stepped smartly forward and saluted. 'Permission to speak, *Generalmajor.*' At the other man's nod, Martin continued. 'What is our destination, sir?'

'It is Stalag Luft Three,' he replied with the hint of a smile touching his lips. 'In your English miles, it is about a hundred south of Berlin. You vill find you are treated vith respect there.'

'Thank you, sir. And can I just add, sir, that the men and I are honoured to have met you. You have proved to us that the bond which binds us continues even during the darkest days.' He turned to the men behind him. 'Attention,' he said clearly, then snapped back to face Baumann. 'Salute!'

Franz Baumann felt his heart swell with pride as he smartly returned their salutes – pride not

414

only that he had done the right thing, but in the spirit of kinship that ran so powerfully through them all. They would all remember this day long after the war was over.

Danuta heard the news through the underground grapevine and would have celebrated with a glass of wine, but she was busy helping to sabotage the ammunition dumps the Allied bombers had missed in preparation for the great invasion. Hopefully, once this war was won, she'd be able to celebrate their victory in the warm, welcoming arms of Peggy, and all those she'd come to regard as family. There was no place like home, and she was becoming impatient to be there.

Anne received the news as she was helping in the dairy. She flung her arms around the startled vicar and gave him a smacking kiss before rushing into the farmhouse to tell Vi, laughing and crying all at once. Work came to a halt and everyone – including the prisoners – gathered in the kitchen to celebrate with Vi's home-made, dangerously alcoholic parsnip wine.

Kitty and Charlotte had been attacking the brambles and weeds that clogged the pocket-handkerchief front garden when they heard the distant rumble of a heavy engine straining its way up the narrow lane. There was something about this unusual noise that stilled them – something that made them reach for the other's hand and wonder if the thuds of their hearts could be heard.

And when the cheerful young airman told them the news they'd hardly dared to hope for, they threw their arms around him, their tears of relief dampening his pristine uniform and making him blush to the roots of his dark hair.

Ron and Bertie sat on one of the stone seats that were dotted along the promenade, watching the bomber squadron head across the Channel. The relief of the moment brought them closer than ever as they shared the half-bottle of whisky that Bertie had tucked in his jacket pocket.

'Here's to all the brave boys,' said Ron. 'And to the brotherhood of airmen. May the ties that bind them continue and bring them all home safely.'

Peggy was surrounded by those she loved in her kitchen as they tearfully and joyfully celebrated the news that their boys were all alive and well and would stay out their war in a proper POW camp.

As the glasses chinked, the happy chatter went on around her and Harvey leapt about in delight, she sat in her usual chair and stroked a purring Queenie. Lifting her glass to salute the many photographs on her mantelpiece, she whispered, 'We'll try to be patient, but it will feel like an age until you come home.'

Dear Readers,

Thank you once again for reading this next chapter in the Beach View Boarding House series. It's lovely to hear from you through my Facebook pages and website, and I take heart from all your encouraging words.

The story of what happened to the airmen is, unfortunately, based on fact. There were indeed 170 men captured and sent to Buchenwald as spies and saboteurs, and I was stunned to learn that the kinship between airmen of all nations was powerful enough to rescue them. Again it was a very difficult tale to tell, for the concentration camps are an emotive subject and needed to be handled with great care, which is why I have not dwelt too long on the horrors they must have really encountered.

For the historians amongst you, I confess that I've changed the timeline of those events to fit my tale. The original pilots were shot down during August 1944 and transferred to Buchenwald a week later, where they were prisoners for two months before the Luftwaffe officer went to speak to them and gain their release to Stalag III.

Stalag III has its own interesting history, for it was on what happened there that the film *The Great Escape* was based.

I do hope that, although the subject matter is distressing, there is a wonderful moral to the story, for even in the darkest hours, honour and the bond of kinship can still burn brightly.

Ellie x

A Map of Cliffehaven

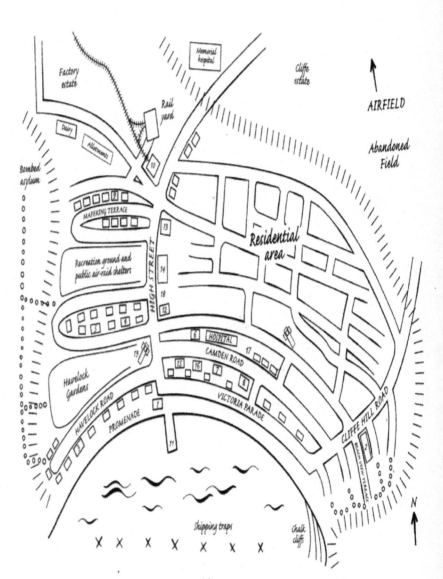

Factory estate

Memorial hospital

Cliffe estate

AIRFIELD

Abandoned Field

Dairy

Rail yard

Allotments

10

Bombed asylum

MAFEKING TERRACE

13

Residential area

HIGH STREET

14

Recreation ground and public air-raid shelters

18

12

19

HOSPITAL

17

CAMDEN ROAD

16

Havelock Gardens

HAVELOCK ROAD

VICTORIA PARADE

PROMENADE

7

11

BEACH VIEW TERRACE

CLIFFE HILL ROAD

N

Shipping traps

chalk cliffs

The Characters

PEGGY REILLY is the middle sister of three, in her early forties, and married to Jim. She is small and slender, with dark, curly hair and lively brown eyes, and finds it very hard to sit still. As if running a busy household and caring for her baby daughter wasn't enough, she also did voluntary work for the WVS before getting a job in the local uniform factory, yet still finds time to offer tea, sympathy and a shoulder to cry on when they're needed.

She and Jim took over the running of Beach View Boarding House when Peggy's parents retired, for her older sister, Doris, thought it was beneath her, and her younger sister, Doreen, had already established a career in London.

Peggy has three daughters, two sons, and two grand-daughters. When war was declared and the boarding house business no longer became viable, she decided to take in evacuees. Peggy can be feisty and certainly doesn't suffer fools, and yet she is also trying very hard to come to terms with the fact that her family has been torn apart by the war. She is a romantic at heart and can't help trying to matchmake, but she's also a terrible worrier, always fretting over someone – and as the young evacuees make their home with her, she comes to regard them as her chicks and will do everything she can to protect and nurture them.

JIM REILLY is in his mid-forties and was a projectionist at the local cinema until it was bombed. He was a young Engineer in the last days of the First War, in which he served alongside his elder brother, Frank, and father, Ron, and now he's again been called-up to fight for King and country – in India and Burma.

Jim is handsome, with flashing blue eyes and dark hair, and of course the gift of the Irish blarney he'd inherited from his Irish parents; which usually gets him out of trouble. He likes to flirt with women and although he would never be unfaithful to Peggy, she likes to keep tabs on him – even if he is on the other side of the world. Jim also likes to make a dishonest quid here and there, and is not averse to 'borrowing' bits of army kit to make his life in the tropics a bit more comfortable. He's enjoying the camaraderie of being a soldier, but the conditions and dangers he's encountering in the jungles have somewhat dampened his enthusiasm, and he treasures the letters and cards from home.

RONAN REILLY (Ron) is a sturdy man in his mid-sixties who often leads a very secretive life away from Beach View. It turns out that the contacts, experience and skills Ron gathered in the previous war are useful in these current hostilities. Widowed several decades ago, he's fallen in love with the luscious Rosie Braithwaite who owns The Anchor pub, and although she isn't averse to his attentions, she's refusing to let things get too intimate.

Ron is a wily countryman; a poacher and retired fisherman with great roguish charm, who tramps over the fields with his dog, Harvey, and two ferrets – and frequently comes home with illicit game hidden in the deep pockets of his poacher's coat. He doesn't care much about his appearance, much to Peggy's dismay, but beneath that ramshackle old hat and moth-eaten clothing beats the heart of a strong, loving man who will fiercely protect those he loves.

ROSIE BRAITHWAITE is in her early fifties and in love with Ron, but as her husband is in a mental asylum, she is unable to get divorced. She took over The Anchor twenty years ago and has turned it into a little gold-mine. Rosie has platinum hair, big blue eyes and an hour-glass figure – she also has a good sense of humour and can hold her own with the customers. She runs the pub with a firm hand, and keeps Ron at bay, although she's not averse to a bit of slap and tickle. And yet her glamorous appearance and winning smile hides the heartache of not having been blessed with a longed-for baby, and now it's too late. Peggy is her best friend, and the family living in Beach View Boarding House has taken the place of the family she'd never had. Her greatest wish is to start a new life with Ron – even though he's exasperating at times.

HARVEY is a scruffy, but highly intelligent brindled Lurcher, with a mind of his own and a mischievous nature – much like his owner, Ron. Clever and intuitive, he hunts for game with Ron, and has become a heroic rescuer of people trapped in the ruins of their homes. He's recently had to suffer the arrival of Queenie, a black kitten with a withered leg who thinks she owns Beach View and has certainly put his nose out of joint. He sleeps on Ron's bed, steals food from the table, and has recently blotted his copybook by seducing a pedigree whippet and producing a son, Monty, who now lives with Rosie at The Anchor. Harvey adores everyone but Doris.

DORIS WILLIAMS is Peggy's older sister, recently divorced from the long-suffering Ted. She lives in the posh part of town, Havelock Road, looks down on Peggy and the boarding house, and is a terrible social climber and snob. She's a leading light – or would like to be – in Cliffehaven society, and is clinging onto her position on the board of several charities because it brings her into contact with Lady Chumley, who actually thinks she's a bit of an upstart fool.

Doris insists upon calling Peggy 'Margaret' because she knows it winds her up like a clock, and she regards the evacuees she's been forced to take in as unpaid servants to be bullied. Doris constantly berates Peggy for marrying beneath her, and filling her house with waifs and strays – and loathes Ron because he calls a spade a shovel and refuses to change his nefarious ways. And yet, despite her snooty ways and her refusal to un-bend, Doris is a lonely woman. Ted has refused to come back and their only son has now married and moved away. Travelling restrictions mean she has yet to see her first grandchild.

TED WILLIAMS is the manager of the Home and Colonial Store in Cliffehaven's High Street. When his wife, Doris, discovered his long-running affair with the woman who worked on the fish counter, he felt quite relieved; now he had a real excuse to leave the house in Havelock Road and set up home in solitary splendour in the flat above the store. The affair is long over, and although he's done his best to try and repair his marriage to Doris, he's soon realised he prefers to be on his own, away from her nagging tongue. If only Doris was more like her sisters, Peggy and Doreen, there might have been a chance of reconciliation.

ANTHONY WILLIAMS is the son of Doris and Ted, and before the war, he was a teacher at a private school. He's now working for the MOD, and has recently got married to Suzy, who was a lodger at Beach View Boarding House. The MOD has sent them to the Midlands where they've set up home and are now the proud parents of a little son they've called Teddy – after Anthony's father – which has rather put Doris's nose out of joint.

DOREEN GREY is the youngest Dawson sister and although she loves Peggy, she can't stand Doris and they usually end up having a huge row. Doreen has long been divorced from her ne'er-do-well husband, Eddie, and now her two little girls are safely evacuated to Wales, she's working for the MOD. Dark-haired and pretty, she fell in love with Archie Blake, who was tragically killed whilst on leave in London. Having returned to Cliffehaven and Peggy to recover, she's now in Wales with her daughters and working at a local school whilst she awaits the birth of Archie's precious baby.

FRANK REILLY has served his time in the army during both wars, but now he's been de-mobbed due to his age and is doing his bit by joining the Home Guard and Civil Defense. He's married to Pauline and they live in Tamarisk Bay in the fisherman's cottage where he was born, which is now haunted by the ghosts of two of their three sons, who were killed on their minesweeper out in the Atlantic. Their surviving son, Brendon, is now enlisted into the Royal Naval Reserve and is based in London. During a visit to his maternal grandmother in the West Country he met Carol Porter, and they've married following a whirlwind romance. But with Carol in Devon and Brendon in London, there is little chance of them being together until the war ends.

THE LODGERS

CORDELIA FINCH is a widow and has been boarding at Beach View for many years. She is in her late seventies and is rather frail from her arthritis, but that doesn't stop her from bantering with Ron and living life to the full. Cordelia has a twinkle in her eye, loves being an intrinsic part of the lively household, and enjoys singing along to the wireless and having too many sherries in The Anchor. As deaf as a post, she regularly forgets to turn on her hearing-aid, which can lead to many a convoluted conversation, and although she tries very hard with her knitting, it usually turns out to be a disaster. She adores Peggy and looks on her as a daughter, for her own sons emigrated to Canada many years before and she rarely hears from them. The girls who live at Beach View regard her as their grandmother, as does Peggy's youngest, Daisy.

RITA SMITH came to Beach View after her home in Cliffehaven was flattened by an air-raid. Her father is away in the Army, her Italian neighbours who took her in have been interned, and so she goes to Peggy's, whom she's known since childhood. Rita is a small and energetic tomboy who is a fully qualified mechanic, having been taught from an early age by her father. She has a motorbike that she roars about on, and can usually be seen in heavy trousers and boots, a WW1 leather jacket, and flying helmet. She works for the Fire Service, and has been organising motorbike races to raise money for a second Cliffehaven Spitfire in her spare time, as the man she loves, Matthew Champion, is a pilot at RAF Cliffe.

FRAN is from Ireland and works as a theatre nurse at Cliffehaven General. She has been living with Peggy since before the war, and has become an intrinsic part of the family. Fran is a little inclined to wear her heart on her sleeve, and has already had an unfortunate run-in with an over-persuasive and very married American service-man. She's a dab hand at hairdressing – much to Ron's disgust – but has proved to be a very talented violinist. She plays the violin at The Anchor for the sing-songs, and has fallen in love with Robert – an MOD colleague of Anthony Williams.

SARAH FULLER and her younger sister, **JANE,** came to England and Beach View after the fall of Singapore. They are the great-nieces of Cordelia Finch, who has welcomed them with open arms. There has been no news of Sarah's fiancé, Philip, or of their father, Jock, since the Japanese over-ran the island – but at least their mother and little brother managed to escape to Australia. Sarah works for the Women's Timber Corps, and Jane has now left Cliffehaven for a secret posting where she's deciphering codes.

IVY is from the East End of London and was billeted for a time with Doris, where she was expected to skivvy. Having moved in with Peggy following a close-call at the munitions factory, she's now working at making tools. She's stepping out with Fire Officer Andy, who is the nephew of Gloria Stevens, who runs The Crown pub in Cliffehaven High Street. She and Rita are best friends and the untidiest pair Peggy has ever met – other than Ron and Harvey.

PEGGY'S CHILDREN

ANN is married to Station Commander Martin Black, an RAF pilot, and they have two small girls. Ann has moved down to Somerset for the duration, and although she is teaching at the local village school and getting on with her life, she misses Martin and of course her mother, Peggy.

CICELY (Cissy) is a driver for the WAAF and is stationed at Cliffe Aerodrome. She once had ambitions to go on stage, but finds great satisfaction in doing her bit, and is enjoying the new friendships she's made. She has fallen in love with a young American pilot, Randolf Stevens, but now he's been sent to Biggin Hill, they rarely see one another. Although life is exciting, the war has brought great sadness, for the life-expectancy of a pilot is becoming less with every operation.

BOB and **CHARLIE** are Peggy's two young sons of fifteen and thirteen, who are also living in Somerset for the duration. Bob is serious and dedicated to running the farm, whilst Charlie is still mischievous; when not causing trouble, most of the time he can be found under the bonnet of some vehicle, tinkering with the engine.

DAISY is Peggy's youngest child, born the day Singapore fell. She can sleep through air-raids, throws awful tantrums, and simply adores pulling Ron's wayward eyebrows. She and Harvey are the best of friends, but she has yet to truly know her father, or her siblings.

The publishers hope that this book has given you enjoyable reading. Large Print Books are especially designed to be as easy to see and hold as possible. If you wish a complete list of our books please ask at your local library or write directly to:

Magna Large Print Books
Magna House, Long Preston,
Skipton, North Yorkshire.
BD23 4ND

This Large Print Book for the partially sighted, who cannot read normal print, is published under the auspices of

THE ULVERSCROFT FOUNDATION

THE ULVERSCROFT FOUNDATION

... we hope that you have enjoyed this Large Print Book. Please think for a moment about those people who have worse eyesight problems than you ... and are unable to even read or enjoy Large Print, without great difficulty.

You can help them by sending a donation, large or small to:

**The Ulverscroft Foundation,
1, The Green, Bradgate Road,
Anstey, Leicestershire, LE7 7FU,
England.**
or request a copy of our brochure for more details.

The Foundation will use all your help to assist those people who are handicapped by various sight problems and need special attention.

Thank you very much for your help.